T5-DHJ-816

The Saviors

BY HELEN YGLESIAS

How She Died
Family Feeling
Starting: Over,
     Anew, Early and Late
Sweetsir
The Saviors

Helen Yglesias

The Saviors

Houghton Mifflin Company

Boston 1987

Library of Congress Cataloging-in-Publication Data

Yglesias, Helen.
  The saviors.

  I. Title.
PS3575.G48S2   1987   813'.54   86–21377
ISBN 0-395-35419-6

Printed in the United States of America

Q 10 9 8 7 6 5 4 3 2 1

This book is for
Kristina, Justin, Matthew,
Nicholas, and Aaron Jacob.

I

O N the first lap of the march, the demonstrators took over the southbound lanes of Highway 95, twenty miles north of Boston. It was four-thirty in the afternoon and traffic was heavy. Though the action was premeditated, not all the marchers were privy to the plan. Maddy Phillips hadn't known of it, but she joined in gaily, rushing in headlong. Police and newsmen sprouted on the spot. Converging squad cars flashed their lights, their claxons squeaking and bleating. Camera crews blossomed.

The day was a clear, bright June perfection: wonderful light. There was a stillness in the air, typical of the season, in spite of the rising clamor of sirens, of shouted slogans, and of passing drivers sounding their horns, some in sympathy with the marchers, some in derision. Beyond the commotion, the powerful patience of the natural world lay in wait. So it seemed to Maddy Phillips, in the front-line of protesters. She knew herself to be a part of, even a leader of, this uproar, but in her deepest self she too waited, aloof as the china blue cloudless sky under which the event boiled.

Traffic was being brought to a halt. Only the marchers

moved ahead now, the old deliberately put in the vanguard, to keep the police hesitant and polite. There were two noisy helicopters above. *Choppers*, she amended. *Hovering*. One must use the current lingo. A busload of police inched through the stalled cars and the demonstrators on foot. She looked back. In a lift of soft wind, the banners and flags of an endless following contingent billowed and danced.

It was then she stumbled. A moment earlier she had been a handsome elderly woman, waving a silken standard and calling out slogans vigorously, but in the instant that she tripped, she collapsed into a pitiful old creature. The words she had been sounding out in unison with others faltered into garbled nonsense.

Two young people rushed to her side. She didn't want them and tried to push free, but they held firm, leading her to a truck pulled up at the side of the road and urging her to mount. Photographers and reporters clustered. She wasn't about to make a fool of herself clumsily climbing into a truck at her age, with all those strangers watching.

She reached out aimlessly in a witless irritability. Her voice emerged strong, loud, querulous.

"Who are you people? What? What? What do you want?" And then, without transition, "Why is it so damned hot?"

A woman slinked through the guardians protecting her and pushed a mike into Maddy's face.

"Are you exhausted, dear? Aren't you exhausted? Isn't this too much for you?"

Bewildered was the word she would have used herself. A dense inner fog, hot and dark with panic, obscured her name, this place, this action, its purpose, her role in it, and friend from foe. The young people restricting her movements were strangers to her, and looked so like all other youngsters in existence that she wouldn't be able to place them even if she knew them. They were dressed in what seemed to be nineteenth-century pioneer costumes: ruffles, fringes, flounces, hats with large, floppy, theatrical brims. Had she been seduced into some outlandish masquerade? She looked down at her own dress for reassurance: indomitably messy yet trim seersucker skirt and blouse. That was all right, then.

"You'll be so much more comfortable in the truck, Mrs. Phillips, with Mr. Phillips and the rest of the group," the young woman guardian said, inserting herself between Maddy and the reporter.

Inflamed by insecurity, Maddy yelled, "What are you talking about? What is this? What year is it? Where in the world are we?"

The reporter pressed in with her mike, calling to her crew. "Here, over here. Get a shot of this. This is good."

A mocking voice she knew she knew called out, "Come back to the truck, Maddy, honey, come back with us where you belong and stop acting like an old fool."

She could not account for her obedient response, but she labored into the truck with the help of a stepstool and an undignified boost. A memory surged of the suppressed titters of her classmates when a grade school teacher returned from the lavatory with her dress accidentally tucked into great gray drawers. She must be making a similarly disgusting spectacle of herself. How ridiculous to have come to this old, old age. She had promised herself to walk all the way, right to UN Plaza in the front-line of protesters. What a piece of arrogant vanity — at her age.

A trick of the sun blotted everything into swimming black forms, and temporary clarity blurred again. Only the glowing eyes of her keepers shone through. She heard a frightening uniform roaring and, oddly close and sweet, a crowd singing, "Phillips is our leader, we shall not be moved."

"Stop that," she demanded testily, fighting the surge of sweetness, and struck out at the young guardian gently forcing her to sit down in a canvas chair. The young woman's eyes flooded with such concern that Maddy experienced a pang of shame. Only for an instant. They liked to advertise their feelings, these new young people, like generals sporting medals. See how much I feel! See! See! All false. A kind of preening.

"They love you, Mrs. Phillips," the young man said. Fake glow. Self-congratulatory glow. "You and Mr. Phillips and the others here with you. They love you all for joining us. We all love you for it."

She had lost again the details of where she was and why, but, under that surface uncertainty, she knew what she knew. She was part of an action under attack: the long, steady roaring sound was the music of battle, as was the singing and the cheering, noises that banged at her heart with fear yet roused up courage. She knew that the back of the truck held not only banners, slogans, American flags, but a band of friends who made it home for her, though at the moment she would have been unable to name one correctly. Even her husband wavered into mist as he smiled indulgently at her. She was being settled down between him and her best and oldest friend, who had mocked and called her back to the truck. They were her family, her allies, her brothers and sisters, her lovers and comrades, and she was glad to be returned to them. Then why was the scene glitteringly lit up by the force of her anger? Why did she want to hit out and shout? Because they were probably losing their goal, whatever it was, as they generally did one way or another. Because she was deathly tired. Because she had been here so many times before.

"That's enough." She cut off the young man gushing at her. "Quite enough nonsense now from you two. Joined you, indeed. Other way around, I should say, quite the other way around."

"Beg your pardon?" the young woman said.

"You certainly should. Beg my pardon. We were here first, you know. It's you who joined us. We've been out here forever and ever."

And then silenced herself when she realized that a TV camera was recording the whole exchange.

While the march proceeded southward throughout the night, the old people riding the truck rested in a Boston hotel. They would make up the distance the following morning. It was Victoria who insisted on a suite at the Ritz-Carlton. Accommodations at the homes of people in the Boston area had been volunteered, but Victoria wanted none of that possible discomfort for herself and offered to pick up the tab for all.

"There are only six of us," she said, "and a three-bedroom suite will do it."

Such a typical grand-lady Victoria gesture held no surprises for Maddy, though Elena Dasinov, also typically, resented Victoria's generosity, if not to the point of refusing it.

"She's so showy," Elena grumbled in secret to Maddy. "I know she's your oldest and dearest friend. But you must admit she's *showy.*"

"Nature of the beast," Maddy said, and turned away.

They watched the television coverage of the demonstration on the 7:00 news, seated on the comfortable couches and armchairs of the living room of the suite, while eating thin grilled American-cheese sandwiches and drinking apple juice from paper containers, all brought in from a luncheonette by the same young man and woman assigned to their care. Victoria's generosity had stopped short of Ritz-Carlton room service charges, and they were all much too tired to venture out in search of a reasonably priced meal, though Maddy herself had miraculously recovered and was ready for anything. The blurry landscape of her head had returned to focus, names marshaled, memory almost intact, even strategies clear again. With the help of the youngsters she had put her husband, Dwight, to bed, and then Bernard Lewis. Only Arthur Brownson remained with "the girls," also known as "lovely ladies," as he steadily sipped away at his pocket flask.

"I haven't seen one of those things in thirty years," Victoria said.

"Look," Maddy said. "There we are."

There they were, on camera, pitilessly exposed in all their lame, deaf, halting deficiencies. There was the back of the truck. And there she was, seated between Dwight and Arthur Brownson in the front row of director's chairs, American flags flying from each side of the vehicle and long streamers proclaiming slogans whose messages the hot wind whipped out of shape.

Set off to the side, in the second row, Bernard Lewis slept in his canvas chair, or pretended to, his large head hanging between his shoulders like a tired dog's. To his right, Victoria Younger and Elena Dasinov flashed on and off the screen.

The cameras closed in on Bernard Lewis. Even to Maddy, who knew Lewis well, he was an astounding sight, a natural wonder, the parchment of his skin as thickly furrowed as a carpet or the tiered rock excrescenses on the Maine coast. His nose and ears had grown into enormous protuberances. An effect of living till ninety-eight? He opened his eyes. They were a young brilliant blue, smilingly suffused with sweetness. He promptly shut them and went back to sleep.

"Good for Bernard," Victoria said. "He accomplished more with that smile than a dozen slogans would have."

The camera shifted to a close-up of Dwight Phillips. Color TV rendered Maddy's husband to perfection. Smooth pink skin; baby blue eyes, palely pleasant; a squared-off, perpetually smiling mouth, showing nicely even dentures; the bonus of the deeply cleft chin. Everything about him was a reassurance — his well-tailored chambray suit, white shirt and striped tie, even the little peaked cotton cap he wore to protect his nose from recurring skin cancer. The camera was

6

so in love with his impeccable appearance, it panned to his white Top-Siders and white socks, while the voice-over described him as a leading peace activist, extending back to the First World War.

"A face as smooth as a baby's ass," Victoria said. "Eighty-eight years old and not a wrinkle."

"Princeton man," Arthur Brownson said, as if that explained it. "Class of nineteen sixteen."

"Money," Victoria said. "Inherited money guarantees pink, smooth skin from the cradle to the grave. The effect of sitting under grow lights while clipping coupons."

"What a mess I look," Maddy said.

The camera centered on her now.

"No," Victoria said, "you look good. Serious. One of us women needed to look serious."

"I look perfectly serious," Elena Dasinov objected.

The camera produced Elena in her carefully chosen, subdued print dress. Her hair was dyed and lacquered into an indestructible French knot, a style she had worn for the last forty-five years.

It was Victoria who looked spectacular in a voluminously cut, clinging black dress, her hair wrapped turban style in a red silk scarf, her face heavily made up into a pale mask adorned by excessively lush, long black false eyelashes and a full red-lipsticked mouth. On her chest a collar of weighty silver pendants hung, sparkling with semiprecious jewels. An amazing octogenarian sight.

"You're the one," Maddy said. "You're the sensational one."

"No," Victoria insisted. "Sloppy is better. Sloppy is serious. Virginia Woolf. Eleanor Roosevelt. You."

Elena Dasinov had other complaints. The cameras had caught only a fleeting view of her, and the voice-over hadn't named her with "the distinguished radical octogenarians and the ninety-eight-year-old war resistance leader, Bernard Lewis."

"Why am I always left out?" she wailed.

"Because you don't look a day older than seventy-nine," Victoria said.

The camera shifted to Maddy again, picking up on her earlier odd outburst. To herself, she seemed a queer, demented old woman.

Then Dwight, delivering a mini-lecture on camera in his deep, measured voice.

"My wife is entirely correct. Young people hold the erroneous view that the peace movement was born with them. In fact, the peace movement goes back to the middle of the last century." He paused to smile his reassuringly all-American, square-toothed grin. "Not counting Jesus Christ, of course." And held the grin.

"There were international peace congresses as early as eighteen forty-three and eighteen fifty-one, accompanied by huge demonstrations in London, Manchester, Birmingham, and dozens of other major cities of the world. In New England a man named Elihu Burritt, unknown to most of you, no doubt, propagandized very successfully for world peace worldwide, and founded the League of Universal Brotherhood in eighteen forty-six, whose members pledged themselves never to enlist or enter into any army or navy, or to yield any voluntary support or sanction to the preparation for or prosecution of any war. Surely I do not need to remind you of the examples of Tolstoy and Gandhi —"

A reporter interrupted. "Does that discourage you, Mr. Phillips, that so little progress has been made in the field of world peace?"

Dwight appeared momentarily at sea. Still, he smiled and, after a gap, spoke again.

"Discouraged? At my age? If discouragement could reach me, wouldn't I just lie down and die?"

"And when he does," Victoria said to the viewers at the Ritz-Carlton, "he'll sit up and make a speech to the undertaker."

The camera shifted to Maddy in her wrinkled seersucker, her face lifted to Dwight's sun, a flushed, disheveled flower.

The crowd sang, "Phillips is our leader, we shall not be moved."

The newscaster's voice-over supplied the information that "other prominent elderly sponsors of the peace movement, including perhaps the world's most renowned spiritual leader, will be joining the group for the final lap of the march, whose ultimate goal is the United Nations. The massive demonstration hopes to affect the administration's deliberations on the potentially explosive issues of —"

"Turn that damn thing off," Arthur Brownson said, "or I'll have to send out for another bottle."

"They're giving us a terrific play," Victoria said. "You see what a good idea it was to lead off with us?" It had been Victoria's idea. "It gives the newscasters a hook. They like a hook."

"What hook?" Elena said.

"We're old. We're old," Victoria said. "When you're as old as we are, it's an accomplishment, a triumph, a distinction."

"Don't be silly," Elena said. "It's because of who we are."

"Who are we?" Victoria said.

"I'd rather be twenty-two again," Maddy said.

"You'll always be twenty-two to me, my darling," Victoria said.

"Bullshit," Maddy said.

"Exactly," Victoria said.

"Maybe we should all die in our sleep tonight. That would be a good hook," Maddy said. "Make a splash. At the Ritz-Carlton."

The cameras had returned to Maddy. An unseen woman reporter put questions in the rapid delivery newscasters were so good at, looking for dissension — marital, feminist, political — probing to pierce a spot that would yield blood. Maddy hated how bewildered she appeared to herself

9

on camera, how red her face was, how messy her scraggly white hair. Though she was listening intently, her heart banged so hard in her ears that she couldn't hear what the image of herself on screen had said. And then they were all gone and the TV news was on to the next item. She pushed herself outside the present and invited an undefined longing to invade her. For what? Goneby youth and beauty. Ridiculous sentimentality. She let a huge yawn possess her entirely.

"Everybody's tired," Arthur Brownson said. "Let's go to bed, lovely ladies. Hard day ahead of us tomorrow."

He rose, tilting slightly, and pressed a button on the TV. The color picture spiraled backward into nothingness. He proceeded from woman to woman, tenderly kissing each good-night.

"Sleep well. Sleep well. Sleep well, my darlings."

Controlling the slight tilt with an almost military hold, he carried himself out the sitting room door.

"Go ahead and get ready for bed, Elena. I'll be joining you directly," Victoria said.

Clearly, Victoria wanted to be alone with Maddy.

"I'm too tired to talk," Maddy said.

Particularly to Victoria — pessimistic, realistic, cynical Victoria — who always turned out to be right in the end.

"I'm going, I'm going, no need to push," Elena Dasinov said, and did not kiss her companions good-night.

Victoria too was exhausted. With the care of a surgical procedure, she unwound the turbanlike scarf covering her head and neck and detached the false eyelashes, then quickly peeled off her pantyhose. Out from under her chic constraints she looked quite wonderfully young, her thick hair flying disorderly and free, her body voluptuously shapely within the folds of the soft dress.

"We could call for a fire," she said, gesturing to the fireplace before the sofa.

"And romantic," Maddy said, amending her list of Victoria's characteristics.

"Yes," Victoria said. "There's nothing more romantic than a fire."

"The wonders of air conditioning," Maddy said. "To even consider a fire in ninety-degree heat."

Victoria opened her arms. "Come sit beside me," she said.

"When *you're* dead on the undertaker's table, you'll open your arms and invite him in," Maddy said.

Victoria laughed.

"I'm too tired to talk," Maddy repeated, but moved to the couch and settled her head in the silky folds of Victoria's wrinkled neck.

"There hasn't been enough defense of the beauty of old flesh," Maddy said, her lips against the fragrant softness.

"Thinking of starting an anti-face-lift movement?"

"No," Maddy said. "Too much else to do."

"Your flesh isn't old," Victoria said. "Firm and silky smooth. Just as it always was."

"Because we live right — Dwight and I. Nothing to do with your disgusting theory. Clipping coupons! You know perfectly well all we have is a tiny annuity."

"I would have given my right arm when I was young for a *tiny* annuity like yours."

"You wouldn't have given your right arm for anything, Victoria. You needed it for all your grand gestures. Most dancers need legs, but with you it was always arms."

"Couldn't I perform again? Why not? Choreograph a piece where I stay firmly on the floor, seated, using only my upper torso, the head and the arms . . ."

She had moved free of Maddy and was demonstrating.

"Beautiful," Maddy said. "But don't think of it."

"Why not? Vidhya is still performing and he's almost as old as I am."

She switched with magical swiftness into the persona of a precise little man, speaking in the strangely level, penetratingly sweet accent of Indian English.

"Of course you are troubled, of course you are in despair, given the violence of the world we all inhabit, but do not turn to me, do not look about you for help, do not even turn to God, my friends, but gaze into your own heart for the answers you are seeking. This morning, at dawn, when I awoke, I heard the song of a bird. It was raining, yet that bird sang—"

She broke off.

"That's hardly as entertaining as I would be, and he fills Carnegie Hall every time he appears in this country. He's taking Madison Square Garden this year."

Maddy laughed, and obviously delighted Victoria.

"I'm laughing at *you* — not Vidhya, remember," she said. "Everybody bares their breasts now, Victoria. They bare everything. Nobody left out there susceptible to shock."

"They're all dead out there. Nothing but zombies taken in by the most blatant absurdities. We were the last intelligent generation. We could shock them, Maddy. Old age shocks them to death. We should do it. Put together a real show. All of us. Octogenarians on Parade. For Peace. For Sisterhood. Brotherhood. Make a splash before we go."

"Doing what?" Maddy said. "Burn ourselves up in the back of the truck on UN Plaza?"

"Anything," Victoria said. *"Something."*

"I'd better get some sleep," Maddy said, "or I'll die in my sleep."

"I always hate to let you go," Victoria said. "I always did and I always will. I could talk to you forever."

They kissed, on the mouth, holding each other for a long space before they separated.

She had left a bedside lamp on in the room she was sharing with Dwight. He was asleep, his head twisted into a tortured position, his mouth obscenely open and his eyes showing dark pupils through a tiny slit of his open lids. He had always been a thrashing, noisy sleeper, always slept with his pupils showing, always suffered nightmares — muttering indistinct phrases, muffled cries, and weak, unearthly bursts of terrifying laughter — or, speaking in tongues, disoriented, would sit straight up in bed and shout at shadows. Now, in his old, old age, he rose a dozen times a night to walk aimlessly, insisting he had to go to the bathroom he had just visited, or to curse and fight, hearing voices, following or resisting commands issued by recurrent tormenting visions. There was a big doll he communicated with, threatening him back into his babyhood. It was a matter of time before she would have to restrain him, use trained professionals or have him put away in a nursing home. So she told herself every day, trying to accustom herself to a horror that everybody advised was the only sensible solution. Yet the following day he would be perfectly capable of rallying, pulling his wrecked self together into the expected image of Dwight Phillips, and in a public situation reach unerringly into the stock of speeches stored in his head for an appropriate one, delivering it in his deep, surprisingly young voice, as he had today. He could be counted on, still, for that kind of performance.

She kissed him. His sweated forehead was alarmingly cold to her lips.

He rolled over, threatening and cursing an enemy, then settled into a childish position, one hand under a cheek and his knees drawn up into the curve of his body, a moment of victory and comfort in the strange country he inhabited in his sleep. Composed now, he became his usual handsome self.

"Bless you," she said, aloud, and kissed him again, a charm to keep him safe in bed.

The clock built into the wall of the elegant blue and white bedroom of the Ritz-Carlton showed eight twenty-five, an early hour; and indeed, once settled into the twin bed nearest the door, she found her nerve ends tingling with sleeplessness, in spite of having been desperately tired earlier. Images of the long day assailed her. Her blurting stupidity on the TV burned a smoldering ridge in her head that endlessly doubled back upon itself. Her messy appearance and disruptive comment: *We were here first, you know, it's you who joined us, we've been out here forever and ever.*

She had never been any good at politics. Couldn't think on her feet. Dwight at almost ninety could still think on his feet. He had saved her from that slip today. Or had she dragged him into her error? He hadn't actually said what he should have. *We're all in this together, young and old, all races, all religions, rich and poor.*

"I hate politics," she said, startled to hear herself again speaking aloud.

She did hate politics, hated the largeness and coarseness of its generalities.

What was this talent that eluded her? Dwight could be counted on to come up with the right comment; Victoria always made her smashing effect, no matter how outlandish; Bernard Lewis knew enough to smile; Arthur Brownson knew how to hold himself erect and say *no comment* in exactly the right patrician tone.

"But I tell myself I'm finer than all of them — too fine for politics."

Again she had spoken aloud.

The truth was, she was the biggest liar of them all. She had never told any of them that she had been born Jewish. No, not even Vidhya, to whom she told everything, spilling over with her sixteen-year-old cockamamie notions about life, work, success, love, art, liberty, happiness. Vidhya even insisted on knowing whenever her period came around, and she told him. Something to do with being Indian, something to do with the phases of the moon, and of Vishnu and the Gopis, stuff she had forgotten now, stuff from another life. One of her many incarnations, except that she had neglected to die in between. She lugged all her baggage behind, like an itinerant land worker, the long trailing bag for the pickings of the field.

Madeleine Brewster Phillips. Born Bessie Bernstein.

Her mother and father had fussily hurried her into the parlor of the top-floor apartment on Union Avenue in the East Bronx one Saturday morning. She was eleven years old. The formal occasion was to announce that they were moving to Iowa City and would no longer be Jewish. Bernstein was to be changed to Brewster, and in this first new incarnation she could choose any given name she liked.

"You always complain that you hate the name Bessie. So take another name."

Her father was irritated by her mother's suggestion. And even to the child it had the ring of a bribe.

"The name is not important," Daddy said. "It's the concept."

Since the concept was beyond her, she concentrated on the name. There was a new girl in her class in public school, name of Madeleine De Mille, the most beautiful name she had ever heard attached to an ordinary person, so she chose Madeleine. It seemed the right thing to do.

The phone rang. She lifted the receiver at once, though not quickly enough. The sound triggered some excitement in Dwight's arcane night world. He sat up.

"That man's no gentleman," he roared, glaring, and instantly returned to sleep.

"Everything all right?"

It was Victoria. The Boston committee would be using the suite's living room for a strategy session and were requesting a delegate from their contingent.

"Will you represent us, love? You're smarter than I am, and we're the only ones awake."

"I'm in bed," Maddy said.

"A near riot erupted in East Hartford. Hundreds of arrests."

"Is the meeting about that? I'd have to get dressed again."

"Slip into your twenty-year-old Pucci robe. It'll knock them dead. Besides, you're the only one of us who can hear. Except Elena Dasinov — but she doesn't listen."

"I can't stand it," Maddy said.

"I already said you'd join them," Victoria said.

She entered the living room, decked out, just as Victoria had suggested, in the bold pattern of the silk Pucci robe, her long gray hair loosely tied back with a length of hand-painted silk.

She knew almost all the people on the committee, and those she didn't, knew her. They were the usual assortment, five men, five women: a journalist, a filmmaker, a peace worker, a black, a rabbi, a Hispanic, a feminist, a Catholic priest and nun, and a Democratic party activist. There was also a former U.S. attorney-general who wanted to join the group in the truck. He was young, seventy-two, but she agreed.

What else?

Would she be able to round up her people for a press interview right after breakfast, when they were fresh and vigorous?

They had become *her people.*

Yes. Limited questions. Early, because they were all early risers. No later than eight o'clock. No sitting around exhausting themselves waiting for the press.

"We have to catch up with the march, remember," she said.

It seemed that Vidhya would join them in Hartford.

"Hartford? In a near riot?"

"Not East Hartford. Bradley is at the other end. He's on a plane originating in Brussels. The flight schedule is Bangor–Bradley, would you believe that? Works out perfectly for us."

The young man speaking had helped take over the NYU computer in 1969. She hadn't seen him since '70 or '71. From having been a dark, skinny, limp figure floating in a mass of beard and hair, he was now a neat, bald, robust fellow in his forties. Very organized. He handed her a sheaf of photocopied pages.

"Copy of our scenario. This is the way things are supposed to go tomorrow. But don't count on it."

"I won't," Maddy said, and smiled warmly — penance for the day's earlier wrong.

"It was wonderful," he said, as if she had communicated an apology directly, "how you and your husband filled in the history of the movement. We needed that."

His name was Jeff, Jeff Bernstein. The only Jew in the room, she guessed, not counting herself. Perhaps they were even related?

"I'm very tired," Maddy said. "Is there anything else?"

"I'll be in charge of the truck tomorrow, be the one helping out, coming into the city and the plaza."

"Your leader." An extraordinarily pretty young woman spoke. "When Jeff says 'jump,' you jump." Derisively, she made a downward motion with a slim, darkly tanned arm. It was her vivid smile against that deep tan that made her so pretty.

"And Susan," Jeff added, tightly. "Susan and I will be the ones helping you tomorrow."

When she left, the group was already launched into a criticism session. From behind the door she had closed on their discussion, she could hear, *Comrades were hurt in East Hartford, comrades were beaten, black comrades, and white, hurt, jailed and beaten, right down the road in East Hartford, what are we going to do about that?*

What indeed?

What Is To Be Done?

Dwight, quietly asleep in the bed alongside hers, would have drafted a statement, gathered resounding signatures, delivered the letter to the press and then flung it at the authorities stupid enough to have initiated violence.

But had they?

What?

Initiated the violence?

And if *we* did, whoever *we* are?

The phone rang.

It was Jeff Bernstein, sorry to disturb her, but the committee was drafting a letter of protest for immediate release. Could they use their names? The bishop was going to sign! They had already spoken to the bishop and he had agreed to sign!

"Sight unseen?" she said.

"Oh, we'll read it to him first. And to you, of course."

"No need to read it to me," Maddy said. She didn't want the phone ringing again. "Just keep it simple. Direct and simple protest of the jailings and beatings. Use all our names, except Vidhya's."

If a black had tossed a toothpick, that would be violence enough for Vidhya, and he might retreat from the whole project — a thought she didn't share with Jeff Bernstein.

"I understand," Jeff said, as if she had shared it.

"But we should have a copy of the statement before our morning press conference," Maddy said.

"Absolutely," Jeff said.

So much for Dwight Phillips's wisdom on the inevitability of arrests during protests — and how to make the most of them. Jeff Bernstein knew how to manage just as well. Had Jeff been jailed as often as she and Dwight? Not very likely. They had at least twice as many years on him. No beatings, in their case. Lucky Maddy and Dwight Phillips, too white, too seersucker sloppy-neat, too prominent, too classy to be beaten. Too minor to be assassinated, and too ineffectual. What a splash it would make if they were assassinated, all of them at once, in the back of the truck.

She would never fall asleep.

She got up, boiled water in a cup with an electrical gadget they always packed for trips, dropped a tea bag of herbs in the water. She carried the cup back to bed with her and sipped from it, half sitting up, staring at nothing, drifting and daydreaming.

She felt herself no different from the younger self she had been, sleepless, restless and edgy, except that, younger, she would have snacked on an onion sandwich on black bread, and her body would have smelled sweeter. Victoria — what a fool she could be. Always be thirty-five to her — or whatever age she had said. To be young, younger — that was real longing. Never mind socialism, justice, peace. To be younger, young enough to make things happen, young enough to do what she felt young enough to be able to do but couldn't. To die was nothing, a tiny sleep before waking to another life; but what had seized her earlier in the day on the march, her stumbling into mists of forgetfulness and irritability — that was a truly terrible fate. She wouldn't think about it. Drift in other directions, drift to Vidhya, soaring toward Hartford, meet in air, youngsters again, in love, he, the Savior of the world, and she, his handmaiden.

She heard Victoria's mocking laughter.

No, of course she didn't believe in any of that now. Neither did Vidhya. Probably hadn't from the beginning.

She finished her cup of herb tea, put out the light, adjusted her head on the pillow. Sleep. Drift into sleep, or into a place like sleep, a state of quiet where everything was good, sweet smelling, enclosed, safe, like her Maine acre of blueberries under netting, a carpet of hay underfoot, a place of work and joy, tender to the touch, tough to the elements, sacred, enduring, and satisfying, where only natural pain existed and even that was eased, a place she had not yet discovered in life, only in this drifting into sleep, her version of the Promised Land on Earth.

2

I N 1927, Maddy Brewster, fresh out of high school,
boarded the train from Iowa City to New York, antici-
pating the forty-two-hour journey with as much excitement as if it were a trip to the moon. That her mother and
father accompanied her was definitely a dampening element,
but an unavoidable one. She was their only child, not yet
sixteen, and though they were freely sending her away from
them to live among people they loved and trusted in the
Universal Society of Brotherhood, freedom did not yet include a license to travel unchaperoned from Iowa City to
New York.

Her father was clearly nervous about unloosing Maddy
from his grip. He covered his uneasiness with persistent,
rattling talk. He had already recounted the complete history
of the Rock Island Line in his penetrating voice, developed
from years of lecturing at the university. She loved him, she
was sure of that, and certainly loved her mother; but she was
ashamed of the careful speech they had cultivated to mask
their now-imperceptible German accents; and her soft love
for them was enclosed in the hard shell of her opinion that

they were essentially two weak and silly people, whose ideas deviated from the normal and accepted and whose knowledge originated in outdated books. It was clearly their fault that she was probably the most ignorant not-quite-sixteen-year-old in the history of the world.

She appeared older because of her height and the amplitude of her womanly figure. She was as fair skinned as a blond, but her hair was dark and thickly curling, and her eyes strikingly dark blue. She was dressed in what might have been a schoolgirl uniform: a box-pleated skirt and middy-blouse top of heavy navy blue material, with a matching cape draped across her broad shoulders. A hand-painted length of silk hanging at the collar of her middy was the only splash of color in the subdued outfit, except for the effect of her head — a splendid flower-burst of softly brilliant tones.

Her costume, seemingly designed to express chastity and wholesomeness, the modesty of a nun, instead was powerfully provocative. She moved down the aisle of the train with the grace of an athlete or a dancer, turning her head from side to side with a full, swiveling motion of her bust and shoulders in a generous display of physical presence that implied an invitation to dare to storm this bastion. Her parents, helplessly following, appeared both frightened and pleased at the uncontrollable beauty they had somehow loosed upon the world.

When they found their seats and settled in, Maddy made note of the stranger across the aisle. He could not keep his oddly hooded eyes from straying to her. He was studying her closely enough to notice the detail on her hand-painted scarf: a link of naked men, women, and children, ascending, or perhaps descending? Maddy was as aware of the stranger as he was of her, even though he was directing his verbal pleasantries solely toward her mother and father.

Beautiful weather. Unbeatable, this weather. Couldn't pick a better time to be headed for Chicago. You folks been there before? Swell place when it isn't living up to its name, Windy City. If I might dare, I'd suggest you stay at the Drake, on the lakefront.

Mention of the Drake and the lakefront must have triggered *architecture* in Daddy's head, and he launched directly into his Frank Lloyd Wright, Louis Sullivan, the-genius-of-American-architecture lecture. The stranger, listening politely, murmured *that so?* from time to time. Toward the close of Daddy's set speech, the stranger, obviously impatient, wriggled in his seat and bent over to adjust a small traveling case he had tucked behind his legs. The movement of his thighs stuffed into his tight trousers bewitched Maddy. Those trousers led *there*, to a mysterious place nestled into his groin at a point that exactly matched her own mysteries, a celebrated mutual cave of adventure that she had never dared explore. But how did one tell if two people matched? Furtively she studied him. Could they possibly match?

He had seized the first break in Daddy's long speech to rise and introduce himself: Martin Jones, of Chicago. In return, Daddy named himself, Augustus Brewster, his wife Anna, and their daughter, Madeleine. The stranger shook hands with each, holding Maddy's hand in a large, dry grip, just a shade longer than he held the others, looking into her eyes with a steady, self-conscious intent and passing a curiously flat tongue over his full red lips. It occurred to Maddy that he had lied about his name being Jones. He was a man of the world, traveling incognito, hoarding knowledge of a Chicago Daddy had never dreamed of.

He sat down, adjusting his thighs and his groin with the movements of a creature who knew where to seek comfort. She turned from him to the window and, seemingly absorbed in the landscape, shaded her face with a hand, behind which she fantasized his somewhat revolting full lips on hers, one hand on her breast, the other stroking her inner thighs under the pleated skirt. Her groin ached. The car was unbearably warm. She threw back her cape.

22

"Are you hot? How can you be hot? I was just commenting that the car seems chilly to me."

Her mother being maddening.

"It's Maddy's first long trip, Mr. Jones," her mother said, as if in explanation of the hot-cool controversy.

The man's hooded eyes slid toward her again. Maddy studied him openly. He was too old, probably thirty. The throbbing in her groin subsided. She was relieved, yet angry and resentful, as if something had been taken from her — as if she had lost, in both senses of the word: been defeated and deprived.

Daddy had entered upon a monologue she had not previously heard, occasioned by the fact that the train was crossing the Mississippi. Like many of his stories, it meandered as if it would never reach its point, but from experience she knew it would. She barely listened.

"The spring of eighteen fifty-six, when the historic rail connection was being built between Iowa and the East with a bridge across the Mississippi . . . And the significance of such a bridge for Iowa, for the West, for the East, for the spread of culture . . ."

Mr. Martin Jones murmured, "That so?" with less and less enthusiasm as Daddy proceeded.

"Two weeks after the opening of the bridge, a new steamship owned by the New Orleans and Louisville Packet Company — it was the *Effie Alton* — made her first trip north of St. Louis. She had already passed under the bridge entirely safely, *just* passed under it, when her wheels stopped. She jarred, backed, and hit a support of the bridge. One of the ship's stoves fell over. The fire on the ship spread rapidly and engulfed the bridge. Volunteer firemen poured in from all the big and little river towns. They were heroic and managed to save all sections of the bridge except the central span."

It appeared that the story had still not reached its point.

"The New Orleans and Louisville Packet Company refused to pay damages."

Mr. Martin Jones clicked his tongue.

"Not only that, but they turned the case topsy-turvy. *They* opened suit against the Rock Island Railroad, charging that the construction of the railroad bridge constituted a menace to navigation."

"And then," Daddy said, signaling that now, *now* he was reaching the climax of his story, "a well-known Springfield trial lawyer was engaged to work on the case. The gentleman went to the town of Rock Island himself. He talked over the nature of the river currents — with — would you believe it — a twelve-year-old boy. That boy probably knew more about the river currents than all the experts put together. Then the gentleman from Springfield gave his attention to a report on the river that had been done by none other than Robert E. Lee. In conclusion, he came up with the astoundingly simple legal notion that the people of these United States had as much right to travel east and west as they did north and south. The gentleman from Springfield won the case against the New Orleans and Louisville owners of the steamboat *Effie Alton.*"

He ended with something of a flourish.

"And the name of that lawyer as you probably well know was Abraham Lincoln."

"That so?" Martin Jones said, and smoothly inquired if he might escort Miss Maddy to the club car for a cool drink since she seemed to be complaining of the heat.

"The heat?" Daddy said, and glanced at Mother as if to trigger her alarm.

Always obedient to her husband, Mrs. Brewster declined the offer. Maddy reluctantly relinquished the possibility of adventure. The window with its moving landscape was all there was to be? The scene was a disappointment, as was the car itself, for that matter. She had heard of luxuriously appointed trains running to and from Chicago and had built up expectations of carpets, velvet upholstery, beveled mirrors, cut glass in the dining car, exotic food and drink, and, inevitably, a mysterious, importunate stranger. But she had also anticipated, if all else failed, a landscape radically different from Iowa's. In fact, they rattled east across the Mississippi into territory not nearly as beautiful as home, and yet enough the same so as to be dully familiar. After Mr. Martin Jones excused himself and went off to the club car, and her father had settled down into temporary silence and her mother to her book, she watched the outdoor scene becoming uglier and uglier, the acres of corn that were a glowing gold ocean back home here straggling into unkempt and nasty-looking fields around dilapidated farm houses and outbuildings. The dumpy little towns grew dumpier the farther they traveled from the neatness and prosperity of Iowa, and the dirty little cities dirtier. Worst of all was the closing in of the sky, as if the splendid arching dome of heaven had flattened and folded down over this deteriorating landscape, leaving God behind to dwell in the magnificent reaches of the massed clouds and curved blue space of the skies she knew.

Her knowledge of the geography of her country added up to a vaguely muddled classroom map. She knew that they were traveling toward cities of great reputation — Chicago, Boston, Washington, D.C., New York — but where these stood on the real terrain of the country escaped her, or whether on this journey Indiana followed Iowa, or Illinois came before Ohio, or if these tracks would carry them across Pennsylvania on their journey east, or whether they would move directly into New York State from Illinois. She was afraid to ask Daddy, for fear of setting him off on one of his self-congratulatory lectures. But she couldn't resist asking about Pennsylvania, much later, when they were in the dining car and she had noted that Mr. Martin Jones had secured himself companionship in the form of another man about his age and two pretty young women, making for a jolly party at a table some distance from theirs, and pretended fascination in her father's talk so that if Martin Jones happened to glance in her direction he would see that Maddy Brewster could be as vivacious and charming as any girl riding the Rock Island Line.

Daddy had persuaded Maddy to order the tomato bisque for her first course. To her immense disappointment it arrived as nothing but Campbell's cream of tomato soup. She was surprisingly hungry and ate it with pleasure anyway, particularly enjoying the little round oyster crackers that accompanied it, while Daddy thoroughly investigated the subject of Altoona, Pennsylvania.

". . . not to be confused with Altoona, Iowa, which is midway more or less between Des Moines and Cedar Rapids, and also not to be confused with Altoona, Wisconsin, in the vicinity of Eau Claire. Those centers contain populations of no more than one to two thousand. Altoona, Pennsylvania, has a population of *sixty-nine* thousand citizens. A railroad town, with the greatest roundhouse in the world and the famous Horseshoe Curve. Would you believe you can ride that train, lean out of the window, and see the train's own tail on the curve? Wonderful sight. Very important Society people live in Altoona, you know. The Woodwards made their money in mining, actually. Not railroad people at all. They've given a fortune to the Society."

"*Mrs.* Woodward, *Becky* Woodward gave that money," Mother said.

"Woodward money, whoever gave it," Daddy said. "Old John Woodward made it out of the mines."

"Becky Woodward gave the money to build the Society's center in Sydney, Australia," Mother said, "because she had a brother lost at sea there."

"I never heard that," Daddy said. "Who told you that? Are you sure you have that correct? Sydney, Australia?"

Mother wasn't sure, and, highly irritated by the interruption, Daddy began again.

"Charles Dickens, on his American journey, stayed overnight at an inn in the vicinity of Altoona. It's all recorded in *American Notes,* an account of his trip to the Midwest, before the Civil War. Imagine, Charles Dickens himself, put up for a night or two at an establishment in the vicinity of Altoona."

Vicinity of Altoona grated like a knife against a plate, but Maddy smiled vivaciously, on the chance that Martin Jones might notice.

"He paid that modest American inn the choice compliment of declaring that it supplied the pleasantest accommodations he had ever enjoyed anywhere."

"Isn't that fascinating?" her mother said, to make up for her lapse, though the fascinating detail was well known to both Maddy and her mother.

Martin Jones and his companions had finished dinner and were rising to leave the dining car. With a regret as sharp as anger, she watched their departure.

Mr. Jones detached himself from the group and seemed to be approaching. Another chance?

"Won't you allow your charming daughter to join me and my companions in the club car?"

He spoke in a rush, as if he were not quite in control of his voice, or perhaps in a plan to take them by surprise; and after a pause, in response to the cold stares of Mr. and Mrs. Brewster, added his patently false assurances that "the ladies would take excellent care of your young lady."

Her parents declined, nervously, without consulting her. Maddy sat silently, her eyes cast down, studying some drops of tomato bisque that the action of the train had caused her to splatter on the whiteness of the tablecloth. When she looked up it was directly into Martin Jones's strangely hooded eyes, now openly mocking.

"A young girl needs a little fun now and then," he said. "Don't you agree, young lady?"

Some instinct led her to return his glance in a conspiratorial fashion, turning their joint mockery against the parents she loved and who loved her, and even adding hostility and insult, so that this man she cared nothing for should think her wiser in the ways of the world.

He smiled and said, "Well, it's too bad, too bad. Here's hoping you get to enjoy a little entertainment on your trip," with a peculiar emphasis on the word *entertainment*.

She said, "Thank you," tossing her hair from her face, looking bold and knowledgeable, she hoped, as if she could teach him a thing or two if only her parents weren't about.

After Martin Jones left, her mother said, "Why, Maddy! What did you mean, 'thank you!' "

And in a mocking repeat, Maddy said, "Why, Mother! Don't you know what 'thank you' means?"

Daddy gazed at them both, baffled.

She had become very warm again. Dinner rose in her throat. She excused herself and walked through the long dining car to the other end, where the toilet was situated. She was afraid she wouldn't make it safely, but she did and, after all, did not vomit. Locked into the clean narrow cubicle, she studied her flushed reflection in the mirror, where it trembled and jiggled with the movement of the train, a steady bouncing beat that unaccountably aroused her body. What was the matter with her? Tentatively she thrust a hand under her skirt and pressed her palm between her legs while the other hand slid under her middy to caress her breast. She had never touched herself in this way before. She neither understood the pitch of desire seizing her nor how to allay it, but as if her hands knew their own business, they stroked and massaged. The eyes of the pretty girl in the mirror detached their gaze from her hands; they misted and glazed; the girl's lips parted and she moaned, *Oh, oh, oh, oh, God, oh, God,* in the voice of a stranger.

From the outside, the knob rattled. For a briefest second, Maddy's body leaped to welcome Martin Jones pushing his way in, but it was a woman who called. "Occupied? Is it occupied?"

Maddy forced her voice to a normal pitch. "Yes, please," she said, "just a moment, please."

In the mirror she watched her hands flutter out and away from their hard work. She shuddered. A terrible humiliation stabbed her. Who was she? What was she doing?

If her parents failed to follow Martin Jones's advice to settle in at the Drake, it was because they would be doing as well, if not better, as guests of officials of the Chicago branch of the Society, put up in the Voynows' townhouse overlooking the great lake, a few blocks north of the hotel. The Voynows were a childless couple, remarkably colorless, even if extremely rich, who centered upon Maddy as on an object to collect, treasure, and pamper, an attention she found both gratifying and hard to bear. Locked into the immense house with four boring adults, Maddy spent much of her time stationed at the full-length windows facing Lake Shore Drive, longing to escape to the endlessly inviting, wide, long sandy beach skirting the amazing sea that rose and fell directly across from a splendid boulevard heavy with traffic. They had arrived in Chicago on the tail of a storm, which left behind majestic, rolling breakers, while upon the extensive surface of the water, stopped only by the distant horizon, whitecaps jiggled brilliantly in a strong, hot sun, lending a merry and decorative touch to the business of the lake, the huge ships plying its length. It was an astonishing sight — this glorious playground in the heart of a busy city much like New York — though to her fuddled memory, Chicago, on this perfect morning, seemed taller, cleaner, richer, more massive, and infinitely more impressive than the New York City of her eleven-year-old remembrance. The company she was forced to keep subdued her spirits, but it was impossible with such a scene below to be depressed by the confinement of the house, or to envision Society members and precepts as anything but absolutely right. Were not both enshrined after all in a wonderful setting?

She had never seen a place as grand as the Voynow townhouse. Nothing in Iowa City, not even the home of the president of the university, set in long, smooth lawns stretching down to the river, was remotely like it. Maddy's parents' comfortable, roomy place, on its tree-shaded road and its own bit of ground, which was luxurious compared to the East Bronx tenement from which they had moved, paled into nothing beside the Voynow mansion. Only the public buildings of the college were somewhat suggestive of its grandeur.

On either side of an inner courtyard, two long galleries ran the length of the building. The first was filled with portraits of officials, some in Indian dress, some in what appeared to be religious regalia, others attired like members of the wealthy class to which they so clearly belonged. The other gallery displayed photographs, paintings, and drawings of Society encampments throughout the world. At the very top of the house, an enchanting circular room was a library containing Society publications, books and pamphlets in many languages, even in Sanskrit, as Mr. Voynow proudly pointed out. One whole section of the library was devoted to the Society's celebrated occult collection: artists' renderings of thought pictures, Astral journeys, portraits of Society masters drawn from memory, genealogies of Society leaders in their former incarnations and interactions, color figurations of the chemical properties of molecules and atoms as detected in Astral investigations, astrologists' charts, music heard out-of-body on Astral journeys and recorded from memory.

To please the adults, and goaded by her father's expectations, she simulated such intelligent and ardent interest in the displays that the Voynows extended permission for Maddy to immerse herself in these sacred wonders for as long as she wished. She had outsmarted herself and was doomed to stay indoors.

Left to herself, sighing deeply, she turned to the shelf that the Voynows had pointed out to her as holding the greatest interest for a young person. She leafed through the booklets, reading at random, her mind riddled with boredom. Many sentences had been underlined by a previous reader. When she encountered one of these, she made an effort to think about what the sentence meant, and in an exaggerated mimicry of her father in deep thought, she threw back her head and contemplated the ceiling, better to absorb the depth of thought. After what seemed a very long time, which when checked turned out to be ten minutes, she searched for paper and pencil in the top drawer of the massive desk and copied certain phrases that struck her as the pithiest keys to Society philosophy. The exercise would also use up time.

She wrote down:

Divine wisdom is a fountain from which all may drink who seek a universal, eternal principle basic to all life.

The Path to the Good is open to all who wish to pursue it.

The spiritual nature of the universe, and our place in the divine simplicity of its design, is clear to all who wish to see it.

Those quotes were culled from a book by the Indian boy Vidhya, written when he was *thirteen,* for God's sake. She studied the frontispiece photograph: a daffy-looking boy with a sallow, sorrowful, skinny face, long black hair parted in the middle, eyes cast upward and showing a lot of white under the iris. What an odd boy, to be able to write like that at thirteen. But then of course he had been designated the coming Savior of the world. She looked at his unsavory picture for some time before passing on to the next book, *The ABC of Society Precepts for Young Readers.*

Though she could remember nothing of the book's substance, she had already read this pamphlet, in Iowa. Its author was Bishop Beauregard Nysmith; it had entered their house before the days of the scandal now surrounding him. The bishop was pictured full-length, decked out in a long robe and fancy headdress, a huge silver crucifix hanging from his neck, his big, kindly face wreathed in Old Testament flowing white hair and full beard.

She skimmed through, mostly reading underlined sections, from which she copied one sentence.

Faith is the transcendent source of all being and all good.

From time to time during the long wait until lunch, she allowed her attention a rest from Society philosophy and let it stray to the bright outdoor scene framed by the expansive windows of the room, pushing aside the rich, worn golden velvet drapes and filmy ecru curtains that hung between her and the bright world outside. But just before the adults came to fetch her for lunch, she became genuinely caught up in a book by Lady Florence Greenwood, a name much mentioned in talk of the Society. *Womanhood and the Moral Path to the Good*, the book was called. She began by reading dutifully, copying out the sentence:

Our task is to reconcile the existence of an all-powerful and all-good principle that governs the universe with the presence of evil in the world.

Not so much the book itself but the sheaf of clippings stuck into its binding whipped up her imagination. To begin with, Lady Florence was beautiful, very beautiful as a young woman shown in a photo taken with her ratty-looking husband, then viceroy of India, and with her two children, leaning against their radiant young mother, all of them frowning and squinting in the intense sunlight, the whole lot abandoned by her that year, it appeared from the clippings, so that Lady Florence was free to live a wild life alongside George Bernard Shaw and an astoundingly handsome man, Gordon Craig. Her husband sued for custody of the children, citing an unwholesome atmosphere of radical politics, experimental art, and free love surrounding their mother. She was a nudist, a pacifist, a Socialist, a leading speaker for the Fabian Society. He was awarded custody of the children and she was forbidden any contact. Then, forsaking Shaw and Craig (or the other way around), she took up with another incredibly handsome man — a German with a long, unpronounceable name — and embracing spiritualism and Eastern philosophy, she joined the Universal Society of Brotherhood and, along with an ugly Russian woman with another unpronounceable name and Bishop Nysmith, put it on the map in England, India, and Australia. Bishop Nysmith was also a very handsome man, particularly in his youth and all along really, right up to the present, and Lady Florence was pretty even into her eighties. In the latest clippings and photos, she was shown dressed in a white sari, looking a little stout and matronly, true, especially looming above that ugly little man Mahatma Gandhi, he dressed in a ridiculous white sheet, or whatever it was he wore tied around his loins.

The adventure of Lady Florence's life sent Maddy racing to the window to look out again. What a world lay out there waiting for her, where a Lady Florence dared to leave security, husband, and children for the romance of her beliefs, to do something in the world, all by herself, alone and a woman. She wanted to be that kind of woman. She would begin the very next day. Leave her parents and set out on her own, putting out of her mind that she was moving on with her parents' blessing and in the care of the Voynows.

The wind had died down when she was fetched for lunch, and it was served on an outdoor terrace, part of the inner courtyard, an enclosure within an enclosure, as cunningly designed and landscaped as her fairy tale dreams of a secret garden. The Voynows, much impressed with her serious pursuits in the library, offered her goodies in alternate voices: wine as if she were a grown-up, blanc mange as if she were a highchair infant, wooing her either way. The notion passed through her head that she might exert sufficient charm on this couple who were to accompany her to New York and then to England so that they would end by adopting her and she could live a life of luxury with them — a fancy that dissipated as easily as it had fleetingly appeared. Not sufficient daring in that adventure. After all, it wasn't as if the Voynows were George Bernard Shaw or Gordon Craig.

Luncheon conversation, after a long discussion of the Sacco-Vanzetti case, proved to be revelatory, though not about Sacco and Vanzetti. They had been executed a few weeks earlier, and there was nothing more she wanted to hear on that subject. Childlike, she had been led by her elders into their unshakable belief that these "two good men," as her daddy and mother always referred to them, could not and would not be left to die at the hands of a violent state. Yet they had died. What had been put before her as an inconceivable possibility had become a mundane fact, kicking a huge black hole into the sunshiny Society optimism that she had counted on to make everything come out right. What about the clairvoyants who had prophesied it would not come to pass? What about the power of brotherhood to right all wrongs? What good was the Universal Society of Brotherhood with its claimed 700,000 membership worldwide if it couldn't stop the execution of Sacco and Vanzetti? Those were the questions she wanted the four boring adults to answer. She wasn't interested in any subtleties that by-passed them.

On the day the two good men were executed, Maddy had cried and stormed, talking nonsense, raging at this unthinkable outcome.

"It's not as simple as the good guys and the bad guys," Daddy chided her.

Why not, she hadn't dared to respond. Why isn't it the good guys and the bad guys, the angels and the dark powers? Why not? That's the way you always put it to me.

She would not listen now at lunch to after-the-fact pieties that could no longer help the two good men. Yet it was impossible to shut out Daddy's voice reciting Vanzetti's last statement in court. He had memorized the words as if they were a poem by Shelley or Walt Whitman, declaiming as if from a platform. His performance offended her, though she could not have explained why, and in spite of her resistance to responding, she did, tears starting to her eyes and a burning sensation seizing the base of her skull, tightening and expanding, in a frightening, pulsating, rhythmic pain.

"'What I say is that I am innocent ... That I am not only innocent ... but in all my life I have never stole and I have never killed and I have never spilled blood. That is what I want to say. And it is not all. Not only am I innocent ... not only in all my life I have never stole, never killed, never spilled blood, but I have struggled all my life, since I began to reason, to eliminate crime from the earth ...'"

There was no stopping Daddy. He went through Bartolomeo Vanzetti's complete statement, by the end of which tears were streaming down Maddy's face, but whether they flowed from pure sorrow, or angry frustration, or the pain at the base of her skull, she couldn't say.

"'I would not wish to a dog or to a snake, to the most low and misfortunate creature of the earth — I would not wish to any of them what I have had to suffer for things that I am not guilty of. But my conviction is that I have suffered for things that I am guilty of. I am suffering because I am a radical, and indeed I am a radical; I have suffered because I was an Italian, and indeed I am an Italian; ... but I am so convinced to be right that if you could execute me two times, and if I could be reborn two other times, I would live again to do what I have done already.'"

She left the table to blow her nose and wash her face, aware that she had once again won the admiration and approval of her hosts, this time for the depth and strength of her emotions, once again, spuriously. Because what touched her about the case of Sacco and Vanzetti was not the solid stuff the adults discussed, but the romance of martyrdom, the Joan of Arc–ness of their tragedy, seeing herself in their role, hung, burned at the stake, dramatically and nobly submitting to a fate containing an important message for all humanity. Not the sort of imaginings she could share with her parents or her hosts.

Her father was agitating about other matters when she returned.

"Bishop! What kind of bishop? New Church of Jesus! Bishop of the New Church of Jesus! Mumbo jumbo. Phony religiosity — robes, silver crucifixes, masses, funny hats — might as well set up a Ku Klux Klan unit in the Society."

"Come now," Mr. Voynow said, obviously shocked.

"Augustus." Maddy's mother placed a restraining hand on Daddy's arm. "Not for others to question any individual's religious faith."

"Religious phony-baloney," Daddy bellowed. "The Society cannot be allowed to become anybody's plaything. We're not a secret society or a religious cult. We are a rational force for good in the world, penetrating into phenomena not yet examined by science. We endanger our endeavors with Bishop Nysmith's nonsense. If the man wants to found a new church, still another church in a world order that already has far too many, let him, but outside the Society. His kind of mischief has no place in the Society. As long as he keeps his shenanigans outside our Society, there will be no objections from Augustus Brewster and the rest of the American branch. And I say that also goes for his dubious claims about a new Messiah."

"Come now," Mr. Voynow said. "Come on, now."

The mild objection inflamed Daddy.

"What? You're convinced this young Indian boy is the Messiah, because Bobo saw this extraordinary aura emanating from him? This man is not to be trusted. What about the trial? What about the charges of perversion?"

Daddy was shouting as only he could shout.

"This is an unspeakable scandal involving these two, the bishop and his chosen Messiah. The entire Midwest section is up in arms over this scandal. You say the accusations are false. Lady Florence says the accusations are false.

Bishop Nysmith puts forth his spurious theories of hygiene and spiritual serenity. But where does such a scandal arise? Where there's smoke, there's fire. Too much talk. Why would these other youngsters lie about such a monstrous evil? Lie against themselves? It's not conceivable to me."

"Please, Augustus," Maddy's mother said. "Think of the child."

Her eyes fluttered in Maddy's direction, distracting her from asking who Bobo was supposed to be.

"I *am* thinking of the child," Daddy said. "Believe me, I am thinking deeply about the child."

"I mean, the talk." Maddy's mother's voice almost disappeared.

"I know very well what you mean. You mean that we should keep silent before her. But if the man is a pervert, practicing his perversions within the Society, then he must be exposed. He must be exposed. We must all give our attention to this exposure. The Society is more important than any individual member of it. And where is the moral logic of your position? Shall I keep silent before my daughter out of some foolish prudery? Why, this scandal has become public knowledge. It's splashed all over the papers, used to discredit us, all of us. We have been brought to public trial. This cannot be hidden."

"Not 'we,' " Mr. Voynow said. "Only Bobo is on trial."

"He reflects on all of us," Daddy said. "He and his theories, his peculiar practices, his auras and his proclamations of a new Messiah. We're sending our child into the midst of —"

Mrs. Voynow showed a faint flush on her pale cheeks. She held up a trembling hand to stop the rush of Daddy's anger.

"I assure you," she said, "Mr. Voynow and I will watch over Maddy with the same care we would take of the child we've never had. We wouldn't dream of leaving her at the house in Hampstead unless we're entirely satisfied with their explanations. But I must assure you," she added, and reached out, like a white moth, to pat not Daddy's hand but Maddy's, "that I have the soundest faith in Bobo. I've known him intimately for many years and he's a man of many gifts."

"His many gifts hardly interest me," Daddy said before Maddy could ask who Bobo was, anyway. "What concerns me is his moral fiber. My concern is with my daughter. She, too, has many gifts, not the least of which is her own good sense. She will see for herself. I believe that is the best education to be had, seeing for oneself. She will make her own decision. In time. When she is old enough. We deliver into the hands of the Society an innocent child, to study her music and to invite her soul, in the words of the great Walt Whitman. We send her forth on life's great journey. The wheel of life will carry her along in its wake. But we must be sure she's in good hands." Daddy put up a restraining palm. "Don't misunderstand. Not the Society comes under question here. Only some individuals, perhaps only one individual, perhaps more."

"And if Bobo's young Indian lad ..." Mrs. Voynow trembled so violently that the plate of fruit she was passing around among her guests wobbled visibly. "If Vidhya really is the Messiah ... if he really is?"

"If, if, if," Daddy shouted, and laughed too loudly. "Then let him convince us." He was more expansive, suddenly. "Let him convince us and the world himself. Not for Bishop Nysmith to drown us in talk of auras and the rest of his hocus-pocus."

"Surely you're not denying the power of the unknown, whatever you choose to call it — the occult, the supernatural, the divine," Mr. Voynow said.

"Neither denying nor affirming," Daddy said briskly. "That is our special task, our mission, to examine what science has ignored, to journey into unknown territories, to penetrate the mysteries. Meanwhile, we can neither deny nor affirm."

"Why, that's exactly what that Jew said, Lord What-ever-His-Name-Is, that man presiding at the trial."

Mrs. Voynow flushed pinker.

"He said it is not within the jurisdiction of the court to question Society canons, or the authenticity of individual claims in the occult world, and that he would neither affirm nor deny such claims, but he certainly has questioned every other aspect of Society business, even the handling of funds. How dare he? Not for a Jew to question our handling of funds, I should think."

"Now you see," Maddy's mother murmured, as if to herself, "where such talk leads."

But Daddy took the murmur as directed squarely at him.

"Where? Where does such talk lead? Where does it lead? Please keep me informed on this subject, my dear wife, since you are the expert. Where does it lead?"

"Daddy." Maddy also whispered. "Please, Daddy."

Her father flung himself back in his chair and, with a long, hissing expulsion of his breath, proposed that the discussion come to an end.

"If it's agreeable to all, let us put these unpleasant subjects behind us," he said. "And let me apologize to our hosts for allowing it to go so far."

"No apology necessary," Mr. Voynow said. "No offense given and none taken."

"I assure you," Mrs. Voynow said, polite in her bewilderment, and finally brought to rest on the delicately embroidered white tablecloth the now well shaken china bowl of perfect, rose-tinted ripe pears.

The splendid train Maddy and the Voynows boarded for the trip from Chicago to New York should have made up for all the shortcomings of the Rock Island Line, yet Maddy's pleasure in its luxuries was spoiled by an unexpected sense of loss. She had parted from her parents with the briefest of kisses and a surge of relief, but only a few hours distant from them, she was overwhelmed with undefined depression, expanding like heavy mist into despair at herself bereft and lonely, totally cut off from everything she knew and loved. Yet that was exactly what she had wanted, was it not? And in irritation at her own inconsistencies, she broke into tears at the table in the elegant dining car. To the inquiries of her aghast temporary guardians, she offered an invented explanation: she had been seized by a vision and was certain she would never see her mother and father again. Mr. and Mrs. Voynow soothed her, but without conviction. Premonitions issued by innocent young spirits were too powerful to dispel. What the Voynows possessed were gifts of consolation, which they exerted freely, urging upon Maddy's material body the veal medallions, a bit of white wine, and even coffee, if she wished, with her apricot soufflé. As a final consolation, Mrs. Voynow reminded her of a promised shopping tour in New York to smarten up Maddy's wardrobe. And Mr. Voynow assured Maddy that she would be in England for a few months, half a year, at most a year, and could leave for home at any time during those intervals if homesickness overcame her.

Her parents had not supplied the information that New York City had been Maddy's birthplace. Maddy herself remained silent on the subject, and indeed the New York into which they were plunged at the end of the run was so different from her earlier remembrances that she might have been entering a city she had never known. They were met in the cathedral-like lobby of the station by three people: a blond youngster, perhaps Maddy's age, though much shorter than she, a boy so handsome he was positively pretty; a grown-up young woman with strangely hooded eyes very like the stranger's on the train from Iowa; and a chubby, middle-aged Indian, dressed in a Western-style business suit, his head elaborately garish in a pleated silk turban, enhanced by deep purple lips, a blazing white-toothed smile, and skin as dark as mud. Though Maddy was introduced all around, their names blurred, except for the young woman's — Victoria Younger — so romantically storybook, it stuck.

She struggled to keep afloat on the rapids of the allusive conversation while the luggage was claimed and placed in the limousine that carried them from the station to the Plaza. It seemed they were all staying at the same magnificent hotel, all sailing on the same magnificent ship; there was constant reference to the group as a *party* and for Maddy, yes, it became a party, an occasion filled with excitement and false posings, a subtle test forcing her to shine, to toss her hair and widen her eyes, to listen avidly and laugh a lot to cover confusion, to somehow make a splash in these unknown waters where otherwise she would surely sink. Names, places, events, gossip, news, flew by her too fleet and alien to corner, tantalizing in flashes of color, a blaze of intrigue, all hopelessly bewildering. There was a prickliness in the banter of the young woman, Victoria, that enchanted Maddy, creating an atmosphere as light and brittle as crystal, in whose reflection even the Voynows became sprightly conversationalists.

The purple-lipped Indian was clearly a kind of manager, handling tickets, luggage, movement of the party, with a smoothly fussy capability. Victoria seemed to have been raised by the Society and constituted one of its stars, a performer, though Maddy couldn't pin down what sort. The pretty youngster was something of a boy wonder, though details of his wonderful manifestations also escaped Maddy. She listened and smiled, smiled and listened, and by the time the car drew up before the ornate entrance to the Plaza, Maddy had successfully insinuated herself into membership in the *party*, an assurance that came to her in an incandescent melding of sensations while standing under the canopy of the hotel on its imposing square, the street alive with the sounds of traffic and pedestrians, sharp with the smell of horses tethered to the run-down carriages lining the avenue, a homey Iowa smell mingling with the acrid air of the city and the exotic perfumes of the hotel puffing out into the street with each turn of the revolving door, liveried men rushing about, handling the Voynow party's luggage, Mrs. Voynow fluttering at the core of the group, Mr. Voynow a pale moon, the little Indian a steadying light, Victoria a glittering barb, the boy wonder a shining essence, and Maddy Brewster hanging on at the edges, a charming adornment.

Whatever the Society was, and in truth she wasn't sure *what* it was, she knew in that moment on the steps of the Plaza that its attractions were already too great for her to forgo. She could mouth Society slogans as well as anybody — Universal Brotherhood, Individual Peace, the Path to the Good — phrases that came to her tongue in capital letters and with solemn intonations — the Seven Levels to Perfection, the Divine Wisdom of the Elders, the Astral Plane. Long before her parents had joined the Universal Society of Brotherhood, Daddy had dabbled in what he called scientific investigations into the possibility of intelligent life in space, and he had initiated a university experiment in ESP, for a time even using Maddy as a subject in a controlled study of mind communication: Daddy in the basement, Maddy in the attic. They had had surprising success. Maddy had a flair for knowing the answer Daddy wanted.

She had been too shy to ask an outright, dumb question: *What will I do in the Society?*

She would see. She would see when she got there.

Meanwhile, she would feel her way through the confusion of information pouring in. It would have helped her if Daddy's positions were less ambiguous. He had always been her model, and her instinct was to follow his lead, but his attack upon Bishop Nysmith worried her now that she was on her own, abandoned in ignorance among strong pro–Bishop Nysmith forces. Daddy's arguments had bewildered more than enlightened her. Wasn't Daddy a sexually liberated, advanced thinker, always quoting Havelock Ellis and castigating bourgeois concepts of narrow morality? Not that she clearly understood whatever it was he was railing against and whatever it was Bishop Nysmith was charged with, though it was plain enough that it had to be *sexual*. And that business about the Messiah. Hadn't Daddy always said that the Jews were idiots for not going along with Jesus and Christianity?

She knew enough to know that her father's positions were not very popular in the Voynow party, and if she had any doubts on that score she had only to listen to the tones in which they invoked her father's name, *that American, Brewster of Iowa*, a phrase accompanied by a sliding sneer, reserved also for the trial judge, always called in his turn *the Jew, Lord Whatever-His-Name-Is*. Another case of "not as simple as the good guys and the bad guys"? She couldn't sort it all out.

She felt her ignorance so acutely it was like an illness of the body — headache or stomachache. At the core of the Bishop Nysmith trial coiled an inexpressible evil, so shocking that nobody named it. Did she want to know? Even to delicately probe into this dark place sent her body into an uncontrollable nervous little dance, backward and forward, forward and backward, the movement of a spastic. A strange ache invaded her groin. Then there was the odd buzz set off inside her head whenever someone said *Lord Whatever-His-Name-Is, that Jew, the trial judge*, and worse when they said *that American, Brewster of Iowa*.

Cleves, the blond boy, brought the whole matter to the surface with a direct question.

Maddy and he had been left alone among the chocolate smells of Rumpelmayer's after a long day of shopping the Fifth Avenue stores. She felt she knew Cleves better at the end of the day, though they had been separated much of the time, she and Mrs. Voynow taking off for the women's sections of the stores and Cleves and Mr. Voynow for the men's. Victoria had scorned the entire excursion. Victoria was twenty-one, the boy wonder seventeen, giving them both a considerable edge on Maddy. But they had all been together at lunch, and while purchasing luggage as well as a heap of expensive little main-floor items she had marveled at anybody's need for. There had been no wondrous manifestation emanating from Cleves throughout the day beyond a brilliant gift for mimicking grown-up mannerisms and ways of talking. Sometimes he seemed a freak, an adult performer wearing a handsome boy's mask or a midget pretending to be a youngster.

"Do you go along with all this stuff your father is — well — so hot under the collar about?"

"What stuff?" she said.

Cleves had insisted on ordering hot chocolates, though the September day was very warm. They were amazing — mounds of ivory whipped cream topped each cup, and they were accompanied by a plate of beautiful little cakes. She wanted desperately to give her whole attention to the hot chocolate and little cakes.

"Come on," Cleves said, "you know what stuff."

A showdown was the last thing she had expected, and that its source should be the boy wonder was also an uncomfortable surprise. Of all the Voynow party, she trusted Cleves least. She pretended passionate interest in her hot chocolate and cakes, while feeling her way. Her choices were limited. She could abandon her father and go over to their side wholesale, or she could establish an uneasy neutrality. She shrank from a coarse rejection of her father, yet the urge to capitulate was very strong. More than anything, the enchantments of life revealed to her in the last days were too dazzling to jeopardize. Give up the beautiful outfits Mrs. Voynow had insisted on buying her? Give up the room at the Plaza, the stateroom on the *Majestic?* Pictures of what awaited them in Europe had accumulated like quicksilver, its elements breaking up and slipping away as they formed in the rapid talk of the group. But she could not now sacrifice any shining possibilities; not for anything, and least of all for her father's opinions. The problem was to make capitulation credible, natural, and likable. Neutrality seemed the best response, hanging her explanations on her ignorance and youth.

"You know," she said, "I really have a hard time understanding the whole thing."

"You mean the charges? You mean the — you know — the stuff about Bishop Nysmith and Vidhya and the bathing? Naked?"

She didn't know about Bishop Nysmith and Vidhya and the bathing, but she nodded.

"Oh, it's all pretty complicated," Cleves said. "But when you really come down to it, what is it, after all, but a question of love? A lot of people don't know anything about love. You have to teach love. You have to teach people how to love. What's wrong with that? Teaching the meaning of love in all its various manifestations. Perfect and imperfect. Because even imperfect love is acceptable while we all travel on the road to perfect love."

He had been intent on scooping up the sliding mounds of whipped cream topping his cup, but he looked up at the end of his speech. His expression proclaimed an innocence she suspected was false. She had seen him in too many greedy situations that day to believe in the visual effects of the fair, round face, the blond hair parted in the middle over an unusually high forehead, the curling lashes decorating the guileless eyes.

She said, "Oh, I see."

He exploded into a laugh of captivating mischief.

"You don't know what I'm talking about, do you?"

She said, "I don't, I guess, really."

"You'll see," he said, still grinning. "You'll see."

She was safe, perhaps, for the moment.

He began again, this time intently serious.

"We're counting on you, you know, about the separate cabins. We're both dead set on that, Victoria and I. It will be hell if we don't get separate cabins. Victoria does *not* want to

45

share a cabin with you. You'll get on her wrong side if you don't back us up. And believe me, being on the wrong side of Victoria is no fun."

"Oh, you can count on me," she said.

She wasn't sure that they could. Victoria Younger and Cleves Wyndham might make life miserable for her, but as far as Maddy could see, it was Mr. and Mrs. Voynow who picked up the bills. Mrs. Voynow liked her and Mr. Voynow liked whatever Mrs. Voynow did. Why should she do anything to spoil her favored position?

He grinned again.

"You western American girls are so gullible," he said. "It's absolutely *charming.*"

Cleves was American, but he had attended school in England and had lived abroad so much he liked to talk as if he wasn't.

"Iowa isn't the West," Maddy said. "It's practically East."

"It's criminal of them to expect me to share a cabin with Mr. Singh," he said.

"Don't you like him?" she said.

She certainly could understand not wanting to share sleeping space with the little middle-aged Indian. After all, he did have purple lips. But criminal?

Cleves sighed. "It's nothing to do with *liking,*" he said. "I love him, of course, he's one of my masters. But —"

He had finished his chocolate, and checking on her cup he snatched the last little chocolate cake and stood up. He really was a tiny fellow.

"Come on," he said. "You're done. Let's get back to the hotel, and I'll teach you how to stand on your head. It's easy as pie, you'll see."

Without premeditation or any clear consciousness of what she was about, Maddy asked Victoria to help her. It was the

morning of the third day of the Voynow party's New York
stopover. The following afternoon they would board the
Majestic. Maddy seized a moment when she and Victoria
were alone at breakfast. They had both been late.

"I want to ask you a tremendous favor," Maddy said.

Victoria's expressionless eyes, hooded by the deep, blu-
ish lids, put her at an unapproachable distance. She turned
to look behind her as if Maddy might have been speaking to
someone else, then turned back.

"What could I possibly do for you," Victoria said, elim-
inating any question from the words.

"The problem is that I must go see somebody, but I
can't tell you who or why or anything at all about it,"
Maddy said.

Victoria was attentive.

"And I know Mrs. Voynow won't let me go alone. I'm
perfectly capable of going by myself — it's perfectly safe,
it's in the Bronx — but they won't let me go by myself, I
know they won't. It's very important to me or I wouldn't ask
you, but I know you'd understand if I could tell you, I know
you would, so I thought you'd help. You could say you want
to show me the sights, something like that."

"In the Bronx," Victoria said and seemed to sneer.

Maddy said nothing.

"Why should I help you," Victoria said.

"I thought we were supposed to help each other,"
Maddy said.

"It's to do with the Society," Victoria said.

It was disconcerting how Victoria asked questions, delivering them as flat statements to which she expected no
sensible return.

"No," Maddy said, "nothing to do with the Society."

Victoria said, "Let's see, now, how old are you again.
Fifteen."

"Almost sixteen," Maddy said.

"It's an affair," Victoria said.

47

An affair! What profound flattery! Her heart pumped in her ears. She had begun this foray without a plan beyond her desperate desire to visit the street in the Bronx where she had lived, but she had also been longing to tear through the remoteness of this older young woman almost from the first moment she had met her in the domed space of the train station. Her request might just accomplish both.

"I can't tell you," she said. "I wish I could." And added, "It's not an affair, honest."

"Why not ask Mr. Singh," Victoria said.

Maddy burst into laughter, an uncontrollable reaction to a vision of the round little man with the purple lips and elaborate turban on the streets of the East Bronx. Victoria looked pleased by the response.

"Why not Cleves," Victoria said, watching her closely.

The subject of Cleves was too complicated to pour into the concoction she had already set to boil. She avoided this danger with a shrug.

"You don't want Cleves's help," Victoria said. "You don't trust Cleves. You don't like faggy boys."

Victoria followed that shock with another. She asked a question and let her voice rise.

"Don't you like fags?" And then, after a pause, "Do you know what I'm talking about?"

Maddy produced what she hoped was an airily sophisticated hand gesture.

"I read *The Well of Loneliness*," Maddy said, "just before I left Iowa."

Victoria laughed. She was irresistible when she laughed.

"Excellent preparation for leaving Iowa," she said. "I'm from Lincoln, Nebraska. I didn't leave until I was almost nineteen, but I read *Psychopathia Sexualis* and *Sanine* before I left."

Maddy was lost. She tried to return Victoria's mocking

smile with a warmly neutral one of her own. After a while, Victoria began again.

"I suppose I could suggest to Les Voyeurs that I take you to the Bronx Zoo. They know I like to study animal movements for my work. It's a beautiful day. Cleves will kick up a fuss, probably insist on coming along even if he doesn't want to, just to be a pest. I can manage him one way or another."

"I don't want him to come," Maddy said. "Please."

"How long will it take — whatever you have to do — once we're where we're going."

Again she laughed.

" 'We're where we're,' " she said. "Listen to me."

"What?" Maddy said, bewildered.

"We can ask for three hours," Victoria said. "Will that be enough time?"

It was a marvelous freedom to be in Victoria's charge. Their trip was a game in which the rules Maddy had established were part of the fun. Victoria would deliver Maddy to Southern Boulevard. Maddy would then walk to her destination. No following, Victoria swore. They would meet again at the same corner two hours later. No questions asked. They would be back at the hotel in time for tea and the important visitors scheduled to arrive with messages and gifts for Society members abroad.

Victoria knew the Bronx. She took Maddy by subway and then trolley car, because she loved to ride streetcars. She bought a Peter Paul Mounds at a candy stand under an elevated train and shared it with Maddy after they boarded the airy trolley.

"I know everything," Victoria said. "You're an anarchist courier picking up a package to be delivered to a secret agent who is a functionary of the Universal Society of Brotherhood. A bomb."

"Something like that," Maddy said.

"Your father's right, you know," Victoria said.

Her head was turned away from Maddy, attentive to the lively, squeezed streets outside the trolley's windows. "He's right about the facts, that is. He's wrong to do what he's doing."

Maddy said nothing.

"Do you agree with him? You probably agree with him. You're very agreeable," Victoria said.

"Oh, Victoria," Maddy said. "Please don't be mean to me."

Victoria mimicked her. " 'Oh, Victoria, please don't be mean to me.' "

Her intent was cruel, perhaps, but the effect was of pain revealed so baldly, it hurt Maddy to glance at its distorted face.

"Mean!" Victoria said. "Didn't I share my Peter Paul Mounds with you? Didn't I? Didn't I? The thing I love more than life itself? And what am I doing on this trolley in the Bronx if it isn't to please you?"

"I'm sorry," Maddy said. "I meant I just want you to like me so much."

"Why? Do you like *me*?" Victoria said. "Don't answer that, I don't want to know."

"I can't help it if I'm young and don't understand everything — hardly anything, as a matter of fact," Maddy said.

"That's right," Victoria said. "You don't, do you."

Maddy didn't speak.

"Well, if it comes to that," Victoria said, "neither do any of us."

"Yes, you do," Maddy said.

They rode in silence.

"You can ask me to explain anything," Victoria said, then. "I'd get a real kick out of explaining things to you."

Her face was oddly distorted again.

"Why do you all say 'that Jew, Lord-Whatever-His-Name-Is'?"

Maddy hadn't meant to say that. It had blurted itself out.

"What?" Victoria said, startled. And then said, "It's a hard name to remember. Bloomenfield, Lord Aaron Bloomenfield, something like that."

"I mean," Maddy persisted, "the other part, 'that Jew,' that part of it."

"But that's what he is," Victoria said.

"I didn't say he wasn't," Maddy said.

"This is a ridiculous conversation," Victoria said.

Maddy began to cry.

"What's the matter with you? Don't do that!"

Victoria seized Maddy's hand, rubbing hard, a nurse bringing a terminal patient back to consciousness.

"I don't know," Maddy said. "I just feel so strange."

"I should think so," Victoria said.

She was smiling in an attempt to be reassuring, but there was a stiff, painful self-consciousness in her manner that transferred her own pain in the rubbing and stroking of Maddy's hand.

"I'm all right now," Maddy said.

Victoria drew back.

"Why have they left you with Les Voyeurs. Your parents. Leave a young girl, leave a daughter with the Society and then go home to attack it. What are *you* supposed to do?"

Maddy was afraid she would cry again. She swallowed hard.

"My parents love the Society," she said. "I'm going to learn Society precepts and study music. What's wrong with that?"

Victoria turned her head back to the street scene.

"Is that the Voynows' real name," Maddy said, "that name you call them?"

Victoria laughed.

"You think we're bigots," Victoria said. "Jew haters. Why, the leader of the South African section is a Jew."

"Oh, I don't care about it," Maddy said. "It just struck me funny. None of you say 'Bishop Nysmith, that Christian.'"

"What in the world," Victoria said. She turned her hooded eyes to Maddy, searching Maddy's face with hot, open interest.

"What in the world," she said again.

Maddy was silent.

"We all know Bishop Nysmith very well. We don't even call him Bishop Nysmith. We call him Bobo. His name is Beauregard," Victoria said.

"What a silly name," Maddy said.

Victoria laughed.

"It suits him," she said.

"My father says," Maddy began, "that there are certain human beings who are half men and half women, that they're born that way and can't help themselves. Hermaphrodites, I think they're called."

She wasn't sure of her pronunciation or of her facts, or why she was pursuing this conversation at all. Victoria studied her. Well, at least she had thoroughly broken through Victoria's inattention.

"*The Well of Loneliness*," Victoria said.

"Oh no," Maddy said. "That was love. You know, real love. Hermaphrodites aren't normal. They're freaks, I think. In *The Well of Loneliness*, that was just two women who happened to love each other. Hermaphrodites are even mixed-up physically. Half men, half women. You know. Breasts on the men and women with no breasts."

"I see," Victoria said. "Freaks from the waist up."

Maddy blushed. "Maybe down there too," she said.

Something in Victoria's silence prompted her to add, "I guess I don't know what I'm talking about."

"Fair enough," Victoria said. "Neither does anybody else."

Was Victoria angry? She had become coldly closed off. It was a relief to arrive at their destination and to cut the heaviness building between them. Southern Boulevard was an astonishing sight. Maddy had forgotten that the broad avenue lined with run-down belly-fronted brownstones was transformed daily into an open market. She had lived six blocks north of this site, but her memory of it had been wiped out in the antiseptic cleansing process led by her father and acquiesced in silently and fearfully by her mother. They were no longer Jews; therefore the Southern Boulevard open-air market did not exist. It was the world of her grandma, expunged and repudiated by her father, not to be recalled. Yet here it was, stubbornly insisting on its smells, its sounds, its mess, its agitated life, its avid humanity occupying this territory, concentrating all its desperate interests under a dome of noise that vibrated according to its own laws, different from anything she had found in her non-Jewish existence. The shock of the scene rocked her, as if a huge hand had slapped her on the back, forcing her attention.

Pushcarts and horse-drawn wagons became stalls for the selling of ribbons, fish, underwear, jewelry, vegetables, trimmings, meats, socks, nuts, fabrics, sausages, feathered hats, fruits, shoes, mushrooms, pocketbooks, other stuff she couldn't name. Charcoal fires in tin drums heated up the already warm air with the aroma of roasted chestnuts and baked sweet potatoes. Open barrels of pickles, sauerkraut, olives, herring, salted meats, and fish mingled their pungent smells with the rising mist of the horses' hot piss and shit freshly dropped into the gutters, where the animals made a home for themselves, eating from feed bags, stamping a hoof or an unkempt tail at the green flies clustering. Children and dogs swarmed. Vendors and customers alike were Jews, dressed like Mennonites, in long black coats and black hats,

53

their hair twisted into long, crazy curls dangling before their ears.

Did she mean Mennonites? Amish or Amana German, one of those queer Iowa sects. And the drab Jewish women vendors, shapelessly black, wrapped head and body in dark scarves — how like the Amish girl she had seen driving her coffinlike black cart. They had been taking a spin in their new Hudson on a back road in the farm country behind their house, Mother and Daddy in the front seat, arguing about something stupid — the breed of pigs on these farms — Daddy overbearingly sure of his facts, Mother hesitantly stubborn of hers, Maddy bored into a stupefaction into which the black cart, the black horse, and the white-faced girl in the black cloak and bonnet entered like an omen.

Save me, Maddy had silently prayed to the still white face as it went by. *Save me from your fate.*

Iowa and the Bronx were mingling into a confounding juxtaposition. She separated the two by sound. Buried alive there, but sweetly silent. Here a confusion of Yiddish noise.

Everybody shouted — peddlers, customers, children, cats and dogs. Even Victoria shouted.

"It's marvelous. God, Maddy, it's marvelous. Why didn't you tell me? To think I might have missed this. I'm so glad I came. Two hours is too *short.*"

She was moving away from Maddy, heading toward a nearby pushcart piled with what seemed to be a jumble of colorful rags.

"Look, georgette!"

She yelled, how she yelled, just like all the other bargain seekers.

"Georgette, and in that wonderful deep green I've been searching for everywhere. What luck, what luck. If it's long enough, oh damn damn damn please make it long enough."

The length of sheer green material had clearly ended short of her hopes, but she held on to it, hanging it around her neck, and went on searching, tossing, yanking, pushing other shoppers aside. The remnant peddler attached herself to Victoria.

"Where will we meet?" Maddy yelled.

But Victoria was lost to her, deeply embroiled with the peddler woman, a gypsylike creature in black garments and head scarf, a clever beggar insinuating into the business between her and Victoria an instant hot intimacy. She lifted an iridescent fabric to Victoria's face, praising fabric and face for their mutual beauty in a language of grimaces and dancing gestures.

"Victoria, Victoria," Maddy screamed. She could scream as well as anybody. "Victoria, listen to me, where will I find you? Where will we meet?"

And beside herself with a jealousy she could not account for, shouted, "Damn it, Victoria, I haven't come here for your entertainment. Listen to me, where will we meet?"

She had all of Victoria's attention now. Victoria came right up to Maddy and in the midst of that wild hubbub spoke almost in a whisper.

"What did you say."

Her direct, angry gaze pleased Maddy even as it frightened her.

"I was afraid we would miss each other, not be able to find each other."

"What did you say about my entertainment."

"Nothing, nothing," Maddy said.

"What's the matter with you," Victoria said. "How dare you speak to me that way?"

"I just don't want us to lose each other," Maddy said.

"Be careful how you speak to me," Victoria said. "Why, I hardly know you. How dare you."

"I'm sorry," Maddy said. "I apologize. But please, where will we meet?"

"Right here," Victoria said. "In exactly two hours. And I expect you to be prompt."

Maddy walked away, mysteriously pleased by their quarrel. In a few blocks, except for some seepage of sounds and smells, it was as if the tumultuous market didn't exist. This was the street where Maddy Brewster had lived as Bessie Bernstein before being taken away to Iowa, a street smaller and dirtier than she remembered it, oddly familiar, oddly unfamiliar. The row of five-story tenements that filled its length had shrunk, yet everything else was the same: the broken sidewalks and cement stoops, the fire escapes dangling in flimsy disarray, the iron gates and dismal alleys piled with garbage cans, the cats and dogs. She could not be certain which of the dark entrances was the one she had run in and out of in those days of growing up on this block, pursuing her passionate little-girl existence as if it were the only possible one in the world. She moved on to the corner, where a new movie house displayed a silvery poster of a woman in a fur coat, looking at herself in a mirror while a sinister man hovered. Under the coat, the woman appeared to be naked. The street signpost, tilting toward Maddy, carried the name that had slipped her mind, Union Avenue. Yes, 883 Union Avenue, fifth floor back.

Was it possible that her grandmother still lived here?

She entered 883 gingerly. She had always feared the halls and did now. Monsters on the dim landings. Rats. Jack the Ripper. Real enough, even if never encountered. The vestibule was cleaner than expected, its linoleum scrubbed down with some strong-smelling disinfectant that triggered recognition. CN. Her grandmother would send her to the store to buy a bottle of the milky, poisonous-looking liquid. The hallways were alarmingly quiet. This had been a livelier scene when she was here — noise, people, kids. Perhaps it was the hour. A ghostly feeling invaded her sense of the place and of herself. The clatter of her own heels on the stairs scared her. The polished wooden banister was pleasantly smooth to her hand but the stained walls repelled her. Cooking smells drew her in — onions in chicken fat on the lower floor, pea soup on the next — Grandma food. Higher up, a nasty odor of cabbage.

The four apartments on the top floor showed no names, only numbers. On the door she picked out as the right one, there was an odd screw that appeared to be a bell. She couldn't bring herself to ring it. They had never had such a bell. She saw herself banging on the door with her fist, then bursting through.

"Grandma, Grandma, I'm home."

Perhaps she had been too short to have noticed that bell?

It was Grandma she came home to for lunch. Mama and Papa were both working. It was Grandma she came home to after school for a snack. Every Thursday afternoon her snack was a charlotte russe and hot chocolate with a marshmallow. So much for Rumpelmayer's. Grandma had her excesses and extravagances, her touches of aristocracy, whatever Papa's opinion. It was Grandma who insisted she change into play clothes, who combed her hair, made her feel beautiful and adored, smart and useful.

Why had she been separated from Grandma?

To wipe out Bessie Bernstein, a necessity for the birth of the Brewsters. Daddy's idea. Before he was Daddy, when he was Papa, haranguing them at suppers at the kitchen table.

"The Jews were idiots. What idiocy to reject Christ. Spend all your energy on one of the world's great myths, the coming of a Messiah, and then turn one's collective back when he arrives. Jews pride themselves on the fact that they're progressive. Nonsense. A most conservative people. You have to be blind not to recognize the moral and social superiority of the New Testament over the Old. As testament. As literature, that's something else. If you're looking for stories, that's another matter altogether."

Papa's theories. Grandma would walk out of the room before he finished the first sentence. He worked as a delicatessen counterman then in another part of the city, and he attended City College at night, studying to earn a degree. Mama had a license. A license wasn't as fine as a degree, but it was very good. No other mama on Union Avenue had a license. A license meant that Mama could teach in a public grade school, but Papa's aim was higher, and when Bessie was eight years old he reached the heights, earning his degree and a permanent appointment as a substitute teacher in a public high school. He had been miserable as a delicatessen counterman and he was miserable as a high school German teacher in what he called "the worst school in the city system." Every night at the supper table he made it plain just how miserable he was, and soon he was back at night school, trying for a different degree, and no longer ate suppers with them. She missed him, but it was a relief to be alone, cheerful and chatting, with Mama and Grandma.

It was impossible not to love Grandma, but Papa managed it. He never called her Mama. He brought nonkosher food into the house and ate it openly, preparing elaborate sandwiches of ham and American cheese on Bond bread with bright yellow Gulden's mustard.

"Gitel," he would say to Grandma, being disrespectful, using her given name, "Gitel, try some. Broaden your narrow outlook on life, prove to your ignorant self that *traife* doesn't kill. Learn something, Gitel, about the real world."

Remarkable how Grandma's always soft and smiling face could harden. Like a bird, she would leave the room. She stopped talking to Papa and was cold to Mama. To her grandchild, too? Never.

Soul was what she called her granddaughter. *Golden soul.* In Yiddish, of course.

Standing on the dark, narrow, smelly hallway landing of 883 Union Avenue, thinking back to being Bessie, why did she feel safer then, safer then with Grandma than now as Maddy Brewster among Society bigwigs?

Papa and Mama had sat her down at the kitchen table

and told her the whole plan. Papa had not only a new degree but a teaching assignment at the University of Iowa. He had traveled all the way out there and back to set up a fantastic new life for them. He said that Iowa City was beautiful, that a river wound through the town, that the college sat at the top of a steep hill in the very center of the city, that it was America, the real real thing, that Bessie was the luckiest girl in the world to be getting out of the Bronx, that there was a wonderful house available, a dream, an American dream of a house, that they would take a new name, Brewster, that she could choose her own first name, and that they would stop being Jews.

But if they weren't going to be Jewish, what would they be then?

"Nothing. Religion is the institutionalization of the fairy tale. Every civilization creates its own fairy tales. You need religion? Make one up. Worship the sun, like the Egyptians."

Not theology concerned her, but Grandma. Easy enough to yield on abstractions, but what about Grandma? What about all the great-aunts and uncles in Jersey City? What about Passover and the Seder, what about Yom Kippur and pretending to fast for a whole day? What about visiting Grandma worshipping in the storefront temple, everybody dressed in their best new clothes, slithering across the aisle of admiring elders to kiss Grandma's wrinkled silk cheek and bathe in the shining love of her velvet eyes. What about holidays in Jersey City, playing *dreidel* or whatever they called it under the table with the cousins, while above the uncles thunderously slammed down their pinochle melds and the aunts laughed and shouted and quarreled and whispered, serving the men little glasses of schnapps and themselves big glasses of tea with lemon slices, drawing the hot liquid through a sugar cube held between the teeth. What about strudel, and bowls of fruit — dried, fresh, candied, waxed; what about all the nuts in the uni-

verse, and prunes stuffed with almonds and rolled in pow-
dered sugar? What about Cousin Sarah's mechanical player
piano? Did ceasing to be Jewish mean giving up player
pianos?

Even while loss entered, so did the possibility of greedy
gain. Would their new life include Christmas trees and gifts,
Easter baskets and bonnets, exotic Lent, ashes on the forehead, fish on Fridays, and retirement to a nunnery? Did it
mean that at long last she could count herself one with all
the others in this country?

Tentatively she searched out a reassuring answer.

"Are we going to become Egyptians?"

"Very clever," her father said in his most sarcastic manner. "Very clever."

He turned to Mama with a gesture that washed his
hands of both mother and daughter.

"Congratulations," he said. "This girl of yours is devel-
oping into a first-class moron."

Her father claimed to be a German Jew who didn't care
for any of that Russian-Jewish stuff. Mama's brother, Uncle
Ben, had a big fight with Mama about that, counterclaiming
that Papa was lying and that he was a poor Hungarian Jew
without any family. Papa said he had come from a rich family who lived in Stuttgart and drank coffee out of china cups
and saucers. No tea in a glass. No kosher kitchen. No Yiddish spoken. No pinochle.

"So how come he talks Yiddish and Hungarian so perfectly?" Uncle Ben said.

"He's a master of languages." Her mother in dignified
tears. "He also speaks perfect German and very good Russian, not to mention English. Why are you so suspicious of
my husband?"

"Because he's one of the world's best liars," Uncle said.
"And the whole world — except his wife — knows it."

"They'll sit *shiva* for you like the superstitious ignoramuses they are." Her father now, badgering her mother.

"They'll mourn their apostate daughter. Like tribal savages they'll rend their garments and wail. Then they'll put 'Cohen on the Telephone' on the Victrola and console themselves."

"Please," her mother said, "no more talk. I can't stand any more talk. We're doing what you wish. What more do you want?"

"What *I* wish? What *I* wish? You don't agree that this move is the best for our family? You want me to turn down this wonderful chance? I'm sending a telegram right now, right this minute."

That was one of their worst fights.

Within the apartment where she now stood, sounds of movement alarmed her. What if her grandmother should open the door to put her face to face with Jewish mystery and revelation, Jewish love and pain, Jewish excitement and exaltation? In a panic she ran up the final flight of stairs to the roof and let herself out the heavy metal door into a burst of light and air smelling of freshly washed clothes. A line of laundry slapped in the breeze. Her best friend had lived in the next building on the fifth floor and they exchanged visits by way of the roof. Easier than walking down, then up, five flights of stairs. She had forgotten their ten-year-old rituals. They would guard each other making the dangerous crossing, watching while the other ran to the divider, slid across, then down. Warily, Maddy tested the concrete structure separating the buildings. Firm enough — no openings, no treacherous drops. What had they been guarding each other against? Vague dangers — a man on the roof, a rapist, a madman, an exhibitionist.

Her new outfit was short and full enough to allow her to straddle the obstruction, but not without difficulty, and she gained the adjoining roof with a smear of soot on her skirt and a run in one of her silk stockings. There were no clothes drying in the sun on this roof, only silence and the sky. She had hardly been aware of the sky when she had lived on Union Avenue. Sky entered her consciousness with the move to Iowa and the recognition that God lived in the spacious dome of blue expanse and solid cloud above the oceanic plains of corn. She knew that for a fact. Where else in the world would God choose to live? In Iowa there was room enough for God *and* humanity. Here the brave, ragged chunks of sky were only a reminder that the great city existed in endless space, and on sufferance.

The roof door appeared firmly closed. What if it were locked? It opened easily and she clattered down the stairs of a hallway identical to the one she had mounted. Impossible to tell one from the other. Perhaps they had lived in this building and Grandma might emerge from any of these doors. It was a relief to make it down to a street transformed with activity. School had let out. She threaded her way among kids racing off the choking restraints of a day in the classroom. A girl of about twelve, leading her gang of younger followers, paused in wild flight to tug at Maddy's filmy dress.

"Pretty lady, pretty lady, pretty lady."

The girl made a song of the words, lightly threatening and mocking, and her group instantly parroted her.

"Pretty lady, pretty lady, pretty lady."

They circled, linking hands, enclosing Maddy at the still center. From past play on these streets, a magic phrase resurrected itself.

"Bread and butter, bread and butter," Maddy said, smiling.

She ducked through the circle. They let her go, laughing shrilly, plucking at her dress, repeating her ritual phrase.

"Bread and butter. Bread and butter."

She had been ashamed to complain of homesickness after the move to Iowa, since she would be grieving for what had terrified her on the streets of the Bronx — the after-school charge into Mr. Kazdan's candy store along with a gang of girls all making a fearful racket, raiding the penny candy shelves, scooping up at least a penny's worth more than the amount they swore they had taken when they paid Mr. Kazdan two cents. Nothing in Iowa City was as pleasurably shivery as the fierce games of ring-a-levio or jacks, or the evening stoop talk of how babies were made and born, or whether there was a God or not. Iowa City had its mysteries, but none so exciting. In Iowa there were the drawling vowels she must learn to mimic and the long, smiling silences. All activity was bounded by instruction and supervision: dance class, French conversation, Bible class, horseback riding, ice-skating, archery, tennis, and the clubs — Girl Scouts, 4H, Little Helpers, Little Sisters, Little Friends of the Poor, Little Visitors to the Shut-In. And there were her music lessons.

"I'm the new girl," she had learned to say with an appealing smile. Mimicry and silence, mimicry and smiles, mimicry and amiability — these were the paths to acceptance. And a million lies.

The owner of the greengrocery emerged at that moment to guard his barrel of apples from the marauding kids.

"Hold on to your pocketbook, young lady," he said. "I can see you're a stranger around here."

She walked rapidly to the corner, clutching her pretty new pocketbook. She turned in the opposite direction from the market. A glance at her wrist watch indicated that she had been gone from Victoria slightly over an hour, and she didn't want to cheapen the mystery of her errand in Victoria's view by returning before her time was up. There was a nervous quivering in her chest, as if her heart were shaking rather than beating, which made it hard to breathe and walk, especially in her new high heels. She followed an avenue that led toward the library, but when she came upon the structure it was unfamiliar, too sedate and well proportioned and, inside, too airy and light, too quiet, too welcoming and comfortingly anonymous. When she was a kid, it had seemed a forbidding, overwhelming institution.

She settled at a table near a window, where a copy of *Lord Jim* was displayed or had been left by a previous reader. It was the book they had been reading aloud at the Young Reading Circle and in the same leather-bound Malay edition, with its exotic maps for end papers. She caressed the book, letting it make its connections between the mutually alienating places she had inhabited.

The soft afternoon sunlight of autumn poured like mist through the smudged city windows. As if it were a prayer she said to herself, *God's light is the same everywhere.*

But she knew that it was not.

3

SOMETHING bad was happening in the room. There was a peculiar noise that had awakened her. She didn't know where she was, in what room, what city, country; she only knew that she was in a comfortable bed and that she had been having a bad dream, one of her usual heart-banging struggles, this time clinging to a broken iron ladder dangling over black, bottomless space. She was sick of such dreams, endless losing negotiations against space or time, laboring to catch up, to leave mess behind in a landscape of infinite litter or infinite emptiness. The residual fright of the dream clung to her, but she shook it off. She was too old to be concerned with dreams. Reality was trouble enough.

Where was she? If in a bed, then there must be a bedside lamp. She groped, found one to her right, turned a switch. An elegant hotel room, familiar, but where, why? If there was a twin bed alongside the one she occupied, Dwight should be in it, but it was empty. She was very tired. She closed her eyes, wishing herself back in her bedroom in the Maine house, but when she opened them she was in the elegant hotel bedroom that she knew she knew but could not place. Again, she heard the strange noises that had awakened her. Groaning, muttering. Human? Dwight? Where was Dwight, anyway? There must be a bathroom attached, perhaps he was in the bathroom.

She sat up, swung her legs over the side of the bed, stood up carefully, and walked to the bathroom, switching on the light. Monogrammed Ritz-Carlton towels. Yes. Boston, the stopover, the demonstration, Dwight meticulously put to bed last night. Where was he? Now she recognized the groans and muffled words as distinctly his. She looked for him in the passageway of the suite, in the bathroom in the hall, in the living room, switching on lights as she went, padding around in her bare feet, her nightgown made of some stupid synthetic cloth winding itself about her legs clumsily, but he was not in any of those places and the sounds grew fainter. She was dizzy and her throat was cracked and dry and she discovered as she moved about that she desperately needed to pee. She returned to the first bathroom and took care of all her needs, even brushing her teeth and combing her hair. If she was being called on to settle some crisis, she should be in proper shape for the task. Now she could attend to locating Dwight.

She found him on the far side of the bedroom, face down on the pale blue carpet, one of his legs wedged under the wooden panel of the bed he had been sleeping in, crawling backward on his stomach.

She said, "Should you be crawling backward, Dwight? Wouldn't forward be better?"

He raised his head and looked at her without recognition.

He stopped the groaning whimpering she had been hearing, cleared his throat, and said, "Madam, I have no idea what you are doing here."

"I'm Maddy. I'm your wife. Did you want something? Is that why you tried to get up?"

"I stood up, madam. I got up."

She said, "Oh."

"I have to pee," he said. "And I want a glass of milk and a slice of chocolate cake."

"Did you fall getting out of bed?" she said. "Or was it coming back from the bathroom?"

He said, "Madam, I cannot make head or tail of what you're saying. You're a hopeless chatterbox."

She said, "I'm Maddy. I'm your wife. We have to get you on your feet."

"The ship lurched," he said.

She said, "We're in a hotel in Boston for the night. We're part of the demonstration. Tomorrow we'll be in New York City at the UN. You remember."

"Nonsense," he said. "We'll be docking at Southampton in the morning."

"I don't know how to do this," she said. "You're too heavy for me to lift."

He said, "You, madam, no doubt prefer travel by plane, but I cannot see its advantages other than speed, which I loathe."

"I love long boat trips," Maddy said.

"Ship, madam," he said. "A ship is not a boat."

"Do you think you've broken anything?"

She meant his limbs, his bones.

"If reparations are in order, they will be properly and punctually met. Perhaps the deck chair is slightly damaged, it seems to have collapsed on me."

She put her arms around his thick middle, straining to lift him. Maybe it was her touch that brought him around.

"For God's sake, Maddy, get me up," he said. "I have to pee. Do you want me to pee out here on deck?"

"On the rug," she said. "We're in a hotel room."

She grasped his hands, tugging hard to drag him free of the bed. Nothing. He might have been a toppled piano. His hands slipped from hers and she too toppled, landing hard on her bottom. She began to laugh helplessly.

"I can't do it, I can't. I have to get help."

67

"Stop laughing," he said. "Save your strength. We must save our strength. SOS. SOS. Maddy, you can do it. We can do this together. Just a little help is all I need. Come on, now."

"Have to get myself off the floor first, Dwight," she said.

Laboriously she turned herself, struggling to all fours. She could reach the phone now, but as if she had spoken her intent aloud, Dwight warned her.

"You mustn't call on any of these people. If the press got hold of this can you imagine what they'd make of it? Maddy, please," he said.

"I was thinking of Victoria," she said.

"What good would she be?" Dwight said.

"I don't know, but I can't do it alone."

He was holding his head erect, his blue eyes pleading.

"Don't let anybody make me look silly," he said.

She rang Victoria's room.

Victoria picked up the phone instantly.

"Did I wake you?"

"No, I'm usually up by four."

Victoria came at once, in slippers and a bathrobe, applying herself seriously to the problem. She never laughed, not even when Maddy toppled again. She thought up the idea of using the bathroom mat as a prop under Dwight, edging it as far under his stomach as she could jam it. They placed Dwight's hands in a tight grip on the edge of the rug.

"We'll pull. You push."

"Think of it as a raft. Keep inching forward. Not back, Dwight, forward. Forward."

Somehow they dragged Dwight clear of the bed. But they still had the problem of raising him.

"Any bones broken?" Victoria asked as they rested.

"I don't know," Maddy said.

"We should call for a doctor," Victoria said.

"No, no, no." Dwight was very agitated. "I'm fine, damn it, I'm fine. Just get me off this damn blue carpet."

Yet he lowered his face directly into the rug as if he secretly loved it. He had used up all his strength. It was the job of the two women now. They went at it as an impersonal piece of teamwork, using the mat now as a kneeling stool, bunching it up against his thighs, dragging and yanking him to a position on all fours, then to his knees, half upright, then desperately, quickly, so as not to lose what they had gained, they supported him while pushing and pulling, propping him between the bed and an armchair, Victoria holding him and Maddy lifting with all her strength, beyond her strength, her heart smashing against her chest wall, her blood hammering, bursting in her head and eyes until miraculously, suddenly, they had him on his feet.

"I have to pee. I have to pee," he yelled.

Between them they shuffled him to the bathroom. They pulled down his pajamas. He mostly missed the bowl. The air stung with the odor of urine.

"I'm sorry, ladies. I am deeply sorry," Dwight said.

"Don't be an ass," Victoria said.

"Exactly," Dwight said. "One tries not to be."

They shuffle-walked him back to bed. He was exhausted and exultant.

"We did it, my friends. We beat it. We licked it."

But his words slurred into *we slickened it,* and he waved a weak hand in a sort of apology and shut his eyes. The clock on the wall showed four-twenty. The ordeal which seemed to Maddy to have gone on for hours had lasted less than half an hour.

"Lie down, rest," Maddy ordered Victoria. "We'll have ourselves three strokes in unison."

"Actually," Victoria said, "I feel very well. I needed a good workout."

She stretched out on Maddy's bed while Maddy mopped up the urine in the bathroom with a beautifully soft, snowy washcloth. Sacrilege at the Ritz-Carlton. Maddy was laughing again and heard Victoria join her from the other room.

In the bedroom Victoria had switched off the lights, but a soft pink glow, the early daylight of June, irradiated the walls.

"Your gown and robe are color coordinated with the rosy-fingered dawn," Maddy said.

She touched Victoria's bare foot, shaped into a monstrous deformity by the long years of dancing. The toes were icy. She took the foot between her hands and warmed it.

"Thank you for helping me," Maddy said.

She wrapped Victoria's feet in the satin-bound blanket folded at the foot of the bed, rubbing them through the covering.

"Cold feet. You always had cold feet."

"When I was little I was so cold I never warmed the bed I slept in. It stayed a sea of ice all night. My mother always came to kiss me good-night and to tuck me in. One night it occurred to me that she might warm me by lying down on top of me. 'Lay on me,' I begged, 'lay on me.' I was five or six years old, maybe younger. My mother was too shocked to respond. She called my father in to handle me. He lectured me on the subject of sin and evil thoughts. Then they both dragged me to the bathroom to wash my mouth out with soap. Afterward I was put back in my icy bed. Alone."

"You told me that story on the *Majestic*, a hundred years ago," Maddy said.

"I did not," Victoria said, and sat up. "What was that thing they had about washing out the mouth with soap? What did they think they were doing, anyway?"

"And you told it to me again in Cairo. Or Jerusalem, maybe," Maddy persisted.

"I never told you that story," Victoria said. "I never told it to anybody."

"Yes," Maddy said. "You told it to me in Spain, too. In Ultramorte, where you said it was colder than death and it was, that March and April in the stone house."

"Sometimes I think it couldn't be worse if we were married, you and me," Victoria said.

"Would you rather I forgot your stories?"

"Stop calling it a story. It's not a *story.*"

She stretched out, put her head sideways on the pillow, closed her eyes. Without her elaborate make-up and costume, she seemed like a vulnerable girl.

"It was terrible," Victoria said with her eyes closed.

"We mustn't think about *then,*" Maddy said. "Now is bad enough."

"Now is fine," Victoria said. "I now have a very efficient electric blanket."

Maddy slid in under the covers, fitting her body to Victoria's, spoon fashion. She wound her legs about Victoria's icy feet, pressing them against her warm calves.

"If we hurry we can sleep for at least two hours," Maddy said.

Glowing pink light flushed the room, penetrating even behind Maddy's closed eyelids, starting her laughing again.

"Now what?" Victoria said. "What's funny?"

"All this hot pink symbolism," Maddy said. "The East Is Red."

"The East is crawling with Capitalist Roaders," Victoria said.

"Pray to God we make it through tomorrow," Maddy said.

"To God?" Victoria said, and let it hang, adding after a pause, "And I did *not* tell you that story before. I did not."

4

ON the second morning of the voyage, well out to sea, Maddy was too sick to get out of bed. She had started to vomit the night before; now there was nothing left to bring up but thin strings of green bile. In the tiny, dark inside cabin she had been assigned, she slept and retched, retched and slept, enclosed in a dank, dark tunnel of unmarked time. She felt herself unloved and abandoned, totally deserted in a way she could not have imagined. Mrs. Voynow visited her several times, an ineffectual, irritating presence. Cleves looked in briefly, demonstrating pleasure in her discomfort. The ship doctor, brisk and impatient, ordered pills, which she vomited promptly. Stewards appeared carrying trays of food she turned from in horror.

On the fourth morning, Victoria opened the cabin door and stepped in full of willful, decisive action.

"Up, up," she said. "Up on deck with you. It's a beautiful day. No more of this."

She had brought a stewardess with her. Between them they dragged Maddy to her feet, into a robe, down the corridor for a hot shower and a rub with a rough towel. She resisted but felt much better cleaned up. They dressed her in underthings, worked stockings up her legs, pinned them to her garter belt, stuck on shoes, a skirt, and a blouse. Victoria brushed her hair. They half lifted, half dragged her to the deck, stopping twice to allow her to retch up nothing. Daylight blinded and dizzied her. Beyond the ship railing a dazzling sea heaved to the edge of a rising and falling darker line.

"Don't look at the horizon," Victoria said. "Don't look at the water. Not yet. Let your body go with the ship. Let it go, let it go. Nothing will happen, I promise you. You're done with that. It's over."

She was placed in a deck chair in the sun, among passengers busy with their activities. It was an outrage to her that ordinary life had proceeded through the long night of her desolation, that others had continued to play, talk, laugh, eat, dance, drink, sleep, and wake, that a child could dash across the sun-drenched deck on her own bare little legs, her soft curtain of blond hair floating and falling as she ran.

"I'm freezing," Maddy said, and showed her chattering teeth.

"Breathe," Victoria said.

She wrapped Maddy in a blanket.

"Breathe," she said. "In. Very deep breath. Out. Good. Now again. Breathe. In. Very deep breath. Out. Good."

The air was surprisingly sweet and warm.

Cleves came by.

"God, I've never seen anybody quite *that* color," he said.

Victoria waved him away.

"Scram," she said. "On about your stupid business."

"You don't own her, you know," he said. "Nobody said she was your exclusive property."

He walked away at the rage in Victoria's eyes.

A steward appeared with a bowl of clear liquid and a

few large biscuits. Victoria forced her to swallow the first tiny spoonful of broth, then another and another. Heaving and rumbling began in her stomach. She retched.

"You're fine," Victoria said. "You're through with that, you're not going to do any more of that. Breathe, don't retch, breathe."

She fed Maddy bits of biscuit, then more broth, more biscuit, steadily, slowly, as if on a job, feeding materials into a machine.

"What time is it?" Maddy said during a rest.

"About eleven," Victoria said.

"Friday morning?"

"If the sun's in the sky it's morning," Victoria said.

Maddy's eyes filled with tears.

"Ah, too harsh," Victoria said. "The little joke was too much to bear."

"I meant what day, to check the day."

"Fourth day out. Friday. You were down there two and a half days. Killing yourself with self-pity. Not while I'm around. You'll have to wait until I've gone."

Maddy shuddered, a spectacularly theatrical shiver. Victoria rubbed Maddy's legs, starting at the upper thighs and ending at her ankles, using vigorous strokes, handling her with a dispassionate strength more reassuring than tenderness.

"There's nothing wonderful about illness, you know," Victoria said. "Not lovely, not romantic, not interesting to be ill. Health is beautiful. Strength and health."

"I'm cold," Maddy said. "I'm just cold."

"I was always cold when I was little," Victoria said. "I slept alone in a big bed and could never get that huge bed warmed up. One night when my mother came to tuck me in I asked her to warm me by lying down on top of me. 'Lay on me,' that's what I said. I had no idea what the phrase meant to her. I would have asked the dog if I had one. That bed was torture, every untouched spot remained icy. I was four or five, maybe six years old. They washed my mouth out with soap; my father lectured me on the dangers of a dirty mind and sent me back to the empty icy bed, gagging and weeping."

"I'm sorry," Maddy said.

"Are you getting warmer?" Victoria said.

"Yes," Maddy said, but her teeth chattered.

"Breathe," Victoria said. "With me. Deep breath."

"I wasn't killing myself with self-pity, what you said, I wasn't. I was seasick. Anybody can get seasick."

"Where are you going?" Maddy said, after a silence.

"What?" Victoria said.

"Where are you going — and when?" Maddy said.

"To India, in November, with Vidhya, if the trial is over by then."

"And if it isn't, will you stay?"

"In England? No, I have nothing to do with the trial. It's Vidhya who must stay. I'll go in any event."

"Vidhya," Maddy said. "What's he like? Do you like him?"

Victoria laughed. "That's refreshing. Like him? We're supposed to love him, to adore him."

"I meant, y'know," Maddy said, "what's he like?"

"Oh, Vidhya . . ." Victoria said.

"What will I do in England — in the Society? What do you do?" Maddy said.

"What you're told. In exchange for faith, food, shelter, divine guidance, and fun and games."

"Don't make fun of me."

"I wouldn't dream of it," Victoria said.

"What do *you* do in the Society?" Maddy said.

"My own work," Victoria said.

She was ashamed to admit that she had no idea what Victoria's *own work* was.

"I'll be teaching this year, in India and at the Australian encampment. You'll probably teach music. Unless of course Bobo has his way and pushes you into secretarial work. He'd like us all to be secretaries, all the females."

"Will the Voynows stay with me in England?"

"I don't know," Victoria said. "I think they're going to Spain to set up the encampment at the Castle."

"Then there'll be nobody to stay with me," Maddy said. "Or will I be sent somewhere?"

"If you're lucky you'll stay in Hampstead, where it's civilized, so pray for that."

"Isn't it civilized in India?" Maddy said.

"Ah, India . . ." Victoria said, letting her voice trail off into mystery. And then, briskly, "Now we're going for a walk — get your blood circulating, generate a little natural heat in your body."

"I can't —" Maddy began, and stopped herself.

"You can," Victoria said, pulling her upright. "Come on, the world is waiting for a beautiful girl like you."

The deck heaved and swayed under Maddy, but Victoria anchored her.

"Don't look down. Or up. Let yourself go with the motion. Let your body go. Let it be. It knows how to manage the sea. Trust it," Victoria said. "Now. Walk."

"Nobody's waiting for me," Maddy said. "The world doesn't know I'm alive. You're teasing."

"Don't mind me, love," Victoria said. "I have to tease. It's my way of showing affection."

Throughout the rest of the day she heard Victoria's words echoing like a song, and not only the words, *love, my way of showing affection,* but the tone of the words, the melody, the charm, softness, the surprising revelation of a different Victoria underneath the harsh one. Victoria watched over her, sent her off to bed happy, so that she slept soundly for the first time on the trip and woke the next day reborn, eager for everything. It would be the last day at sea and she must make the most of it. She walked the deck before breakfast, greeting everyone she passed without her usual self-consciousness. Only Cleves was seated at the breakfast table when the bell rang. She astonished him with pleasantries and by eating heartily — even the lamb chops — and then ran from his talk to walk the deck again, searching for a glimpse of Victoria, drinking in the air, warmer than yesterday's, sunnier, perfumed with the nostalgic sense of land nearby, visible any moment. She saw Victoria striding toward her, strangely got-up in trailing, ragged-looking garments.

"How are you this morning?" Victoria said.

"I'm fine," Maddy said. Then quickly, before shyness intervened, "May I walk with you?"

"I'm not walking," Victoria said. "I work out every morning. I'm on my way now. Sorry."

She didn't understand what Victoria meant, except that it was clearly a rejection.

"The captain set aside a little gym for my use just for an hour every morning."

She had not slowed her long, swift stride. Maddy kept up, nodding, without knowing what she was nodding at. Her agony at having been rebuffed must not show. Perhaps *affection, love,* in this strange world meant only the absence of active dislike.

"Walk along with me," Victoria invited. And then, "Maybe you'd like to come and watch. The piece I'm working on is almost finished, so I don't mind an audience."

Maddy's joy had her heart slithering and slamming around in her chest.

The little gym was a bare room with a smooth wooden floor, a railing along three sides of the green painted walls and a couple of folded mats tossed into a corner.

"You can settle down over there," Victoria said, "on the mats."

Obediently she scrunched herself into the indicated corner, her knees drawn up, her skirt pulled down between her legs. Victoria was rearranging her odd garments, taking

77

some off, then putting one back on but in a different order, ending clothed in a covering shaped like a tent, made of some stretchy stuff of a brilliant red color. She had stripped her feet bare, but now she stooped to bind cloths around the lower legs and over her arches, anchoring the mess with high socks from which the toes and heels had been cut off, without ceasing her stretching, bending, bouncing, twisting. She loosened her hair. It fell in a straight, long, shining curtain, springing from her too-prominent forehead, with its touching and vulnerable nobility. Now she bent into a slow, dipping circling, then up, wider and freer, larger and larger, her bare toes and heels splayed out flat, powerfully rooted to the boards of the floor, her body arching higher and higher, lower and lower. She grew wings. The room burst open beyond its walls. Her face, too, was transformed, masklike, intensely serious, the eyes focused beyond space. Suddenly she was perfectly still. Then a movement that drew the senses inward, powered by the very core of the dancer's body, a pulling in of the soul, more secret and more revealing than any gesture Maddy had ever seen. Then an offering out, and again in, and again out. Now the body softly collapsed upon itself, yielding, the arms rising free as birds, the feet dancing a fast, charming, and, yes, funny little jig, the head undulating from side to side and the hair running after in a long running stream. Beautiful, bright movement, making Maddy want to laugh aloud.

She did, and then choked on her alarm that she may have insulted Victoria.

But Victoria was untouched, securely in her own world, beginning a repeat of the wide, sweeping, dipping, circling, that lifted beyond the narrow space of the room out into eternity. Then everything stopped. Victoria slumped to the floor, her legs spread wide, her upper body inclined toward her head, a figure at prayer, swaying back and forth to a slow beat, her hands gripping her shins, her hair moving like water, forward with each rhythmic bend, backward with each return.

"How beautiful," Maddy said. "How beautiful."

Victoria was silent.

"I didn't mean to laugh," Maddy said.

"You laughed when it was funny. Why not laugh?"

Victoria's voice was again different, pitched lower, more breathless, its brittle edge buffed husky.

"I've never seen anything so beautiful. I've never seen anything so wonderful," Maddy said.

Victoria sat up.

"Did you like it?"

Again Victoria's face was a new one, lit up, the eyes soft and gleaming.

"Did you really like it?"

"It was beautiful," Maddy said. "It was the most wonderful dance I've ever seen."

The light went out of Victoria's face, and a familiar mocking expression took over.

"What have you seen? Who? Where?"

Maddy swallowed her words.

"Ballet companies came to Iowa City."

Victoria laughed. "Ballet, tap, ballroom," she said.

"You're always laughing at me," Maddy said. "I don't care. It was wonderful, it was extraordinary — I know it was."

"I mustn't waste this time talking," Victoria said. "Can you sing 'Oh, Shenandoah' or 'Can She Bake a Cherry Pie'?"

"I'm not sure I know the first one."

"Sing," Victoria said. "It's hell working without music."

Maddy sang the opening lines of a melody, without words.

"That's 'Down in the Valley,'" Victoria said. "They told me you're a musician."

"That's Daddy's idea," Maddy said. "I'm not anything."

"Try the other," Victoria said. She hummed the tune herself, lending it a fast, jazzy beat, accompanying herself to the jiglike part of her dance.

Maddy picked up on the music. " 'Billy Boy, Billy Boy,' " she sang. " 'Can she bake a cherry pie, charmin' Billy?' "

"No words," Victoria yelled. "Shit. No words. Just the melody."

Maddy sang "la la la la la la la," altering the beat when she saw it would better fit into Victoria's variations.

"That's good," Victoria said. "Could you do that on the piano? Could you work it out with me, do you think?"

Maddy nodded and felt a blush rising to her face like a flag lifted in victory.

After lunch, on her own, supposedly meditating in her cabin, she decided it was time to begin keeping the journal that Daddy insisted was necessary to any proper journeying. She took the red leather-bound notebook he had presented her as a going-away gift and went in search of a suitable corner. She had noticed a small salon on the main deck, furnished with ladylike writing desks and manly lounge chairs. In the softly lit room stiff with propriety, she chose a table facing the farthest wall and opened the notebook to its first page. Daddy had made it sufficiently clear that this was not a silly girl's diary, with tiny allotments of space for each day's passing gush of feeling, but a commodious masculine arena, built for serious and important notations by a young, intelligent, and curious mind seeking to find itself. She sat for a long time staring at the blank page, imprinted as clearly with Daddy's imperatives as with its own watermark, a surface too intimidating to violate. Then she lifted a pen from its cunning inkpot on the table and wrote in a careful round hand, using little circles as dots over the i's and the j, in a mannerism copied from her teacher at the Iowa City public school.

I love her. I love her. I love her. Oh, God, how I love
her. She is the most wonderful person in the world!!!!!

She had not had any intention of writing down what
appeared on the page. The ink flowed unevenly, the pen
scratched and spluttered, and the last exuberant exclamation
point became a messy splotch. Where had this unseemly
outburst come from? She glanced about uneasily, then
picked up a dainty blotter, a part of the furnishings of the
writing table, and covered her words. Her heart had risen to
her throat to choke her. The hush of the room, the shock of
her feeling violently expressed, the replica of the *Majestic*
imprinted on the blotter, the pen in its holder — all advanced and receded as if charged with a private will over
which she had no control. She looked around the room for
help.

In a lounge chair near the french doors opening out to
the deck, an old man was asleep, a collection of magazines
sliding down his lap. At a distant table a very large lady was
displaying the mixed contents of a very large carrying case:
a comb and brush, a box of hairpins and one of pills, another filled with powder and a series of little rouge pots. These
she pushed aside to make room for a collection of folded
pieces of paper and worn envelopes. Maddy heard the loud
breathing, just this side of snoring, of the man in the armchair and a muttering accompaniment to the large lady's
dithering with her bits of papers and envelopes. Maddy
dared to lift the blotter and reread what she had written. The
words on the page remained an astonishment to her, unbidden,
gushing like blood. Nothing to do but clean it up. Slowly
and carefully, she tore the page free of the sewn threads
that bound the book, then, turning the journal over, she
removed the blank matching page at the back, carefully destroying the uneven remnants, patting and smooth-

ing the book to the original shape of its pristine dignity. There. Nobody would ever know.

🙰

Brotherhood House was one of a tall, skinny line of Victorian homes overlooking Hampstead Heath, the first and lowest of the row, with its high stooped front climbing the rising ridge of the curving street and its back sliding down to nestle at the edge of the pond. In heavy rains the pond seeped into the basement and first floor of the building, leaving behind a perpetually musty smell. Maddy was assigned a room at the very top. She loved her tiny space at first sight, though it was shockingly cold and there was no way to warm it. Not even Iowa at the height of its punishing winters was as cold as the house on Hampstead Heath.

"Rising damp," Cleves informed her. "Hell on structures and hell on human bones. Doesn't bother me a bit. I love the cold. You Americans overheat terribly. Very unhealthy, very."

His room was warm, shared by Conrad, a boy of Cleves's age, very blond, Australian, generating health and body heat. Plus their room had a coal-burning tile stove. Maddy's quarters were too small to accommodate anything more than herself, a single bed, a narrow dresser, and a narrower wardrobe. Its one window was as broad as the width of the room and as high, floor to ceiling, an expanse of diamond-shaped leaded panes. When the sun shone the effect was exalting, cathedral-like, but the sun shone rarely. Wind, cold, dampness, and rain seeped through the rattling seams; beyond, mists rolled, clouds heaped dramatically, skies shifted — a backdrop for a romantic melodrama or a parody, and an irresistible invitation to loaf and invite stormy moods.

But that was later. The first week in the house, Victoria was still in England and Maddy rode on her wings. The household was too confusing for Maddy to sort out, and she didn't then try, except superficially, concentrating her main

82

efforts on pleasing and impressing Victoria so as not to be forgotten by her when she left. Victoria had scheduled a performance of a new small dance for her last day in Hampstead. Maddy had become, inconceivably to her, part of the performance, shoved into the role of Victoria's composer. They practiced in the formal music room on the first floor, a space set aside for their use during the morning hours, and later used for yoga in the afternoons and for lectures, meetings, and performances in the evening.

It wasn't easy working with Victoria. She got mad. She yelled at Maddy. No wonder. Maddy didn't know what she was doing. But she plunged in. The melodies she worked with were all traditional tunes hummed to her by Victoria. Maddy strung them together, beat them into new rhythms, quickened or stretched, made plaintive or lively, closely following what she saw as the needs of Victoria's movements. There were moments when the experience was pure glory; more often it was torment. Victoria had named her ballet *American Theme, Inside Out.* Maddy took her cue from that, pulling familiar melodies into inside-out forms and tones. It was lucky the dance ran only fifteen minutes, or she couldn't have stuck with it.

Victoria yelled under her breath so as not to be overheard by the others. Yelling was frowned on in the Society. She said *shit* a lot, too, also under her breath.

"Keep it tinkly, keep it tinkly," she yelled. "Shit. No chords. Don't let it go maudlin, keep it tinkly."

At the last rehearsal, the morning of the performance, she yelled all the time.

"Damn it, stop trying so hard to match the music to my steps. Make your music mean something by itself. Shit. We're not trying for a *thé dansant.* Keep it tinkly, tinkly light, tinkly funny."

At the end of the session, she hugged Maddy.

"It's great, I think. Isn't it? I think so, I think so, what do you think?"

Maddy was too tearful to speak.

She couldn't tell whether the performance itself was a success. It was too difficult to gauge this strange audience's responses. Or Victoria's unpredictability. On the program — carefully drawn up by Victoria herself — to Maddy's amazement, the little dance wasn't called *American Theme, Inside Out* but *Aura #1*, "choreographed and danced by Victoria Younger, music composed and performed by Madeleine Brewster." *Original* was implicit in the phrasing. During the criticism session, Bishop Nysmith, Mrs. Voynow, and Lady Pansy discussed the piece in a way that made no sense to Maddy, citing Indian folk influences and Society concepts manifest in the choreography and in the music. Later, Victoria, laughing, threw light on some of the mystery.

"They had no idea *whose* aura, so they didn't dare criticize too much."

"I don't understand," Maddy said.

"It doesn't matter," Victoria said. She was jubilant. "It was good, it was good. And we weren't doing it for them, anyway, just pretending to. And it *was* good. Oh, for God's sake, Maddy, say it was good, can't you?"

"*You* were wonderful," Maddy said.

They were setting the music room to rights before going to bed. Victoria would be leaving at dawn the next morning.

"What will I do without you?" Maddy said. "I'll be empty. Lost."

Victoria laughed.

"Nature detests a vacuum," she said. "Something will rush in to fill you up. Somebody. Never fear."

Their farewell was surprisingly formal. Victoria took Maddy's right hand in both of hers, cradling and shaking in one gesture.

"I'll be back," she said. "Try not to forget me."

☙

Without invitation, the mood that took over the next day was grief and loneliness. She skipped breakfast to stare out her window at the pond active with birds, swans and ducks, easily identified, and others she had never seen and couldn't name, particularly the dizzy, darting little white birds coming and going in droves. She named them *coots* and took to following their flights, returns, matings, and bird heartbreaks, telling herself touching romances of bird sensitivity and longings, in which her own loneliness and sorrow merged and made its escape.

She was totally adrift again. Victoria, Mr. Singh, and the Voynows were gone. Of this strange new household only Cleves was someone she knew and only Cleves was an American. The others were English, Indian, Australian. Cleves, to whom she looked for information while mistrusting his explanations, told her that the house belonged to Lord Harkness and Lady Pansy. She had not yet seen Lord Harkness, who was mostly absent, busy attending to his civic duties having to do with government housing. He arrived for short stays of two or three days and made no secret of a pleasantly jolly contempt for all of them and for what he termed "Brotherhood balderdash," treating all the acolytes with the same lightly dismissive scorn while reserving for Bishop Nysmith and Vidhya a comically exaggerated astonishment in their "daily exercises in commercial sainthood." Most amazingly, nobody seemed to pay any attention to him, except Maddy and his three daughters. Against her will, Maddy found him funny and her laughter obviously delighted him.

He was a very large presence because of his height, his large nose, and very large hands, which sought and found vulnerable parts of Maddy's body, patting, surreptitiously touching, rubbing, sliding about. Once, in an accidental meeting in the downstairs gallery that led to the music room, he smiled a truly terrible smile, pressed her up against the wall, kissed her, thrusting his large and active tongue deep into her mouth, holding her head back with one oversized hand while the other moved directly under her skirt to her mound, thwacking and massaging, like a machine, until a noise made him stop and break away.

"There, that will do you good," he said, matter-of-factly.

She thought she would hate him too much after that to ever find him funny again, but the next time he visited for a few days she found herself laughing at his comments just as she had before the incident in the passageway, which he seemed to have totally forgotten, as if it had never happened.

He always requested mustard, jam, and chutney at table, spreading one or the other, sometimes all three, over everything served.

"Have to impart some taste to these vegetarian concoctions," he said. Lady Pansy shook her head at his breaking the rule of silence.

At the end of the meal, the others having left for more serious occupations, his three daughters and Maddy stayed as an admiring audience while he drew stick figures with his black ink pen on the white tablecloth, women with tiny round O eyes, their little line eyebrows tilted into comical frowns, their stick legs bent in an uncomfortable squat, skirts up and drawers down, bright yellow mustard spattering from a crack in each squared-off buttock.

"Dysentery in India among the English ladies," he explained, adding a little more mustard.

The girls, Maddy too, laughed till they choked.

Lord Harkness and Lady Pansy were rich, Cleves told Maddy, but not very rich.

"They're the sort of rich who think they're poor," he said.

It wasn't their money that ran the house in Hampstead, though some of it did. Most of the money came from a really rich American woman, heir to a fortune made in steel or rubber, mail-order, cars, maybe it was department stores —

Cleves wasn't sure which. At the moment the rich American was *on the Continent* with her daughter, a phrase that teased Maddy's snobbish nerve and touched a jealous one when she was further told that the rich American and her daughter would be joining Victoria on the voyage to India. *The voyage to India.*

"It sounds like *The Arabian Nights,*" Maddy said.

"Jerusalem would be more like it," Cleves said. "I think Mrs. Dasinov is Jewish. They say her husband was a Jew boy."

She ran from him to her room. It was a mess. She was supposed to do for herself up here, but since nobody checked her quarters, she let everything go to pot from Wednesday to Wednesday, when she was assigned fresh linens and did a halfhearted general cleanup. She took a bath that day, too. There was a *loo* on the floor below, but the bath was one floor below that, and so discouragingly icy that she never wanted to bathe.

She was learning new words like *loo,* and old words with new meanings, *knickers* and *pudding;* she was learning how to be meaningfully silent, even more silent than before, pretending depth. She had mastered standing on her head, chanted her mantra dutifully, meditated when she didn't fall into a nap first, and mouthed key phrases of Brotherhood ideology. She wanted to believe. She requested books to help her understand more about the movement and made a show of carting two or three at a time to her room. Though she picked up enough of the jargon to seem more knowledgeable, the truth was she fell asleep after a page or two. The stuff was boring, and when it wasn't, it seemed to be nonsense. Perhaps that's why she found Lord Harkness so funny.

More interesting than Brotherhood theory was fitting the population of the house into the philosophy. Inconceivable, for one thing, to place Lady Pansy in a bed with her husband, Lord Harkness. They had produced three daughters and a son who had died, proof enough of Lady Pansy's subjugation under Lord Harkness's large hands and athletic tongue. She refused to imagine anything further, cringing, as she imagined Lady Pansy must have cringed from the initial violation. Poor, pale, wilting, strange Lady Pansy. Apparently there was a more powerful Lady Harkness somewhere behind and above this one, so that this Lady Harkness bore the ridiculous title of Lady Pansy. But then all the names were ridiculous to Maddy. The Harkness daughters were called Daphne, Millicent, and Marigold. They were horsy girls, with prominent blank blue eyes, irregular bony frames, and thin, greasy hair. It bewildered Maddy that they were always described as *pretty, charming, lovely,* by all the household when they were clearly as plain as weeds, and anemic as well. Lord Harkness was difficult to deal with, to say the least; Lady Pansy was kind to Maddy in the vague Voynow manner, from whom she now saw it had been copied; but the three sisters were the rudest people she had ever met, ruder even than Cleves. Had they been his model? She added to the sum of her information of British imperviousness to dirt and smells, British insolence. She shunned the company of Daphne, Millicent, and Marigold. The most ordinary exchange of pleasantries became with them as abrasive as skinning a knee.

"What do they do in the Society?" Maddy asked Cleves.

He stared incomprehensibly.

"They're petitioners, like us. They're learning."

"Yes, but to do what?"

"Why, nothing," he said. "They come with Lady Pansy. They're her daughters, after all." And added after a pause, "The others, Mari and Daph, can't do much of anything. But Milli's wonderful with numbers. She helps Mr. Singh and the Center people with the accounts. But mostly they're here because of Lady Pansy and *she's* glued to Vidhya. She's Vidhya's fairy godmother. Lady Florence put her in charge of Vidhya when things began to get, y'know, bristly, between Bobo and Vidhya. And she has all the free time and the money . . ."

Who else stayed at the house in Hampstead? Mr. Singh, who had returned with a young, jolly fellow called Jag since his full name, Jagannathan Varadarajan, was too hard for others to remember. There was Bishop Nysmith, Daddy's fabulous enemy, the man on trial, the man called Bobo, who turned out to be a delight, a huge Santa Claus of a man. Maddy found herself treacherously liking him, but Bobo returned no interest in Maddy apart from the possibility of her training as a stenographer-typist, a wish he made plain whenever he noticed her. There was Cleves, and Conrad, the Australian. At the bottom of the heap was the household help: an Indian couple buried in the basement and two giggly English girls tucked away at the top of the house alongside Maddy in an even smaller room than the one she occupied.

At the palpitating center of the establishment there was Vidhya.

She had had her vision of Vidhya before she met him, fed by the odd photograph in the book he had written. The young Savior would be Gandhi-like, ugly, with dirt-colored skin and purple lips, dragging an emaciated body, lifting an ascetic's turbanned head, casting downward his black, saintly eyes, or upward, showing a lot of saintly white under the iris. He wasn't in Hampstead when their party arrived and didn't show up until a week after Victoria left. She met the flesh-and-blood Vidhya just before dinner on the day he returned.

His skin was the color of dull gold. His full lips, the color of a deep red rose, smiled in repose, resting upon each other in a sensual caress. His teeth were remarkably white. He was slim, muscular, his neck a golden column rising above his smartly tailored English suit, white shirt, silk tie. His hair was parted in the middle and combed back like

Cleves's but was black, silky, dense, alive. His eyes were extraordinarily long, almond-shaped, thickly fringed by black lashes, the eyes themselves a light gray and the whites a startling blue, a visionary's eyes, focusing beyond her and beyond what was beyond her to an unseeable region.

He was the most beautiful man she had ever seen.

How was she to greet him? Sink to her knees? Make an attempt at the graceful hand gestures of the Indian greeting? She fumbled, blushing and speechless. He laughed, a long, artificial trill, like the ringing of a bell, while taking her hand and shaking it, democratic fashion.

"Welcome, Maddy," he said. "I have heard so much about you."

He spoke like an Indian, in the expected rapid singsong, too sweetly, though he had learned to temper his speech by the upper-class English intonation of the shade of malice they affected.

"You are happy to hear, I am sure, that the trial is ended and all is settled in satisfactory conclusion?"

She hadn't heard but she nodded.

"You must write to your papa at once. The good man will have no more worries to trouble him. Isn't that fine?"

Was he mocking her? Behind him, Bishop Nysmith seemed to glower at her, his Santa Claus beam extinguished for the moment. He rested a huge arm around Vidhya's shoulders, squeezing, caressing with his fingers. She thought she saw a wincing withdrawal on Vidhya's part.

"Well, what did you think of our Vidhya?" Cleves asked her.

It was the following morning. Cleves's tone was juicy, conspiratorial, inviting mockery. They were alone, sorting the mail in the center hall.

"He's the most beautiful man I've ever seen," she said.

"Man!" Cleves said. "He's only eighteen. Just five months older than I am. Man! That's ridiculous. Don't be fooled by them, they mature early physically but stay children all their lives."

She seemed to have expressed her admiration badly and outraged Cleves.

"You females are impossible. You all go gaga over Vidhya. What is it about him that so appeals to females? The only sensible one is Victoria. She keeps her head. As if Bobo's adoration isn't enough, he has this gaggle of gaga women trailing after him with Lady Florence at the head." He ended in a sort of growl.

"Does Bobo adore him?" Maddy said.

"Well, we all *adore* him, naturally," Cleves said. "But Bobo found him, y'know, discovered him, playing in a gutter in his village. Bobo saw his remarkable aura and that was enough to convince him . . ."

He paused, then continued as if he were convincing himself as well.

"I mean, it wasn't like the usual *favorite*, y'know, like with me or Conrad. It was different with Vidhya, anyone could see that, and then Lady Florence going along about Vidhya being exceptional, out of the usual mold of Bobo's favorites, and everybody agreed, even I, though God knows I couldn't help being jealous, just as Conrad was, though *his* time was over years ago, really. And Vidhya's no fool, y'know, in spite of doing so badly on tests. Don't fool yourself about Vidhya, he's no fool, he knows where he's headed. It took a while, but he's thoroughly convinced by now that he has a very special mission on earth."

He laughed.

"Why shouldn't he?" he said. "He'd be an idiot if he didn't. Everything to gain and nothing to lose."

Enlightenment was what was needed, more enlightenment. She took books to her room to read, falling asleep over repetitive ideas by Beauregard C. Nysmith, by Lady Florence Greenwood, and by Vidhya, *First Steps to Perfect Brotherhood*, this book written when he was fifteen. Its authentic authorship had been attacked at the trial, as was the authenticity of the earlier one. The books were all so much alike that in attempting once to win over Bishop Nysmith by repeating a quote from his book, she had mistakenly quoted from Vidhya's. Bishop Nysmith didn't seem to take offense and in fact seized the moment as another opportunity to urge Maddy to study stenography and typing instead of music.

Surely he was right. In the music room where she had been so absorbed in working with Victoria, she now pursued her solitary practice, her hands stiff with cold, the Mozart never progressing beyond its current level of heavy-handed diligence. Her "musical talent" was clearly nothing but another Daddy notion gone wrong. She overheard Bishop Nysmith reporting to Lady Pansy that he had listened at the door.

"The girl can't play for toffee apples," he said, clearly referring to her. "Typing is what she should be studying."

"But she did compose music for Victoria," Lady Pansy said. "Perhaps it takes the form of composing rather than performing."

"That was Victoria's lead," Bishop Nysmith said. "The girl's a lost sheep without her shepherd."

Miserably depressed and sick with fear of a chance bruising encounter with a member of the household, she sneaked up the back stairs to her room, where, lying on the bed, bathed in the light of the sky's dramatic effects, she shook out her heart in an abandonment of lonely despair. What a strange life, in which crying had become one of her satisfying indulgences. If she could have run from the house on the Heath she would have, but where to? Crying out for her mother and father to save her would be a defeat she couldn't absorb.

Meals at the house were especially difficult. Vegetarian food served under the rule of silence. She wasn't prepared for either observance. There were times when she considered silence a blessing (easier to stop pretending for a space) but mostly it was a torment. Certainly it was morally wrong to kill animals and eat their flesh, too cruel and disgusting to think anything else, yet secretly she lusted for meat.

As part of their daily routine they walked in a group along the paths of the Heath; but once a week they strolled into the streets of Hampstead. Smells of fish and chips and the aroma of roast beef leaked from the restaurants. Her mouth watered. She had never known what that phrase meant until it actually happened to her. During meditation and while standing on her head, she imagined American hamburgers, french fries, pickles, cole slaw, mustard, and ketchup on a toasted bun. She was losing weight. In the mornings, awakening to illusionary odors of bacon and eggs, often sick to her stomach, she went down to a breakfast of raw fruit, whole grains, and bitter herb tea.

She blamed herself. It was unworthiness that made her dissatisfied. She was a beast, a carnal being entwined in the lower needs of her body — food, warmth, sleep, and sex. She meditated, she practiced yoga and breathing, she read, she reviled herself, but still her mind and body escaped discipline. She daydreamed butter, milk, eggs, spaghetti, candy, layer cake, fish, meat, fowl, ice cream. Oh, ice cream! She daydreamed a lover and her hand crept down to the part of her body she had discovered in the lavatory of the train from Iowa. She put the pillow over her head so that no one might hear the strange cries tearing from her throat, lying alone on the bed in her room overlooking the pond while her hand did its work.

These transgressions did not interfere with her acceptance in the Society as a petitioner for election. Within a month she was elevated to Level Seven in a ceremony that bewildered and scared her. As she understood it, she had been the heroine of an out-of-body adventure, which took place without her normal awareness but with her full participation on the Astral Plane. Bishop Nysmith had transported her. The Elders had welcomed her. She had sworn fidelity to the Society, vowed adherence to the struggle toward perfection, and had promised to perform the duties and services that would lift her to the next highest rung, Level Six. In Bishop Nysmith's report, the Elders had been pleased by Maddy's age, health, and enthusiasm and had encouraged her to take up the study of stenography and typing.

To the congratulations and applause of her fellow petitioners and initiates, she smiled and blushed. Nobody but the Elders knew that she was unworthy and in their wisdom they had preferred to overlook her failings. So far so good.

She had the daily routine under her belt. Breakfast, individual study (music for Maddy), private chores, elevenses (fruit juice), group instruction in Society precepts, lunch, meditation, daily walk, tea, instruction from Vidhya, individual reading, study, yoga, etc., supper, Bobo's messages from the Elders, and bed. Of these the instruction from Vidhya was her favorite. Now that she had been ushered into the inner circle, she basked in the comfort of belonging. At these sessions, Vidhya spoke only to the younger people. They sat cross-legged on the floor, Vidhya at the center, dressed usually in the soft, loose ecru cotton trousers and shirt that she far preferred to his English suit. There would be a space of silence during which Vidhya looked deeply into the face of each person in the circle, smiling lovingly.

"This morning the first thing I noticed when I awoke was a little white cloud in the sky."

He usually began with some such opening.

"I studied that little white cloud in the vast sky. What is it accomplishing there? I asked myself. Nothing? Or is it perhaps accomplishing everything it is destined to accomplish? There it sat, the little cloud, supremely itself, an entity in a harmonious universe, an integral part of that harmony, fulfilling its unique cloud function, in its being entirely itself and always supremely itself. We would be astounded if the cloud questioned its role as a little puff in the vast sky, would we not? Yet who among us does not constantly question what should not be questioned? What is there to learn from this little cloud, what can we learn, we who are troubled and distraught, what can we learn, to-

94

gether, putting our heads together, as we used to say when we were little children, observing the cloud for its message to us, for indeed it has a message for us, as every living thing on earth has a message for every other living thing on earth . . ."

She listened, silent, entranced, face lifted to receive wisdom from this beautiful young man proclaimed a kind of god, or the son of a god, or the embodiment of a powerful spiritual truth. Whatever Vidhya was, she listened to his words as if to music, floating free on the sweet sounds of his rounded vowels, the singsong lilt of the melodic line, the clarity of his consonants — like the sharp note of a violin cutting across elaborate and decorated embellishments of variations on an endless repetition. Later, trying to make exact sense of his discourse, digging for a usable direction, some answer to the perpetual question — *How shall I live my life?* — she became depressed as if faced with a dreary exercise, the practice of scales or Czerny finger exercises in the cold music room, alone. She put aside this response as part of her unworthiness, a failing she must work hard to rise above.

Then, suddenly, there was a hullabaloo she couldn't make head or tail of. It began with Bishop Nysmith announcing the joint promotion of Daphne, Millicent, and Marigold to Level Five, all together at the end of a day that had brought floods of rain since early morning. Bobo made a party atmosphere of the occasion and it was a nice diversion after the long, dreary day; but Cleves made it plain to Maddy that there were scandalous machinations behind the communication. Millicent herself had reported the event. She and her sisters had met with the Elders without Bobo's assistance, she swore, and the Elders themselves had elevated all three to Level Five.

"If you want to know what I think," Cleves offered, having sought her out in her room, Conrad in tow, "Millicent topped old Bobo on that one. What could he say? 'No, my dear, you never went anywhere last night, and never met the Elders in your life, Astral or otherwise, unless I say so.' She did a perfect copy of the sort of thing he does. Even her description of the Elders was word for word his. So what was there left for him to say? I understand he questioned her for hours without turning up a single discrepancy, some detail or other he was hoping he could catch her up on. Nothing doing, nothing doing. He didn't get anywhere with Milli."

He laughed breathlessly, without enjoyment.

"Here we are, Con and I, working like niggers to move up to Level Five, and there go Daph, Milli, and Mari, sailing right by us."

"And did you notice," Conrad said, "that Daph and Mari didn't corroborate a single detail. 'I don't remember.' 'If Milli says so.' Rotten little liars."

"After all, that's the way Bobo reports elevations, isn't it," Cleves said. "Goes off when it suits his fancy, traipses off to Cairo or Delhi or Jerusalem or wherever the Elders are supposed to be that particular night and carries along anyone he pleases. If the initiate doesn't remember the journey or anything else, that's no skin off Bobo's teeth, the petitioner hasn't reached a high enough level of awareness, that's all. Then Bobo comes trotting along home with stories of the Elders accepting this one or that one, promoting this one or that one. Goes in for the same song and dance with Lady Pansy every time she takes a step up, doesn't he, and poor Lady Pansy without a clue where she's been, Victoria Station or Katmandu, whatever Bobo says it's all the same to her. So why shouldn't Milli copycat the procedure for herself and her sisters? What's sauce for the goose, y'know."

He stopped. His prominent blue eyes rolled wildly. He clapped a hand over his mouth.

"Oh," he said in a choking voice. "Oh, oh, what am I saying?"

His speech had fired up Conrad. Mimicking a girl's

voice, he spoke in a mincing falsetto, while his Adam's apple bobbed up and down ludicrously.

"Dear me, dear me, is that what happened to me last night? Dear me, dear me, I don't remember a single thing! Oh, how mysterious, how exciting, how spiritual!"

"Shh, shh," Cleves said. "What if someone hears us?"

"I don't care who hears us," Conrad roared. "It's sickening. Sickening. And followed by that ... that ... that garbage about their contribution being recognized. What contribution? Sitting around filing their nails, that's Daph and Mari's contribution. If anybody thinks I'm going to comply with Bobo's suggestion that I make *my* contribution wiping little kids' arses in Sydney without even a promise of an elevation to Level Five just because Bobo has fallen in love with the city of Sydney and just because I was born there I'm supposed to go back to the one place I worked like a madman to get away from and spend my life teaching little kids how to weave straw baskets and potholders ..."

Cleves clasped Conrad around the middle, trying to pin his gesticulating arm and stop the flow of words, but Conrad was so big Cleves clung like a little monkey to a tree trunk. In a frenzy of irritation, Conrad threw him off.

"Cleves, you little runt, get off me, stop hanging on me."

Maddy thought she would disgrace herself and laugh aloud.

Cleves said, "Oh, oh," in a choked voice.

"Don't you believe in the Elders?" Maddy whispered. "Don't you believe in the message Bishop Nysmith brings back, and Vidhya and his reports?"

She had shocked both young men to a total halt.

"Of course we believe in the Elders, silly," Cleves said.

"Of course we do," Conrad said. "It's nothing to do with the Elders."

He turned to Cleves in bewilderment.

"Cleves!" he said. "What's the matter with her? Doesn't she understand anything?"

Cleves made a gesture as if he were about to settle the matter to everybody's satisfaction. He came up very close to Maddy. Now he, too, whispered.

"Listen, Maddy, it's not the Elders, Maddy, it's not Bobo or Vidhya. Nobody's questioning the Elders or Bobo or Vidhya. It's Milli. It's that bitch Milli. It's *Milli* we don't believe. Don't you see? Where's her verification? Did she come up with a single smitch of verification?"

"Well, the others don't either, do they?" Maddy said.

Cleves was choking again, covering his mouth with his fat little hand. Now Conrad came close to her, his usually ruddy face pale.

"*Nobody* is questioning Vidhya or Bobo or the Elders or the messages, *nobody* in this room. We aren't and you aren't. Isn't that right?"

She agreed that he was entirely right.

Whatever she didn't understand, she certainly understood their fear. Bobo could be terrifying. Though he had never displayed anything more than benign indifference toward her, she had seen his anger in action against a minor infraction on Conrad's part — sleeping when he should have been meditating.

Not to feed Daddy's fire, she wrote only good of Bobo, how kind he was, jolly, interesting, how delightful his stories of the Elders and of his own adventures as a young man, containing deeds of heroism as exciting as in a boy's adventure book. She avoided saying that his real interest was centered on males and that the young women were excluded from a number of activities. Twice a month Bobo held a special all-male session in a basement room Maddy had caught a glimpse of, filled with what looked like exercise mats. She didn't want to write any of this information to Daddy. How did she know that outgoing mail wasn't read? Mr. Singh took the mail to the post office.

She didn't know whether incoming mail was read either, even though it was she and Cleves who distributed it every day, so it was just as well that Daddy was busy revising his version of the trial against Bishop Nysmith.

I had a long, reassuring missive from Lady Pansy Harkness, who appears to be a very fine person in every way.

So he wrote in his latest letter.

She finds the trial verdict entirely just and reassures me that Bishop Nysmith is not the unwholesome being I had been led to believe he was. She explained the circumstances that led to the original misunderstanding on the part of the unfortunate boy who started the proceedings. It seems that he misinterpreted some advice on a matter of personal hygiene given to him by the Bishop. It's true that aspects of Nysmith's theories are quite bizarre, but then again so are Havelock Ellis's, so perhaps I just have to admit that I'm a bit behind the times on the modern approach to health, hygiene, and wholesome sex. In fact I should apologize to you for not having been more forthright in discussing sex with you, since it is the modern view that the more openness the better, and particularly between parent and child.

I trust you continue to keep your diary up to date. Mother sends her love.

An amazing suggestion. In the Bronx, when she was six years old, she had surprised her father in a state of undress. (Nothing to do with sex. In fact it was her belief, now that she was sixteen, that her parents had never had any sex other than the once when she was conceived.) Bursting into her parents' bedroom with some piece of childish news, she had found her father after a bath, standing naked before the mirror, his body twisted into a position that allowed a close scrutiny of an ugly boil on the back of his hairy behind. But it was the front of his body that seized her attention. She had never before or since seen a naked male. She considered her daddy a generally unattractive sight, all that hairiness, muscle, mottled skin color, but the most astounding aspect was the whole complicated, messy attachment in front that she didn't know existed. It was Daddy who was the more horrified of the two of them, a development that wildly frightened her. He screamed right out loud, and an entirely new expression took over his face, making his eyes very wide and open and shooting his eyebrows way up his forehead almost to his hairline. There was a pair of shorts lying on the bed, which he snatched up and held before the bunch of odd things between his legs. He was in a trembling, ungainly panic that was pitifully comic. He bent over, and in a squatting hop he reached the back of the bed and hid behind the headboard. From behind that shield, with only his head exposed, his eyebrows descended and his eyes returned to normal; he reassumed his father face, father stance, and father voice and dramatically ordered her to leave his bedroom.

"And don't you *ever, ever, ever* again enter a room without knocking, do you understand?" he said.

Despite that vivid lesson, she did it again in the house on Hampstead Heath, entered a room without knocking, Lady Pansy's upstairs sitting room, on a routine mail delivery, at an hour when Lady Pansy was supposed to be in the basement kitchen supervising the day's menus. Yet there she was, sitting upright on the ornate Victorian couch, her thick ankles in her heavy laced Oxfords resting solidly on the Persian rug, her head lolling about oddly, the wrinkled lids of her eyes shut tight, and her open mouth emitting soft, exulting moans. It was Vidhya spread across her lap and stretched the length of the couch, barely clothed in filmy ecru cotton pants and sleeveless shirt, his long, elegantly shaped feet bare, his limbs and muscled back, his wriggling legs, his round buttocks manifest under the gauzy fabric. His bare golden arms were entangled in Lady Pansy's bosomy amplitude, his face buried in the general softness, and his black, black hair spread breathing at her neck. The room also held the distinct sound of sucking.

What? What? *What* had she seen? She desperately needed Victoria. She fled the room unnoticed, but there was nowhere to go, no one to run to with her questions. What? What was this? What had she seen? What did it mean? Why wasn't Victoria here to help her?

Instead there was Millicent, in the center hall.

"You're red as a beet," she said. "Are you . . . You're not coming down with a fever, are you, Maddy?"

Though Millicent's tone was characteristically hard, and there was a hint of great inconvenience to her in the possibility of Maddy becoming ill, Maddy pushed herself to believe in Milli's concern. After all, there seemed to be more to Millicent than had originally met her eye. One had to admire the dash of her promotion coup, whether authentic or not. Besides, it was unnatural not to have a single friend among the group. Perhaps Milli would do.

Maddy said, "No, no, it's just . . . I don't know . . . sometimes I get so confused, Milli. Do you think we might have a little private talk — sometime?"

Millicent was longing to have a closer connection with Maddy, it seemed. Conspiracy was a game Milli loved to play. In a second she had arranged for them to walk together on their daily outing that afternoon.

For privacy, they simply fell behind, but when Millicent asked what Maddy had wanted to talk about, it was clearly impossible to bring up the scene between Vidhya and Milli's mother. How in the world could she ask Milli about her own *mother*? And anyway, as the day had progressed, the notion had grown that she hadn't witnessed that scene at all but conjured it up from a sick imagination. It couldn't be; it couldn't have happened. To Millicent she presented vague doubts of her own worthiness, of a general lack of faith, and of overwhelming ignorance of profound aspects of the Universal Society of Brotherhood. Wonder of wonders, Milli suffered similar doubts; and so they were launched into talk.

Straight off, she learned a new word — *bugger* — though not its precise meaning. Millicent blushed and said "never mind, then" when Maddy told her she didn't know what a bugger was. It was hard for Maddy to believe that this awkward, blushing girl was twenty-three, the oldest of the younger people, seven years older than Maddy, whose sixteenth birthday had gone by unnoted except for a dreary birthday letter from Daddy, heavy with advice, and her mother's postscript, *Happy Birthday, Dear Daughter.*

"It's clear as day," Millicent was saying, "that Vidhya's attachment to Mummy is pathological. Just as her response is pathological as well. We all understand, naturally. It has to do with Vidhya never having had a proper mum, and on poor Mum's side there's the tragic death of our brother. But understanding doesn't make it any easier to live with, does it now? It's all very hard on Daddy. And on my part, naturally, I do want to be Mummy's favorite, even if I am a female. So there I am, jealous of Mum, jealous of Vidhya, because she's first on his list and he's first on her list. And then there's my own passion for Vidhya, cooling its heels, so to speak, sitting around waiting for him to fall madly in love with me, but how can he when he's so pathologically tied to Mummy? And besides that, there's the question of our ages. I *am* five years older than he, you know. It is complicated, isn't it?"

She smiled at Maddy cheerfully, displaying an expanse of red gum.

"Do you love him?" Maddy said.

"Everybody loves Vidhya," Milli said. "I'm *in* love with him. And then, Mari and Daph adore him as well, though they don't dare hope as I do."

This babbling was delightful. How pleasant to walk along the now bare paths of the Heath, in the cold and the wind, her arm linked to Milli's, close to another warm body, luxuriating in intimate gossip. It was a revelation that Milli could be so animated and attractive. It was true that she looked somewhat like a horse — the long, pale face and prominent teeth, the short blond eyelashes stuck straight to the lids of her eyes, the lanky mane of hair falling from the sloppy bun, but this animal likeness was touching and appealing. She saw why Lord Harkness called his daughter *Pet*. She *was* a pet.

"But aren't you afraid? Doesn't it scare you that he's, you know, the ... the Second Coming ... the Messiah ... whatever ... you know?"

"Here's how I look at it," Milli said. "There's Vidhya the carnal being, the boy we play volleyball with and accompany on walks and make jokes with and die laughing with, and then there's Vidhya the legend and the promise of a spiritual being surpassing all others, and I never mix the two."

Maddy saw Vidhya's gauze-covered legs and round buttocks and his bare, golden feet writhing on the ornate couch in Lady Pansy's sitting room.

"How can you do that?" she said. "And if you can do it now, what if he really is the manifestation of the Second Coming, what if he really does turn into the Messiah?"

"Well, Mary loved Christ, didn't she?" Milli said.

"Wasn't it Joseph?" Maddy said.

"Joseph?"

Milli was lost for a second. Then she plunged on.

"Oh, I see what you mean, at least I think I see what you mean. But I've been meaning to ask you if you know that the case was reopened in India."

"The case?" Maddy said. "You mean the trial?"

"All the old worn-out charges that we thought had been put to rest. And worse this time because an uncle of Vidhya's has joined his father in the suit, claiming that Society leaders are making a laughingstock of him with all this Second Coming talk, turning his head and making him unfit for normal life."

"Who?" Maddy said.

103

"Vidhya," Milli said. "The attack is mounted against the Society and Bobo and even Lady Florence and my mother, but it's Vidhya all this really harms. Those charges against Bobo — corrupting a minor, undermining his customs and his religion — that rubs off on Vidhya."

Milli blushed deeply, then giggled, glancing sideways at Maddy.

"Sorry," she said. "I didn't mean that that way."

"What?" Maddy said.

"And just when your father's fears had been put to rest.

"They're suing for custody, too," Milli added, following a wildly disconnected laugh, more like a horse's whinny. "Lady Florence is terrified that Vidhya will be kidnapped. Until the case is settled again, he's not to set foot in India."

"What if the case goes against —" Maddy began.

"Impossible," Milli said. "No court in the world will take the word of some Indians against our Bobo's."

"Milli," Maddy said, "what kind of Indian is Vidhya?"

"Whatever do you mean?" Milli said.

"Well, Cleves was explaining to me that India is so large, and all that, and that there are different parts and different kinds of Indians, so I was wondering, what kind of Indian, y'know, I mean, is Vidhya Christian? Isn't he Hindu or Buddhist or something like that?"

Milli paused.

"Well," she said. "Well."

"I mean, does he speak Indian, for example?"

"Goodness," Milli said. "I'm sure I don't know half the answers to your questions. But I think Vidhya was a Hindu and a practicing Buddhist, though I've no idea what language he spoke, Hindi maybe, though I vaguely remember Mum saying something about learning *telegu* of all things years ago when Vidhya could speak hardly any English whatsoever, but he doesn't speak anything other than English now, he doesn't even recall that other language, whatever it was, and you do understand, don't you, that in the Society all people, all religions, everyone and everybody is equal, and beliefs, differences, I mean, are swallowed up in the larger precepts of Brotherhood?"

She flashed a big-gummed smile.

"Oh, I do understand," Maddy said. "I was just wondering . . . I was just wondering," she pushed herself to continue, "why Jesus? Mightn't a Messiah come in some other form?"

"Oh, absolutely," Milli said enthusiastically. "Any form at all, but our Lord came in the most perfect form so it's natural that —"

"Isn't it more logical to suppose that Vidhya would reappear in the form of Buddha or Mohammed? . . . I mean, why Jesus again?"

"I don't think Mohammed has anything to do with this," Milli said, somewhat coldly.

"It's hard to explain what I mean," Maddy persisted. "You know, on the feast of Passover, the Jewish holiday, a door is left open so that Elijah the prophet can visit every home . . ."

Her throat was very dry. Milli stared at her in wonderment.

". . . Their religion promises the Jewish people a Messiah, lots of religions promise a Messiah, so why shouldn't Vidhya be the Messiah of the Arabs or the Hebrews or a completely unexpected, new Messiah? I mean, why Jesus again?"

"Why, what a funny thing to say," Milli said, ceasing to walk for a moment. "How funny. 'Why Jesus again?' And anyway, I can't see your point at all, since Jesus *was* the Messiah of the Hebrews, wasn't he?"

She peered into Maddy's face.

"What a funny thing to say," Milli repeated. " 'Why Jesus again?' You say that as if he failed."

"Well, if he didn't," Maddy said, "why are we still waiting?"

Such conversations, having a friend, pairing off with

Milli, was a little like being back in the Bronx, living the exciting stoop life of play and discussion. During their daily walks it was accepted that Milli and Maddy strolled together, left to their endless, rambling conversations, which never strayed far from the topic of Vidhya — his nature, his looks, his spirituality, his occult powers, his words, his future, their future in following him, and, of course, the trial, always the trial.

The new case with old scandals repeated was widely reported in English-language newspapers in India. Clippings were sent on to Hampstead, but by the time the slow mails delivered them, the London papers and magazines had taken up the story, having fun with headlines. BOBO AND THE BOYS. TALES OF THE WILD(E). MESSY MESSIAH MESSAGES. Maddy carried the clippings to her room and avidly read the charges and countercharges, accusations and defense, copying down any words that mystified her for later investigation into their meanings via a huge old leatherbound dictionary in the library. That yielded mystery upon mystery.

Sodomite (1) an inhabitant of Sodom. (2) a person who practices sodomy.
Sodomy (1) unnatural copulation. (2) bestiality.

At table, she studied Vidhya, probing for the unnatural beast beneath the sensitive boy. There had been a defiant fight on his part for the right to eat with his fingers, and he had won it with the clever argument that Bishop Nysmith's injunction of silence would be more carefully kept by the practice, since eating with the fingers eliminated the clatter of cutlery against china. Nothing bestial about his method. With fastidious speed and expertise, he scooped up rice and vegetables, using bread and broad leaves of lettuce. The messy part of the food never touched his fingers. He caught her watching him, and without breaking the rule of silence he smiled and gesticulated an invitation to eat Indian fashion, but dropped his eyes and lowered his hand to his lap when Lady Pansy indicated disapproval by shaking her head at him.

Maddy imagined him suffering excessively from the ugly exposure of the trial. She longed to ease his pain, but how? His attention, though it had been directed at her for only a few seconds, created an inner agitation she could not shake off. She carried it back to her room — along with more clippings.

A former Society member, now disaffected, a young Indian who had been a close friend to Vidhya, testified to an unnatural act that he claimed to have seen with his own eyes, having opened the door of Bishop Nysmith's bedroom and surprised Bobo and Vidhya in the very process. The defense talked of hygiene, modesty, chastity, cleanliness, care of the easily infected foreskin, proper bathing techniques. The disaffected young Indian had misinterpreted a lesson in hygiene. What he had seen in Bobo's bedroom, Vidhya naked on Bobo's naked lap, was Bobo conducting a lesson in hygiene.

The defense also argued that Vidhya's father had grossly neglected the child Vidhya after the death of his mother. His present filial interest was a mask for materialistic concerns. He knew that Vidhya's grooming for his world role was nearing completion, and, more to the point, he knew that Vidhya had been made financially independent.

"Money is what his father is after," Cleves told Maddy. "These people know how to smell out money, regular Jews at it."

"What money?" Maddy said, quieting the buzz set off in her head.

"You knew that Mrs. Dasinov settled a lifetime income on Vidhya, didn't you? Just a few months before Vidhya's father instituted the suit?"

She hadn't known.

"But isn't she Jewish?" Maddy said.

"I don't know," Cleves said. "Maybe her husband was. Anyway, what difference does it make whether she is or not? We're all equal in the Society of Brotherhood."

He spoke as if it were she polluting their talk with prejudice.

In the following weeks, more charges were carried by the newspapers, attested to by new witnesses, white witnesses, participants in former Society ceremonies and encampments. An American boy, two English boys, and an Australian came forward to accuse Bobo of teaching the practice of masturbation. The young men were described as having been *prepubescent* and *pubescent* males at the time. Again she needed the dictionary.

> Pubescent (1) The state or quality of being first capable of begetting or bearing offspring, which is marked by maturing of the reproductive organs, with the onset of menstruation in the female and the development of the secondary sex characters in both sexes; the period at which sexual maturity is reached. The age of puberty varies in different climates and environments, being from thirteen to sixteen in boys and from eleven to fourteen in girls, and is commonly designated as fourteen for boys and twelve for girls.

She gave up on definition number 2, something to do with the age at which the lower animals begin to lay eggs. What worried her was *twelve for girls* and *secondary sex characters*. Didn't that mean she was practically ancient? And what if she never developed any of those secondary sex characters, whatever they were?

She went on to locate *masturbation*, passing on the way a full-page illustration of the Muscular System of Man, figures 1 and 2, frontal view and dorsal view. Both views, carefully labeled, showed nothing between the legs of the muscular figures. Was Daddy a freak? Papa, she meant, since he had been Papa then, back in the Bronx. Perhaps that was why his eyebrows shot up to his hairline and he hurried in that peculiar stooped hobble to the cover of the headboard, clutching the little piece of underwear to cover his front. He didn't want Maddy to know he was a freak. Bessie. She had been Bessie then.

She turned back to the M's.

Masturbation. To practice onanism. *Onanism.* Self-pollution.

It was hopeless. Everybody knew that boys masturbated. It gave them pimples and made them nervous and if they did it too much they went crazy. That was common knowledge on the stoop. But girls? She knew what it was that she was doing in her room with the diamond-paned windows, alone in her bed. Was she a freak too? Did nobody else do what she did to herself?

And what did it all have to do with *love?* Somewhere buried beneath these obfuscating definitions was the link between that place between the legs — and *love.* Somewhere in this mess lurked *love,* the state of being she most longed for. Somebody must love her. She must love somebody. That was what life was all about. But *love* had been cast in a new light, suffused with a terror and danger that drew and repelled, repelled and drew. She moved about now in an aura of lust, perpetually aroused and faintly nauseated.

Beneath the decorum of exterior appearances were dark, passionate secrets. Underneath Society spirituality lurked the unthinkable happening in Lady Pansy's upstairs sitting room, the all-male sessions in the basement room, Bobo's theories of hygiene. Behind Milli's insipid jabber, a carnal longing for Vidhya; behind Vidhya's saintliness — what?

She shuddered away from her fancies and shuddered toward them, obsessed by sexual imaginings and puzzled as to which bothered her more: the recognition that evil existed alongside all the striving for good in the house on the Heath, or the dismaying fact that she seemed to be the outsider in this circling intimacy of incestuous passion.

5

IN the hotel room that continued to glow with an unearthly rosiness, Maddy Phillips tried hard to go back to
sleep. She must have drifted off for a second, because
she awoke frightened, her heart beating too fast, her body
painfully stiff from the constraints of lying carefully alongside Victoria to give her enough room. The eerie light in the
room shifted rapidly, a series of soft alarms — bright rose to
softest pink, a sudden blare of gold, an abrupt darkening like
a bereavement, then a bright, steady trumpeting of morning
sunshine. Her body responded to these astral signals with a
wild alert. There was menace in the room, a black amorphous shape at the doorway, visible from the corner of her
eye. Accost it with a sudden turn. Nothing. Strange noises
from the corridor. Listen. No, in the room. Victoria and
Dwight breathing, moaning, sighing out the dreadful complaints they would not utter awake. Aaaah, sssss, grrrr,
fffttt, ooohhh.

She quit the crowded bed, shuffled into slippers,
slipped on a robe even older than the Pucci, a light woolen
plaid she had bought on a trip to England with Dwight
twenty-five years ago. The formal living room of the suite

had not been tidied since last night's picnic. She did not stop herself from the reflexive act of picking up. It steadied her, normalized the nightmarish fears. She would have liked breakfast on a tray, fresh-squeezed orange juice, real coffee, good bread. Coffee was forbidden, but she would have ordered it anyway except that it was only five o'clock and surely not even the Ritz-Carlton supplied room service at such an hour. She walked the length of the pretty patterned rug, tracing a trailing branch in the design — a child's game — then detoured to the windows at the far end of the room. She pushed aside the inner white curtains of the many-layered draperies and surveyed the Public Garden, jolly with colorful blossoms under the gold of the fully risen sun. A beautiful morning. The weather would help the demonstration.

Nothing stirred on the scene. Then, on an outer path, a jogger appeared, a woman in a yellow costume; after a little space a couple in matching black and white; then a single male, naked to the waist and wearing a red headband, bouncing along at the bottom of the slope, gradually slowing as they labored uphill, finally running on beyond her range of vision.

She remembered that the Shaw Monument was somewhere in that direction. What if she went out in her dressing gown and jogged her way up to the monument to make her obeisance? Nobody would take the slightest notice. She was tempted. But it was a stiff climb. She might become short of breath, turn an ankle, trip, stumble and lose her bearings as she had yesterday.

Anyway, the monument had been messed up by anti-black protesters. She didn't want to see that beautiful work marred and mocked.

Bury one's head. Look away from the screen when horrors appeared on the evening news. Living holocausts in changing geographies. The wheel of life crushing human beings in its downward plunge, taken from any hidden corner of the world and caught on the color TV. Retaliation or succor following on the morning news. The wheel of life quiveringly turning upward. Three steps forward, two steps back. The spiraling whirl of history. Round and round, up and down, seesaw, seesaw till the end of time. Which might easily occur almost immediately. We shall overcome. When? A split second before we spiral downward again. Down and out this time. Nothing salvaged. No more good wars. The war to end all wars and everything else.

She was stretched out on the couch, lying in a jagged half-conscious state of fleeting images and thoughts.

Was it a simple matter of having lived too long? She was in no hurry to go. She, to whom it wasn't supposed to matter whether she stayed or left. Had she lost her solid faith in reincarnation? There had been an interview a few months ago in which she had been asked the usual run of questions and responded with her usual answers.

Q: *Maddy Phillips had never had a child. Did Maddy Phillips regret never having had any children?*

A: *There is nothing to regret. I've had hundreds of children in my other lives and I'll have hundreds more in future incarnations. In this life it was ordained that I be childless, but this life is only one of my many lives.*

Q: *Are there advantages for women in remaining childless?*

A: *It left me free to care about the fate of all the children of the world instead of just my own.*

Q: *Did Maddy Phillips mean by her statement that mothers were too selfishly involved with their own children to care about the state of the world or the fate of the world's children?*

A: *I am speaking solely of myself. But, yes, I do believe that in general we exist in a dangerously selfish-minded world.*

Q: *Did Maddy Phillips consider herself a feminist?*

A: *Yes, absolutely.*

Q: *An advocate of zero growth? What were her views on marriage and the family? The new life styles? Pornography? Lesbianism? Who were her heroines? Betty Friedan, Simone de Beauvoir, Simone Weil, Gloria Steinem, Jane Fonda? Did she feel that she had seen everything, done everything, experienced everything in her former lives? Was current life nothing but déjà vu? Could she describe those sensations? For example, what about punk? Anything resembling punk in her former lives? Had she had a former life in ancient Rome? Babylon? And what if there is no future life, nothing to be reincarnated into except a smudge of radioactive ash?*

A: *I believe in the continuation of life in the universe. There are other planets, other forms of life. No, I don't embrace the possibility of nothingness. And now, no more questions, please.*

If they repeated those questions at the press conference today, she might just put back her head and howl. She let her head roll back and was instantly asleep and dreaming. They were all in the rear of the truck, seated on the director's chairs, a fierce joy in the air, Victoria's scarf billowing like smoke, Dwight looking into her face with a fixed smile, Vidhya standing forward addressing a huge assembly of people listening in a subdued hush. Behind them, the truck was ablaze, but there was no discomfort, no heat or smoke from the flames, as if the fire were a photographic trick. Close to her ear, Victoria's mocking voice.

"Good show. Good show. A most accomplished charlatan. Best in the world."

Someone said, "Are you suggesting he's not to be trusted?"

"It doesn't matter. He's a good showman. A hunger strike is fine, just fine, better than anything any of us came up with. If we're putting on a show, make it a good show, is my approach."

"You're impossible," someone said.

Maddy opened her eyes. She, the voices, and a number of people were gathered in the living room of the hotel suite. Had she been sleeping in public with her mouth open, snoring and dribbling? She sat up. She saw first Victoria, in the costume of the previous day, make-up firm, eyelashes in place, hat and scarf anchored. The young couple who had assisted them yesterday rushed to her side, whispering *good morning,* urging speed, the press conference was due to begin momentarily, breakfast was about to be served by the hotel porters. The young man seemed fresh and alert, the young woman sluggish, her breath thick with the smell of cigarettes. They had deliberately allowed her to sleep on while they took care of Dwight, helped him dress. Dwight, impeccably put together and planted in an armchair, greeted her with a grin touched with competitive triumph. *See, I can manage on my own, I'm even ahead of you today, on my toes, fit as a fiddle.*

At the opposite end of the couch where she had been lying, Arthur Brownson, Brooks Brothers casual, fussed about Bernard Lewis to the steady flow of Lewis's objections.

"Not a soul will notice my socks, Arthur. Please cease this undue attention to my socks. One of our great contemporary failings, a foolish obsession with details of no consequence. 'Protocol,' 'saving face,' 'standing tall' — flimsy nonsense, top dressing. Mismatched socks are not a disaster, Arthur. Our policy in Africa, in Central America, in Latin America, is a disaster. The Middle East is a disaster. The selfish, headlong rate of industrial development is a great social disaster. Nuclear power. Nuclear weapons. World disasters. But one navy blue and one dark brown sock on the same set of feet is of no consequence, and for you to bring all your formidable literary intelligence to this problem is a vast waste of your considerable talents."

Dwight laughed and applauded.

"Bernard," Arthur Brownson said, "I really resent the

way you say 'formidable literary intelligence.' I really do resent it."

Bernard Lewis closed his eyes and fell into an instant sleep.

"Maddy," Victoria called out, "are you up, alert, compos mentis? Vidhya is on a hunger strike. He announced it this morning."

Maddy nodded, and rose to make her way to the bedroom to make herself presentable. The day had definitely begun.

6

AT long last there was a letter from Victoria in among the mail that she and Cleves sorted every morning. The envelope, by itself, set her heart smashing against her ribs — heavy creamy paper, thick slashing lines written in black ink. It was addressed to Lady Pansy and she let Cleves take it up for delivery to Lady Pansy's upstairs sitting room, preferring no further contact with that space.

In the evening, Bishop Nysmith read sections of the letter aloud to the group. He had just returned from India, once again cleared of all specific charges, though having been reprimanded for "advanced" theories and practices and accompanied by still another young Indian boy with a remarkable aura — Ramlal, instantly shortened to Ram. And because Milli, Mari, and Daph considered the new boy to pose a risk to their beloved Vidhya's sovereignty, they teased him unmercifully, running a taunting circle around him on the daily walk, chanting:

> "Cowardy, cowardy custard
> Your face is the color of mustard."

It was Vidhya who befriended and made life bearable for the new boy in the house in Hampstead.

Victoria's letter described a train journey in the service of the Society.

> We traveled in great style. The Maharajah put his private coach at our disposal — living room, dining room, bedroom with twin beds, and *two* baths. Kitchen and servant quarters, of course. Lady Florence brought her personal servant, and mine, nonexistent, as you know, was also invited, but we managed with just one between us. The Maharajah had gone to the trouble of ascertaining what Lady Florence preferred to eat and ordered the cooks to prepare those dishes. When we went to bed our sheets were turned back, a glass of cool water was placed at the bedside, etc., etc., exactly the sort of attentions yours truly is not particularly accustomed to receive.
>
> The Maharajah didn't appear to be disturbed by the scandal of the trial, at least not to the point of withdrawing his patronage of Society events. He's a great admirer of Lady Florence's, though he apparently disapproves of her politics. The night before we left Bombay, there was a splendid dinner in Lady Florence's honor given by the Maharajah at the palace, and there was the usual heated talk pro and con on the subject of Home Rule and Congress, Gandhi, etc., and that led to a disagreement about the design for the viceroy's house. The Maharajah has the sweetest way in the world of disagreeing, but disagree he did, pointing out that the architectural concepts for the buildings at New Delhi ignore Indian traditions, insult the Indian people, and at the same time require that India underwrite the whole extravagant shebang financially — his words exactly. He became very bitter about it, but Lady Florence is a master at smoothing things over, even if she and Sir Edwin are related, which made for a bit of awkwardness there for a moment. She made it perfectly clear that her political views are hers personally and

that the Society never intrudes into the political life of
any country in which it sets up an encampment — and
is most sensitive to the particular problems of India.
She stressed that we are above divisions of nationality,
race, creed, or political persuasion, so all ended happily.
I think we can definitely continue to count on the Maharajah for support.

The encampment is beautiful — so beautiful —
words cannot describe the beauty of this scene — the
low buildings in the exquisite setting of water and hills,
palms and beach, and above all, the color of the light,
the tinted, perfumed color of the light.

My love to all of you. Tell Maddy that I have discovered some wonderful folk melodies to work into our
music for a new dance. Also inform her that nobody
ever bothers to answer my letters. Will she be different?

She reverberated with the wonder of having been sin-
gled out. The specific content of the letter was beyond her;
the details floated off into romance; the Sheik of Araby and
Scheherezade were as real to her as this maharajah and Lady
Florence. But the last lines, the blessed last lines! They let
Maddy in. They let her in. And sent her flying back to the
Bechstein in the music room to try again. And fail again, in
her own expectations. She couldn't *feel* any musical talent.
Wasn't one supposed to feel something? She knew she had a
flair for rearranging melodies composed by others, manipu-
lating them into a kind of parody — at least under Victoria's
push. But that was cheating, wasn't it? And without Victoria she couldn't even do that. A lost sheep without her
shepherd. But surely Victoria didn't want her to spend her
life cheating?

Now when she should have been meditating in her
room, she wrote intense, anguished pages of ungrammatical,
chaotic thoughts to Victoria. The challenge of *will she be
different?* rang in her head, but in the end she never mailed
those outpourings. She wrote instead a short note, stiff yet

gushing, hinting at hidden unhappiness, and at unexpressed love, and mailed it to that far-off, exotic place where Victoria pursued her glamorous life. Later she burned with shame that she had sent such a poor messenger of her feelings. Almost immediately, she started on an impatient watch for a reply, though she knew that it took months for the mails to work their way back and forth.

Her father's letters with her mother's postscripts arrived with greater regularity. He too pressed her forward in her music studies. She had been trying to impress him with a newfound passion for poetry, but he would have none of that.

> There is more poetry in a single musical phrase of Mozart, more poetry in a few bars of Beethoven's Ninth Symphony, than in the entire body of sentimental verse written by ladies like Elizabeth Barrett Browning or this latest enthusiasm of yours, Elinor Wylie . . .

For the first time, his contempt enraged her. She didn't answer. She put his letter in the diary he had given her. She had written nothing in it since the day on the *Majestic* when she had torn out her first entry. Defiantly, she read more poetry, spent more time memorizing sonnets, could recite the whole of "How do I love thee? Let me count the ways," and during the weekly ritual hair-washing she and Milli shared, she shouted out the lines, " 'I could reform the world / In those lost hours while my hair is curled.' "

And then Elena Dasinov joined the household, arriving with fashionably bobbed hair and her childlike, knobby-kneed legs, striving to look daring in square-cut above-the-knee dresses. She was the daughter of the rich Mrs. Dasinov who had settled a lifetime income on Vidhya. Was it this bite out of her inheritance that accounted for her melancholy air, or only the inevitable effect of her long nose and drooping eyes?

Perhaps it was the overwhelming presence of Lady Florence, the fabulous Lady of the books and the clippings and Victoria's letter. She had picked up Elena from a boarding school in Paris and escorted her to Hampstead. Lady Florence was very old, but she was very beautiful. Her skin was unlined and her hair was a luxuriant, shocking black, drawn tightly around her head to a low knot, Spanish fashion, creating a sharp frame for her large, flirtatious, violet-colored eyes and oval face, glowing with her conviction that she was a most enticing and clever woman, justifiably entitled to the charmed life she led and fully intended to continue to lead.

But it was Elena Dasinov who held Maddy's real interest. Beneath Elena's studied sophistication, beneath the artificially straightened shingled hair, Maddy recognized a self-conscious little Jewish girl she might have played jacks with on the Bronx stoop, or another cousin giggling under the dining table at holiday gatherings in New Jersey, younger than Maddy and even less sure of herself. In a spasm of relief that there would be someone more vulnerable than herself in this formidable household, she tenderly befriended the new girl. In no time, she had earned herself her very own satellite, an adoring pet, circling and running at her heels as Cleves ran at Conrad's and she did at Milli's.

Elena Dasinov had cast Maddy in the role of sun to Elena's growth, winding herself around Maddy, to use Bishop Nysmith's description, "like a clinging vine, gathering substance from a young sapling hardly strong enough to nourish itself, but never mind, never mind . . ." accompanied by a condescending pat on the head of each, more slap than caress. ". . . It is nature's way with young girls and nature will find its way to balance the scales, all in good time."

His comment deeply discomforted both Maddy and Elena. Maddy gave no sign of the queasiness he had caused her, but during the long afternoon walk Elena cried, choking out between sobs that Bobo knew she was a failure in life and that even her mother, who loved her dearly, longed in her secret heart for a truly beautiful daughter. Aghast at such open emotional display, Milli ran from them to join the others.

The two girls walked on alone, Maddy offering the comfort of linked arms and a steady murmur of sympathetic noises. After a long time, during which Maddy ceased to listen, Elena exhausted her supply of grief and fell silent.

"You must learn to laugh more," Maddy said.

She had determined to be brisk and mature with this sad little girl.

"Laugh!" Elena said. "Laughing is what I'm really good at. Would you like to laugh? Shall I do Lady Pansy for you?"

And she immediately became Lady Pansy, driveling on about Vidhya and the depths of her own soul, from time to time falling into the open-mouthed, trancelike pauses that seized Lady Pansy in mid-speech.

Elena could ape anybody. Victoria dancing was one of her favorites — a turn Maddy enjoyed in spite of a twinge of disloyalty, perhaps even laughing more because of guilt. Elena did Vidhya communicating his wisdom to the group, Bobo pontificating, Cleves affecting his postures of arrogance.

"They're easy," Elena said. "They caricature themselves."

New turns appeared in Elena's repertory regularly. The pair of giggling servant girls were rendered in a dialogue consisting entirely of glottal stops. An impersonation of Milli raised horsiness to human complexity, so that one ended loving Elena's Milli, tossing her head, exposing her teeth and gums and speaking in neighs.

"Can you do me?"

There was trepidation in Maddy's request.

"Never. No. I don't do anyone I cherish."

Her drooping eyes conveyed her adoration.

Impossible not to love Elena, Maddy's special satellite, and so clever and amusing besides. Impossible also to refrain from acting unaccountably mean to Elena, hurting her by a

display of moods, aloofness, joy in the misery she was caus-
ing. She played Elena off against Milli, shut her out, ignored
her for a whole day at a time, drunk with the pleasure of the
power to wound another. Did she use these games for the
sweetness of the moment when Elena broke into tears and
they made up?

Not that Maddy apologized. Never.

"That's the way I am, Elena," Maddy said. "Take me
or leave me."

She knew she was in no danger. She knew she com-
manded a slavish love from Elena. Why, even though their
mysterious estrangements were always Maddy's doing,
Elena wrote long impassioned pleas for forgiveness when
they occurred, pages and pages of scribbled love, slipped
under Maddy's door.

> Tell me what I've done to upset you. Whatever it is I
> swear I'll never do it again. I miss you horribly. It hurts
> as if a big hard ball were stuck in my throat. I can't
> even cry, I'm so sad. At lunch I saw the sun strike your
> hair into gold and I had to leave the table before I
> choked on my tears. If I should lose you I don't know
> what I would do. My feeling for you has melted me to
> the core and our feeling for each other has reformed me
> with you at my center. Do you understand what I am
> saying? I must become worthy of you so that I stop
> doing the things that turn you from me . . .

It was immensely enjoyable melodrama. There were
melodramas all around Maddy. Of course she must have one
of her very own. She discussed all aspects of the Elena-
Maddy relationship with Milli to keep the drama on the boil.
Didn't Milli think her unworthy of Elena's adoration? Did
Milli think their love was sufficiently spiritual? Sufficiently molded into Society mores? Did Milli consider Elena a
"genius," and if so, of what sort? Might it be said that
humor and mimicry qualified as serious talents? Questions
like that.

Maddy didn't care what Milli said as long as she went

on talking. She would have liked the discussion to never end. Her very own drama, a gift from Elena. Of course Maddy loved Elena for such a gift. And for something else, for being Jewish. The fact of their Jewishness created their closed world; while estranged, they were closer than they were to any of the others; they knew they would make up, renew their sweet, secret compacts; they would babble nonsense, mingling silly ideas, lofty dreams, ignorant theories. They would laugh. They would laugh and laugh and close off their world to the others.

"I'm Jewish," Maddy said, almost in a whisper, on one of their daily walks. "Or at any rate, we *were* Jewish before Daddy changed us."

"Are you? You don't look it at all," Elena said, and was off on her own concerns. "God, I wish I looked like you. Why do I have to look like this, why?"

Another reason to love Elena, treating Maddy's tormenting information as if it were nothing at all. Yet, to her astonishment, Maddy found herself betraying their secret relationship, not the Jewish part, but the love part. She confided in Vidhya. She hadn't intended any intimate revelations when she sat down with Vidhya for help in her individual struggle to attain inner harmony on the Path to the Good, an innovation put into practice that week by Bishop Nysmith, who proclaimed *the girls*, sometimes called by him *the maidens*, to be particularly in need of private guidance, so much so that, in fact, they remained the only ones receiving it. Maddy's appointment was the last of the week, late on a dismal Friday afternoon. A heavy, cold rain had been falling all day. In the unheated music room, Vidhya sat cross-legged on a high cushion. He motioned Maddy to sit before him. His aspect was bored and forbidding. The intense cold of the bare wood floor penetrated through Maddy's woolen skirt. She reached for a pillow but was reprimanded.

"There, that is typical of your attitude, your bad attitude. You look always in the wrong direction, in the direction where there is physical comfort. You must think more of the spiritual. Why do you not think more of the spiritual? Think about that. Instead you are drawn to ways that are typical of young girls of your upbringing, especially American girls, who are pampered and smothered in unnecessary and harmful physical comforts."

"Yes," Maddy said, and returned the pillow to its chair.

Like a juggler adding more and more balls to his performance, Vidhya piled failure on failure in a display much like her father's ill-tempered attempts to reform her thinking. The cold floor penetrated her flesh and entered her spine. It seemed to wither her ability to think. She heard herself succumbing to and even encouraging the attack.

"Yes," she said. "Thank you, Vidhya, that's true, yes."

"You must try to think in a positive direction," he said. "You must study to become more quiet. You must learn to cultivate stillness of the soul. Marigold has been working on this problem and is showing much improvement. You must be more like Mari. You are too forward in your manner, too bold, always smiling. You must cultivate some seriousness. You must not smile so much, Maddy."

"Yes," she said. "That's true. Yes."

"And humility," he said, gazing above her head with bored, vacant eyes. "You must study humility. Perhaps you have noticed the great improvement in Daphne. Daph has been making great strides in development of humility. You must try to be more like Daph and let your head droop a bit. You carry your head too high. Pride cometh before a fall."

He frowned.

"Goeth," he said.

Maddy dropped her head to hide tears of humiliation at being compared unfavorably to those ninnies, Daph and Mari.

"Now," Vidhya said, more briskly. "Are there any

questions? Special problems in your struggle on the Path to the Good?"

"Yes," she said. "Yes. Thank you, Vidhya," and fell silent.

"What is troubling you, Maddy? Speak up."

"I'm a very bad person," she said in a rush. "I must be. I am unworthy. I must be very bad or I wouldn't be so cruel to Elena. I love her, I really do, and still I'm cruel to her. Why am I like that? And she loves me so much and is never, never, never cruel to me. Help me to understand why I am so bad. Why am I so bad to her? I want so much to be kind and good and loving. And with this dear friend who loves me so much and is so generous with her love, I am unkind and cruel. It must be that I have a bad character, that I am unworthy . . ."

She was enjoying this outpouring of words and had a gratifying sense of her own nobility in exposing her faults, but the effect on Vidhya was unexpected.

"Elena?" he said sharply.

She had riveted his vacant, wandering eyes to her face at last.

"Elena?" he said again. And then again, "Elena? What in all the wide world has Elena to do with the Path to the Good? Why are you talking of Elena? The Path to the Good is through *me*, not Elena. You should not be thinking of Elena or talking of Elena. Elena is a child, a nobody, except for her mother she is of no importance. I cannot believe you are having problems connected with Elena. Are you sure that you are not mistaken?"

She was frightened and said nothing. There was a long silence. He studied her face.

"Ah," he said. "Now I understand, now I see. You have been immoral together. You have been naughty, that is the problem. You have been indulging in immorality, that is it, is it not?"

It was a bewildering comment, until in a shocking flash his meaning came clear.

She said, "If you mean . . . if you mean . . ."

She shook her head no, and blushed.

"No, oh, no," she said.

"Well, what is the problem, then? You girls are always fussing, always fussing."

He was immensely irritated.

"I want to be a good person, kind and loving and generous. I must have a bad character . . ."

Inanely, she repeated what she had said before. The joy had gone out of confession, however.

"Why are you not troubled about *me*? You have consistently refused to learn typing, for instance. Is that kind and loving and generous?"

The skin of Vidhya's face was very dark that day, perhaps because of the cold room. Except for his head and his bare feet, he was entirely wrapped in a warm, loose garment. The black big-toe sticking out, showing a purplish nail, grotesquely started a refrain running in her head:

> Eeny, meeny, miny, mo
> Catch a nigger by the toe
> If he hollers let him go . . .

The following afternoon a bright spell made their daily walk unexpectedly pleasant. Milli and Elena had gone off to Harley Street, Milli to the dentist, Elena on a mysterious visit she would not discuss, she said, "until I return." Maddy fell behind to tie an undone shoelace. Vidhya dropped back and joined her.

It was Marigold who initiated the story that Maddy had deliberately placed a pebble in her shoe to entice Vidhya into her clutches — Mari's words exactly — but there wasn't any pebble at all, and the idea of entrapment had never entered Maddy's head. Entrap Vidhya? With a silly trick like pretending to have a pebble in a shoe? The coming Messiah? Their guide on the Path to the Good? Did they think her so stupid? Her shoelace had come undone and she had stopped to retie it. She jumped up on a bench that was the driest object around and, crouching, worked at the lace. And there was Vidhya at her side, helping her.

"You have very pretty feet," he said.

"Too large," she said, embarrassed by the compliment.

He laughed and dropped his voice.

"Have you noticed Millicent's? They are the size of a punt."

His wonderfully pealing laughter rang out.

"And Daphne's . . . larger than mine, larger than Bobo's, much larger than mine."

She remembered his golden feet writhing on the couch in Lady Pansy's sitting room; his big black toe sticking out from under his warm garment yesterday.

"Shall we walk together?" he said.

His manner was delightfully invitational. She couldn't lock this playfulness into any pattern that fit the Vidhya she thought she knew. Remembering also the criticisms he had made of her arrogant bearing, she shortened her normally long stride, lowered her head in her little hat pulled down straight over her eyes, and was careful not to smile and talk. It was Vidhya who babbled on as they walked up Parliament Hill.

"Have you noticed sometimes that you become stuck on a particular word? Like a needle on a broken record. There are many occasions when I become like that. I repeat the same word over and over and over. This week it is the word *trouble* that troubles me. I have fallen in love with it, it seems. Next week it will be sickening to me and I shall stop using it. Are you like that?"

Oh yes, she agreed, she was exactly like that. There were days when she could hardly speak in decent English, she assured him. Not that she meant that the way it sounded. She didn't mean that there was anything wrong with *his* English at all, at all. She meant —

He understood, he understood perfectly. Gradually her

head in its little hat returned to a pertly proud angle and a tiny smile of triumph pulled at her lips, try as she might to keep a solemn face. What an extraordinary turn of events, that Vidhya should be singling her out for his playful attention. It was a wonderful walk, all the way home to the house at the edge of the pond. And reaching it, he took her arm and whispered in her ear.

"Forget what I said yesterday, Maddy. I was in a bad mood. Don't allow your head to droop. You carry yourself like a queen, a royal princess. You should be the tutor of these English girls to teach them proper carriage. Really, you should."

Alone in her room, excited beyond her body's capacity to control, a fleeting, darkening thought sobered her. Perhaps Vidhya thought her an American heiress like Elena? Abroad, all American girls were reckoned the daughters of millionaires. The idea was unworthy, surely, of so exalted a being as Vidhya and should have been rejected by herself, an adoring disciple. Still . . .

At dinner, necessarily silent, she never let her eyes stray in his direction, so that he would see that she had not placed any mistaken significance on the afternoon's incident.

Lord Harkness had arrived for the evening and lingered at the table, requesting Milli and Maddy to stay with him. He was obviously upset, depressed, without appetite for anything but jams, mustards, and chutney, his heavy groans floating into the silence imposed on dining. He had caught at his wife's hand as she went by in Vidhya's wake, requesting her to stay for a moment, but Lady Pansy dropped a perfunctory kiss on his broad, red forehead, murmuring something, and followed Vidhya and the others to the library, where a game of charades had been promised after a reading of messages from the Elders by Bobo.

"You'll forgive me, Bishop," he called out, "for detaining Maddy and Milli, just for a moment. I know *I* won't be missed, but we'll all be along shortly."

"You're a sensible girl, Maddy." He plunged right in as if he had never shoved her up against the wall in the gallery and put his hand up her skirt and his tongue in her mouth. "Everything I see and everything Milli reports about you confirms that judgment. I do need your help. I've turned to Milli and to Daph and Mari, I've pleaded with my wife to help me understand, but it seems they can't, they simply can't. Her obsession with this boy, Vidhya, is beyond my comprehension, really it is. Perhaps you might enlighten me. Oh, he's charming enough, but surely by now . . . It's more than two years. She's lost to this occult stuff, to this nonsense. Not to be dignified with the word *philosophy.*"

"Father," Milli said, "you promised not to say such things about . . . about . . . It's very wrong of you to speak this way . . ."

"It's very wrong of me not to," he roared.

Milli cringed away from him. His voice broke when he spoke again.

"But my dear child, don't you see that I'm abandoning you, I'm abandoning all of you if I don't speak out?"

"Oh, Father," Milli said, "you wouldn't cut us off, would you?"

He mimicked her cruelly.

" 'Oh, Father, you wouldn't cut us off' . . . Silly melodramatics, stupid histrionics . . . I'd sooner cut off my arm. Why doesn't some of that higher consciousness work in my direction? Why can't you understand *me?* Your mother babbling about higher consciousness and an awareness so intense it approaches ecstasy — babble, babble, babble. Makes my flesh crawl. Where's the enlightenment in that? He's just a boy, just an ordinary boy, not even a bright young man, an ignorant boy who can't make the hurdles into Oxford or Cambridge, in spite of the pots of money spent on tutors."

Milli stood up, her face white.

"Daddy, I can't listen," she said. "I shan't listen."

She fled from them. Maddy wanted to run with her, but, painfully embarrassed, stayed. Lord Harkness hung his big head in his enormous hands. Was he crying?

"I'm not a Philistine," he said. "Why do they treat me as one? I fought my battles against my own parents. I understand how it feels to be adolescent and dependent. I never dreamed that with my own children, with the wife that I adore ..."

He threw himself back in his chair. His eyes showed red but tearless.

"I fought my battles. I understand. My parents chose the army for me, failing that, the navy. My father, really. My mother stood alongside him and agreed with everything he said. I refused. I refused the church. They couldn't afford the diplomatic service and they failed to use their influence to work me into the consular service. My father called me into his study. 'There's nothing left but the Italian police or the Egyptian police. Which do you choose?' As if there was nothing else to choose. I'm not that kind of father! They're girls, only girls, everybody tells me, but they're my darlings, they're all I have left. I had a son, you know. But my girls are free, they're free to do as they choose, but I don't want them hurt, mangled in a bunch of nonsense."

Had he finished? Might she join the others now? He began again.

"My father extracted a promise from me that I would cease to read poetry. Imagine! I had refused all the important things so I agreed in that case. He particularly objected to Shelley. Of course, I didn't stick to my promise. One needs a bit of beauty in life. I know that. I understand their dreams, their hopes. I wanted to lead a useful life when I was a young man, a life that did some good in the world. And don't I, don't I?"

He asked so fiercely she felt obliged to nod in assent.

"I do. I perform good and important work, and while I'm at it I earn enough for all of us to live on, and live well, too. There's very little comes to us from Lady Pansy's money, and most of that is spent on this . . . this . . . this enchantment that's taken hold of her. It will ruin us, ruin our family. She was thirty-eight years old when she began to follow him around. Before then I didn't really take it all that seriously. What is it that she's found? Do you understand it? Can you explain its grip on her? Can you help me?"

Vidhya burst into the room.

"Why are you lingering here? I must have Maddy on my team. We've thought up a wonderful phrase for the others, they'll never guess it, but they have thought up some very difficult ones themselves. Please, please, Maddy, you must, you are indispensable."

She ran off, calling out, "Please do excuse me, Lord Harkness, Vidhya needs me," and put Lord Harkness out of her mind.

In a matter of days it was a part of the accepted routine among the disciples that Vidhya was *in love* with Maddy, apparently a fluid state of being that he floated in and out of with great ease. Nobody in the house at Hampstead was surprised by the development. What was for Maddy an alteration in the color, the shape, the very vibrations of the physical and spiritual world she inhabited seemed to be given no more importance by others than a change in the weather. Less importance.

And the weather had changed, rushing into spring with an endearing and precipitate ardor. It rained a lot, but between downpours, the sun shone hotter than it had all winter. At the ends of barren twigs and branches, leaves and blossoms budded and leafed out in a glorious outburst. In what seemed like a split second of Maddy's inattention, Hampstead had become a garden.

Vidhya told her that the English spring was a pitiful display.

"You think this is a blossoming? This is nothing, nothing. In India our blossoms are an explosion. An explosion of beauty! You will see with your own eyes," he said.

He had extracted a promise from her that she would return with him to India as soon as he was allowed to go. Yes, oh, yes. She promised. She would do anything Vidhya asked of her. Her intimacy with Elena disturbed him? She would mask it. As if in cooperation, Elena took off anyway. Agitated, distraught, and upset, she offered mysterious excuses for her leave, promising to explain all on her return. Her mother would be meeting her in London; they would be staying in their manor house in Devon.

"Do you promise to love me no matter how changed I am?" she said, compounding the mystery.

Maddy promised. Promises were thick in the air. Maddy promised Milli that whatever Vidhya felt for Maddy, or Maddy for Vidhya, would make no difference in her friendship with Milli. She promised Daddy to go on with her study of music, no matter what, and immediately afterward promised Vidhya to give up music for the study of shorthand and typing. It was more important to him that she become proficient in shorthand and typing than in any other study — music, dance, yoga, meditation, occultism, Society precepts, vegetarian cookery. He desperately needed a skilled secretary, an intelligent, understanding, spiritual being with a fine command of the English language. What Bishop Nysmith had failed to effect with all his pressure, Vidhya accomplished with his first request.

"Will you do this for me, my sweet Maddy?"

Now, early every morning, she walked up a steep tree-lined street to a genteel school less than a mile away, where a little bird of a woman led her through the paces of the Gregg method of shorthand and the touch method of typing, followed by mid-morning tea and a practice session. She returned in time for lunch and private meditation, yoga, study. Then, daily in the late afternoon, for an hour before afternoon tea, she attended to Vidhya's thoughts and messages from the Elders, taking them down in the squiggly marks of the Gregg method and transcribing them onto fine white bond paper on the new Remington typewriter that had been especially bought for *her work*.

A fuss had been made over *Maddy's work*. There had been celebrations and congratulations on her decision to give up music for shorthand and typing; there had been serious joint discussions as to which method — Pittman or Gregg — which school — Hampstead or London — which typewriter — Remington or L. C. Smith — and now that she was advancing so brilliantly she was extravagantly complimented on her aptitude and growing skills and held up to Daphne, Marigold, and Millicent as a paragon for them to emulate. They did not, any more than she would have in their boots. What made for the difference between her compliance and their defiance was the fact that she had Vidhya and they did not. She had Vidhya's love — or the appearance of it — which would do for the moment.

She had imagined *love*, true love, the one and only love, singular, particular, simple, transcendent, a happiness beyond expectation, quiet and satisfying. Instead she was thrown into a boiling cauldron of passionately mixed ingredients.

There were the external elements. She was envied. She liked that. All the young women envied her, her close buddies, Milli, and Elena, who left with the news of Vidhya and Maddy *in love* hot and fresh on her mind. Maddy was noticed now. She was no longer passed over as if she hardly existed. Lady Pansy's pale blue eyes no longer sailed by Maddy with vacant good humor, but rested on her with penetrating calculation. Now when events and talk soared beyond her comprehension, she clung to the strings connecting her with Vidhya, trailing his kite. Vidhya was her security, as Lady Pansy was Daph and Mari and Milli's, as Mrs. Dasinov was Elena's, as Bobo was all the young men's. That was an improvement.

In other ways she felt externally more exposed and threatened. For wonder of wonders, if Vidhya was her security, she appeared to be also his. She put all her weight on him; he put a lot of his on her. They leaned on each other, facing an imminent joint collapse, shoring each other up against mutual, terrifying ignorance.

The very first time she arrived at his room ready to take down the talk he was preparing for an enlarged meeting of the London Society, she found him wildly upset. His routine included a daily afternoon session with Bobo and Lady Pansy. Had something bad taken place there?

"Come in. Come in. Sit down. Sit down. Do not expect me to do any work. I am very troubled, almost crazy with it. Sit down. Sit down."

He was shouting, gesticulating, violently rude.

"I do not understand you English. You are incomprehensible to me. Especially Englishwomen. What is the matter with you women?

"Sit down, sit down," he shouted. "Please pay attention to me. Sit down."

"I'm American," Maddy said. "I'm an American."

She sat down cross-legged on the floor.

"I'm not even slightly English," she said.

"Don't upset me further, I beg you," he said.

But he was shouting, not begging.

"Why are you so upset?" Maddy said.

"It is bad enough with Bobo, but when Mother refuses to understand me, I have reached the end. It is the end for me. That is all."

What Mother? His mother was dead, she knew that from the trial. He called Lady Pansy *Mother?*

"She is refusing to understand me. She understands well enough but suddenly she is refusing to. She no longer wishes to. She is shutting her eyes to the truth.

"I cannot understand Englishwomen," he said again.

She would have liked to flee this encounter, with its

mystifying torments. She had been looking forward to her time alone with Vidhya all day. She had bathed and dressed as for a tryst, and it was a stabbing disappointment that Vidhya was totally preoccupied with himself and problems having nothing to do with her. Was it all over between them? He was already through with her? Their great love would have amounted to nothing more than their walks on the Heath, his arm through hers, and an insistent pressure of his fingers on the palm of her hand?

He was continuing his shouting complaints.

"What more do they demand of me? I have given my best. My best. There is nothing more to dig out of my poor brain . . . What do they expect of me? If I cannot pass their tests then perhaps it is the tests that are idiotic. Why do they not consider that possibility? Now they tell me once again I cannot enter their idiotic Oxford or Cambridge. They are killing me. Killing me."

He was dressed in filmy clothing, barefoot; his hair drooped across his cheeks; his face was contorted into babyish grimaces; his words emerged in a whining singsong; and he paced the room like a four-year-old in a tantrum, raising his legs high and flapping his arms. At that moment, he was ludicrous to her. Tears came to her eyes to blur the image.

"I shall kill myself one day. I shall. I must. There is no other way. Why have they chosen me? Why? To torment me? I cannot bear this life they have thrust upon me. I shall kill myself."

He stopped pacing, dropped to the floor before her, kneeling, and looked directly into her tear-filled eyes. His eyes also teared and reddened.

"Oh, Maddy," he said, "what can I do? What shall I do? Must I kill myself to solve my problems?"

He was really looking at her now.

"How kind you are. How kind — to suffer with me. Your eyes, the tears in your eyes, how kind, how kind, the tears in your beautiful eyes. You are the only one who feels for me. Ah, Maddy, I am so miserable, so miserable."

He lunged forward awkwardly and pulled her toward him by the upper arms. His head dropped into the side of her neck, his tears, or sweat, wetting her skin. They fell backward together to the floor. He moved her under him and pressed down upon her. She wasn't frightened of his body; it was all smooth, silky, perfumed. The hardness growing at his groin, at her groin, didn't alarm her. She liked the sensation; there was a flattering urgency in this bulging, pleading presence beating its way in. It made her powerful. She had begun by lying limply under him. Now her arms wound themselves around his smoothly muscled back and she too pressed, pressed closer. Through his thin cotton clothing she could feel him as if he were naked, and she herself was wearing only a silk blouse and skirt and a thin cotton chemise. They rolled and pressed. He kissed her on the mouth, opening her lips and mingling his tongue with hers. Her hands moved to his head, stroking. His hair was as silky as a girl's, heavy and rich and smelling of spices. How nice. How nice to cuddle this way. She was having the loveliest time of her life, in Vidhya's room, on the floor, during that hour when she was supposed to be engaged in taking down sublime messages transported through Vidhya in the Gregg system of shorthand, transcribed on her new Remington typewriter.

7

RUSHING to shower and dress for the press conference, she pushed against a sense of distance, of being slowed as if by drugs. Bad night. Not much sleep. Everything now seemed muted — the air surrounding her body, her consciousness fogged over. Dreams. Bad dreams. She had a lot of bad dreams lately. Why? She had lived a good life, done good all her life. Tried, anyway, hadn't she?

The Path to the Good.

How beautiful Vidhya had been. In the publicity shots she saw of him from time to time, he was still beautiful, but then, then, almost sixty years ago, when she had last seen him, then he was beautiful. A fake? Unbearable to contemplate such a notion, even now. An illiterate Indian boy, picked up in a poor Indian village and told his remarkable aura singled him out for elevation to the Savior of the world. The ignorant little kid was supposed to become *sincere* under such circumstances?

The Path to the Good. The Seven Levels to Perfection.

He had salvaged what he could, poor Vidhya. Poor Vidhya! He was a phenomenal success. One of the world's respected philosopher-gurus. He filled Carnegie Hall, Madison Square Garden.

And Bobo? A fake? Almost certainly. She could face that realization now without a qualm. There had been a recent biography sorting the lies from the truth in the reported life of Bishop Beauregard Nysmith. Even if it were all lies, what harm had been done?

The boys in the basement in a ritual act of mutual masturbation. No harm done? Who knows? Maybe some future society will be all in favor. Surely the silly girls were made sillier, and the older women, roped in for their money and their services, were misused. And if, instead, they weren't used at all? They believed. They believed. Bobo and the Elders. Astral voyages. Seven Levels to Perfection. The Path to the Good. Peace, harmony, and the Kingdom of God on Earth, established without an act of violence or a drop of blood. Why not believe?

She was late. She couldn't find what she needed in these strange surroundings. The plush Ritz-Carlton bathroom confused her. Where had she put her bobby pins and hairpins? She hurried into the bedroom, found them on the wicker dressing table. She combed her straggly gray hair, twisted it into a messy little knot, pinned the knot in place at the nape of her neck.

What would Vidhya think of his Maddy now, she wondered, studying her old-woman image in the mirror. Not much. But she was eager to see him. After all these years.

8

VIDHYA was her *lover*. They were *lovers*. That was Vidhya's designation for what went on between them. In the Society, the term used was *Vidhya's infatuation with Maddy.*

After some months she became alarmed by heavy bleeding, which stretched out her menstrual periods for days, accompanied by pains that twisted her insides. Secretly she visited a Harley Street gynecologist, who asked the inevitable question when he completed his examination.

"Are you having a relationship with a man?"

She knew what he meant. The cool word *relationship* stood for what had been hotly called, at home, *going all the way*. She was desperately embarrassed. Impossible to supply a precise answer from what she and Vidhya actually did. Everything. But Vidhya had never entered her *there* where the doctor had examined her and had found reason to believe she was no longer a virgin. He repeated his question. She nodded dumbly. He prescribed a powder for use in a douche daily and mumbled the suggestion that it was better to shun foreign objects. Fingers? Tongue? The heel of Vidhya's palm? Were these foreign objects? She was too shy to pursue such discriminations, or to inquire further about the douche. What was it? Where did one get such a thing? He was an older man, kindly, but as easily embarrassed as she. With his white-haired head bent over his prescription pad, he spoke softly of his hope that marriage to the young man was in the offing.

"Marriage is the best cure by far for these minor infections," he said. "Until then . . ." He stood up. "Until then . . ." He shook his head. "Try to be a good girl." He made an effort to look stern as well as sad.

To be *good*, by Vidhya's standards, or the Society's, was exactly what she was aiming at. She was very busy at the try, day and night. Between *love* and *work* it was an exhausting try. Most exhausting was the trial of never being alone, except for the few hours she spent back in her own bed, having stolen as quietly as possible from Vidhya's. It was always Maddy who crept about in the night. It wouldn't have done for Vidhya to be discovered tiptoeing from her room to his. The risk must be hers. She liked that. It gave their *affair* the illusionary cast that it was Maddy who was in control, the aggressor, a hussy almost. In fact she never made the night journey to his side without a whispered invitation delivered during Vidhya's good-night greetings to all before he left for his private quarters.

"I shall be waiting for you, Maddy."

In the house in Hampstead, getting soundlessly back to her own room from his meant crossing the width of the hall, then climbing from the lowest floor to the uppermost, without being seen. That was difficult enough. To add to this, a daily douche was impossible. She had bought a douche bag when she filled the prescription in a pharmacy close to the bus stop, a place large enough to insure anonymity. A douche was a hot-water bag equipped with a rubber pipeline ending in a long nozzle, an attachment she had never seen before. She smuggled the stuff into the house and read the instructions, hidden in her room. They seemed impossibly complicated. The powder was to be dissolved in warm water before filling the rubber container. Hot water on demand was the first stumbling block. Privacy, the use of the bathtub, free time, even the problem of hanging the gadget to dry after use — how was she to manage all this? During a carefully planned solitary walk on the streets of Hampstead, she threw the whole outfit into a street litter basket. She would suffer through this minor infection, count on her strong constitution to overcome it. It was too difficult to do anything else. But her condition gnawed at her, especially when she bled or felt pain. Was there a judgment, and a punishment, implied? Was she being punished for being bad? She buried these thoughts, too ashamed to share them with anybody, and most particularly with Vidhya. Divine Vidhya, who should know and understand all. Now that she was seventeen, nineteen didn't seem so wise and old, after all. What if he knew no more than she did?

Love and work and being good — these were the imponderables to try to grasp, and of the three, work was the easiest to put her hands around. She had been taken into London to the offices of what was called the Center, once she was graduated from the business school and declared competent and fully trained. She and Milli were picked up by a chauffeur-driven Society car and delivered to an ugly area dominated by a water tower, where the Center occupied an entire small office building. A discreet plaque announced the Universal Society of Brotherhood in a ladylike italic script. Inside all was efficient bustle, from the printing presses in the basement to the quiet, comfortably furnished offices at the very top. Here Lady Florence and a tall, soft-faced, extremely serious-looking Indian, introduced as Nityianda, presided over the business of the Society.

Lady Florence herself took them around. Her explanations were no more than titles.

"Finance and Administration," she said of the office at

the top, while the man she called Nityia let his wonderfully black, serious eyes rest on Maddy with open sexual interest.

"Membership," she said on the floor below, filled with files, brochures, and two middle-aged, pleasant-looking Englishwomen.

"Editorial, Publications, Reception," and so on, down to "Printing," with its cheerful clack, clack, clack of the presses, attended to by two elderly, dour men.

"These are our Nursery girls," Lady Florence had said when she introduced them to the man she called Nityia. He said he had met Milli before.

"Many times," Milli said loftily. "It's Maddy who is new around here."

"And very nice, too," Nityia said. "A very nice new addition."

They were having tea in the cozy top-floor office.

"Why do you call it that — the Nursery?"

Maddy surprised herself by her boldness. The term bothered her. She had heard it before as a way of describing the house in Hampstead. She had taken *Nursery* in its worst interpretation, a kindergarten for babies like herself, ignoramuses like Daph and Mari.

"The Nursery is our Soul," Lady Florence said in her voice too resonant for small places. "The Soul of the Society, where our most precious Babe has been tended and reared for his Mission."

She smiled at Maddy. What a beautiful woman she was, to be so old and so smooth-skinned, with such black, black hair and enchanting, flirty eyes. Her too-resonant voice looped around the tiny room, rebounding and echoing.

"The Center is our Heart. Just as the heart in the body is a machine, so is our Heart the machinery of our Society. We like all our members to know everything about the Society, but we also wanted you and Milli to have a further look around. You might elect to work here, Milli in Finance and you, Maddy, in Editorial and Publications. Someday," she added, as they looked dismayed. "Years and years ago I worked in Editorial at the Fabian Society. It was most exciting. I did enjoy it."

⌣

There had been an open drive to cast her in the role of general servant to anyone in the top echelon needing secretarial services. Vidhya fought hard to keep her his exclusively, and won that battle. She took down Vidhya's speeches as he delivered them, later transcribing her notes into articles for the *Society Journal*. His speeches demanded little alteration — some smoothing of the grammar, correction of slight errors of fact, some substitution of words to avoid repetition. It seemed she had a natural flair for this work.

At first, she offered changes with considerable trepidation, but he mostly accepted editing without comment. Perhaps he never even noticed. Later speeches would incorporate her additions and corrections as if they had been his own. However, he was as volatile here as elsewhere. What had been welcome one day was unacceptable the next; one day he would pass over her changes without comment, the next day kick up a storm, ripping the typed pages to shreds, yelling that he would not be constrained by what he called *your documents, your heavy, stupid documents*. He put great store in extempory talks, what he termed *speaking from the heart* and *speaking from the soul*.

"You will kill my ability to speak from the heart," he would plead, "from the soul."

Whichever way he spoke, from a written speech or "from the heart and soul," it made no difference in his power to enchant an audience. They loved him in either form.

His first public talk, given in Hampstead, was delivered impromptu at his insistence — otherwise, he said, he would be unable to talk at all. The gathering was held in a small theater up on the hill, a few doors from the cinema. Before he went onstage he was sick, vomiting into the sink of the tiny dressing room. Maddy held his head, as her grand-mother used to hold hers when she was ill. She bathed his face with a cool washcloth. He returned her kindness with rage.

"Stop it. Stop. You are babying me. I'm all right now."

He refused to allow any of the others into his dressing room. Nobody but Maddy could be near him, and he could barely tolerate her.

Surely flattery would help.

"You're a wonderful speaker," she said.

"I must speak for an hour and ten minutes. Do you re-alize how long — an hour and ten minutes. That is a very long time," he said.

"Speak as you always do," she said. "Just as you do every day. You often speak that long, sometimes longer."

"Are you saying that I am long-winded?" he said.

"You're a genius," she said.

Genius was a word much in vogue in the Society that year. Bobo was a genius, Victoria was a genius. Above all, Vidhya was a genius. Maddy was a genius at the typewriter.

He paced the room.

"The auditorium will be empty. It will be a colossal failure. I shall be a terrible failure."

She smoothed the collar of his light gray English suit.

"Why am I wearing this ridiculous suit and tie, these shoes? Tell them I must change immediately. Tell them to bring me proper attire. It is a mistake for me to appear in Western dress."

It had been his decision, after endless discussion. She told him he looked wonderful.

"All of this is useless, anyway. The auditorium is emp-ty. I know. I know."

A knock on the door made him hysterical.

"No, no. No one may enter."

Maddy slipped outside, closing the door behind her. It was Lady Pansy, checking.

"Is there an audience?" Maddy whispered. "He's afraid that nobody will come to hear him."

"Well." Lady Pansy's soft face tightened into an almost comic haughtiness. "Well. How extraordinary. What an extraordinary idea. Of course there's an audience. The hall is quite filled. Let me reassure him."

She called out his name and opened the door, but he rushed to hold it closed, screaming that only Maddy was allowed in. But alone in the room again with Maddy, he erupted in a new cluster of fears.

"I shall be an awful failure before a houseful. They will hiss and boo. I shall become the talk of the town. What are they expecting of me? God knows what they are expecting. I shall be a colossal failure before a full house."

Bobo knocked, announced himself, strode in, magisterial in a richly embroidered robe. She saw in Vidhya's eyes a fear of Bobo stronger than any other he suffered.

"Stop your nonsense," Bobo said in a voice she had never heard him use before — commanding and contemptuous. "You have five minutes. The program begins in five minutes. I shall speak first, then Lady Florence. We shall utilize no more than five minutes between us. Then you begin your talk."

"That is *ten* minutes that I have, then," Vidhya said.

Bobo slapped Vidhya, more a punch to his jaw with an open hand, hard enough to send Vidhya staggering.

"Close your mouth as soon as you finish speaking," Bobo said. "There is nothing uglier than a gaping mouth. I have made this clear again and again. Do you wish to be taken for an idiot?"

He grasped Maddy firmly by her arm. It was so unusual for Bobo to touch her, she was too startled to object. He led her out of the room.

"We shall leave you to yourself to compose yourself," Bobo said without looking at Vidhya.

Fear of Bobo was contagious. She took the seat reserved

for her in the front row. The auditorium was indeed filled; there was a scattering of standees. Her legs shook, her stomach swooped and churned. What if Vidhya utterly lost himself up there on this public platform?

Bobo spoke first, welcoming the audience, then Lady Florence, dressed in a white sari embroidered in gold thread, burst into an exalted call to Vidhya to "lead us out of our unnatural darkness into the natural sweetness of light and reason." Her voice rang like a trumpet in the hall.

The smell in the auditorium sickened Maddy. The hall was filled with women predominantly, drenched in the heavy scents of perfume and make-up, and the last arrivals had come on the heels of a sudden shower, bringing wet rubber and umbrella smells. She held her breath. She must not be sick. She repeated to herself *Vidhya Vidhya Vidhya Vidhya Vidhya*, a magic incantation to help him in his awful moment.

He entered from the wings on the right. His modulated, slow walk seemed to float him to the chair set up in the exact center of the stage. A hush descended on the fidgety audience.

Vidhya's composure was so complete, she felt her banging heart quieting. Thin applause broke out, thickened, then swept across the house, flushing the audience with a throbbing expectation. Vidhya gracefully slid into the chair, his hands clasped before him, his enormous eyes, luminously gray and vacant in his dark face, fixed on his listeners. In another beautifully modulated gesture, he inclined his head in greeting. His audience sighed with pleasure. He had not yet said a word.

Vidhya invented himself that afternoon on the platform of an obscure hall in Hampstead. She could not have explained to herself or to others exactly how, but that he became the personification of a healer-philosopher was as clear as the steady spotlight illuminating his superbly serene presence. He radiated spiritual grace, inner peace, intellectual wisdom. His listeners drank deep. The silence was intense and thankful.

Vidhya's hysteria, the scene in the dressing room, Bobo's slap, and Vidhya's submission surely belonged to someone else's experience, nothing to do with the beautiful young man onstage sharing the insights of a saintly yet practical wisdom with his eager audience. His well-cut English suit was a reassurance. The melodiously sweet tones of his Indian-accented proper English added the right touch of exotica. The flow of his poetically articulated creed faltered only once. When it did, he recovered magnificently. He put a hand to his forehead, maintained a longish, restful pause, then resumed, repeating part of his opening and continuing without a break, coming to a graceful ending precisely an hour and ten minutes after he had begun.

He had begun with the usual lyrical invocation:

"This morning a tiny goldfinch flew into the garden outside my window to suck at the blossoms of the daisies in the flower bed. A breeze tossed the blossoms about but the little bird clung to the yellow center of the flower and rode upon its movement. What was its purpose . . ."

It was the form perfected in his informal daily talks before the acolytes. He drew a moral message from the incident of the goldfinch, then approached the big topics: brotherhood, the unity of all living matter; the self, the selfless self (good) and the selfish self (bad); the imperatives of an orderly universe; the interaction of all living things in the universe and the individual's responsibility in striving toward the Good. He did repeat a bit, particularly certain phrases — *what we shall consider together; putting our heads together; what we shall discover together* — bringing his audience close, closer, closer yet, until they dissolved as separate listening units and became one responsive heart and soul.

It was the opening lecture in what proved to be a startlingly successful tour. Vidhya was scheduled for public appearances in York, Birmingham, Dublin, Edinburgh, ending with a large London gathering. No matter how testy, how nervous, Vidhya was, no matter his vomiting backstage, once on, he always came through with a commanding performance. His audiences grew from stop to stop. Word-of-mouth enthusiasm flew before him, whipping up interest. Some certainly came out of curiosity, to see with their own eyes the skinny, black Messiah-to-be; others came prepared to be overwhelmed, and were, staying to join the Society and donate money. Even the critics, looking to make hash of the Vidhya phenomenon in the evening papers, were mostly respectful.

They were a large party, traveling with Vidhya on tour. Maddy; Bobo with a boy in tow — that season the boy was Ram; Nityia to help Bobo pull the whole show together, the staging part and the money-raising end; Lady Florence, for the contacts and the grand touch of her introductions; Lady Pansy, naturally, Vidhya's nanny; Milli, on the business end, carefully overseen by Mr. Singh and Nityia.

It was exhausting. Maddy and Vidhya were blessedly left to themselves during the train trips between stops. That was fun. They nibbled on fruit and nuts, cuddled and kissed and dreamed upon the passing landscape; they were silly, they giggled at nonsense; sometimes they seriously devoted themselves to one of the games Vidhya loved, Twenty Questions, poker. Bridge was a new craze with him. He practiced his skills in their compartment, laying out four open hands on the little folding table, scolding Maddy scorchingly when she came up with the wrong bid or the wrong play. Oddly, it was Bobo who arranged for their private time alone before the performance. Lady Pansy fussed. She argued that Vidhya should be with her, studying, reading, plotting out the scheme of his speech.

"She thinks we spend all our time kissing and petting. I know, I know what she thinks, how she thinks. Mother is like that."

That was one of the things they giggled about. To Bobo, he conveyed a more sober plea.

"Mother worries too much about me, that has a very bad effect on me. I know she is concerned with my good. I know that very well. But then I try too much to please her, and I am made very nervous. With Maddy I relax, at least until I actually enter the hall. That is better for my nerves."

To appease Lady Pansy, Maddy proposed that they memorize a poem during each trip. It would improve Vidhya's accent and his vocabulary. They memorized "Let me not to the marriage of true minds" and "Season of mists and mellow fruitfulness," and both shed tears for "Now more than ever seems it rich to die."

How could others live out their lives lacking the great motivating forces of Vidhya and the Society? She was inexpressibly lucky — reborn — growing up and growing out, growing intertwined with Vidhya and the Society, her work cut out for her, her place assigned and safe and high in its importance, the indispensable helper of Vidhya, carrier of a great, healing message to the world. She wound up the speaking tour in a state of hysterical exhaustion, but on fire with pleasure, gratification, and triumph. The Society had become her family, moving ahead on a momentum beyond her control, on which she rode in an ecstasy of excitement.

Vidhya loved her. He told her over and over again that she was indispensable to him. He wrote down the words on a note attached to a bouquet left outside the door of her room in Hampstead.

"My Maddy, my darling, you are indispensable to me. Would it be possible for me to have a clean copy of my scribbles in this envelope?"

Elena Dasinov was with her when she picked up the flowers, the note, the manuscript in the envelope.

"Nobody on earth is indispensable to Vidhya but Vidhya," Elena said. "You don't know the darling as I do. Remember, I've known him since he was a mangy little lad."

This was the new Elena, returned from her time away in an incarnation so different from the former one that Maddy's promise to love her, no matter what, was a total irrelevancy. Gone forever was the drooping-eyed, long-nosed, clever Jewish girl who might have been a playmate on the stoop in the Bronx. Plastic surgery had opened her eyes, snubbed her nose, and rounded off her chin; dentistry had capped her teeth and stretched her lips into a perpetual smile; a new cut freed a mass of short curls, Clara Bow fashion, now bleached reddish blond. Her figure had "developed." Two bouncy enticements shaped the flat cut of her stylish clothes, and a small, firm backside slithered under the slim skirts, which showed a lot of sweetly curved leg in clocked silk stockings and high-heeled pumps. No saris for Elena Dasinov. No tweeds, either. But she had worked up small talk that lilted and dipped in a perfect copy of a daffy English upper-class nitwit. Elena had become one of her acts.

The two remained close, but in a new way. Elena was no longer Maddy's exclusive, adoring slave. Elena had broken out of the tight circle of the Society; she had met a female heir to the Borden millions, a fellow big-nosed pioneer in the hands of plastic surgeons, who had introduced Elena to a tight crowd of heirs, royal and otherwise — there was even a Rothschild among them. They found Elena to be bright, daring, a success, something she had never been in the Society. She urged Maddy to come with her to her friends, but Maddy resisted. For Maddy, Elena's new crowd was a group of lost souls, part of that great mass of unfortunates who did not have the incentives of Society life and the love of Vidhya to lend meaning to an empty existence.

Then the good weather settled in, and everybody from the Nursery spent most weekends at the Dasinov manor house in Devon near Tiverton. *Devon near Tiverton* — what charming music the name itself made. Weekends lengthened to three, four, sometimes five days. The landscape was new to Maddy — the narrow, dipping roads lined with hedgerows, the storybook thatch-roofed houses and plots of meadow and pasture, the flocks of sheep, the birds in the blossoming roadside barriers. But everything else about the manor house and Mrs. Dasinov, its host, was gratifyingly familiar, out of Maddy's aunt's house in New Jersey, though infinitely grander and richer — a plenitude of furniture, rugs, cut crystal and china, linens and towels, comforters and pillows, even a cathedral-shaped radio and the player piano and phonograph in the music room, plus all the rest, the fun and the games, and the food, food, and more food, down to the waxed fruit — all presided over by Mrs. Dasinov, Elena's mother, a welcoming bosomy presence exactly like Aunt Molly, the soft-skinned, shining-eyed, black-haired, youngest, and prettiest of Maddy's Jersey relatives.

The Devon visits were pure holidays. Apart from yoga and meditation, the days were given over to play — tennis mostly, bicycling, and, in the late afternoon, croquet and complicated imaginative games of hide-and-seek. At night Maddy came to Vidhya in an unused studio beyond the kitchen garden. The studio was empty except for a large table and a bed covered by a tapestrylike coverlet, coarse to the skin of their naked bodies, and she would carry back to Hampstead the bruised lassitude and melancholy fulfillment that followed their lovemaking, forever associated in her mind with the Dasinov place in Devon.

In the middle of that summer, Elena ran off with a man of thirty-five, heir to a rubber fortune, lamed in one leg, English, and, according to Mrs. Dasinov, of defective intelligence. Mrs. Dasinov ran after them, accompanied by her old friend Lady Florence. They located the couple at the Hotel Claridge in Paris, already married, and found Elena in a state of deep depression. The marriage was annulled. Elena was only sixteen, for one thing, and for another, nonconsummation was claimed. They brought her back to Devon, where she was kept incommunicado. Lady Florence reported that "the poor child" wanted to go home to Riverside Drive in New York City, back to the Lincoln School and then to Finch College, like a real American girl.

"There's some difficulty about funds, too," Cleves told Maddy. "The crash hasn't totally wiped out the Dasinov millions, but Mrs. Dasinov needs to get back to the States and see to money matters."

They sailed for home that week. Everybody talked of nothing else. It became known as *the incident of Elena Dasinov's total breakdown.*

Milli's contribution to the talk was hysterical wailing.

"Terrifying, too terrifying, absolutely terrifying, terrifying, I can't think about it, I can't talk about it."

Cleves and Conrad conveyed cool information picked up from Bobo.

"Elena's not going back to school. Who do they think they're kidding? She's straight off to a sanitarium and a psychiatrist."

"It's all the rage, y'know, psychiatry, analysis. Mrs. Dasinov is quite sold on it."

"So am I." Conrad wound up the talk. "If I had their money, I'd dive right in myself. Why not?"

Vidhya said, "I do not wish to discuss the incident of Elena Dasinov's total breakdown. I forbid you to talk about it, Maddy."

Did it frighten him, as it frightened Milli and, yes, frightened her? Maddy's excitement and drive had come to a full stop with Elena's departure. She missed Elena, of course, and missed Elena's mother and the familiar pleasures of the weekends at the Dasinovs', but it was something else that gnawed at and depressed her. She lay on her bed in her room at the top of the house in Hampstead, staring through the diamond-shaped panes at a sky spattered with innocent white clouds, and cried her heart out. Was she crying for Elena? It was amazing to her how hard she cried, wildly and for a long time, as she used to do during those early months when she was so unhappy and knew that she was unhappy.

She heard nothing from Elena until a package arrived from the States some six weeks later, addressed to Maddy and with no indication of the sender, containing a dozen pairs of silk stockings. They could have come only from Elena. The stockings were a godsend. She had mended and remended the old ones. Now she could throw them away.

Pocket money — spending money for stockings, toothpaste, soap, sanitary napkins, a new brassiere — had become a great problem. All her important needs were taken care of. It stuck in her throat to ask for pocket money. And to whom would she go to ask?

She managed. She was adept at mending and laundering her clothes carefully. She accepted whatever was passed on to her, usually by the older women, since she was a large size. Theirs were fine garments of wonderful fabrics, French-seamed and hand-hemmed. She altered skirts to fit herself, added a belt to a dress, gathering extra material under it. She always looked pretty. She had learned too that if she dug her fingers deep into the upholstered chairs and sofas in the library and sitting room, she would come up with coins dropped out of the men's trouser pockets. It had been an accidental discovery that she then carefully mined to take care of minor purchases.

She buried these troubles along with her dark broodings against her parents. What was wrong with them — or with her — that they could so easily put aside their only child as their special object of care? She wrote and tore up a dozen bitter letters to them. Their letters — Daddy's really — had been promising a visit for months, postponed repeatedly, because of their obligations elsewhere — to the university, to the Garden Club, to the Chicago branch of the Society, to the child labor movement, in which they had become activists. Now a visit was definitely promised for early September. Daddy had been granted a sabbatical leave, and they had both made arrangements for their other obligations.

She was puzzled by references to her superb money-managing abilities, in Daddy's letters and in comments made by her companions in Hampstead.

"We are a perfect pair," Vidhya said, more than once. "I am a spendthrift and you are tight-fisted. We balance each other to perfection."

He had developed subterranean methods of quarreling with her. Perhaps this was one of them.

"You're always teasing me about money," she protested. "You must imagine that I'm an American heiress. I have no money, Vidhya, none."

"Aha! Aha!"

He laughed his most exaggerated tinkling sounds.

"I don't, Vidhya. My father is just a university professor."

"Aha! We all know about you and your money, about your savings, Maddy. You cannot pull the wool over my eyes. Aha! Aha! But believe me, I admire it, I admire you, I deeply admire such thrift, honestly, honestly, I am expressing admiration, do believe me."

It was when Milli pressed her on her plans for her accumulated savings that Maddy finally asked what Milli meant by her "savings."

"The money you've not touched, never drawn on. The money your father sends monthly for you."

For a second she thought her heart had stopped.

"I've forgotten," she said, trying to sound casual. "What does he send?"

"Well, I can't say precisely, without looking at the books," Milli said, "but it's generous, very generous, and not only the Society's share, but your own, your pocket money and clothing allowance, and he never stopped the money covering special fees — music and the secretarial school fees — all that, you know."

"What do you mean, the Society's share?" Maddy said.

"The donation part, naturally. And then there's the money covering all your costs, whatever that entails — food, lodging, train travel, purchases of clothing, your typewriter — you know, whatever it is that particular month."

"My daddy has paid for everything, then?"

"Of course," Milli said. "Whatever did you think? Why, didn't you know?"

"Of course I knew," Maddy said, and fled to her room.

She was immensely agitated and deeply happy, wanting to be alone with this blaze of corrective knowledge scorching her bitterness against her parents. She had never loved them so much, longed to be closer to them, to hug them, kiss them, make amends, return them the real love they had shown for her, apologize for the wrongs she had done them in her brooding thoughts. She rushed from her room and sought out Milli.

"You know, I was about to approach the office for some funds, for underthings and some toiletries. Who do I go to?"

"To me. Or Mr. Singh or Nityianda. You let us know before three o'clock and we'll have the money for you the following noontime. You can't draw more than ten pounds without your father's permission, you know. We can go to the office right now, if you like. How much would you like?"

"Ten pounds," Maddy said.

Ten pounds! There were one hundred and eighty-four pounds in her pocket money and incidentals account. A fortune! On her way to the underground, she bought a snakeskin wallet and carefully tucked away her money in it. In London she went directly to Fortnum and Mason, but ended buying nothing, though she indulged in the forbidden — tea and scones with butter, jam, and whipped cream. The endless possibilities of what she might buy, if she pleased, overwhelmed her. She walked to the Burlington Arcade and again bought nothing for herself, but in the window of one little shop she became enchanted with a tiny tie clip in the shape of a snake, gold, with a red-jeweled eye. It cost two pounds, the sales clerk informed her. Her knees shook, but she said she would take it.

"American?" the young, dapper clerk asked.

She nodded.

"I could tell on first sight," he said, congratulating himself. "A gift, is it? Care to have it specially wrapped?"

She had agreed before he informed her that there would be an extra charge. No matter. She was out to show Vidhya that she wasn't the skinflint he was pretending to admire.

When she gave him the charming paper bag in which they had placed the beautifully wrapped package, his surprise was a gratification. That was soon over. He was afraid of snakes in any form. The red-jeweled eye he believed to be an opal, and opals were bad luck. It was lovely of her to think of him, but he couldn't possibly wear the little tie clip, it would give him the willies. She understood, did she not, his darling Maddy?

She hid the little box in her drawer and asked Milli to let her know the next time she was going shopping — perhaps they might go together? In spite of the trip to the shops having been something of a disaster, she felt wonderfully grown-up and liberated. One hundred and seventy-four pounds in her account and seven pounds and change in her wallet, with more deposited monthly by her sainted, generous, loving, thoughtful mother and father, the best in the whole wide world.

Once again their visit was postponed. Then Cleves Wyndham was called home, and on the day he left for Southampton, she astonished everybody by bursting into tears when saying good-by to him. It wasn't that she wanted to go home with him, but his departure triggered an undefined homesickness, if not for the actual home she had left behind, then for any old solid home furnished with parents demanding her presence, as Cleves's parents demanded his. All the young people were leaving, and particularly the Americans, who had dwindled down to Maddy alone. The Universal Society of Brotherhood was contracting into an Anglo-Indian club, where again she felt herself the outsider. Especially since Vidhya would be going on a tour without her, to Paris, Rome, Geneva, Evian, and Florence, not a speaking tour, but something to do with inner Society matters — money raising, Conrad thought it was.

Disconsolate without Cleves, Conrad hung about Maddy, hoping to keep her interest by relaying the kind of gossip Cleves excelled in. It was a horrible wrench to have Vidhya led away by Bishop Nysmith and Lady Pansy. For some reason, Marigold was one of the party, though Lord Harkness had fought to have her stay with him and Daphne in Wales, where, as he said, "my girls may relax among normal young people." The fact was that Elena's breakdown seemed to be infectious. Both Daphne and Marigold had gone queer, indulging in fits of tears, melancholy, strange nervous spasms in which their legs and arms jerked helplessly. They reported sleepless nights spent fending off alarming sensations, grotesque distortions of the transporting visions promised on the Astral Plane.

Maddy had overheard Lord Harkness shouting. He and Lady Pansy and Milli were in Lady Pansy's upstairs sitting room. Daphne and Marigold had been banished to the library, where Maddy found them crouching in a corner like impoverished foundlings. She was so sorry for them, she knelt and gathered them to her, the angular, lank-haired, horsy pets.

"They'll all be driven mad before this nonsense is stopped."

They could hear Lord Harkness clearly.

"I have some rights over what happens to my daughters. If you've lost your senses, I still have some rights, some say. They are coming with me to Wales."

"My dear, my dear," Lady Pansy said, over and over.

Milli shouted, like her father.

"And what of my rights? I have the right to decide for myself. I want to stay right here, right here. I'm old enough to decide for myself. God knows I'm old enough."

"He'll never turn from Maddy to you, you goose," her father said. "He'll turn from Maddy, you may be sure, but not to you, you goose."

"My dears, my dears," Lady Pansy said.

In the end, Daph went to Wales with Lord Harkness, Mari went to the Continent with Lady Pansy, Vidhya, and Bobo, who, of course, took Ram with him. Conrad, Milli, and Maddy, left behind in the house in Hampstead with Jag and Mr. Singh, entered upon a looser existence than usual. They did as they liked. Maddy went into London often, whenever Conrad or Milli was willing to take the little trip; many other times she went alone. Conrad and she sneaked off to the cinema. She had fallen in love with the cinema and Conrad had long been a secret devotee. With Milli she went to the shops. Alone she acted the tourist, visiting Westminster Abbey, the Tower of London, Trafalgar Square, and the National Gallery, the great palaces and museums of London. She knew she was an ignoramus. Perhaps going about looking would help correct that, fill in the huge gaps in the wobbly packet of information she carried in her head. But the details of English history bored her, the kings and queens, even if the proofs of English conquest did not. American history was more fun, more like a movie; it flashed by faster, caught in the fist like a trophy, a stunning win.

Her work on Vidhya's book brought her to the Center in London once a week. Nityia was always most agreeable, smoothing her way with the persnickety editorial people and with the impatient printers in the basement. At the sight of her, Nityia made his pleasure plain. His liquid black eyes bathed her in a continuous caress. On the surface he was always the perfect gentleman.

She returned to Hampstead dreamily aroused by contact with Nityia. He smelled so good and moved with such gliding ease. He was so clearly a man, not a boy pretending. Milli told her that Nityia had a wife and three children at home in Delhi. He was a lawyer, a member of a family prominent in Indian political circles, as was his wife's family. One of her brothers had been jailed for anti-British activities.

"Not our sort at all," Milli said. "It's just as well she doesn't come with him to England."

Nityia's wife, Milli meant. Milli told Maddy that Nityia was twenty-nine.

Vidhya was gone forever, it seemed. In the beginning it was virtually unbearable. She didn't know how to reach herself; she felt cut off from the person she had been beginning to be, separated in two, each piece at the end of a long rope. Then suddenly she began to feel free and Vidhya's absence was a relief, as if she had thrown off hampering ties. Not to be thinking of him first, what luxury. Like flying, her head intoxicatingly empty of thoughts of others. She had money in her purse and she was on her own, or with Milli or Conrad, if she liked, for whom she felt only the slightest responsibility. Vidhya wrote her every day — the equivalent of their time spent together preparing his speeches and articles — long effusive letters in the lyrical Vidhya manner, punctuated with passionate endearments, dashes, dots, exclamation points, and underlinings, outpourings of love, carefully composed in the style of his public writings.

> When I woke today you had flown directly to my heart, my darling Maddy. You appeared in the charming shape of a butterfly I spied sitting on a flower outside my window . . .

She read these distanced and cool, a critical audience watching a performance. If the letters expressed his true emotions, why hadn't he insisted that she accompany the party on this tour?

Other information came her way. Nityia told her the money raising was going very well.

"Rich women have only to meet Vidhya and their pocketbooks fly open," Nityia said.

He told her that Vidhya had taken up golf and was very good at the sport. He was good at many sports, apparently. He swam every morning and rowed on Lake Geneva in the afternoon.

Then a letter from Mari to Milli arrived with different details. In a quick trip to Monte Carlo, Vidhya had been lucky and won enough money to buy a car. *An Isotta Fraschini, if that's how it's spelled — absolutely dazzling!!!* There was a newcomer in the group, a niece of Lady Florence Greenwood. She had joined them in Paris. She was beautiful, twenty years old, tall and slim, dark eyes and dark hair, and very white skin. Rosamund Keats. *Vidhya is head over heels in love with her,* and Marigold added, *please don't tell Maddy.*

Milli turned the letter over to Maddy the morning it arrived, observing Maddy closely as she read it. Were they supposed to moan and groan in unison their shared, spurned state? In Milli's presence, Maddy laughed and tossed aside the bad news. In the privacy of her room, Maddy paced and burned. After all her loyalty and submission — this? The minute they were separated? But what did she understand loyalty and submission to be? Hadn't those manifestations been the showings of *love?* Didn't she *love Vidhya? Everything* she was, everything she did, was at his bidding. Wasn't that *love?* To respond to his pleas, the urging of his bulging desires, to be at his side when he called, for love, for taking notes or typing, absorbing his thoughts and dispelling his anxieties, to make herself his slate and his sponge, wasn't that for *love?* Even the infection and the bleeding, gone now, had been a manifestation of her love, and all the acts she didn't enjoy, or like, had *dis*liked, if the truth be told, all the strange ways of doing it, permitting anything, any entrance but *there*, even *taking it in your mouth*, as he called it, telling her that way she would be safe, her virginity undisturbed and no pregnancy threatened, could she have done any of that without *love*? And if it was for *love*, then all other talk of loyalty, of submission, of everything done for him, with thoughts of him, him first, before everyone and particularly before herself — wasn't all that jabber hypocritical self-justification, if, in fact, she had done it all for *love*, since love was its own reward, soaring above all else — the whole meaning of life? Was she going to end up in her own books unworthy even of *love*?

But that wasn't the trouble. The trouble was, wasn't it, that Vidhya didn't love her. His involvement with her had been a surface emotional entanglement, *Vidhya's infatuation with Maddy*, as the others called it. If that were true, did it alter everything, cast the exalted state she had imagined herself in as something ugly, deformed, foolish? Must she realistically judge herself to be not only unworthy but as deluded as Milli?

In her room overlooking the pond, she paced and brooded, her thoughts and her long, strong legs tracing a narrow repetitive circle from which at that moment she could see no exit.

But the Society moved ahead under its inexorable momentum, and, caught up in the motion, she kept going. Early in the autumn, the manor house in Tiverton was used for a weeklong Society retreat. In Mrs. Dasinov's absence, Lady Florence traveled from the Continent to preside, as host and in her own official Society role. She brought news of the successful tour, news of Vidhya, and news of Rosamund Keats, rising through Society levels at a clip. Lady Florence harnessed Maddy to her side to help with the Devon housekeeping arrangements. At her other side was Nityianda, organizing the business of the retreat, the formulation of the winter task plan, and the coming spring encampment in Spain.

She was glad to be busy, glad to be in Devon, glad to be working alongside Nityia. She bustled about in a state of heightened awareness, because of his attentive gaze, enjoying the intense physical sense of her own flesh in movement, the sway of her breasts under her sweater and the slide of one thigh against the other under her thin wool skirt.

He came to her room the first night of the retreat. That was the first difference between him and Vidhya, that Nityia came to her. His lovemaking was entirely different from Vidhya's. He was sure of himself, direct, quick to reach satisfaction, eager then to turn to hers. Everything about his lovemaking was natural and easy, nothing like Vidhya's.

So much for the theory she had worked up that Vidhya's odd rules of lovemaking were typically Indian — the way *they* did it.

Nityia cried out that he loved her, and he called her by name, but only at the moment of climax. Done with the act, he reestablished a certain formal distance, even after the first time. They grew no closer, oddly enough, only more familiar.

Technically, she reminded herself, he had taken a virgin, but so much perverse play had gone on down there, there had been no sense of violation, of conquest. It was the first time she had actually been entered; but the event came and went with no great significance attached. Some pain followed by true pleasure. An air of social affability throughout. Reassurance. (*"You have nothing to concern yourself about, Maddy, I have undergone a vasectomy last year."*) A warm climate of polite continuation — Must do this again soon — very much as one might schedule a series of games of tennis or bowling.

They did do it again in Devon, and in London throughout the winter, on the couch in the top-floor office of the Center after Lady Florence returned to the Continent, rejoining the others. Nityia was sweet, a real comfort to her.

He understood that she was *in love* with Vidhya. She

understood that his deep feelings were with his wife and three little girls. He soothed her about Vidhya.

"Don't worry about this Rosamund Keats. That is mischief-making, all that talk. Poor Vidhya gets carried away. He is not so sure of his own mind, his own heart."

He always referred to Vidhya as *poor Vidhya*.

"What will happen to that boy?" He would begin most conversations about Vidhya in this manner. "He will die of tuberculosis in these terrible climates, poor Vidhya."

"What will happen to that boy?" he said, just before Vidhya's new book was set for publication. "Sometimes I think they will tear him apart, poor Vidhya, with their ambitions for him." Nityia was afraid the new book would be a failure, but it sold out through Society channels, though it wasn't much more than a repetition of the earlier one.

Nityia never came to the house on the Heath. She saw him only on her once-a-week trips to the Center. He explained that the Nursery made him uncomfortable. A look of sick distaste spread over his round, dark face.

"The higher-consciousness experiments in the basement . . ." He shook his head.

"Nobody's there now," she said. "Bobo isn't, or any of the . . ." She trailed off.

"Poor Vidhya," Nityia said.

Late in January he told her that he would be leaving the Society following the Spanish encampment. They were drinking tea in the cozy top-floor office. It was a raw, wet day.

"It's not a secret," Nityia said. "But I wanted you to be the first to know — from my mouth."

He explained that Society work kept him away from his family too much. His little girls were growing up and needed him. His wife was lonely. He wanted to return to his law practice and to his own country.

"I am needed there, in my country. So many problems." He sounded out the o's very round.

Jagannathan Varadarajan was in training to move into Nityia's spot at the Center. He had even taken some courses at the London School of Economics. The orderly calm of the projected change made it more melancholy. Could Nityia leave so easily? Could anyone? Shouldn't there be more of a fuss? What if she should leave? Where would she go? What would she do?

9

THERE were so many reporters and cameramen crowding the press conference that Maddy Phillips had to force her way back in. She sat down in an empty chair alongside Dwight. He was flushed and breathless, obviously in the middle of a speech that had been going on for some time.

"... reiterate that nationalism is the greatest danger of our times, an international scourge cloaked in the high-minded platitudes and the untouchable mantle of patriotism. But we must not indulge this travesty, whether on the part of other nations or of our own. Yes, it is true that terrorism surrounds us, but it is not the terrorism of small revolutionary bands that endangers us, but the powerful terrorisms of the state, those great armed states who control the destiny of mankind through atomic warfare . . ."

Dwight drew breath and a reporter seized the pause to rush in with a question.

"Miss Younger, a question please. Miss Younger, there are reports that you have agreed to appear in a musical comedy, a Broadway musical comedy, during the coming —"

Victoria brightened, raised her head, opened her lips, but Arthur Brownson, apparently in charge, answered for her.

"No," he said. "Not true. Ridiculous. There will be three more questions, ladies and gentlemen. May I remind you that we agreed questions were not to go beyond the subject of this demonstration—"

He interrupted himself, nodding and pointing to one of the many raised hands. The cameras lingered on Victoria, smiling and shaking her head in denial. Two reporters stood up, speaking simultaneously.

"What are the specific demands attached to the Indian guru's hunger strike? Does Mrs. Phillips continue to believe in reincarnation, and how do you rationalize such a system of belief today, Mrs. Phillips. My question is directed to Mrs. Phillips, please. What does the guru, Vidhya, hope to accomplish —"

"We cannot accept any questions directed to individuals not present at the press conference," Arthur Brownson announced, but Maddy was calling out her answer to the other question, at the same time.

"Nothing to it," she said. "We'll all return as radioactive ash."

"What does this group hope to —" a reporter shouted.

Arthur Brownson said, "This is the last question."

"What does this group hope to accomplish by this display of —"

"To bring the governments of the world and particularly our own administration to its senses . . ." Victoria was saying.

"To bring about the settlement of disputes by civilized means . . ." Dwight was saying.

"To make the negotiating table the center . . ." Arthur Brownson was saying.

". . . talks, mediation, détente, yes, détente, and the consummation devoutly to be wished . . ." Bernard Lewis was saying in his surprisingly deep, vigorous voice, though he had been asleep up to the moment he began to speak. "The end of killing, the end of the arms race, peace on earth at long last."

Some applause broke out. The young man assisting the contingent of the elders stood behind Maddy, whispering barbaric sounds in her ear. She had totally forgotten his name.

"I can't hear you," she said.

"Whoosh, whiish, sh, sh, js, js," she heard.

"A huge anti-apartheid demonstration, feeding in from Harlem . . ." he was saying.

"I haven't had any breakfast," Maddy said. "What is this demonstration, anyway?"

"Whoosh, whiish, sh, sh, js, js," she heard.

"Speak up, speak up," Maddy said. "Can't you speak clearly?"

"There's fresh orange juice and some melon. Is that okay? We didn't know about the South African protest. But it's good, isn't it?"

"Of course it's good. It's excellent, if they keep it non-violent. If I could just have some orange juice," she said.

His name was Bernstein, Jeff Bernstein. Remembering his name made her feel much better about him, more warmly toward him.

"Thanks, Jeff," she called after him.

Dwight shushed her. A reporter was insisting on asking Bernard Lewis to briefly describe the regimen to which he attributed his long life and excellent health. But Bernard Lewis had sunk back in his chair and his eyes were closed.

"There will be no more questions, ladies and gentlemen, thank you for coming," Arthur Brownson said, cutting off and closing the session.

"Cat naps," Victoria called out. "That's the secret."

Someone handed Maddy orange juice in a paper cup and four thin slices of honeydew melon on a paper plate. She sipped and chewed, enjoying the coolness and lightness of taste.

His face alarmingly scarlet-splotched, Dwight, in great distress, indicated the young woman assistant in the doorway, handing out what seemed to be press releases.

"What is that material? What is she doing without our permission? What is that she's distributing?"

"I don't know," Maddy said.

"What is that girl doing?" Dwight said, as if she hadn't spoken.

"I don't know," Maddy said.

"Well, why are you sitting here so calmly munching on melon while that girl is distributing leaflets in our name?" His eyes blazed blue in the mottled flush of his face. "This has been a total fiasco. A fiasco."

It was then that Maddy noticed Elena Dasinov was not among them.

"Where's Elena?" she said.

Jeff Bernstein had obviously heard Dwight's outburst. He hurried to their side with a sheaf of handouts: position papers on El Salvador, Nicaragua, Central America, the Latin American debt and Fidel Castro, the sanctuary movement, the Middle East, a defense of security at Athens airport and at Rome airport, an explanation of social security and cost-of-living increases, papers on abortion rights, South Africa, the defense budget, and a brochure on the growth of censorship in the country. Maddy put them aside to study later.

"Where's Elena?" Maddy said.

Dwight was shaking the papers and shouting.

"This is ridiculous. Who allowed this? Who sanctioned this? Young man, young man ... Why, they might just as well have put in some documents on vivisection, and AIDS."

"We had a long discussion about what to include, sir, and —" Jeff hurried to explain.

"Don't be such a nincompoop," Dwight said, more enraged. "You nincompoop."

Victoria would know about Elena. Maddy pushed through the crowd of admirers surrounding Victoria. One of Victoria's eyelashes had been attached out of kilter, lending a touch of daffiness Victoria could have done without.

"Your left eyelash is pasted on crooked," Maddy said. "Better fix it."

Victoria's hand flew to cover her left eye. She moved rapidly out of the circle.

"Where's Elena?" Maddy said.

"I have a note she left for you, in the bedroom."

She followed Victoria into the bedroom Victoria and Elena had shared. Victoria fidgeted with her false eyelash at the dressing table mirror. Maddy read the note Victoria handed her. The envelope was hand addressed to Maddy Brewster, wiping away Phillips as if Phillips had never happened, MADDY BREWSTER underlined in heavy black ink in the style they had all affected in their youth, back in the days they wrote madly to one another, two and three letters a day, splattered with underlinings and exclamation points, an aping of Vidhya's style then, who had copied it in turn from Bobo, who not only underlined the person addressed but also his own signature, BISHOP B. NYSMITH, or more intimately, BOBO, underlined twice, the second line thicker and longer than the first, in the manner Elena had now ended her note — a bold, capitalized, twice-underlined ELENA.

She took in the letter in a gulp, a dive into unpleasant waters it was necessary to cross, a plunge back into the suffocating enclosures of their life together as girls in the Society, within which Elena remained inexplicably entangled.

You have always put others ahead of me, always chosen others before me, and I am no longer so foolish or deluded as to expect anything to change. It is six o'clock and I am leaving! Pray for me that this time it is for good! You asked me to be a part of this farce for your own reasons. Whenever you want me about, it's for your own reasons. I do something for your immense ego. You are insatiably selfish . . .

She stopped reading, folded the note into its envelope, and stuck it in her handbag.

"Breakdown?" Victoria said.

She was studying the effect of the repositioned eyelash, her attention on her image in the mirror.

"Is she falling apart again?"

"I shouldn't have asked her to join us," Maddy said.

"Never mind," Victoria said. "She made a hefty donation. It was useful. Has she asked for it to be returned?"

"Don't be coarse," Maddy said. "It suits you too well."

She ignored Victoria's furious glance.

"Boohoo, boohoo," Victoria said. "Boohoo, poor Elena. You like that better? I will not pity her. I refuse to pity her. Pity is the last thing she's looking for and the first you always offer her."

"I seem to be everybody's punching bag this morning," Maddy said, and left.

In the living room of the suite, there was a general air of confusion and indecisiveness. The young man and woman had been marshaling the group to leave the hotel, but there was a telephone call and everything came to a stop. Dwight motioned to Maddy to come close. Another rebuke? She sat next to him, leaning her head to hear clearly. In his still red-blotched face, his blue eyes were now serene and cool.

He said, "I want you to know that whatever occurs today, my life with you has been worthwhile, important, filled with accomplishments, and it has been happy. I want to thank you for your love and companionship."

Was he joking? He wasn't given to making sentimental pronouncements. She smiled and kissed him full on his beautifully modeled lips.

171

"Good," she said, lightly. "Thank you and thank *you*. Are you expecting something awful to happen?"

"Yes," he said. "I feel it in my bones, as you would say. We have just heard that thousands of police are deployed along the line of march."

"Nothing will happen," she said. "We're not blacks in South Africa or the poor in Chile."

Jeff Bernstein rushed into the room, whispered something to the young woman, whose name refused to come to Maddy's mind. From the doorway she made a mumbled announcement.

"What? What?" Maddy said. "Why can't they speak properly?"

"Delay," Arthur Brownson pronounced clearly. "Fifteen-minute delay. If they are saying fifteen, count on at least half an hour, more, most likely."

"Busybody," Dwight muttered under his breath. "Damned busybody."

They settled into an uneasy wait. Their numbers seemed to be dwindling. There was Bernard Lewis, dead asleep in his chair, his huge head hanging loose and heavy. Perhaps he was dead; any breath drawn could be his last. There was herself, and Dwight, also asleep, or resting in his more self-contained, well-mannered fashion, holding himself firmly upright, two hands placed on his tall cane, his cleft chin nesting on the back of his manicured, brown-spotted hands. Elena was gone. Vidhya was off on his own, inventing a private play. Where was the former U.S. attorney-general who had pleaded for permission to join them? Never showed, apparently. In the doorway Arthur Brownson and Victoria stood chatting with the young woman. *Susan.* What a relief to have snatched her name from the blank abyss.

"Susan," she called out. "Make them sit down. They'll be worn out before we start."

Victoria looked up. *We're not mad at each other?* her

glance inquired, and then, smiling radiantly, telegraphed the answer. *We're not, we're not!*

The three moved to sit, continuing their murmuring conversation. Maddy heard snatches.

"When the judge released us, we promised we wouldn't sue for false arrest. That's what the lawyers told us to do. Hate those fellows. So somewhere there's a photograph of me with my arresting officer, a darling young man, Irish of course, and my fingerprints, and a record of my arrest."

"When was that?" Susan, pink with excitement.

"Sometime around the Kent State killings. We should have sued. Like the Mayday people. They even got money, some of them, didn't they, Arthur?"

"I don't approve of suing," Arthur said. "Except in freedom of information cases."

"Don't be silly," Victoria said. "Har*ass* them." She had accented the last syllable.

Arthur Brownson corrected her, accenting the first. "*Har*ass," he said. "*Har*ass. However, the point is it's the citizens who pay. One must ask oneself, Who is paying for this harassment?"

"Horses are the worst," Victoria said. "Worse than tear gas. Rearing horses are the scariest."

"Clubs are the worst," Arthur Brownson said. "They always go for the head."

"Yes," Susan said, breathless, eager. "Sixty-eight. I've seen the photographs."

"I was thinking of fifty-two, or earlier, at Union Square," Arthur Brownson said.

"The Rosenbergs," Victoria said. "The night they killed the Rosenbergs."

"No, no," Arthur Brownson said. "Korea, the Korean War and the Stockholm Peace Petition."

"Last night," Susan said, her tone soft with awe, "somebody was telling us about Peekskill and they said that you were there, Miss Younger."

"When the authorities used horses against our pro-Loyalist demonstration on Fifth Avenue," Arthur Brownson said. "It was nineteen thirty-eight or late thirty-seven, at the Spanish consulate. I knew then it was all over for Spain. If they were using horses, it was all over."

"Of course I was there," Victoria said. "Because of Paul. Paul Robeson was one of my dearest friends. My manager was with me. My then-manager. He was an important party member, donated a lot of money and had a lot to do with those immense pageants put on at Madison Square Garden. He got me out of there without a scratch, early, even before Paul left."

"Remember Bella?"

Arthur Brownson was laughing. He was transformed into a young man.

"She came tearing out of her car, brandishing a Coca-Cola bottle at those rock-throwing thugs, and they ran, they ran. Big woman, Bella."

"I didn't see any of the violence," Victoria said. "My manager got me right out of there. He was afraid I'd lose all my bookings. All my bookings! It wasn't as if I had a mass audience. Only the left liked me then."

"Jeff tells me you were in Jackson — Mississippi — in nineteen sixty-four, running a Freedom School, when the three were lynched, the voter registration volunteers."

"Oh, for heaven's sake," Victoria said. "One couldn't be everywhere. I was on tour, as a matter of fact." She leaned her head against the back of the couch. "Do you think there's a drop of juice around?" she said.

"No, I meant Mr. Brownson," Susan said, getting up.

"That must have been Dwight and Maddy Phillips," Arthur Brownson said. "I think. It certainly was not I. Bernard was there, I believe. Jessie was still alive then, and I think they both went down. Bernard Lewis, and his wife."

"It would be wonderful," Susan said, "if we could have a discussion sometime about the Communist party and your disillusionment —"

"Balderdash," Bernard Lewis called out.

He was wide awake, as was Dwight. Dwight began a recitation.

"While Titian was mixing rose madder,
His model he spied on a ladder,
The position to Titian
Suggested coition . . ."

Victoria took up the line.

" 'So he climbed up the ladder and had her,' " they declaimed together.

Arthur Brownson frowned. "A frightful nonsequitur," he said.

Victoria laughed.

" 'So he climbed up the ladder and had her,' " Dwight repeated, savoring the lilt.

"Fiddling while Rome burns," Bernard Lewis said.

"A frightful cliché, that," Victoria said.

"Don't waste your time with all that balderdash out of the past," Bernard Lewis said. "Work on current history, girl, there's work enough at hand."

"You're not allowed to call them 'girl' now," Dwight said. "Even if they're six months old."

Susan flushed.

Victoria said, "Cut it out, Dwight."

"I had a wonderful nap," Dwight said, "and I'm feeling silly. Can't I be silly in my old age?"

"Arthur," Bernard Lewis called out. "Come sit beside me. I've been meaning to discuss something with you."

"Would anybody else care for some juice?" Susan said.

"You cannot embrace both writers, Arthur. I've been thinking about that introduction you wrote. It's not feasible to attempt to fit Tolstoy and Dostoyevsky into the same philosophical system. You're simply building an arbitrary construct that ignores empirical judgment."

"Yes," Arthur Brownson said. "I would love some

juice. I'm going to need some nourishment, given this sort of talk."

But he sat down close to Bernard Lewis, his face eager for combat.

"Tolstoy, the quintessential humanist," Bernard Lewis continued without interruption. "And Dostoyevsky, flagrantly nihilist . . ."

"Wrong," Arthur Brownson said. "Absolutely wrong. Grossly incorrect. A gross *mis*reading of a great writer, a *great* writer. Sublime. In fact, sublime. Think of that moment when Grushenka plays upon the hypocrisy of Katerina Ivanovna, like a cat with a mouse. 'What if I take to Mitya again. I liked him very much once — liked him for almost a whole hour . . . You see I'm so changeable—' "

"What are you mincing about for?" Bernard Lewis interrupted the other's dramatic rendering, but to no effect.

"What a scene, what a marvelous scene. She holds Katerina's hand but withholds the great honor Katerina has bestowed on this degraded woman. Grushenka does not kiss Katerina's hand, though Katerina has kissed *her* hand. 'Do you know, after all, I think I won't kiss your hand,' and laughs a merry little laugh."

"You miss the point," Bernard Lewis roared. "Stop mincing about and listen to me."

"Sublime! Sublime! 'So that you may be left to remember that *you* kissed my hand, but I didn't kiss yours.' What subtlety, what psychology. Let your Marxist critics analyze that scene for what it yields in true class consciousness. From the lowest of the low, a telling blow. 'So I shall tell Mitya how you kissed my hand, but I didn't kiss yours at all. And how he will laugh!' The subtlety of that scene, with its social and moral overtones. The subtlety and the profound irony."

"Social and moral overtones!" Bernard Lewis said. "Depravity and degeneracy, though God knows what you're talking about. I certainly don't know what you're babbling about, and I've read every word of *Crime and Punishment* and *The Possessed*."

"*Brothers Karamazov*," Arthur Brownson said.

"You miss the point, the basic point," Bernard Lewis said. "We're not discussing a sleight-of-hand literary trick. Nobility of thought and the elevation of humanity are at stake. I've heard you on the subject of Romain Rolland, and your dismissal of *Jean Christophe* on the basis of literary skill. Balzac and Proust you admit to the pantheon —"

"This is ridiculous." Arthur Brownson turned to the room. "Why, I daresay the man hasn't read a novel since nineteen thirty. *Jean Christophe*. It's embarrassing. Proust is to Romain Rolland as —"

"No!" Dwight joined the fray. "No! You may not quarrel about Marcel Proust this morning. I won't have it, I won't. I forbid you to mention his name. Over my dead body, over my dead body."

"Oh, shut up, Dwight," Bernard Lewis said. "Not funny at all, not at all."

"I'm dead serious," Dwight said.

Arthur Brownson screwed his lips into a little locked purse. Bernard Lewis closed his eyes and seemed to fall instantly asleep.

10

LATER, not only much later when it was reasonable to expect old age to muddle memory, but when she was still very young, being shepherded from country to country, from one Society encampment and guest house to another, a member of a *party*, the Lady Florence Greenwood party in Paris, the Voynow party in Spain, the Bishop Nysmith party boarding the ship in Alicante bound for the East, the Lady Pansy Harkness party in Jerusalem and on to India, even way back then as a participant at the palpitating center of the dramas of that life, she hopelessly confused geography so that reality, what happened where and in what order, became unreal, a movie screened before a series of painted backdrops.

Certain scenes are sharp; the event and the place are clear.

In the stone house on the Costa Brava, Victoria became her lover. They meet again, Maddy and Victoria, after the long break, as if they have never been apart. Victoria is subtly different, tougher, clearer in outline, and Maddy too has changed, but they come together easily, joyously, plunging into talk with the eagerness of lovers, though they are not yet lovers.

In the stone house in the little village of Ultramorte, they have come together to discuss certain aspects of programming at the coming encampment farther down the coast. Mornings they confer with Lady Florence, Nityia, and Jag; their afternoons are free.

On the coast a pebbled beach curves its white shell shape into the vivid sea, a semiprecious stone in a rough-cut setting. Inland the little town of Ultramorte broods apart, a dry, still center under the hot March sun. From the house they bicycle to the beach or to the plaza, its trees and flowers blossoming, fluttering with birds and birdsong. Every day street cleaners wash down the paths of the plaza with buckets of water and straw brooms. One end of the sleepy plaza holds a kiosk, the other a café. Maddy and Victoria drink forbidden coffee at a teetering cast-iron table. The waiter steadies it by placing a folded cloth napkin under one leg. Maddy and Victoria smile into each other's eyes in unspoken understanding. They also talk and talk and talk, enjoying spoken understanding. Every day dawns beautifully sunny. The nights in the stone house in Ultramorte are unbelievably cold.

"I was always cold," Victoria says.

It is Maddy's first night in the stone house. Maddy's and Victoria's rooms are side by side. Maddy has prepared a hot-water bottle to warm Victoria's bed. Victoria is in a thin nightgown, her ugly dancer's feet bared to the marble-cold floor.

"I was always cold," Victoria says.

Once again Victoria tells her story of childhood naiveté and adult incomprehension. When she finishes, Maddy tucks her into bed, adding the rubber warmth to Victoria's ice-cold toes. Victoria shudders. Maddy shudders, but her body feels very warm.

"Lay on me," Victoria says.

Victoria is smiling, an ugly smile, diffident and pitiable. Maddy is sickened as if by the sight of an uncovered organ — a pulsating lung, a jellied spleen, a bloody, quivering liver. Maddy lies down quickly. She prefers Victoria to be Victoria — in command — and so she obeys. But she also *wants* to lie down with Victoria. She enters into the embrace of Victoria's strong, aggressive arms, sighing with the pleasure of a child coming home. Here perhaps she will find a mothering safety, a haven from the surprising pain of Vidhya's sudden treachery, of her own shocking infidelity.

Under the covers, skin to naked skin, it is much like lying down with Vidhya, though in some ways Vidhya is more feminine. His flesh is softer than Victoria's; his hair is silkier and thicker. Victoria is muscled, tense, alert; she is more embattled. With Vidhya what happens in bed flows dreamily; Victoria works harder at lovemaking. Maddy doesn't allow herself to think of Nityia.

Maddy winds her arms and legs around Victoria, binding her close. The bed heats up deliciously.

Even so it remains technically correct to say that *Victoria became Maddy's lover.*

Maddy loves Victoria. (Of course Maddy loves Victoria.) But there are two kinds of love going on, out of bed and in bed. In bed, Maddy cannot bring herself *to love Victoria back.* She talks to herself in evasive phrases. *Why can't I love her back? There are different ways of loving. I don't love Victoria that way.* She explains herself to herself. And admits that she desperately wants to be loved by Victoria *that way.* Isn't that acceptable? In *The Well of Loneliness* one woman acts the male, the other the female. Surely it is correct for Maddy to act the female? She will lie still and allow herself to be adored.

In this game of statues, after some time Victoria flings herself out of the tableau.

"You don't love me," she says. "You don't love me."

How can Victoria make such an accusation? Maddy *adores* Victoria; Victoria is her *idol.*

"I love you," Maddy says. "I do love you."

"Bullshit," Victoria says. "Merde. Lovers love each other. Lovers are lovers. They're not best friends and a bit of sex play for topping."

Maddy lowers her head. Open talk of sex frightens her.

"That's right," Victoria says. "Cast your eyes down like some fucking Victorian heroine."

Victoria has picked up some new rough talk from two American artists she has become friendly with in Spain. She pals around with them, hangs out in bars. They are helping her design a set for an elaborate new dance she will not allow Maddy to see until it is more finished.

But where are we now? In Barcelona, at a café on the Via Layetana. Maddy is a part of the Voynow party, en route to the Society encampment in Alicante, with stopovers at the Hotel Colón, opposite the cathedral, and another at a stone villa in Alicante province. Here, in Barcelona, Maddy and Victoria are out on the streets at an hour when the city closes down for its midday rest. They are in search of privacy for a conversation demanded by Victoria. First they sit on the cathedral steps in an agonizing silence under the oppressive heat of the sun and the fear of being observed by one of their party from the windows of the hotel overlooking the plaza. But inside the café around the corner, it is dark and cool, permeated with strong smells — cleanser, seafood, wine, and the saturated wood of the mahogany bar. Sawdust on the floor, overlaid with lunch debris — dirty napkins, shells of shrimp, lobsters, tiny clams, the remains of sardine heads, odds and ends of squid, and the scaly black outer hide of the *percebes,* ending in a hideous yellow nail. The floor in the back part of the spacious café is swept clean, and two young girls are on their hands and knees, scrubbing the marble. They are singing in shrill, off-key tones that simultaneously convey a light happiness and the heavy tug of nostalgia. The café's patrons are all men; the space resounds with deep voices and barreling laughter. The waiter seems to be a child, he is so tiny, until up close he shows crinkled eyes and a thinning hairline. He makes his unhappiness clear: Maddy and Victoria have arrived at closing time. Victoria explains in her excellent Spanish that they wish only refreshment, a little orange juice will do. Because they are foreigners, the waiter makes a gracious exception.

As soon as his back is turned, Victoria resumes.

"Unrequited love never interested me. Not interested, damn you."

Maddy can hear Victoria grinding her strong teeth.

"No, nor sainthood, either. Don't confuse me with Vidhya. I believe in gratification. Lineaments of gratified desire . . ."

Again Maddy hears her grinding her teeth.

"Don't get me wrong," she says. "I'm begging for nothing. Not even fair play. Turn and turn about. No, that would be a horrible humiliation. Doing your duty toward me — with revulsion."

Maddy was about to say *I love you* but the waiter is upon them, serving two glasses of orange juice in tall, stemmed cut-glass. Her face contorted, Victoria drains her glass at once and orders another. Maddy twirls the stem of her full glass, concentrating hard on the motion of the liquid, waiting for the waiter to depart. But the moment he does, Victoria is speaking again.

"It's not as if I'm hard to love," Victoria says.

"I love you," Maddy says.

Victoria speaks through Maddy's words.

"Poke me with a finger and I come. Just like that."

Her upper body rises and stretches, the long neck soars, she raises both arms and snaps two fingers of each hand in parallel gestures of completion and triumph.

"Like that," she says. "*I* don't have any trouble coming."

Again she snaps her fingers.

"Like that," she says.

The attention of the men at the bar turns toward them. The waiter informs the patrons in Spanish that the two women are foreigners and shrugs his shoulders in expressive dismissal. The men comment privately and roar out public laughter. Could they have overheard and understood? That Victoria is shoving sexual failure in her face, as lover and loved? Tears choke Maddy.

"Don't you dare," Victoria says. "Don't you dare cry. Turning the facts around, making yourself the aggrieved one. You would have gone on as we were. Until Vidhya comes back to you. The truth now, tell the truth for once. If he beckons won't you run to him?"

Maddy's fingers slip on the stem of the glass she is twisting. Orange juice sloshes over the clean white tablecloth. The tiny waiter, arriving with Victoria's reorder, lingers to sop up the spill. Like the mahogany bar, the body of the waiter is saturated with odors of seafood, wine, and cologne. *Good enough to eat.* Her groin responds to the notion. Blood flares into her face.

Victoria drains the second glass of juice, then slams it to the table.

"It's meaningless to you, whatever you do," she says. "We can talk about anything, you and I, except the things that really matter. Why don't you answer me? Will you go back to Vidhya?"

"Go back?" Maddy hears herself ask like a defective child. "Isn't he coming here?"

Victoria groans and puts her head in her hands.

"Stupid, ignorant kid," she mutters. "I must have been out of my mind, hoping for anything . . ."

"I love you," Maddy says. "And I love Vidhya. How could I not? If he decided it was me he loved all along and that this Rosamund Keats was all a mistake? Go back, I mean."

Victoria shakes her head in disbelief.

"All a mistake," she repeats. "Can the pure Vidhya make mistakes? Is it a mistake that he wears pale gray spats? That his shoes are made to order and his suits — at Meyers and Mortimer — not to mention his shirts — at Beale and Inman — and that he wouldn't be caught dead wearing a tie other than a Liberty, or hand-initialed handkerchiefs?"

"I don't understand," Maddy says.

"Do you know that your sainted Vidhya went to London first to renew his wardrobe and get his hair cut at Trumpers?" Victoria says.

Maddy shakes her head.

"And to garage a pale blue seven-seater Lincoln convertible with silver lamps and cut-glass flower holders —"

"I don't understand," Maddy interrupts. "Are you saying that Vidhya is a fake?"

"Ah," Victoria says. "The girl knows how to speak directly, after all . . ."

"I thought you would never speak to me that way again, after . . . after . . . everything," Maddy bursts out.

"And I thought . . ." Victoria begins.

Overheated, Victoria is letting off steam, in a long exhalation of breath.

"Oh, what's the use?" she says.

She is silent, staring ahead. Maddy doesn't know what to do. The strangling silence grows between them, a palpable mist, asphyxiating, killing. The singing maidens approach closer and closer on their sea of suds. The men at the bar depart in a noisy, hailing group. The waiter hovers, eyeing Maddy and Victoria with an expression sadder than theirs. They are robbing him of his midday break. But they cannot help themselves or him. They are immobilized, bewitched into a misery so deep they cannot speak or move.

Like the house in Ultramorte, the villa in Alicante is also made of stone, but its design is simpler and rougher, and its large, wooden-floored rooms are barely furnished. There is a bathroom on each landing, complete with the newest plumbing, but without running water. Buckets of water stand ready for flushing; buckets of heated water are supplied for bathing in the sparkling porcelain bathtub and washbasin. The countryside surrounding the villa alters itself dramatically, almost from acre to acre. On the sea side, stunted olive trees dance away from the rude two-story structure. Beyond the olive grove, the salt marshes stretch, geometric squares of brilliant seawater, startlingly green against the white heaps of salt and borders of gray-brown sand. On the inland side of the house, behind the kitchen garden, there is an astonishingly tender, pink, perfumed almond orchard in full blossom. And beyond that, the hills begin their soft ascent into the sky.

Vidhya arrives at the villa the day after Maddy does, dressed just as Victoria described: spats, Liberty tie and initialed handkerchief, English-cut suit and English-cut hair. In his room next to hers on the upper floor of the villa, he takes Maddy's arm, leads her to his bed, and kisses her on the mouth. He has changed out of his European clothing into clinging soft folds of Indian cotton. His golden beauty is irresistible, and she does not resist.

Only a handful of Society leaders are staying in the villa at Alicante: Vidhya, Bobo, the Voynows. (Do the Voynows own the villa? Maddy thinks so. They are very much in charge here. But she doesn't know for a fact, and isn't very interested anyway. The mysterious ways of the Society have assumed a normalcy for her.) Jag and Mr. Singh are part of the company, but of the younger women, there are only Maddy and Milli. The others are seventy miles north on the Mediterranean coast, readying a place referred to as *the castle* for the most ambitious encampment ever planned by the Society, to take place in April.

Society leaders have made the decision that the long years of grooming Vidhya as the coming Savior of the world must come to a close. The pronouncement of the fulfillment of the Elders' promise will be the climax of the events at the Spanish encampment. Underneath his impeccable British clothing, his well-arranged hair, and his irresistible golden skin, Vidhya is a mess. He feels himself under siege.

"I am surrounded. Surrounded. I must capitulate," he says. "I must. What else can I do?"

The villa is built of two unequal stone blocks, connected by an inner courtyard. Vidhya's and Maddy's rooms and their shared balcony are isolated on an upper floor of the smaller block. Here they are free to do as they like, free even to cry their hearts out, as Vidhya is doing now.

"Why me? Ah, Maddy, why did they choose me?"

After her first efforts to soothe him with reasoned words, she no longer answers in words. All words, any words, drive him into a rage. She offers instead the safe harbor of her body — hugs, kisses, more if he wishes — always holding herself prepared for rebuff.

"They know I am full of doubt. They know how profoundly I doubt myself," he cries out.

His strange gray eyes remain tearless, though sobs rack his chest.

"How can they demand so much of me, knowing that I am torn in pieces with doubt?" he cries out, dramatically.

How can the Society not demand so much of Vidhya? He has been the promised Messiah for almost ten years now. One day he *must* arrive. Otherwise they are all simply ridiculous. But Maddy doesn't say this to Vidhya.

At the same time, work proceeds on the talks to be given by Vidhya at the encampment. Jag and Bobo have insinuated themselves into this work. They are striving for a subtle change in tone, an air of the Master, a hint of capital letters, *I, Me, Mine.* Phrases are inserted: *I bring peace; My voice speaks within you; Come with me.* Jag deletes *we* wherever he finds it, and all communal appeals, Vidhya's great favorites, *putting our heads together, reasoning together, talking together.* Bobo has decreed that now is the time for a divine voice speaking with the authority of the highest powers of the universe, a single voice, embodied in Vidhya.

But can Vidhya be counted on to deliver these speeches to audiences in the form in which they are written? He has never been faithful to a written speech. He hews close to the same personal formula. It has been spectacularly successful. Dare they tamper with it? Lady Pansy joins them in Alicante to help make decisions. She arrives with Rosamund Keats. Maddy studies the dark-haired, white-skinned, rosy-cheeked girl, satisfied at last that she is not as beautiful as reported. Nevertheless her presence is a bother. It bothers Maddy that Rosamund and Vidhya are pointedly cool toward each other. It bothers Maddy that she is bothered. She would like to soar above such petty reactions.

She is working very hard. Daily lengthy sessions are held, at which Maddy is welcome because of her shorthand skills and from some Byzantine notion that she will influence Vidhya in the directions thought proper by Bobo and Lady Pansy. She emerges from these meetings exhausted, with a raging headache. Why, they have even discussed the possibility of dramatic reenactments of Jesus walking on the water, driving the moneylenders from the temple, and, of course, a miracle healing. A contemporary equivalent, naturally, nothing ridiculously contrived, but such talk gives Maddy a headache.

For respite, Maddy has taken to walking about under the blossoming almond trees, alone. In the soft wind, the blossoms flutter to the ground, creating an enclosed bower of almond blossoms in the canopy above and the carpet below. Here it is silent and sweet, and the possibility of uncomplicated, blissful happiness is strong. Maddy goes to this special bower every afternoon, directly after the sickening meetings, to wash away the disquieting nervousness they leave behind.

And here in the almond orchard after a particularly trying session, Maddy sees Mr. and Mrs. Voynow approaching across the floor of blossoms, obviously seeking her out, two gray-faced, misty creatures, solemn, burdened, and frightened. They warn her first that they have terrible news, and then tell her that her parents have been killed in a head-on collision. At two o'clock in the afternoon of a bright, sunny day, a drunken driver steered his truck diagonally across the straight new highway running west out of Chicago, to hit her mother and father full on. Maddy cannot comprehend the message. She rattles the details out of the murmuring Voynows, shakes them again and again for further information, but they know only the little they have been told. No, the accident was not caused by her father's bumbling driving. Yes, it was entirely the fault of the drunken driver of the truck. Yes, her parents were killed outright. Quickly. No, they could not have suffered pain. She asks again. Again, they repeat. But she cannot absorb the information.

The Voynows gently escort her back to the villa. She is embraced and consoled by all in a beautiful ceremony that Bobo quickly invents for the tragedy. She is enveloped within an aura of adulation and respect that surprises her. Why this careful treatment? Because of death? Yes, and more. Maddy doesn't remember the incident, but it seems she had foretold her fate in a prophetic statement. The Voynows recall the scene in detail. In the elegant dining car of the Chicago–New York Express, having bid her parents a light-hearted good-by in Chicago, Maddy had burst into tears and cried out, *I know that I shall never see my parents again.* The Voynows remember Maddy's exact words and other bits as well, such as their urging Maddy to order the apricot soufflé, which proved to be delicious. The Voynows cannot stop themselves retelling the story. They repeat and repeat until its significance is clear to all — proof of Maddy's psychic powers, the highest of all attributes sought after by Society petitioners.

After some days of observance of Maddy's mourning, Mr. Singh requests a conference. In one of the downstairs rooms that Milli and Mr. Singh have set up as their office, Maddy sits on a stiff-backed chair in the barely furnished room and Mr. Singh talks to Maddy of life insurance, pensions, savings, property investments, her father and mother's wish to leave a certain percentage of their money to the Society, and sums up Maddy's financial situation in a final gush of reassurance.

"You shall be collecting a nice little annuity," he says. "A nice little annuity. Yes, a nice little annuity. Nice little annuity."

He apparently loves the sound of these words so well he goes on pronouncing them over and over. For Maddy, the words are like a strong wind tearing into the amorphous mist of her grief. She has lost her mother and father and she is alone in the world, but new concepts take shape. Free and independent. Independent and free.

She would like to take time out to think about this new state of being, but the routines and concerns of Bobo and Lady Pansy and Vidhya have a relentless force of their own and she is drawn into their activity again as if nothing has changed, apart from the new respect she encounters. There is one particularly wearing session in which Bobo discusses Society long-range plans to follow the successful conclusion of the Spanish encampment: speaking tours for Vidhya in the USA, in India, and, finally, in Australia. Bobo rattles on enthusiastically about what he calls the "wilderness territories" of Australia and America. He invokes the "vast spaces" of Madison Square Garden and the Hollywood Bowl, of immense mass meetings where Vidhya will rule the emotions and arouse the faith of thousands. He calls California "the new promised land" and claims that its soil and air are breeding a "finer race of humanity. Look at Maddy!" he says. "Maddy was born out there in the West. And does she not come close to the perfection of the Aryan ideal?"

Maddy doesn't know where to begin to correct the multiple errors in his rhapsodizing.

"No, no," Maddy says. "California isn't . . . Iowa isn't really anywhere near . . . Not the West at all, and anyway I wasn't exactly born . . ."

But her denials are viewed as modesty, another prime virtue.

Soon Bishop Nysmith announces Maddy's promotion to the highest level of petitioner. She listens to Bobo's account of her out-of-body encounters with the Elders as to a fairy tale. He recounts that Bobo and Vidhya were her escorts to the mountain retreat in India where the Elders received her most cordially. He reports that she behaved with her usual charm and that the Elders were most pleased with her inner and outer demeanor. The Voynows also materialized before the Elders to attest to Maddy's spiritual nature and psychic powers. She was jumped, skipped, practically catapulted to her present eminence in the Society's system of promotions, after which, Bobo says, she was offered a sweet, cool drink, a slice of melon, and a thin rice wafer. Then Mrs. Dasinov materialized, transported from the estate in California she had recently bought, to speak of the possibilities of California as a new territory in which to develop the ideal Aryan race envisioned by the Elders. This section of Bobo's tale continues for some time and Maddy loses the drift.

The whole wonderful rigmarole of events is supposed to have happened during the night before. Though Maddy can almost taste on her tongue the cool drink, the melon, and the thin rice wafer, she is shaken by his report, since she knows very well how she spent the night. She and Vidhya never went to sleep at all. They had been up all night. How then had their spirits been transported from their sleeping bodies as Bobo told it?

Maddy steals a questioning glance in Vidhya's direction. He isn't looking at her, only at Bobo, nodding now and then in corroboration of Bobo's recital, his eyes glowing and vacant, fixed on scenes beyond her capacity to envision. She looks to Vidhya for reassurance that the actual night she and Vidhya spent together does not invalidate Bobo's version, but Vidhya never turns his head from its devoted attention to Bobo. She wants desperately to believe. And if Vidhya believes, how can she not? Okay, there is a slight discrepancy here. Vidhya and Maddy were supposedly transported to India while their physical bodies slept in Alicante. But they never went to sleep at all. They had talked and made love all night, made love and talked, Vidhya wildly questioning everything, alternately aroused, violent, soothed, passionate, and spent, but never calm enough to fall asleep, no, not for a split second. Might they not have been together in his bed in Alicante and together in their out-of-body trip to India? Surely the hand of God, or Whoever, with his or her unfailing genius for the miraculous, was capable of anything?

Now Vidhya himself in his sweet manner of speech is verifying Bobo's account.

"What a wonderful, wonderful night we spent, ah, how wonderful this night has been," Vidhya says, nodding his head.

Vidhya, then, had been present at the ceremony held by the Elders and had seen it all with his own out-of-body eyes? Was it possible that Vidhya, intermittently raging at his position in the Society, intermittently loving her body and his own, could leave both behind him, go off on this extraordinary adventure and keep the whole incident from her at the same time? The convolutions of the reported event are dizzying. She clings to the faint taste of melon, of wafer, struggling in her memory for substance. *Something* must have happened, if she can taste melon, surely.

In his room later, the disquieting scene and the questions crowding her brain have made her unusually unresponsive.

"Are you sulking?" Vidhya says.

She is aware of the effort he is making to control his anger.

"This is how you greet me? After everything I have done for you?"

"What have you done for me?" Maddy says.

"Your promotion. Do you think I had nothing to do with your promotion?"

"I thought the Elders were the ones who promoted —"

"Don't be childish," he explodes. "What is the matter with you? Are you a child? You know very well how things are here, how they come about, promotions, everything. Why are you pretending to be stupid suddenly?"

"Maybe I'm not pretending," Maddy says. "Maybe I'm just plain stupid, plain old stupid."

He draws a deep breath and makes a fresh start.

"Come, Maddy," he says, "I know that you have been put through a great deal these last weeks, good and bad, the terrible news of your parents, a terrible blow, and the excitement of your promotion and the hard work we have all been called upon to perform, but we must not make life worse for ourselves, is that not so? . . ."

Why is he talking to her as if from a platform?

". . . We are here to improve the earth, is not that so? That is our primary duty on earth, to make it a better place . . ."

She springs up from the bed, outraged by his manner and fortified by new concepts: independence, annuity.

"What about Rosamund Keats?" she says, straight out.

"What about Rosamund . . ." he repeats, startled, and then laughs his characteristically artificial cascade of notes, not his real, helpless, full-bodied laughter. He spreads his hands wide. "Rosamund and I . . . Rosamund and I are comrades. What do you mean? We are friends and comrades."

"Marigold reported that you were head over heels in love with her," Maddy says.

"Marigold!" he says. "Can it be that you are seriously quoting an opinion of that ninny girl?"

He laughs again. The burst of controlled sound grates maddeningly. Maddy doesn't answer.

"How can you pay attention to a report from Marigold? Maddy, I am ashamed to see you so gullible. She is head over heels in confusion, that girl. Everybody knows that Mari is quite unreliable, head over heels unreliable."

"And you and I," Maddy says, the tears starting, "what are we, please, friends and comrades?"

"Yes," he says, "yes."

They stand facing each other, saying nothing for a bit.

"Why do you stare at me with accusations and tears in your eyes, Maddy? Have we not had wonderful times together, has it not been beautiful, our time together?"

And after a pause, during which she says nothing, he speaks again.

"Maddy, are you saying that I have been mistaken in you?"

He clutches at his head as if she is driving him mad.

"Maddy, can it be that we do not understand each other, as I thought we did, understand each other in our souls, our secret souls?"

She says nothing.

"Do you not love me anymore?" His voice is a child's wail.

"And you?" she says. "Do you love me?"

"How can you question my love?" he says. "All the world, everybody knows how much I love you, everybody knows it. Don't you believe me?"

"I don't know what to believe anymore," Maddy says. "Were you there last night, where you say you were?"

Now he really wails, clutching his head and rolling his eyes.

"Oh my God, oh my God, I can't bear any more, I can't bear it, I can't, I assure you, this is intolerable . . ."

"Shh, shh," she says, "the whole house will hear you."

"Don't you understand that I must, I must, I cannot do otherwise, there is no way out for me, don't you understand, why are you torturing me, why have you ceased to love me?"

"I haven't," she says. "I do love you, Vidhya, I do, I do, only I don't know what to think . . ."

"You're not supposed to think," Vidhya wails. "Oh God, stop trying to think."

"I don't know what to do, I don't know where I'm going, I don't understand, there's too much I don't understand," Maddy says.

"Trust me, trust me," Vidhya says.

He puts on an air of calm and approaches Maddy with authority.

"You must listen to me," he says. "You must trust me. Let us become secretly engaged. It will be fine. Everything will be gorgeous again between us. Come now, is it agreed? Now we are secretly engaged. Nobody must know, only you and I. We will keep this beautiful secret hidden in our hearts, until the proper time arrives to burst forth with it. Isn't that fine?"

He reaches out to seize her and smothers her head against his silken-skinned chest, bared under the loose, open cotton jacket.

"Let me hear you say yes, Maddy, darling, let me hear yes, yes."

She is crouched uncomfortably to nestle into his body, but it is a relief to no longer look directly into the overworked, overexcited face and lying eyes. Why not believe? How delightful to be secretly engaged. She is free and independent, the mistress of a nice little annuity and secretly engaged to Vidhya, the coming Messiah of the world.

194

"Yes," she says, her face hidden in his silken-skinned breast. "Yes, yes."

There is much confusion at the Spanish encampment. Hundreds more than were expected have arrived, lured by the possibility that the Messiah is to be revealed. The campsite is set up on the grounds of an actual castle, seventy miles north of the Alicante villa, complete with moat, battlements, and a façade of gold-tinted granite.

As a part of the inner circle, Maddy is housed in a tiny room within the castle, with its own w.c. attached. She is told that her body wastes empty directly into the moat, where ancient carp attend to the sanitary task of cleaning up, a detail that horribly stirs up Maddy's imaginings. Outsiders — visitors, petitioners, acolytes, all the others — mill about in an area of communal tents on the high ground below the moat and above the brilliantly colored sea. How beautiful this campsite is to Maddy. The cloth of the tents, dyed in the hot colors of the sun, has been brought from India; the soft reds, oranges, and golden yellows radiating outward to the pillows and throw cloths flung out on the hillside are repeated in the flowing garments of the pilgrims, and in their head scarves and turbans. On the spindly tables set up here and there, a sleepy wind blows the fall of yellow cloths on which sit the large pitchers of golden orange juice and the copper bowls of ripe figs — the only nourishment allowed during the two-week retreat. Along the edges of the site, shrines made up of silken prayer cloths in the same hot colors are combined with garlands of shrubs, leaves, and flowers decorating a photograph of Vidhya taken on the beach below, in which a trick of the sun and the flow of his garments create the illusory effect of a walk on the water. In the constant wind, bells ring out over the repetitive complaint of stringed instruments and a moaning and humming buzz as from a colony of bees.

Maddy would rather be here than in the castle, with its huge reception rooms hung with Goya tapestries of street games, canvases of tender Murillo children, and an immense, cruel Ribera, which so terrifies Maddy that she has only looked directly at it once. And the carp in the moat.

The young count who inherited the castle and has passed along its use to the Society is nothing like Maddy's version of a prince of a castle, this or any other. Pini (everybody calls the count Pini) is short and squat, and his overlarge head, rounded and wreathed in smiles, is that of a court jester. Milli and Mari, too old now for childish games, nevertheless run around Pini, chanting, "I'm the king of the castle, and you're the dirty rascal," to which taunts the count responds with his usual good cheer. Pini speaks English, French, German, Russian, Italian, but all so badly that nobody understands him.

Cleves, returned from his visit home unchanged except for his hair, now parted on the side and slicked back behind his ears, insists the count is retarded. Conrad retorts that Cleves is rotten jealous of Pini's wealth and of the fact that everybody loves Pini for himself as well as for his money.

Very little rain falls here, but Lady Pansy is distraught with a vision of the chaos of a downpour on the tent site.

"It will not rain," she is assured by everybody.

But it does rain one afternoon. Rounds of crystal liquid as big as American silver dollars splash down through golden sunlight, shining throughout. The shower lasts for five minutes. The whole camp rushes out into the pelting splatter, mad with joy, leaping and dancing ecstatically, then falls silent when the rain stops, as though in the presence of a miracle. It is a crowd thirsty for miracles.

Vidhya speaks to the pilgrims every afternoon as the sun cools down. The camp is mysteriously and totally hushed, listening to him. Only the indifferent sea maintains its murmuring conversation with the earth. Nobody admits it, but Vidhya's speeches are subtly off stride. Perhaps his followers' expectations have been raised too high. They are listening for *His Words* and leave disappointed. In the evening their spirits are buoyed by the golden campfires, by the singing and dancing and the instrumental music that never ceases.

Victoria and her company are supposed to perform every night, but though a week has passed, they still have not appeared. Yes, Victoria's company is there, a troupe of twelve dancers she is training in the Victoria Younger Technique, all women, three of them Indian, of whom one is an exquisitely tiny creature with a perfectly modeled head and a dramatic fall of black hair, like a spill of India ink. She is known only as Indira, and is clearly Victoria's lover.

"Does this situation bother you?" Victoria asks.

She and Victoria are alone for a moment, walking away from a distressing meeting.

"Indira and me, I mean," Victoria says.

"No, no," Maddy says. "I want you to be happy."

Victoria laughs harshly, then surprisingly her eyes show tears.

"I never want to hurt you," she says. "It's funny. Almost as if you were my child. I don't want to hurt you even when I do."

They are interrupted. There is too much going on for Maddy to really think about hurt, jealousy, love, the truth of her own feelings. She is secretly engaged to Vidhya and has no right to any feelings about Victoria. Or about Nityia, who is just ahead of them, walking rapidly away, the maleness of his back and shoulders in his thin cotton shirt arousing her, quite against her wishes, particularly since he has withdrawn, as if they had never been lovers. Maddy shoves her heaving emotions aside for the work at hand.

Victoria is at the center of a tremendous fuss. She is insisting on adhering to her set designer's color scheme: white, gray, black, and an occasional splash of red. The demand on her is that she stick to the prevailing colors — the sun colors.

She refuses. She is adamant. In addition she puts forward her own demands. She wants a platform built so that her dancers can perform on a smooth, flat surface. All the others are opposed: Bobo, Mr. Singh, Nityianda, Jag, Lady Pansy, the Voynows, Vidhya. The earth is sacred. *They* all speak and stage events upon uneven ground. How can Victoria refuse to perform upon the body of life-giving Earth?

Maddy is the unwilling recipient of Victoria's diatribes against the Society. She tries to shut them out.

"Bloody Philistines. They don't want to spend the money. Money is their whole objective in running this encampment. Why do you think they insisted on a rigid diet? Money, nothing but money. Orange juice and figs, what could be simpler or cheaper. No need for cooks, waiters, dishwashers, cleaning squads, and then there's the added twist that the whole dimwitted congregation is hallucinating from lack of nourishment."

Victoria's company have set themselves up somewhat apart from the others on a protecting elbow formed by a dip in the hill, hidden from the heights above and the beach below. A feast is in preparation: a soup of potatoes and leeks; rice, roasted artichokes, string beans, sliced tomatoes; a flat bread shaped like a matzo, but not so thin; Spanish melon and hot herb tea. Victoria has forcibly led Maddy here a few days later, primarily to feed her, but also to bluster at her so that Maddy will plead with the leadership to accede to Victoria's demands. But Maddy can barely move her own body, a result of ten days on the sun diet. Her mind is melting along with her limbs. The sun itself is an invading lover, dissolving her organs, blurring her vision, slurring her speech. She cannot follow the intent of Victoria's comments, though she has a firm sense of Victoria's anger. Something to do with their past? Maddy thinks of a month earlier as *the past*. Maddy has thought up a joke about Indira, very funny, if she can only hold on to it in her slippery brain. She believes that she is laughing out loud but hears herself whimpering, and tears roll down her cheeks. She feels herself sliding into a hot darkness, frightening yet somewhat pleasant.

When she comes to, she is lying on a makeshift bed in a tent, her head propped up with pillows. Victoria, Pini the count, and a group of young men are lounging nearby. She recognizes the American artist who designs Victoria's sets and another American new to Maddy. The others are all Spanish. Maddy feels her dignity at stake before these strangers and tries to get up but flops about helplessly. The American she doesn't know laughs and helps settle her against the pillows. Then he goes away and returns with a bowl of soup, which he spoon-feeds to Maddy. How delicious, how delicious food is. Victoria commands him to stop after half a dozen mouthfuls, and he does. Maddy remembers Victoria taking care of her on the deck of the *Majestic* and tries to recall the scene for Victoria but hears how her paralyzed tongue has garbled the message. Again she means to laugh but issues only cries and whimpers. The young man smiles and feeds her a few more spoonfuls. Up close, his face explodes into garish colors and disintegrates into bending shapes. She closes her eyes. When she opens them she sees a real American head, square-jawed, with a dimpled chin, a full-toothed smile, and wonderfully cool blue eyes, so reassuring that she instantly falls asleep.

A wild hubbub has awakened her. Victoria is in the tent with two Spaniards, rough-looking men, workers. She yanks Maddy to her feet, supporting her. The men are pulling apart the wide couch in order to slip in between the straw stuffing. Victoria rearranges the covering. The bed is a lumpy mess now. She pushes Maddy down, turning Maddy on her side and raising her skirt so that her naked thighs are exposed.

"Close your eyes. Pretend to be asleep. Don't say anything no matter what happens," Victoria says.

Victoria is tearing off her own clothes. Naked, she

places herself back to back with Maddy, curling inward, breathing heavily. Through the thin bed covering, Maddy feels the bodies of the men under her, their stringy tensed muscles and sharp bones. Outside, there is the sound of women screaming, a loud thumping of boots, shouted orders in Spanish. Then the tent is invaded. Maddy keeps her eyes closed. Victoria turns heavily, flinging an arm and one leg across Maddy's body, spreading her legs wide. Though Maddy cannot see Victoria, she sees her vividly. A violent, tearing noise forces Maddy's eyes open before she can stop herself. The tent flap has been ripped off. It is being held in the gloved hand of a soldier or a policeman gotten up in a fantastic costume, and, with an expression of exaggerated disgust, he is flinging the drapery over Maddy's and Victoria's nakedness. There is a troop of these men. Dressed as they are — black patent leather hats, heavy capes — they are too picturesque to be considered dangerous. Who in his right mind would dress this way in such heat? Some costume drama must be taking place, nothing serious. The troops seem to be wearing drawn swords. Is this possible? No, a long pistol, the sort used in duels of honor. Ridiculous. The soldier directly in front of Maddy waves the weapon and shouts at her. He is very young. Under his costume-drama shiny black hat, his liquid black eyes meet hers in fear and embarrassment.

Maddy stares into these charming eyes, sits up, says *oh, gosh*, and then, recalling Victoria's orders, lies back and pretends to have fallen asleep again.

The officer in charge laughs. He shouts an order in Spanish and clumps around the tent, his men following him. Again the sound of cloth being torn, and the screeching of women. Maddy is sure she can feel the soft nose of the man beneath her being crushed. What if she smothers him? Impossible to hold her eyes closed. She opens them. The sides of the tent are being torn down by the troops, but with care, almost politely, so that Maddy and Victoria are not hurt by falling posts. When the tent is totally dismantled, the company marches off, down the hillside toward the beach below.

"Don't move," Victoria whispers. "Wait."

Maddy waits, covering her head from the invading, blazing sun with her arm, and though she is terrified, and terribly uncomfortable in her attempt to ease her weight resting on the small man beneath her, she apparently falls asleep. When she awakens, the sides of the tent have been re-built, the two men are crawling out from under her, and she is being rolled to the end of the couch by Victoria. Victoria has wrapped herself in a tent drapery. Pini, the count, is also here, with a couple of Spaniards and Victoria's set designer and the square-jawed, smiling American who spoon-fed Maddy. They are all removing articles of clothing and trying them on the two Spanish workmen, searching for a good fit. The main problem seems to be with the workers' haircuts.

"Motoring caps, and scarves," Victoria says. "That would do it."

Pini and one of his friends go tearing out. This quick activity starts Maddy's stomach heaving again. Her vision wavers. She wanders outside and sits cross-legged on the grass, staring off into a little hollow in the near distance where a mass of tiny golden folk have gathered in busy con-ference. The dimple-in-the-chin American joins her. He nods, then carefully surveys the scene, turning slowly full circle.

"What are you doing?" Maddy says.

"Checking," he says.

He speaks in a deep, pleasant voice, without any accent, regular East Coast American, and she loves to hear it. He inclines his head in a courtly little bow.

"I'm Dwight Phillips," he says.

"I'm Maddy Brewster," she says.

"Yes," he says. "I came here to see you. I knew your father and mother. We worked together in the child labor movement. They sort of sent me to you with their blessing."

"All the way from the USA?" Maddy says.

"Well, no, not exactly," Dwight Phillips says. "I was coming here anyway, but they thought we'd get along."

She nods.

"I'm terribly sorry," he says. "Terrible, that accident, terrible."

His fair face flushes with the effort to pass over this emotional moment.

"I'm so sorry," he repeats. And then, "Are you feeling better now, I mean than before, when I fed you?"

Maddy nods.

"You should eat more food. There's lots left."

Again he circles, checking out the surroundings. On the heights, Pini and his friend are running toward them in caps and floating scarves of white filmy stuff.

"What is all this?" Maddy says. Her voice exhibits the crossness she feels. "What's happening? What was *that* all about?"

"Your friend Victoria is a wonderful person," Dwight says. "Rare, very rare."

She is astonished by the *ping* of jealousy she records internally.

"She said we could count on you, whatever you knew or didn't know."

He pauses.

"We have to keep those men safe for a couple of days." And then, "How do you like my get-up?"

It is only now that she notices how charming he looks. His pants and shirt have been exchanged for the bright blue work clothes of one of the hidden men, and to cover these he has draped himself in two lengths of cloth, one orange and the other sun yellow, tied with a sash of soft red, above which costume his thoroughly American face shines happy as a kid's in a pageant.

"Victoria dolled me up," he says.

"Who are they?" Maddy says. "What have they done?"

"They're a couple of anarchists," he whispers. "Separatists. Republicans, naturally. They're almost certain that Alfonso Trece will abdicate today or tomorrow, then they'll be able to return to the village."

"They can't be all three," Maddy says. "That's ridiculous."

"Not the *party*," Dwight Phillips says, and laughs aloud. "The concept. A republic."

"Well, they must have done *something*," Maddy says, "if those soldiers were after them."

"Guardia civil," he says, and smiles. "I hope to God they've done something, more power to them."

"Don't you know?"

He shakes his head.

"Who knows then?"

"Pini," he says.

"The count? That's impossible."

"Why?"

"Because he doesn't know *anything*. At least that's what everybody says."

"Very good cover for a clandestine worker," Dwight Phillips says, and nods sagely.

Maddy is quite lost. She clings to what she can grasp.

"Are they good men, then, those two Spanish workers?"

"The best. Good and brave and true to their ideals."

"Like Sacco and —"

She stops herself, ashamed of such simple-mindedness.

"Exactly," her new American friend says. "Do you think we would have asked for your help if they weren't?"

"Have you come for the retreat? To Spain, I mean."

"Oh God, no," he says, and laughs. "I don't have much faith in your Society for Universal Brotherhood. Hope I'm not hurting your feelings." He apologizes. "I came to see Pini. He and my closest friend were at Cambridge together.

Wonderful fellow, Arthur Brownson. You may know him."

"No," she says. "I thought you came to see me?"

He smiles.

"Not even my daddy could convince you, about the Society?"

He smiles and smiles. "Not even your charming mother. We saw eye to eye on almost everything, your mother and father and I, except all this occult stuff. Sorry."

"You're not sorry at all," she says. "Perhaps those little people can help, down there."

She points out the hollow where the tiny golden creatures are dashing back and forth, their arms raised and their fingers waggling in a frantic sort of activity. Dwight Phillips looks in the direction Maddy is pointing. He studies Maddy's face, looks again to the hollow, then back to her.

"Come and show me," he says.

He extends his hand and helps pull her up. She enjoys leaning on him. He is solid, a little taller than Maddy, and his body emits a calm strength that soothes and pleasures her. They walk silently to the spot where she saw the golden little people, but once upon it there is nothing in the rugged declivity but tall, feathery grasses, drenched in sunlight.

"Oh, they left," Maddy says. "They slipped away."

"You're serious, aren't you?" he says. "You really believe in fairies."

"These were angels, more likely," Maddy says.

Dwight laughs out loud.

"How delightful, what a delightful girl you are, hallucinating angels, angels and fairies."

"I'm not hallucinating," Maddy says. "They were there and slipped away."

"I think we'd better stoke up on a little more food," he says.

When Cleves arrives, looking for Maddy (Vidhya is frantic because of her long absence), the group is gathered in the tent, eating. The men have been arguing theory: anarchism, anarcho-syndicalism, communism, socialism, and social democracy. They have indulged in a sort of futurism too, prefiguring the coming state of the world now that the Bolshevik Revolution has changed everything. Apparently, Dwight Phillips is quite a theoretician. He is listened to carefully. Pini translates what Dwight says into Spanish. (What about Pini's language difficulties? He is suddenly clear as a bell in English.) The two workers, utterly changed by their playboy clothing, listen intently, but, like Maddy, say nothing. Victoria is off to one side in agitated private talk with her set designer and Indira. But all conversation comes to a total stop when Cleves steps into the tent.

Maddy is caught up in confusion at having been found eating forbidden food. Cleves makes no comment and then sits down to join them, helping himself to everything at the table.

"What in the world?" Maddy says.

"Oh, for heaven's sake, Maddy, don't tell me you didn't know we've all been supplementing the diet."

"Well, *I* wasn't," Maddy says. "And what about Vidhya?"

"How did you expect us to function?" he says. "We have to go on functioning, you know."

"What about me?" Maddy says. "I could have died."

"Don't be silly," Cleves says. "The sun diet is perfectly adequate for a short period of time. It would take months for someone to fall ill, years, probably, to die."

When he finishes his snack, he stands up.

"Come on, Maddy, let's go. Vidhya speech time. And he's beside himself, so let's go, let's go."

She rises, automatically obedient, following Cleves, while a mocking voice and the click of fingers snapping accompanies their movement.

"Yeah, kiddo, make it snappy." Click, click, click. "Let's go, let's go. Can't keep the boss waiting." Snap, snap, snap.

It is Dwight Phillips, his lips fixed in his charming full-toothed smile, pleasant as could be.

Cleves hurries her out. They are crossing the bridge over the moat when the sound of loud singing makes Maddy look back. Straggling up the hill, headed toward the swirling mass of pilgrims gathering at the point where Vidhya will speak, comes a carefree band of playboys, Pini leading the way, a clown camping up an Argentine tango, trailing lush-colored Indian draperies and partnering a slim little fellow in a chic white suit, a Panama hat, and a long white silk scarf, the smaller of the Spanish workers, while at the rear is Dwight Phillips, snapping his fingers and singing along with Pini, off-tune but at the top of his lungs, partnering the other worker, this one in a motoring cap, plus a long white silk scarf.

"Adiós muchachos," Pini sings.

He executes an exaggerated dip with his clumsy partner.

"Adiós muchachos," Dwight Phillips repeats.

"Compañeros de mi vida," Pini sings.

They are so enchantingly happy. Maddy longs to be with them, tangoing up the hill. She waves and throws kisses as she hasn't since she was back home.

"Compañeros de mi vida," Dwight Phillips repeats, and waves and throws kisses to Maddy.

"What idiots," Cleves says. "Nothing in their empty heads but amusing themselves."

And then, out of his need to be in the know about everything always, he supplies the information that "Adiós Muchachos" is all the rage back home at the moment.

An extraordinary manifestation occurs at the close of Vidhya's talk.

The speech itself is routine, except that it is delivered later in the day than is usual. Maddy's fault. Her absence has disturbed Vidhya; now he needs additional soothing time. Rested, nourished, she turns eagerly to fulfill the task of nursing the nervous little boy he becomes before an appearance.

He whines, he rages, he cries for a bit. They lie on his bed then, kissing, caressing, bringing each other to gratification. They sleep a tiny sleep. Together they rise, together they wash. Then they dress him. During the retreat, Vidhya has chosen exclusively Indian attire, and now he is wrapped in garments of creamy white. Very lightly, they review his speech. Then he applies finishing touches to his hair, kohl to his eyelids, and composes his face into a mask of beatitude. His eyes question Maddy's. Am I perfect?

"You're perfect," she assures him. "You are beautiful, serene, perfect."

Maddy rushes to dress herself: a white shirtwaist of Indian cloth styled in Western design. She subdues her extravagant hair under a plain white scarf. Sandals on her bare feet. No jewelry and no make-up. It is Bobo who has supervised the costuming. Everybody is to be in white. Maddy was not granted the honor of wearing a sari like the older women. She is not yet a part of the inner, *inner* circle. The scarf covering her hair is her individual touch, for which she has asked no permission.

They walk as a group, a shimmering of white, from the castle to the open encampment: Bobo, Lady Pansy, Lady Florence, Jag, Mr. Singh, Nityianda, Vidhya — and Maddy Brewster. Behind them come the young women, all dressed like Maddy, except for her head scarf: Milli, Daphne, Rosamund Keats, and young women representatives from the various European branches of the Society. Victoria is conspicuously missing. A group of Indian musicians follows. The tenderly solemn Indian music disperses into the heated air, mingles with the humming expectation of the immense crowd spread out before them, and draws in the pervasive sound of bells and the darker sound of the sea. All the movements of the group have been choreographed and rehearsed by Bobo. Maddy, Jag, Mr. Singh, and Nityianda detach themselves from the others and sit cross-legged on the ground before the first edge of the standing audience. The young women arrange themselves on the ground to another side. At a gesture from Bobo, the gathering seats itself in a great rustling, sighing exhalation. The leaders stand on the height from which Vidhya will speak.

Lady Florence greets the pilgrims. She is magnificent in her splendor, but babbles incoherently. Lady Pansy fades beside her and announces the final days' events in a voice so faint it is drowned by the wind. The instrumental music and the ringing of the bells gradually hush. It is a revelation to Maddy that the bells are not stopping of their own accord as Vidhya begins to speak, a miracle she had believed in up to that moment when she sees with her own eyes that Cleves, Conrad, Ram, and an assortment of young men are sheathing the tongues of the bells with wadding while Bobo introduces Vidhya. Then Vidhya begins.

"This morning when I awoke, I made my solitary way on the heights above the sea . . ."

The gathering listens in profound silence.

". . . A solitary bird joined me, solitary as myself . . ."

Only the sea still speaks, mingling its voice with Vidhya's.

Maddy has typed and retyped every word of Vidhya's talk, but what comes forth is newborn. God's sky turns itself inside out for Vidhya's dramatic backdrop. Vidhya becomes a darkened shadow outlined against the blinding gold of the late-afternoon sun, the light dazzling into indistinction the contours of a merely human face, the visionary eyes and the oracular, lushly carved lips, leaving bodiless words, *His Words*. As he speaks, the fire of the sun extinguishes itself in a plunge into melancholy. A thick band of indigo blue dominates, against which Vidhya's form shimmers into a transformation of a white angel. Now he exhorts in the name

of joy, of virtue, of peace and acceptance. A wild prodigality
of colors takes over the sky and burns on the earth and sea,
heir to the sun, already set. Vidhya has ended his talk. He
bows, raises his pressed palms to the pilgrims, then stretches
his body upward, head thrown back and arms extended to
the pulsating, charged sky. His white garments and black,
black hair swim with the current of warm wind blowing
from the sea, and as if part of this flow, the pilgrims rise to
their feet and rush toward Vidhya, flinging themselves on
the ground before him, chanting *the sun, the sun* (or *the
Son, the Son*), and the acolytes and pilgrims shout out the
glorious news and flow out to touch in adoration and to
make obeisance before the miraculous figure of *His Presence*
made manifest in Vidhya.

Some saw a vivid blue shaft of light envelop Vidhya.
Some said it was a column of ice; some said crystal. Some
saw Vidhya consumed by an orange flame. Some saw him
transformed into marble; some saw ash and swore it crum-
bled into petals. Some saw liquid gold pour from the sky.
Some saw a reverse fall, a river of gold flowing upward,
drawing Vidhya into the shifting mass of colors of the sunset. Some were entirely seized by their own sensation of
melting, dissolving, of fiery substances or icy elements
piercing their bodies — flame, ice, swords, trees, horns of
animals. What beasts had attacked? A unicorn, one young
woman swore.

And Maddy?

She is paralyzed with fear that she will be trampled to
death. Or Vidhya will be. She is strung on anxieties. Is she
part of the adorers, or part of the adored? How is she expected to perform? She has no directives, but if all the world
is bowing down before Vidhya, then surely Maddy Brewster must bow down.

Vidhya has been elevated to a pedestal covered with a
cloth of gold. Jag, Ram, Conrad, and Nityianda, in their
white garments, guard the four corners of the pedestal.

Has this manifestation been planned all along, without her knowledge?

Behind the stand on which Vidhya is enthroned, Lady Pansy and Lady Florence pose, their arms upraised, their white saris flowing gracefully in the hot wind. She has not seen them prostrate themselves, but she knows that they must have. Now Milli is kneeling before Vidhya, with Daphne directly behind her. She sees Rosamund Keats pushing her way through a crowd of pilgrims. None of the girls have covered their heads. Should she rip off her head scarf? She feels more devout with it on, and Bobo had not objected. Where is Bobo? Rosamund Keats has reached the pedestal and throws herself to the ground before it. She rises clumsily and joins the women behind Vidhya. Milli and Daph are already there, with upraised arms.

Maddy tells herself to hurry. She can no longer arrive *first* at Vidhya's feet, but she must at least arrive *soon*. She presses through the sweaty, delirious crowd, her fear of them subdued by the greater one that she will be left out of this singular occasion. In her desperation, she barges in with two overweight Dutch girls, volunteers at the first aid tent set up by the Dutch branch of the Society. They are adolescents, but immense for their age. The three collide in the act of going down full-face to the ground.

"Oh, I'm sorry," Maddy says.

The young girls are too exalted to notice her. They are chanting *the sun, the sun*, or perhaps *the Son, the Son*, their eyes fixed in adoration on Vidhya.

At the base of the pedestal are heaps of petals, clearly placed there for the purpose of sprinkling on Vidhya's feet, buried up to the ankles in flowers. Maddy grabs a handful when she rises and throws them. The wind returns them to her, spreading a marvelous scent of jasmine. She is too confused to even look at Vidhya. Those who have completed their genuflections are being directed away from the area by Cleves and two young men from the German branch, but Cleves shouts at Maddy and waves her the other way.

"Back there with the others, Maddy, back there," he says.

It is almost as if the women were a receiving line. They welcome her with rapt faces, streaming tears.

"He has come, He has come," Lady Florence says.

She kisses Maddy, holding her hard by her upper arms, and then passes her along to Lady Pansy, who clutches Maddy to her damp, hot bosom and seems unwilling to ever let go. She is sobbing and moaning.

"He has come, He has come," Lady Pansy says. "Oh, my child, He has come at last."

Maddy can't breathe. She is about to choke and expire on this lack of breath, when it bursts out in intense sobbing; she is gasping in air and sobbing out breath, uncontrollably.

"There, there," Lady Pansy says. "Here is Milli."

She turns her on Milli. Milli is shaking, sobbing, swaying, doubled over, her arms gripping her lower stomach, as in the throes of menstrual cramp. She lifts a terrified, ravaged face to Maddy and intones the same words.

"He has come, He has come, He has come, He has come . . ."

Her lips curl back from her prominent teeth like a crazy animal's. Maddy cradles Milli, rocking back and forth, crying with her, joining her in the chant. Daphne, sobbing and snuffling, clings to Maddy's back, kissing her head.

"He has come, He has come."

Daphne's chant screeches into hysteria. Rosamund Keats offers her open arms. They are steady and constrained, and her cheeks are dry.

"He has come," Rosamund says once, flatly.

"Yes," Maddy says.

"He has come, raise up your faces to Him."

It is the directorial voice of Bobo reminding them. Where is he? Nearby, under a tree, where it has become solid night. There is a broad band of purplish red and a heartbreaking streak of jeweled green in the rim of sky holding the daylight, but night has claimed the ground below.

Around the far edges of the site, torches light up the prayer banners decorating Vidhya's photograph and campfires illuminate the streams of pilgrims making their way back to their quarters. The bells have been unsheathed and add their faint ring to the music of the instruments. How smoothly this miracle unfolds.

Maddy obediently raises her face, and her arms, to Vidhya. From where she stands she sees only his back, the back she knows so well that she feels under her upraised palms the silk of its fleshy masculinity, the round buttocks, the long valley and the hard ridge of spine. She feels his black silky hair lifting in the wind. His hands that bring her to delight, raised in blessing over this vast community, rest upon her, grope inside her, loosening something, opening her out so that she lets go as if an organ is discharging itself from her body with a pain so overwhelming that she screams aloud.

"Aaaaagh!"

She screams and screams again and again and again. First for the loss of Vidhya, who is discharging himself from her body, and then for her father and mother and for her grandmother, in a series of terrible discharges, a ghastly litter of loss emerging from the center of her body. They stand a little apart from her, but in their real forms: Vidhya first — not the god upheld on the gold-cloth-covered platform before her, but her solid Vidhya she has embraced all over; and her father — not the stern lecturer of his letters, but the early loving father of her childhood, to whom she runs from the stoop on the block in the Bronx because he has brought her a present, a book, *Black Beauty*, as a reward for earning two A's and two A+'s on her report card, a good, smiling father, who leaves her hand in hand with her mother, sadly, gently waving good-by, arm in arm with Grandma, oddly all dressed up, as Maddy seldom saw her, in a longish skirt adorned with a fashionably gored hem so that it flares out as she walks away from Maddy, her head averted in infinite sorrow, pulling Maddy's mother away, out of the very center of Maddy's body, all, all leaving her in a gush of pain so intense she drops to the ground.

Maddy wakes in Vidhya's bed. She puts aside the troubling issues of finding herself in bed with Vidhya, given the significance of the events of last night. It is light outside and there is a confusion of noises, voices, movement, penetrating the room, but Vidhya is asleep, his head covered by his golden bare arms, and Maddy lies still. Through the open windows she distinguishes chanting: *Vidhya, Vidhya; the Son, the Son.* There is a knock at Vidhya's door. She startles at the prospect of being discovered in a scandalous situation, but Vidhya responds from behind his tent of crossed arms, calling out *enter,* and when Bobo does, followed by Ram and Jag, none of them exhibits surprise or horror. She congratulates herself on being fully dressed, in the clothes she wore last night, and on the good chance that she is lying on top of the covers. Vidhya is clearly naked, covered by a thin sheet. He unwinds his head, opens his red-rimmed, swollen eyes, flooded with anguish.

"Stay with me, Maddy, stay with me," he whispers.

She reassures him, and he drops his lids. There are heavy black rings under his eyes. Perhaps the kohl has run.

Bobo's directives are as much for Maddy as for Vidhya. Vidhya must be readied in order to bless the departure of the pilgrims. The retreat has been cut short. The abdication has created turmoil. There is trouble in the big cities with anarchist takeovers rumored in Barcelona and in nearby Almería, but Bobo declares these reports unreliable and exaggerated. Tourist ships in the port of Alicante stand by to take on American and British passengers. Foreign governments have been calling on their nationals to leave the country at once. Many of the European pilgrims have already left by train. The city of Alicante is functioning smoothly, actually in a holiday spirit of intense gaiety and excitement, Cleves has reported, recently returned from driving a group of younger pilgrims to the railroad station.

Bobo announces that the trip to the Middle East will now take place immediately. He is arranging passage for that night or the following one.

"Where are we going?" Vidhya asks.

"The trips we planned to make later in the summer," Bobo says. "Cairo, Jerusalem, Athens — the places we've promised you will appear — and, finally, the encampment in India."

Bobo speaks very carefully to Vidhya, as if contact with Vidhya contains a new and dangerous explosive now. And Vidhya explodes.

"Am I being punished? Is this a banishment?" Vidhya says.

He sits up, speaking with his lids cast down, unable or unwilling to look at Bobo.

"Banished?" Bobo says. "We're all going. We are all part of the same party.

"That was an extraordinary triumph last night," Bobo adds.

Through the window the pilgrims call, *Vidhya, Vidhya,* and Bobo creates an inclusive gesture, wrapping together that sound outside and Vidhya on the bed.

"Jag tells me we have never raised so much so quickly," Bobo says.

Vidhya laughs, then claps both hands over his mouth. The scene, as a sequel to last night's manifestation, strikes Maddy as so inappropriate it is bizarre, much like her ludicrous sprawled position, which a paralyzing shyness makes her incapable of changing. Ram and Jag seem as much at sea as she is. They stand behind Bobo, absolutely still, their faces expressionless in the wiped-clean cover-up adopted by servants.

"I must have time, I must have time," Vidhya yells. "I

must sort out my thoughts. Do you want to see me collapse?"

"No," Bobo says.

The patriarchal old man and the golden young man stare into each other's face. Bobo rubs a trembling hand over his forehead, down his beak of a nose, and lets the hand rest, gently pulling on his white beard. Has this gesture inflamed Vidhya? His eyes bulge with craziness. He rises to his knees. For a moment, he is naked, the entire golden torso exposed, but he seizes the thin sheet and wraps it about himself closely, tucking it in to cover his groin.

"I must have time to think and to recuperate. I am tired, very tired. I must sort out what has happened to me. I must think about my future. I am not anybody's puppet."

Maddy has seized the moment to stand up, close to the bed, her head down and her face composed into blankness, like Ram's and Jag's.

"What is it?" Bobo says. "What is it you want?"

"Maddy must be with me — for my work," Vidhya says.

Bobo nods.

"And Rosamund," Vidhya says.

Again a nod.

"And I wish to be incommunicado to everybody on this trip. To everybody. I do not tolerate everybody barging in whenever they please. I must think. I must think and prepare myself and study. If I am to be what I am to be, then I must study how to be that. Otherwise I shall collapse, I warn you. I am very, very tired."

"There comes a point" — Bobo speaks with great deliberation — "when one must consider that perhaps one's material is too intractable to mold into shape. One must seriously contemplate . . ."

"What?" Vidhya explodes. "What? Who is this 'one'? This mysterious 'one'? Do you believe in me or not? You, yourself, tell me."

215

"Absolutely," Bobo says. His voice is rich and caressing, as only Bobo can make it. "I saw your remarkable aura. I found you. I love you. Remember?"

"Of course I remember," Vidhya says. "But what have I said that is wrong? I cannot be watching every word in that way. What was wrong with what I said?"

"There are obligations to be met in Athens and Jerusalem. We can skip Cairo if you insist, but Athens and Jerusalem —"

"Yes, yes, yes," Vidhya says, "all that is perfectly in order, I understand, that wasn't what I meant at all, I recognize my obligations and promises."

"Well, good," Bobo says. "We have a perfect understanding, then, and everything will be splendid. And now, the pilgrims. They won't leave without your blessing."

He glances at Maddy significantly, indicating that she is to hurry Vidhya along. Bobo turns his back, but Jag stands with his head bowed and palms clasped, clearly asking for a blessing. In confusion, all follow suit, Maddy, Ram, even Bobo. There is nothing for Vidhya to do but bless them in the gesture he invented the night before, but when the door closes on the three men, he slumps into a condition of despair so wild Maddy is afraid to step in to console.

"I cannot," he moans. "I cannot."

But he does everything he is supposed to.

Victoria comes by the bridge over the moat, the scene of the blessing, looking not for Vidhya or his services but for Maddy. She asks Maddy to come away with her for a walk on the beach, where they can be alone and talk.

"I'm going," Victoria says. "I'm leaving today."

She means *going, leaving;* she is departing from the Society for good. Like Nityianda.

"For good," she says, "it can only be for good. What a relief to turn my back, to finish with Bobo's mumbo jumbo, all of it, Vidhya's tricks and Lady Pansy's hysteria. I wash my hands of all of it. See, I literally wash my hands of it."

216

They are on the edge of a flat, slanting slab, a granite runway dipping into the sea, where Victoria crouches, wetting her hands in the warm green-blue water.

"How could I have hung around this long?" she says. "Because I was afraid, not ready to go out on my own. Because it was easier to stay, everything I needed given to me, everything taken care of by the Society. Does that disgust you?"

"I don't believe it," Maddy says. "You were learning a lot. I saw you doing that."

"Sure," Victoria says. "It was rotten opportunism on my part. I should disgust you. But I'm through, forever."

"Was it last night?"

"Oh, last night," Victoria says, and laughs.

"You don't believe in — last night?"

"Are you kidding?" Victoria says. "You can't be serious."

"I don't know what to think," Maddy says. "I'm going to tell you something that you mustn't tell anybody. Vidhya and I are secretly engaged."

Victoria bursts out laughing.

"Don't do that," Maddy says. "I'm sorry I told you."

"So am I," Victoria says. "Now I won't have a moment's peace. I worry about you. Are you going along on this Mideast trip?"

"Vidhya wouldn't go without me," Maddy says. "He loves me."

"They did something bad to him, Maddy, they disconnected him at his center."

"Me, too," Maddy says. "That happened to me, too."

Victoria shakes her head.

"You're only eighteen. He's a grown man, he's almost twenty-one . . ."

After a pause, she begins again.

"Listen, Maddy, I'll always let you know where I am. If you need someone. I'll write care of the Center in England so that wherever you are . . ."

"I'll be fine," Maddy says.

"Are you sure?" Victoria says.

They have been strolling up the beach along the water's edge. Beyond the granite slope they have descended to a thin crescent of brownish sand where bathers gather to swim these hot afternoons, but it is noon and the tiny shell-shaped beach is empty. On the overhanging hill above, a boy no more than a child has driven his herd of goats to the edge of the cliff, where they mill about, a charming grouping in black, gray and white, the cry of the goats beguiling against the sea's murmur. There is a sudden rushing noise of water, then a descending flood of putrid stuff, emitted from an open pipe.

"Shit!" Victoria yells.

And so it is, shit, pouring down with other garbage and a light cargo of grayish deflated little balloons. Victoria scrambles back to the safety of the granite height, leading Maddy along.

"What is it?" Maddy says.

Maddy is trembling. She wants to cry and to vomit. The smell, the sight, the violence of this onslaught are too disgusting.

"What is it?" Maddy says again.

"Shit!" Victoria repeats.

"But what is it? Is it coming from the goats?"

"It's our shit," Victoria says. "Goats — why, goats could never . . . The latrines are cleaned out every day at this hour. Why didn't I remember that?"

"Ours?" Maddy says. "What do you mean? And what are all those little balloons?"

Victoria looks at Maddy sharply, then bursts out laughing.

"I never knew I could be so amusing," Maddy says. "Why are you laughing *now*?"

"Never seen a condom? What do you do, keep your eyes closed all the time?"

Through some mental telegraphy, Maddy comprehends

what a condom is used for, though in fact she has never seen one. The mucky stream empties itself into the innocent green-blue sea, the bulky mass sinking quickly but the little balloons, the *condoms*, stay afloat, sailing about in sad little whirling dances before going under in the rising tide.

"But there are so many," Maddy says. "Millions of them."

"Hundreds, surely," Victoria says. "The only activity that could possibly top last night's show is screwing. So everybody screwed."

She is scrambling up the hill using a shorter, easier path than the one they had used coming down, a trail leading to the main road below the castle.

"Let's get away from this stink," she says. "We'll walk back along the main road."

She stops short.

"Wait a minute," she says. "Doesn't that bastard use anything? If you don't know what a condom is, what the fuck is he doing, anyway?"

Maddy cringes from this crude onslaught into what she and Vidhya do, how they do it, secret matters she cannot look straight in the face. Is she ashamed of their lovemaking? No. But panic attends the exposure of love to clinical examination, to *condoms*; and that Victoria should be her interrogator is more shocking than the gush of shit and garbage and condoms from the open pipe.

"I can't say I understand your need for men in your life, but at least I accept it, that you insist on your very own set of cock and balls. What I can't accept is ignorance. Don't you know how to protect yourself? Do you want your whole life smashed? Want to wake up one morning pregnant at eighteen and by Vidhya, for God's sake, of all the men in the world . . ."

"I'm perfectly safe," Maddy says, but so low that she must repeat it for Victoria to hear her. "Love is more than . . . love isn't only . . ." Maddy adds.

They have reached the blacktop road now, empty of

cars or any other vehicles, its tarred surface steaming in the heat. Far up ahead, an unidentifiable object wavers toward them.

"Ah, yes," Victoria says, "do tell me about love."

The word *sex* sticks in Maddy's throat, but she gets it out in a rush.

"Love isn't only sex."

Victoria again comes to a full stop.

"You've been seduced by spiritual baloney, haven't you — the higher manifestations of love, all that garbage necessary to neurotic, repressed women like Lady Pansy. Is that what's happened to you?"

She takes Maddy's face in her hands, forcing Maddy to look directly into her hooded eyes. Her long neck gives to her head the authority of a queen's.

"What do you want me to do?" Maddy says.

At that moment, she is ready to do anything Victoria says, follow her to the end of the earth, however unhappy she might be, however much a failure, however lost in Victoria's power and brilliance.

"They have their own reasons, these daffy English, because of their obsession with India. It has nothing to do with us. Come home, come home where we belong."

"With you?" Maddy says.

Victoria drops her hands, strides on, leaving Maddy to catch up.

"You think I'm jealous of that bastard's penis? You think all this is because I'm trying to win you back? I just don't want you to ruin your life. I don't hate men, I've nothing against men, even sexually. I've screwed them, they're okay. Women are lovelier, that's all. They are. But I don't want anything from you that isn't there. It isn't that, it's that I worry about you — you're so soft, you pull like homemade taffy wherever you're yanked."

Surely Victoria pummels and pulls her about as much as anybody? Maddy makes an effort to keep her voice soft.

She doesn't want to quarrel with Victoria just before they are to separate.

"Don't call him names," Maddy says.

"I'll call him anything I damn please. He may be some kind of god to you, but he's skinny little Vidhya to me. I've known him too long."

"You do want to harm me," Maddy says. "You want to shake me in my faith."

Victoria stops walking to stare at her in disbelief.

"Your faith? In what? Vidhya? The Society? Bobo and his Astral journeys, his higher-consciousness theories of exaltation, better known as mutual masturbation?"

"Stop it," Maddy says.

"Are you really looking for something genuine here?"

"Weren't you?" Maddy says.

"Of course. But I knew when I didn't find it," Victoria says. "I stayed because I had no place to go. I had nothing but wild ambition. The Society took care of me. Lady Florence encouraged me. Mrs. Dasinov staked me. Nothing to do with faith."

"Where would I go?"

"Anywhere. Anywhere in the world. You even have a little money."

"I want to do good," Maddy says. "I want to be good. I want to make the world a better place, leave my mark on it, like Lady Florence."

"Lady Florence!"

"Yes. Yes. She's worked hard to fight poverty, and injustice. Don't sneer at her and her efforts. She's struggled against the violence and cruelty she found in the world. She didn't have to. She was rich and secure and settled. That's faith. Faith to change the hearts and souls of men and women and slowly, slowly change the world. That's what Vidhya wants. And he can do it. He has the power. You saw that last night, we all saw it."

She is firing up the faint glow of conviction simmering

at the heart of her faith, making it blaze for herself as much as for Victoria, who is staring in disbelief.

"I know that evil exists, that it lives in our hearts and, yes, even in the Society, in Society individuals, anyway. But that doesn't negate the good in the ideal. One must fight harder, struggle harder, to be worthy."

She holds back on expressing the supreme exaltation she experiences at a further thought. What if Vidhya is truly *He*? What an extraordinary gift, what a blessed fate to be singled out to serve *Him*, to assist *Him* in *His* labors for the sake of all humanity.

"Poor Maddy," Victoria says.

"I'm not poor," Maddy says in a rage. "I'm rich. I'm happy. I'm a million times happier loving Vidhya than I would be loving some ordinary stupid person. I'd rather be in my shoes, believing in something, working for something I believe in, than leading a silly, empty life, striving . . . for what — ambition, fame, fortune."

"Is that what you think of me?" Victoria says. "And of my work?"

"No, no," Maddy retreats. "I know you have higher aims, in your work —"

"Nothing like Vidhya's, though."

"You don't understand Vidhya," Maddy says. "He suffers. He's in agony. Right now."

"Oh God, let's not talk about Vidhya anymore," Victoria says.

They walk on, silent now, coming closer and closer to the strange bobbling object moving toward them. Then Maddy begins again, hoping to appease Victoria before they part.

"What are you going to do?" Maddy says. "Where will you go?"

"I didn't think you gave a damn," Victoria says.

"How can you say that?" Maddy says. "I love you. I love your work. It's important, it's marvelous, it's unique.

The world must have what you produce, it's starving for your work."

Victoria is clearly pleased. She puts her arm around Maddy, and her voice is rich with gratitude, though she pretends to mock Maddy.

"Oh, what do *you* know?" Victoria says, smiling. "You're my friend. Naturally you think I'm great."

She launches into the kind of talk she loves to bounce off Maddy — plans, places, projects.

"Paris is first on my list. Shankar is there performing now and I must see him again. But I don't want to stay. I want to get home as quickly as possible. To New York. I can't wait to get to work where I belong. I've wasted so many years, not entirely wasted, of course, but not properly narrowed in on what should have been first . . . I'm going to be the greatest dancer of our time. I am. Nobody is doing what I do . . ."

But Maddy's attention is split between what Victoria is saying and the odd shape advancing toward them, more and more clearly defining itself as a huge moving pile of barren twigs, an arching fan of the kind of debris their yard boy in Iowa City would clear out of trees and shrubs in the early spring or late fall: dead brush, brittle and sweet smelling, to be burned in a ritual of blue smoke and rich scents at the edge of the lawn. It seems to proceed of its own power, jogging and wobbling forward, until it is close enough for Maddy to see that a very old man is at the center of the burden, bent so that his back flattens to accommodate the unwieldy mass. It is tied to his body with an old rope trailing in an unraveling tangle, and he helps support the load by extending his arms and curving his hands upward, while he holds his head upright at an excruciatingly uncomfortable angle to see where he's going.

Victoria, too, is stopped by the sight.

"What an effect," she says. "I have to use that. I know exactly where I can use that image. And the face, the face.

He's old enough to have been here with the Phoenicians. He's a figure on a vase, the wall of a tomb."

She bends over, extends her back into a table, copying the old man's carriage, the awkward position of his head, the legs splayed like a weak animal's, the arms extended in their painful clutch, copying also the agony in the dim eyes, adding each formally composed bit until she feels it complete, then loosens her limbs and grounds her feet on the earth, turning everyday tragedy into a dancer's formal stance, fluid and strong. Jogging past them with his wobbling gait, the old man shifts his pupils into the extreme corners of his eyes, trying to keep the two women in his sight as long as possible. Then he is past them. They continue their separate ways, until Victoria turns and shouts out the current slogan she has picked up from Pini and his political friends.

"Viva la República, viejo, viva la República."

From the surprising distance the old man has already traveled beyond them, he returns a thin corrective cry.

"Viva la humanidad," he calls, once only.

I I

THEIR part in the demonstration was disintegrating.
The action had gotten too big, too dangerous; the
organizing committee was nervous about letting
them participate further. And a plane hijacking had occurred,
still another one, with more than seventy Americans onboard. The number was still not clear, nor who the hijackers
were, or their motives and demands, but between the two
uproars, the old people's little attention ploy was getting lost
in the shuffle.

Why chance their safety or their frail health? The plans
were altered. Bernard Lewis, in the care of Arthur Brownson, was placed in a limo and driven to Kittery Point, where
he lived. Arthur Brownson would spend a day or so with
him until his housekeeper returned. Only Maddy and Dwight
Phillips would go on to the UN session. Victoria Younger
was returning to her New York apartment.

They were put on a shuttle flight to New York, traveling three abreast in a space barely adequate for one, as an
outraged Victoria made clear to the entire plane. Dwight fell
asleep as soon as he was buckled in, and Maddy settled into

the discomfort of her middle position between Dwight's spreading limbs and hanging head and Victoria's animation. Fortunately, Boston to New York was a short flight.

Maddy would have preferred the window seat, always, even when there was "nothing to see," a phrase she rejected. There was something to see even if it was nothing but the dark or white blankness. At the moment the view was charming. Past Victoria she looked out on brilliant sunlight above and a solid bank of white clouds ranged like the Alps below the plane. She liked the sense of false solidity the dense white clouds conveyed; they might well form a plateau for the plane to rest on in an emergency.

She cut into Victoria's outrage at the airline's poor accommodations.

"Remember the Spanish encampment? When Vidhya was made manifest as the Messiah?"

"Oh, that mess," Victoria said.

"Do you think the Society planned the event in advance? I could never figure it out."

"No," Victoria said. "Bobo's genius for seizing the moment. And Vidhya's. Never underestimate Vidhya."

"Oh, I don't," Maddy said.

Victoria handed her a mint.

"For the ears," she said, "until we're properly aloft. They used to hand out chewing gum and cunning little toffee candies, but they don't do a thing these days."

"We've been aloft for ten minutes," Maddy said. "What moment?"

"The commotion started with some villagers dashing in to tell those two guys — remember the anarchists we were hiding? — that Alfonso Trece had abdicated . . ."

Dwight, startled awake by the shuddering of the plane as it entered the cloud bank, instantly embarked on a little lecture.

"Alfonso Trece, a playboy, yes, but he understood the inevitability of the formation of the Republic, he understood the needs of his country and valued the progress of his nation above his own selfish interests, and he wisely stepped down. That was a period during which all of Europe might have successfully entered into the era of socialism, a democratic socialism that could have spared the world the horrors of the Spanish Civil War, the Second World War, the Holocaust. If the Weimar Republic had succeeded, think of the suffering averted — think of the Jews alone —"

"Oh God, can't you turn him off?" Victoria said.

And then, as he continued, she began a harangue to accompany his.

"Let's inject a little reality, now, shall we? Some reminders here, like the Hitler-Stalin pact and the archipelago, Zhdanov and artistic freedom, Afghanistan and the whole unbelievable attitude toward the Jews — Can't they just be allowed to emigrate, if they want to. What barbarity to keep anyone from living where they wish to live . . ."

"Could we save comments for the question period, please?"

Dwight, at his most mannerly.

A well-groomed man passing through the aisle stopped to listen and look for a moment, then smiled as if at a trio of children and moved on.

"Where was I?" Dwight said, reaching out for Maddy.

"We're on a shuttle plane to New York," Maddy said. "Go back to sleep."

Victoria said, "I can't believe how he goes on and on making the same speech over and over. Like Vidhya . . ."

She turned her head away from Maddy to address her more intimately.

"Vidhya's the real reason you involved us in this preposterous event. You wanted to see him, to confront him."

"Confront. What a word. I want to see Vidhya. Look at him and talk to him. Not *confront* him. Anyway, I won't. He's in Hartford, starving himself to death."

"Fat chance," Victoria said.

"But you said . . ."

"Want to bet he'll be at the UN, holding forth?"

Victoria went into her Vidhya routine, mixed English and Indian accent, the voice unutterably sweet, resonant, and delicately monotonous.

"The great conflagrations raging across our Mother Earth begin in the individual breast. First we must tame the violence in the individual breast. From the fount of the human heart peace will come to the cosmos, to the Earth, to the country and to the individual town and village, into the home and into the breast of man, from which it all began. First we must conquer the terrible violence that shakes our individual hearts, then violence in the world at large will come to an end. Think of the wonders that bring us together, our shared Earth, our shared heavens, our one God, no matter what our religion. Let us learn to live like the human brothers and sisters we —"

"You do that very well, you know," Maddy said with real admiration. "But what's wrong with his philosophy. Given our world."

"If you don't know yet . . ." Victoria said. "It's bullshit. À la mode. That's what's wrong with it."

"Why are we so querulous?" Maddy said. "We used to be able to talk. Now we only seem to quarrel."

"We *always* fought. We were never able to talk. You like to tell yourself fairy tales."

Victoria pauses, then begins again, in a whisper, a signal to Maddy that this is a serious quarrel indeed.

"You want me to act your lover till we're both dead and buried. I'm not your lover. We were never lovers. I love you, I loved you, I'll always love you, but that's not what you want, and I will not act the fool for you."

"Is that what you think I want?"

"Yes, yes, yes. You want adoration under the pretense that it's all good health and worthy relationships."

"And you? What do you want?"

There was fury in Victoria's amazingly young eyes.

"Everything. I want everything, just as I did when I was seventeen," Victoria said. "That's the most dismaying aspect of growing old, that I go right on wanting, wanting, wanting everything, everything I had earlier and everything I missed out on. Now that there's little chance, I want more than ever . . . everything, damn it, everything."

"Listen," Maddy said, in a rush of close feeling, "I've been wanting to tell you something for a long time now. I'm Jewish. I want you to know I'm Jewish. Both parents, both grandparents, both sets. I'm completely Jewish."

"Oh, for Christ's sake," Victoria said, so loudly that there was a general stir of interest around them. "That again. Do you know how many times you've confided in me that you're really Jewish? Who cares? Everybody's Jewish. Between the conversions and the assimilations and the intermarriages and the rapes, everybody's Jewish. The Nazis cared and now the orthodox Jews care. But why the fuck should you care? I certainly don't. Unless you're looking for excessive admiration. One of the chosen. I don't go for that, either. Whatever happened to the spirit of universal brotherhood and sisterhood."

"When did I tell you? I never —"

"Dozens of times. Good God, I can't even remember all the different times, except maybe the first, I think it was the first, that Christmas in the early forties before the war. You swore us to secrecy, me and Dwight, and then later that same evening you told Arthur Brownson and made him swear, too. It was at Arthur Brownson's place in Boston, with that great view of the Charles, when he was still lighting his Christmas tree with live candles, remember, and serving fresh pork with roasted onions for Christmas dinner instead of that boring turkey, and you and Dwight ate only vegetables and cranberry sauce, you fools . . ."

The public address system crackled into speech announcing the approach to La Guardia, but in fact they circled for twenty minutes before landing, during which Maddy ate the mints Victoria handed out and maintained a surly silence.

12

BOBO managed to book passage on what had been a small French luxury liner, now badly gone to seed. Lady Pansy worried that the ship wasn't seaworthy. The cabins, generous only in their allotments of space and roaches, also boasted a washbasin, but the bath was down the passageway, locked, and its facilities made available only following complicated negotiations with the steward. There were common toilets in the passageway as well, men's and women's, which after a day or two smelled and ran over and ran out of tissue. There were finer staterooms and worse ones, but no classes onboard. The decks were shared by all passengers.

Of their party, Vidhya, Bobo, Lady Pansy, and the Voynows had the best cabins, with attached baths and adjoining deck terraces, where they were able to keep entirely to themselves. In a large cabin on a lower deck, Maddy had one of four berths with Milli, Daph, and Rosamund. She was lucky. They let her have the berth with the big round porthole directly above it, and she spent much of her time watching the sea splash at the rim of the opening, the water dirtied by their yellow wake. Ugly seagulls trailed the ship's garbage. She took in these sights at her eye-level post, sitting cross-legged on the sagging mattress, escaping the forced companionship of her bunkmates, lulled and mesmerized, substituting a kind of contemplation for the required meditation.

She longed to be alone, in spite of a feeling of isolation to a point of illness, a chronic case, terminal, fatal. She saw very little of Vidhya, and after a day and a half of cross-legged hypnotic contemplation, she dressed and explored the public spaces of the ship. There was charm to its run-down, passé elegance, an old lady clinging to past prettiness, unable to keep a brisk pace, and, though perfumed, smelling a little bad from insufficient washing.

Settled into a deck chair, Maddy interested herself in the ship's passengers: an elderly American foursome, Mid-westerners on a tour of the world; a large group of German tourists, seeming even larger because of their clothes and their voices and their laughter; and a party of French, actually more numerous than the Germans, but paling beside them, except on the dance floor, where every afternoon and evening they crowded in to move about in tight circles to the music of the dreary little orchestra that did so badly by the new American songs, endlessly repeated, "Ain't Misbehavin' " and "All of Me" and the outdated "Yes, We Have No Bananas."

And there was a larger group of young Americans, Jews on their way to settle in Palestine. They, too, crowded onto the dance floor, making hash of the formalities of the French, singing along with the orchestra in mocking sentimentality and sexy innuendo, until someone spoke to their leader, or whoever he was, an older man, described to Maddy as a well-known theoretician and activist in the Zionist movement, Zalman Weingartner, tall, good-looking, very suave, who persuaded them to leave the dance floor to those who took it seriously. They gathered instead on a lower deck to sing Yiddish and Hebrew folk songs and dance in a circle of linked commitment and athletic exuberance. Maddy watched, smiling and clapping along with the beat. Zalman Weingartner wanted her to think about joining a kibbutz in Palestine and spent hours of the next few days proselytizing. She listened, smiling and nodding, her arms resting on the railing of the ship, the sea air caressing and warm, the color of the water full of promise. She did not respond in substance until they were nearing Naples.

"I didn't know you accepted non-Jews," she said.

He looked at her for a long space, during which she felt compelled to look back. There was nothing grossly Jewish about him, whatever she meant by that. He was fair-skinned, freckled, blue-eyed, blond, with a small, somewhat pug nose and a ready, full-toothed smile. The nationality he would immediately be assigned anywhere at a moment's glance was American.

"Actually," he said, "we do. But . . . I did take you for a Jew. Shall I apologize?"

"I wonder why," she said.

"Because you look so much like my niece," he said. "And because you told me you were bound for Palestine."

He paused for a moment. His manner had grown distant.

"Or were you asking about the apology."

"No, no, of course not, don't think of it . . ."

She was blushing, in a stupid confusion, ashamed and irritated. Why didn't he leave her alone, for God's sake.

Like a trolley, the ship advanced at a crawl, pulling into different ports every day. At one, they took on a group of English soldiers, at another a contingent of French. The English were got-up in ridiculous little-boy uniforms, like Boy Scouts; the French in ridiculous costume-drama outfits. They were bunched into two isolated units, eyeing the young women on deck but making no move toward them.

At these stops, passengers were restricted to the ship,

but Maddy stood at the rail to watch the life of the port and try to penetrate the city beyond. On the gangplank, men like the old man on the road in Alicante picked up and carried burdens to the hold of the ship, an endless line of men, endless bags of burdens, an endless series of bent backs.

They anchored in the Bay of Naples for two nights and a day. Vesuvias blinked its homey light. Of the group, only Maddy and Rosamund had never seen Pompeii. To broaden the young women's knowledge of the world, the Voynows would accompany them on a trip to the famous buried city. Vidhya, who had seemed buried by his own concerns, wanted to join them.

The trip became Vidhya's game. He planned and blocked the outing as if it were one of his public appearances. The girls must wear white. He appeared on deck in a white flannel suit and Panama hat, looking thinner and darker but quite dashing. Rosamund and Maddy, like schoolgirls in uniform, wore matching white shirtwaists, their manifestation outfits, the only white garment each owned.

The city of Naples was a disappointment close up; it had seemed so airy and charming from the harbor, a string of delicate lights, but inside its heart, it stank, it was unbearably hot, and everywhere too many preposterously costumed soldiers, or policemen, whichever they were, too many flags, posters, banners, pictures of Mussolini, and within this bustle of officiousness, an oppressive quiet.

They went directly to Pompeii by cab, since the city virtually closed down during siesta. At the site, more officiousness from costumed officers, messing up the simplest entrances and exits of the tourists. Then at last they were in. She had harbored no advance expectations of this outing, other than a chance to break free of the monotony of the ship's journey and the constant companionship of Milli, Daph, and the uncommunicative Rosamund. If she had hoped for anything, it would have been for some true contact with Vidhya, anything sound and real enough to be of comfort. But though he was certainly there with them, holding one of Maddy's arms and one of Rosamund's, riding between them in a sort of preening victory of the success of his composition in white, his presence was patently false, a representation, one of his appearances, and Vidhya, the Vidhya of their intimacies, continued to hold himself as aloof as he had been since boarding the ship.

But apart from the miserable little museum with its charred bodies, she was enchanted with Pompeii. Not with the actual remains so much as with the sense of this city, ruined but still *there*, still *here*, intact, itself, reconstructing itself into its streets and houses. Wonderfully aromatic grasses pushed through its smashed tiles, lizards darted away from the disturbances of the tourists, the air was fresh and sweet smelling and God's light smiled down on the ancient paths. She broke free of Vidhya's grasp and tried to put distance between herself and the Voynows, intent on imparting book information, like Daddy, and bickering in a husband-and-wife fashion over details and sources.

"There is a most fascinating account, by Tacitus, I believe, of a sport's event some twenty years before the eruption, which ended in a riot. The spectators fought bitterly, the people of Pompeii against the visiting townspeople of Nuceria, because of the games between the two towns held here in Pompeii. Fists, taunts, stone-throwing, and, in the end, swords. Many died."

"Tacitus?" Mrs. Voynow said, her hands beginning to quiver. "Surely you mean Pliny the Younger? Tacitus stops well before the eruption."

"I clearly indicated that I was speaking of a period at least ten to twenty years *before* the eruption," Mr. Voynow said, "but in her usual fashion, my dear wife prefers to dispute my facts. This event of which I speak occurred years before the earthquake that demolished much of Pompeii, more than ten years before the eruption, and the point I was trying to make to Maddy was to emphasize certain similarities within our own society and the gross —"

"I never heard of any of that," Mrs. Voynow said, her hands quaking violently now. "Are you quite sure of your sources?"

Mr. Voynow was so upset, he stammered.

"It is no news to anybody, my dear wife, that your education suffers from a number of blanks. Latin is certainly one of them. It has always been a source of wonder to me what you girls were taught during those years you spent at that women's institution of so-called learning you attended . . ."

"How dare you speak to me in that tone!" Mrs. Voynow said.

"Maddy, I appeal to you," Mr. Voynow said.

But Maddy had turned away from them, acutely embarrassed by this passionate quarrel between two people who should have considered themselves far too ancient to display passion of any kind. They were spoiling the sweetness of this experience, the intense awareness of then and now, the closeness alive on the ancient paths between her feet and the ground, between her hands and the old stones she picked up and rubbed between her fingers, between the skin of her face and the soft, hot air that fanned it, connections beyond Mr. and Mrs. Voynow's comprehension, safe from the explanation in any book of history written in Latin a million years ago, a continuation linking then and now in the blood of her veins so that she knew at that moment and would know forever that she was indeed immortal, as immortal as the sweet grass growing between the ancient shards of tile under her sandaled foot.

Mr. Voynow was insistent, following Maddy and grasping her by the arm.

"Town life was brutal and disorderly. Promiscuity and degradation throve in an atmosphere of such profound immorality that chastity, modesty, the barest vestiges of human decency could not survive. There are structures back there" — he waved a hand vaguely — "you are not permitted to enter that are shockingly brutal in their graphic depiction of the sexual mores of the day."

Rosamund came running toward them across an open space. Her usually flushed coloring had been drained from her face.

"Come," she said. "Vidhya. I don't know what . . . I can't . . ."

They found Vidhya in a corner of broken wall in what had been a courtyard. He had frozen into position, his open eyes fixed downward where a gathering of grayish lizards lay strangely immobilized at his feet. Vidhya's lips were blue, as if his heart were losing function.

"What's wrong with him?" Mr. Voynow said.

"What's wrong? What's the matter with him?" Mrs. Voynow echoed.

"I turned and saw him, suddenly, in that state, just as he is. I couldn't move him, he doesn't seem to hear or to see," Rosamund said. "I've been trying and trying. I can't think what's happened to him."

"Perhaps the lizards frightened him," Mrs. Voynow said, tentatively.

"We'll get rid of those in a shake," Mr. Voynow said.

He stooped, picked up a handful of stones, and threw them wildly, as a child might. The lizards scattered instantly, disappearing under the remains of the wall.

"It wasn't the lizards," Rosamund said. "The lizards gathered after Vidhya had been standing there for a bit. They came like pilgrims to make obeisance. It was uncanny."

"Why didn't you come for us at once?" Mrs. Voynow said. "You should have come to us at once."

"I was trying to talk to him, to convince him he could move."

"What were you doing back here?" Mr. Voynow said. "There's nothing of interest back here."

236

"We were looking for that other villa, the Villa of the Mysteries, and out of nowhere Vidhya was seized by this odd fit. He put himself into that corner and went rigid, utterly rigid, and didn't answer to anything I said. I was afraid to leave him here alone. And then that strange congregation of lizards formed and I became terrified, it was all too strange, too strange . . . I heard your voices nearby and ran to tell you," she said.

Without a plan, or even a clear intention, Maddy went up close to Vidhya. She was improvising, as she might in one of their games, and, responding, he lifted his eyes imperceptibly. They were lighter, more transparent than ever because of the brilliant sunlight falling across his face. Did he wink? She thought she saw one eye blink in a mocking signal that was gone in an instant.

"Vidhya," she whispered. "Come back to us, please."

He shuddered. He raised his arms and crossed them on his chest in an uncharacteristic pose.

"He moved," Rosamund said. "Oh, thank God."

"I have been here," Vidhya said.

"Yes," Maddy said.

She put out an arm for him to grasp, and unfolding his hands he took one of hers.

"I shall come again," Vidhya said.

"Yes," Maddy said.

She offered herself for him to lean on and he did, slumping and dragging himself. In his rakish white outfit he could have been a drunken playboy. His Panama hat slid to one side of his head, and, as if he were a drunk, she led him away, indicating to Rosamund to support his other side.

What was wrong with Vidhya? Bobo, seeking help from the Elders, brought back messages that Vidhya's states of mind and body were not connected with the high mission to which he had been appointed. The Elders could not account for his physical and spiritual anguish. Lady Pansy became fixed on epilepsy as an explanation for Vidhya's condition and insisted on a visit from the ship's doctor, a small, round, fussy Frenchman with a pencil mustache. Vidhya loathed him on sight. The doctor ordered aspirin every four hours and an immediate change to a meat diet.

"I wouldn't trust a cat to his care," Vidhya said.

Vidhya now fell frequently into one of his immobile states, lying on his back and staring at the ceiling, where a reflection from light on the sea outside his stateroom danced and glimmered.

He was guarded around the clock. Jag watched over Vidhya at night; Maddy, Rosamund, and Lady Pansy took turns during the day and evening. There were a dozen alarms daily: acute pain, onslaughts of rigidity, blindness, failure to hear. Though he complained of excessive cold and then of heat, the thermometer readings showed no variations from normal limits. Yet symptoms continued and multiplied: headaches, clanging noises in his ears, cramps moving from one part of his body to another, stabbing stomach pains.

Mr. Singh's diagnosis was brain fever.

It was Vidhya himself who convinced them that his state was entirely spiritual, part of the preparation for the role the Elders in their wisdom had assigned him. He was in the hands of a power greater than any of them had ever encountered or indeed imagined, the Power that had shown itself on the heights of Alicante and that had come again on the heights of Pompeii. If this Power brought agony and suffering, it also brought the promise of the fulfillment of their hopes. They must submit to its mystery and to its authority, to its anguish and to its glory, to its pain and to its exaltation.

"But we only want to help you," Lady Pansy said. Tears formed in her colorless eyes. "Surely this great and good Power would want your friends to help you."

"I must endure this test alone. It is my time of preparation and testing," Vidhya said. "I must endure it alone."

The problem was Bobo. Bobo wasn't going along with Vidhya's version of the events. For every message that Bobo brought back from the Elders, Vidhya returned with a contradictory one. And then there was the powerful weapon of Vidhya's fits. Vidhya said his piece, and if Bobo's reaction displeased him, he would go off into one of his trancelike states. Difficult to sustain an argument under such conditions.

Bobo withdrew from open confrontations. In private conversations he warned that Vidhya's so-called Power exhibited all the earmarks of a Dark Force masquerading as a good one.

"If I can't understand these mysterious manifestations," Bobo said, "and the Elders cannot enlighten me, what are we to make of his claims?"

He gazed into one's eyes earnestly when he spoke, stroking his soft beard, gently and considerately persuasive. He lost his temper only once, shouting Vidhya down when Vidhya insisted that the Elders had assured him he must pursue the difficult path on which he had been placed and that they alone would inform him when his preparation was complete.

"I wash my hands of this whole damned mess —" Bobo said and then stopped himself from using an unfortunate image.

Some of the party fell into Vidhya's camp, some into Bobo's. They all tried to keep the lines wavery and misty. Ram, Jag, Rosamund, Lady Pansy, and Maddy found Vidhya's suffering beyond reasonable analysis. Mrs. Voynow and Daphne didn't know what to think. Milli and Mr. Singh were convinced that Bobo was right and that Vidhya had been possessed by a Dark Power. Mr. Voynow floated from one position to another.

"I have been thinking about Vidhya," Mr. Voynow said.

He and Mrs. Voynow had led Maddy out of the dining room after breakfast for a stroll on deck before she took on her duties in Vidhya's cabin.

"It is an extraordinary manifestation of self-inflicted

mortification. These painful severities are typical. He is teaching himself governance, self-control. He is purging himself of unruly, buried elements within him, calling up measures of heroic, militant virtue. Of course he insists he must do this alone. One can understand that."

"I can't help feeling," Mrs. Voynow said, "that it's all very un-Christian. Noises in his head and stomach cramps . . ."

"Not at all. There you go again, off target. Very Christian indeed. That's where Bobo goes wrong with his Dark Power theory. Your father would have agreed, I'm sure, Maddy."

"Old Testament, perhaps," Mrs. Voynow persisted. "And then again, how do we know, how can we distinguish a Dark Power from a benign presence . . ."

They were off on one of their bickering, meandering talks. When she left them, Zalman Weingartner, the Zionist leader, approached her to offer assistance. He had heard that the young Indian lad was very ill. One of their group was a very fine doctor, a young man who had given up a splendid career back home, one of the first Jews to be admitted to Columbia Presbyterian. Might he help?

She thanked him, no, and went to her post at Vidhya's bedside. Now she never left the ship for trips ashore. There was only Vidhya and his strange states of being. During those times when she was relieved of her duties by Rosamund or Lady Pansy, she emerged from the darkened stateroom with its grip of pain and spiritual constriction, to heat, sun, dazzling water, light and air, and the life of other passengers, as if released to a magic show.

At one port, all the French soldiers departed. At another, contingents of black and Arab soldiers boarded, in family groups big as tribes, carrying huge trunks, radios, folding tables, stoves, and immense supplies of food, the women shrouded in white or muddy brown, their children silent, clinging, with the inevitable fly draining sight and fluid from the well of their enormous, sad, black, black eyes, and their old people, grandparents, bent out of shape, showing a blind eye turned a sickly, unfocused blue.

Some of the women wore draperies that revealed their eyes, but others were entirely covered, with only a hint of a latticed window of cloth, from behind which Maddy felt them peering with desperate intent to see, to see. Some of the soldiers were recovering from wounds. What battles? Where? And for what? Two polished black men with filthy bloody bandages on their heads, a dramatic touch to their exotic uniforms, perched themselves on the ship's railing, drinking a pungent-smelling beer out of animal-skin containers, swaying dangerously and glaring with bloodshot eyes at anyone whose eyes dared to meet theirs.

Milli had begun to act crazy the last few days, seeking Maddy out to weep and storm at her mother's failure to understand that she could not stand India, she could not, she could not bear it that here she was once again on her way to India, a land she loathed, detested, utterly despised, here she was, so old, old enough to be governing her own life but instead carted about like a child against her wishes. She ended this complaint in midstream to lead Maddy to a lower deck, where there was something she must show Maddy.

It was much hotter in these passageways, and there was an unbearable stench coming from the common toilets. Down here the doors to the cabins were left open, a makeshift drapery hung for privacy, and even that cloth sometimes pulled back to allow more movement of air. Milli stopped at a doorway from behind which came sounds of voices, wailing of children and a whining, maddeningly repetitive singing, a metallic noise, probably issuing from a radio.

Milli called out in her English-accented French. The general din ceased, except for the radio and the crying infants. From a pocket of her skirt, Milli drew an orange and held it out before her. A veiled woman pulled back the curtain enough to show herself and her uncovered eyes. She looked from Maddy to Milli, then bowed her head slightly.

"Entrez," she said.

Though her voice was soft and cordial, the woman's manner did not quite extend the invitation of her words. She clearly judged their visit an intrusion, but Maddy followed Milli in, ducking under the slightly drawn back drapery.

In a space considerably smaller than the cabin Maddy shared with Milli, Daph, and Rosamund, dozens of people milled about, all women and children except for one very old man. The air was blue and choked with smoke coming from a small cooking utensil in a corner and from cigarettes or perhaps incense, something heavily scented and carrying an instant suggestion of sleep. The woman who had bid them enter dropped her veil. She was very young, tiny, pretty, though muddy-skinned, pockmarked, and scarred on her upper lip. She carried a wailing infant in her arms.

"I brought an orange," Milli said in her rotten French. "For the children."

The children stood in a bunch, silent, staring. The women whispered urgent shh, shh, shh noises. The young woman acting as the hostess shifted the crying infant from one arm to the other and threw off her outer garment. Underneath she was entirely in black. Had her husband died? She looked too young to have a husband. Perhaps the infant was her baby sister. Her thick black hair was braided into a long cable hanging down her back. She seated herself cross-legged on a floor cushion and put the baby to her breast, bared under the soft material of her wrappings. The breast was perfectly round, the nipple very large and dirt-colored. The infant drew it into its mouth with a loud, greedy smack.

Maddy said, "Milli, let's go."

Milli offered the orange to the group of children, but none responded. A woman issued a sharper command in the shh, shh, shh language they spoke to one another. A boy stepped forward, took the fruit, holding it awkwardly, smiling and nodding, his black eyes darting back and forth from Milli to Maddy. He seemed to be just managing to restrain himself from bursting out laughing.

"Say *thank you* in English as I taught you yesterday," Milli said.

The boy laughed, shaking his head, then stopped himself laughing with a hand over his mouth. Another boy, looking much like the first one but a bit smaller, stepped forward.

"Thank you," he said, or what passed for those words.

"Ah, there you are," Milli said, "you wicked thing."

Milli fished in her pocket, came up with a coin, and placed it on the boy's pink palm.

"Now you must say *thank you* again," Milli said.

The boy repeated the garbled sound.

"Milli," Maddy said, "we should go."

"Excellent," Milli said to the boy, and clapped her hands. "Excellent. I'll come again tomorrow."

They left behind them a rush of noisy talk and suppressed laughter.

"What are you doing?" Maddy said. "You're bothering those people."

"It's for their good," Milli said. "What good is their French to them? They'll do much better knowing English."

"Where?" Maddy said. "How? Where are they from, anyway?"

"What does that matter? Wherever they're from, it's just nonsense to speak French. There's no sense to their having been taught to speak French."

Later that afternoon she found Milli talking to the two wounded black soldiers. Nobody else was on that portion of the deck. Milli had struck what she obviously hoped was a provocative stance, one hand on a hip, her head thrown back, and a loose smile nervously coming and going. The two blacks kept their eyes cast down and did not respond. She was speaking in English.

What to do about Milli? Maddy needed advice, but from whom? Vidhya had to be protected from everything. She was afraid of alarming Daphne or Lady Pansy. Rosamund didn't care about anybody but herself and Vidhya. She had never confided in Ram, Jag, or Mr. Singh, and the Voynows were too dim and frail and far too talkative. She didn't want to be the initiator of one of their endless bickering conversations. She seized on a moment alone with Bobo to tell him that she was afraid Milli was breaking down.

Bobo was coldly impatient.

"Milli will improve the moment we're settled at the encampment. Milli is a splendid girl, don't trouble yourself about Milli."

"She approached two wounded Negro soldiers on deck. I happened to come along, but otherwise they were alone. I worried that they might harm her," Maddy said.

She shied away from describing Milli's behavior.

"Blacks don't harm Englishwomen, titled young Englishwomen," he said. "You don't understand this world out here. Milli does. She's been to the East many times, my dear."

Later that week a scandalized pair of Voynows reported that Milli had been dancing with a common English soldier at the *thé dansant* held every afternoon in the ship's small salon.

There was a Criticism/Self-criticism session, conducted by Bobo that evening on their private terrace, after the evening meal, the first of its kind Maddy had attended, though she had been warned once by Cleves and Conrad that Criticism/Self-criticism sessions were "worse than the rack for torture." She saw what they had meant. First Milli was asked to tell her story.

She did — a long, rambling tale of an irresistible urge to partake of tea in the salon, complete with little French biscuits, "not a bit as good as our English biscuits," and the subsequent approach to her table of an English soldier dressed in khaki shorts, red-faced and trembling, to tell her of her uncanny resemblance to his childhood sweetheart waiting in Yorkshire for his return and marriage. How could she refuse his request for a dance, the poor thing?

Milli took the reprimands and explanations of what constituted proper behavior very well, Maddy thought, perhaps because she had no intention of following the strictures discussed. She was back at the *thé dansant* the following afternoon, and had dragged Maddy with her. Maddy had come along to protect Milli, but, herself approached by one of the undernourished little English soldiers in his Boy Scout shorts, she was actually very happy to be dancing on the tiny floor to the badly rendered American popular music. He danced very well.

He told her that he was twenty years old, had so many more years to serve he didn't want to think about it or talk about it, and that he hated the East, the Near East, the Far East, and any other portion of the East. His accent was very thick and she had difficulty understanding.

He asked what part of England she came from.

"I'm American," she said.

That information delighted and intrigued him even more. When the musicians took a break, the four sat at a table, Milli and her broad, red-faced soldier and Maddy with her slight, red-faced soldier. He drew a photograph from a wallet and showed Maddy a picture of a girl who looked nothing like her, pointing out the uncanny resemblance Maddy bore to his sweetheart at home. Maddy shot a meaningful glance at Milli but Milli was too entranced with her own unwholesome-looking young man to notice Maddy's signal.

Suddenly he was deeply intimate.

"American's as good as English. 'American cousins,' we always say, don't we, 'our American cousins'? Well then, you should be told. I owe it to you to warn you. You don't want to mix with the natives out here, those chaps I seen, Indian natives or whatever they are, that's not the sort . . ."

He meant Ram or Jag or Mr. Singh. Vidhya had been in his cabin since these troops came aboard. Shock this soldier to death — whip out a photo of Vidhya. Here's *my* intended.

"We don't believe in any of that," Maddy said, "we Americans."

"Oh, come off it," he said. "I wasn't born yesterday, you know. What about your own blacks?"

Mr. and Mrs. Voynow hurried in, obviously alerted to the danger their girls were in. Mr. Voynow seized Milli firmly by her arm, but Maddy was out of reach, on the other side of the scrawny soldier.

"Maddy, you're overdue to relieve Rosamund," Mrs. Voynow said. "Come, we'll all walk together."

Maddy's soldier stood his ground.

"Can't we say a proper good-by? With your permission . . ."

He kissed Maddy, a quick peck on her cheek, a cousin's kiss.

"There," he said, blushing an uglier and more alarming red, "that's all right, then. All in front of your relatives, family like. A proper good-by. Something beautiful to remember where I'm going, something to write home about, explaining to my sweetheart it was really her I was kissing, you know, a reincarnation like."

The band started up again. He took a deep breath and struck out boldly.

" 'Tea for Two.' How about a last dance? We're disembarking first thing tomorrow morning. You won't see me again, or my mates."

He waved a hand toward another table, where his buddies sat watching as if at a drama. Milli's soldier had run back to them when the Voynows advanced. Maddy's was the plucky little fellow.

"How about it?" he said, and held out his arms in dance position.

"Maddy," Mrs. Voynow said. "You're keeping us waiting."

"Am I under arrest?" Maddy said.

She felt reckless and happy and stepped off onto the dance floor as if she were declaring some kind of independence. They were the only couple on the tiny space. The music carried on interminably, however, and she was glad when it ended. She gave her hand to the soldier in saying good-by, but he kissed her cheek, a peck, as before.

"Good luck. Keep safe. And a happy homecoming to your girl," she said.

"God bless you, miss," he said.

He had made himself choke with his sentimentality. The scene was ridiculous, but she was glad she had played the role she had. So much for Mr. and Mrs. Voynow and their copycat English snobbery.

Now she and Milli were subjected to a Criticism/Self-criticism session, after the evening meal, on the terrace, while a glorious sunset and a brilliantly reddened sea lit up their dismal goings-on. Milli was better at self-abasement than Maddy, but even silence was a form of self-abasement, and Maddy listened quietly. It was the word *cheap* that stung her into self-defense.

"Only cheap girls have anything to do with common soldiers," Lady Pansy said.

"I went with Milli to protect her," Maddy said. "But why is it considered cheap to feel compassion for a poor little English soldier going off to fight for England in some awful place, a desert or worse. Haven't you taught me to love humanity? Isn't that the whole point of the Universal Society of Brotherhood? I didn't think I was supposed to make a poor English kid who happens to be a common soldier — whatever that is — I didn't think it was my duty, as you've taught it to me, to make him feel like dirt. So maybe I need that explained to me more clearly," she said. "Why I should make him feel like dirt."

She had brought them to a halt, at least for a moment. They picked up their burdens of explanation soon enough, but they embroidered the message with more care, they admitted some errors in formulation, they conceded Maddy's point about compassion. But she must also confess that she had made mistakes. She should not have danced with the soldier. She should not have allowed him to kiss her cheek. Milli's sins paled beside Maddy's. Milli fell asleep in her chair while they continued to drum away at Maddy until all light was drained from the sky and, out of general weariness and boredom, the session came to an end.

13

GEOGRAPHY had always eluded her. There were maps and there were places. One had nothing to do with the other. New York State: bounded on the east by Connecticut, Massachusetts, Vermont, and the Atlantic Ocean; Iowa: bounded on the east by the Mississippi River; on the north by Minnesota; on the west by South Dakota and Nebraska. Squiggly lines, pastel colors, neat blocks of geometric shapes, a magical recital of mouth-satisfying sounds. Now other names to suit her new condition: England, bounded on the east by the North Sea; Spain, bounded on the east by the Mediterranean Sea; the Mediterranean Sea, bounded on the east by the East: the *East*, the boundless East, toward which they inched lazily.

Off the map, the real thing, the actual places, materialized into stubborn reality. Athens, the fabulous city of schoolbook legends, firmly anchored as another hot, noisy, dusty Mediterranean port, its gangplank another link to the inevitable Alicante man, lifting and carrying, bending and breaking.

On the heights, another great site that must be visited by Rosamund and Maddy for their enlightenment.

Mr. Voynow alone escorted them. First they must view the prison cell of Socrates, where the hemlock was drunk, or so the guide said, hurrying his spiel to sooner arrive at its desired end, the tip. It was unbearably hot, the roads to the miserable hole in the ground with a single barred window were choked by dry dust. Maddy left to Rosamund the task of making Mr. Voynow happy that his little lectures were falling on receptive ears.

In the laboring cab that took them up to the Parthenon, Mr. Voynow delivered a long description of the process of salting olives, a major industry of Greece, he said, and then he returned to the history of Pompeii, which had been interrupted by Vidhya's catatonic fit.

". . . volcanic eruption of A.D. seventy-nine. Rediscovered in seventeen forty-eight, you know — it just lay there undiscovered all those ages, and now there it is, run as a tourist attraction by Mussolini's little bureaucrats. Still, one must give the man credit where credit is due," he said, "much as one hates to. Ever since the end of the war . . ."

Maddy shut him off. She didn't want to hear about the war, an event a generation removed, over and done with fifteen years earlier, a whole lifetime earlier, *her* whole lifetime. If she gave these adults the power, they would rob her of her entire here-and-now life. They used the past to throttle her. She didn't quite know what she meant by that, except that she had had enough of bullying teachers. Too much like Daddy? Yes.

They step out of the cab onto a plateau of marble rubble.

The sun dazzles, striking the shards. Up here, there is a light breeze, the high, bright blue sky balances a handful of puffy white clouds; the atmosphere is governed by an extraordinary stillness, a serenity and harmony that flows from the ruined structure at its edge. Sections of the temple are knocked off, faces of the serene goddesses smashed, limbs missing, supports fallen away, but Maddy has never experienced the presence and the power of an object as she does this ruined building. It settles into her being, a perfect whole, making her different, blessing her.

There are no other sightseers, and the self-styled guide, the driver of the decrepit cab, rebuffed by Mr. Voynow, has remained with his car.

She tries to escape Rosamund and Mr. Voynow, to protect the privacy of this precious moment, but the clear air carries Mr. Voynow's words wherever she moves.

". . . this temple, this greatest triumph of Greek civilization . . . In antiquity the destruction of the magnificent figure of . . . War with Turkey, the destruction by the Turks . . . Lord Elgin . . . The Elgin Marbles . . . The British Museum . . ."

She covers her ears with the palms of her hands and walks into the inner center of this perfection of space, an enclosure and a liberation, simultaneously sheltering and granting the limitless freedom of its open horizons.

As in Pompeii, she is gripped by a physical connection, not here between her feet and the homely ground, but between a core of herself she can only call her soul, and the soul of this serene ruin. She feels this object, this soul, rise like a lump in her chest, into her throat, and fly out of her mouth to soar the spaces of this infinitely gracious ruin. If she were alone she would pray, atoning for the injuries inflicted and giving thanks that something, anything, has remained.

Yet she feels invaded by the experience. Her faith, her immortality, is at stake. Why? A suffusion of evil bloats and distends her body, like a cramp. There is as much evil on this scene as good. The purity of this innocent building, capable of no harm to anybody, has been invaded over and over again, by the Turks, Lord Elgin, grabbing and destroying, while believing they were *good*, doing *good* in the world. And, most terrible thought of all, what if even the original intent to do good, the impulse that built this great work of harmonic beauty, hadn't been pure either but had wreaked its own harm in some way she was too ignorant to imagine? Who made the rules of good and evil? What if it were all a senseless mess, and what one did or didn't do was of no consequence? What then?

She came away subdued. In the silence imposed during dinner her abstraction went unnoticed, but later, when she is sitting with Vidhya, he questions her. It is so unusual for anyone to be concerned with her for her own sake that his attention brings tears to her eyes.

"What is it, Maddy?" Vidhya says. "What is the trouble? You are different tonight. Sad. What is troubling you?"

She hesitates. Of all the people in the world, surely Vidhya must understand what it was that pierced her soul in Pompeii and in Athens. Perhaps he shared this experience, knew precisely what she felt. She struggles to speak so profoundly that he will be dazzled into understanding. Words buzz in a dizzying pattern.

Life, death, immortality, mortality, the past, the confusing present, our future, the world and you and I, humanity, the Alicante man, the men on the gangplanks bent double under their burdens, the Society, love, you and I and grace and human kindness, the future, our future, the path, the mission, your mission, good and evil, the innocent children, the fly drinking the precious liquid of the infant's eye, God's light that shines on all the world, my life, my future, the sickly blue of a blind eye, the beauty, the inexpressible beauty, the loss, the ruins, the lives gone, the past, the present . . .

He rises on one elbow, an extraordinary amount of movement for him these days.

"What is it, Maddy? What is it?"

"I don't know," she says. "I think I'm lost."

That was not what she had meant to say. *I saw God's light shining on pure beauty. I felt the evil of the world in my body like a sick cramp.* That's what she had meant to say. And more. More. *Where does one learn how to live?* And more than that. She wanted to ask: *Are you a fake, Vidhya?* Instead she had whined. Like a stupid kid. *I'm lost.*

Vidhya arranges himself higher in his bed, stuffing pillows behind his back, and when he is disposed to his satisfaction, he smiles at Maddy, with true sweetness, and opens his arms to her.

"Come, Maddy, darling," he says. "Come to me. You're with me. You're not lost one bit, Maddy, darling. You're with me."

14

D O you remember," Maddy said, as they circled over La Guardia airport, " 'The sun never sets on British soil'?"

"Of course," Victoria said.

" 'The sun never sets on British soil,' " Maddy repeated. "That was supposed to make your blood run quicker."

"Now we say that the sun never sets on American bases," Victoria said.

"U.S. bases," Dwight said, awake and alert. "America refers to the entire continent."

"Hear, hear," Victoria said.

"We don't say anything of the kind," Maddy said. "I've never heard anybody say that the sun never sets on U.S. bases now. But then, it was always said, 'The sun never sets ...' "

"Now and then, then and now," Dwight said. "How we love to draw our lines of definition. 'That was then and now is now.' Incantations to buttress our ignorant prejudices."

His voice had deepened to the cadence of a lecturer's, though there were only Maddy and Victoria to listen and they had heard this speech by Dwight Phillips before.

"*Now* is the fruit of *then*. *Then* foreshadows and is the fundamental shaper of *now* as *now* foreshadows and shapes the future. Mankind talks endlessly of human happiness as if it can be delivered by Federal Express, but life is a whole, a continuity of experience. We call it history, the nightmare we cannot escape, but it is the continuity of our own actions. We like to pretend it has been visited upon us, our history, as if it were a natural calamity, earthquakes and floods, but it is we who invented the industrial revolution and the age of technology, it is we who organized capitalism, the system that knows no conscience, just as we structured the slave trade and modern warfare. The First World War led inexorably to the Second World War. The slave trade prefigures the contemporary inner city and all the problems therein. The military-industrial complex prefigured the shuttle disaster, just as it prefigures the world disaster of nuclear war. *As ye sow so shall ye reap.* Violence begets violence. In spite of all the warnings, we continue to develop chemicals and express horror when a leak results in twenty-five hundred deaths in Bhopal, India. Was any intelligent, reasoning person taken by surprise by Three Mile Island, by Chernobyl? It was an inevitable outcome of the development of nuclear power. We are caught in a spiral of violence reaching from then to now to shall be, a continuous becoming, is, was, and shall be — the three sisters — the then, the now, and the shall be of human existence, doomed to continue until we have the wit to alter *now* to insure the future, to study the past so as to understand the now . . ."

"Maddy, for heaven's sake, can't you . . ." Victoria said.

Maddy placed a hand on Dwight's cool, slightly damp forehead. She stroked his fine, papery skin.

"Shh, shh," she said.

"I'd rather hear the lecture on 'The Sin of Exploitation,' " Victoria said. "Or 'Tolstoy, Gandhi, and the Lesson of Nonviolence,' if we must hear any, during this disgusting circling."

Dwight closed his eyes and seemed to fall asleep.

15

THE vessel put into the port of Haifa. There was trouble in Jaffa, rioting and a strike of dock workers. Port workers were on strike in Haifa as well, but the ship anchored in the harbor while passengers and luggage were transferred to a launch, nothing more than a raft, really, with an engine mounted in the center. The steward pronounced it *lunch* so that for some five minutes Bobo refused to allow any of his party to board, through misunderstanding. After all, it was only nine-thirty in the morning. The incident turned them all silly, giggling uncontrollably. Vidhya was especially gay.

Loaded at last, the launch chugged toward an inviting shore of sand, backed by a pleasant slope of greenery. She had expected Palestine to show a harsher landscape. The noise of the engine made talk impossible. A thin plume of acrid black smoke rose from the machinery, and in a few minutes an explosion followed — nothing very sensational, a soft, ineffectual release of heat and steam, a flash of fire, a single muffled noise — and the raft was brought to a shuddering halt. Under an unbearably hot sun, they waited to be rescued.

The men offered their help to the Arab in charge of the machinery, but he was adamant in his refusals. Vidhya's good humor faded. He was frightened of drowning and requested that the women encircle him. Bobo strode about, determined to display nothing but patience and goodwill. At the opposite end of the launch, their offers of help more violently rejected by the Arab, perhaps because some of these Jews spoke Arabic, the group of Americans on their way to a kibbutz sang songs, alternately jolly and sad, and dangled their hands and feet in the cool water.

They were towed in hours later, hot, hungry, thirsty, and exhausted, and then held up on the steep slope leading from the port to the hotel, the Arab in charge of their party's move bringing all his underlings to a stop, demanding more money to finish the haul. Bobo lost patience and screamed and railed. The Arab's passivity was impressive. He lowered his eyes, slipped his brown hands under the beautifully soft folds of his robe. He waited. He said nothing. His turban was arranged with astonishing care, Maddy noticed. Bobo paid what was demanded, and they moved on.

At the hotel, halfway up the Carmel, a woman waited to greet them. She was an emissary of a friend of the Society, a young, rich Arab, son of a sheik, just home from Oxford. The woman was a European now settled in Palestine. She was neatly put together, pretty, perhaps thirty, a German originally, Jewish, a Socialist and a Zionist who spoke German, English, French, Arabic, and Hebrew. She told them all this after dinner, while they relaxed on a terrace whose flower borders of jasmine overwhelmed with their heavy perfume. She talked in a low, deliberate manner that never changed, even when she became agitated. Her employer sent greetings and very welcome invitations to partake of his hospitality.

They were transported to the sheik's quarters in a series of long, smooth cars, their luggage in a sparkling new truck, the caravan sucking up the dust of the unpaved road and whirling it about. Maddy rode in the third car and could see almost nothing of the countryside through the thick haze. They arrived at a castle, a virtual oasis in the middle of nowhere. The son of the sheik greeted them. He was the epitome of a prince: handsome, courtly, in stylish Western dress, though he wore eye make-up and perfume. The house too displayed a mix of styles, every room decorated differently: Victorian English, Moorish, Chinese, art deco, plain old wicker comfortable — the last the sitting room they were ushered into for tea.

Vidhya was alert and social, in training for the talks he was to give in Jerusalem and Tel Aviv. The rich son of the sheik was a proselytizing Communist, *his* talk filled with revolutionary declarations of the need for social justice and the absolute elimination of empire. He asked them to call him Said.

"Only with the end of imperialism shall the problems of the Mideast and the Far East be solved," he said, turning to Vidhya with charming urgency.

"Surely, you agree, you of all people?"

"How can I not?" Vidhya said with equal charm. "When you speak with such passionate love for this troubled part of the world? Peace, peace. The entire world needs peace. That is where I agree."

That didn't satisfy Said at all. He rushed from the room, returned with a sheaf of pamphlets sloppily printed on thin, grayish paper, unevenly cut, and loosely pasted together, and handed them around: *The Communist Manifesto* by Karl Marx, *State and Revolution* by V. I. Lenin, *What Is Communism?* and *The ABC of Communism*, all in English.

Maddy held on to the booklets through the long argument that followed. At one point, Bobo threw his handful of tracts at Ram, who had joined Said's side of the discussion. Bobo was quite wild. He sawed the air with both arms, he whacked the armrests of the wicker chair and seized a chintz pillow behind him as if it were stuffed with communism and other vile ideas, beating it to emphasize his points, *Western Civilization*, whack, *Way of Life*, whack, *British genius for organization*, whack, whack.

"White man's burden," Ram said. "Why don't you say it? That's what you think, isn't it?"

Bobo swept out of the argument and off the terrace. They could see him, in his magisterial robe, stalking about the garden. Lady Pansy murmured her regrets that the evening had taken such a bad turn. Mr. Voynow deplored the entrance of politics into their smooth relations. Ram flung his beautiful head back and looked defiant. Said smiled radiantly. Vidhya had been cornered by Elsa, Said's secretary, who hammered away at him privately. Vidhya kept his head down, nodding seriously and rhythmically at Elsa's words, which Maddy couldn't hear.

The others made a point of leaving behind the pamphlets Said had distributed. Maddy took hers to the room she shared with Rosamund.

"I should have taken mine, too," Rosamund said. "They'll come in useful for toilet tissue."

"Is that a political comment?" Maddy said.

"Toilet tissue is a dreadful problem out here," Rosamund said. "And sanitary napkins. Stock up on any that you may fall upon in Jerusalem. There must be an English pharmacy somewhere in Jerusalem. Elsa will know. Germans make a point of knowing such things."

Vidhya had signaled *I shall be waiting, Maddy*, along with his whispered good-night. Impossible to go to his adjoining room until Rosamund was sound asleep. She was listening so intently for Rosamund's breathing to become heavy and steady that she didn't hear Vidhya on the balcony. He stepped up to the door and beckoned her. Rosamund didn't stir when she rose.

She whispered, "I don't think we should, in this place . . ."

To her surprise he instantly agreed.

They embraced on the balcony, in the soft, warm air heavy with the smell of jasmine. He kissed her, his cushioned lips opening to draw in her lips and tongue. When he released her and began to whisper, her expectations were for some romantic good-night speech.

"Maddy, do you know," he whispered, "what is the difference between the Second International, the Third International, and the Fourth International they are all arguing about?"

"What?" Maddy said.

"This political talk they picked up at Oxford. Even Ram," he said.

"I don't know what you're talking about," Maddy said.

"Neither do I," Vidhya said, and kissed her once more before they parted.

The caravan of cars drove into the city of Jerusalem the following morning. Elsa accompanied them, smoothing their way, putting them up at an excellent new hotel, built with Rothschild money, Elsa told them. Ram, still argumentative, disputed her facts.

"American money," he said. "American money will ruin this country. Tel Aviv as well is being built entirely with American money."

"But we are speaking of Jerusalem," Elsa said, in her flat, unperturbed manner. "I think I know more about Jerusalem than you, with all due respect."

They learned at once that Vidhya's appearances had been canceled. There was a six o'clock curfew in effect; all meetings were prohibited. In the confusion of new planning and delays, it was agreed that Elsa would chaperone Maddy to do some personal shopping and to visit the shrines, since it was Maddy's first visit to Jerusalem.

The sights began with the calm, pleasant piece of the city where Elsa lived with her mother and an aunt, when she was at home, on a street whose buildings might have stood in London, except for the heavy gray dust and the exotic trees that lined the avenue. The spacious apartment reminded her of her parents' house in Iowa City — dark solid furniture, a good piano and record player, a cello upright before a music stand, books lining the walls, Persian rugs, oil paintings, mid-morning coffee in a silver service presided over by the two older women, beautifully dressed and coiffed, their manner affectedly gracious.

Then in a horse-drawn carriage to a part of the city that seemed to be in another country, by way of a wide boulevard: a massive mess of traffic, *droshkys*, cars, buses, donkeys, bicycles, horses, wagons, camels, and even oxen. The noise made talk impossible.

It had been Elsa's intention to show Maddy the Wailing Wall, but they ran into a commotion before they reached the spot. Men in the traditional costume of the Jewish orthodox sect were using their bodies to stop all traffic.

"What are they doing?" Maddy said.

"It's the Sabbath," Elsa said. "They want traffic outlawed on the Sabbath."

She had spoken so quietly that Maddy assumed Elsa agreed with the action.

But she said, "Intolerable, these people."

"Oh," Maddy said. "For a moment, I thought you approved."

"How could I approve?" Elsa said. "I'm a Socialist. I don't approve of fanaticism, of mysticism. I'm a materialist."

They left the carriage and walked to the wall. Elsa explained about the destruction of the temple and the remnant still standing.

"You may write a wish on a piece of paper and place it between the bricks of the wall," Elsa said.

"I'm not a believer," Maddy said.

"It's just a game, like throwing pennies in a wishing well," Elsa said.

The noise here was even more deafening than on the

streets. The wall as edifice was nothing, a dirty, sun-baked, not very tall stone fence in bad repair. But among the men in their prayer shawls and phylacteries, in the midst of their cries and swaying bodies, she was at home, sitting with Grandma on the hard folding chairs at the corner storefront *shul* in the Bronx. She did not write out a wish. She couldn't think what to wish for. And besides, among these men beseeching God she didn't want to play games.

Elsa led her through Old Jerusalem, a warren of covered alleys, up and down stone steps encrusted with filth, crowded with hawkers. British soldiers and an occasional tourist toured the bazaars, but all of the vendors and most of the shoppers were Arabs going about their daily business. The men wore the graceful gowns in which they looked so stubbornly masculine in spite of eyelids heavy with kohl and their hair streaming in a wild, dirty tangle when it wasn't covered by a dirty turban. The women were veiled, only their eyes showing, and under the dark draperies cradled their infants. When she looked at them, they looked straight back. She liked that. She watched a hawker pour liquid from a goatskin container into a tin cup for a paying customer, and another man put down two pennies to dip his fingers into a plasterlike white substance that was a cooked food of some sort. A crowd gathered. They studied Maddy intently from the straw hat on her head down to her white pumps. Elsa pulled her away.

In a *droshky* again on a quieter drive back to the hotel, she asked Elsa why she had come to Jerusalem.

"And your mother and your aunt. Do they like it here? What will they do here?"

"*They* hope to build it into a place of culture. They're trying to form a symphony orchestra now, and they sponsor the Habima theater."

Maddy said, "I see." She knew about orchestras, but not the other reference. "And are you artistic, too?" she went on, feeling like a fool.

"I'm political," Elsa said. "My interests are political."

"Is that why you work for Said?"

"I work for Said for money," Elsa said. "We have to live, my mother and my aunt and me, somehow. Said and I don't agree politically at all. I'm a Zionist, a Socialist-Zionist. I don't know what Said is — a pro-Soviet Trotskyite, even if he had to invent the category single-handedly, perhaps that's what he is, if he's anything definable. He belongs in the camp of the Fourth International."

"Is that here in Jerusalem?"

"What?" Elsa said.

"The encampment of the Fourth International?"

Elsa stared at her, and then laughed.

"Don't bother your pretty head about it," she said.

It was Said's wish that Elsa smooth their way to Tel Aviv and Jaffa, where they would board an English ship for the trip farther east. Again she produced the caravan of long, luxurious cars, the luggage in the bright new truck, and this time a troupe of Arabs swooping out at lunch time with equipment for washing up, dining, and resting — tents, chairs and tables, rugs, cushions, warm water, cool water, towels, light coverlets, cooking equipment, and food — the whole shebang whipped out, served up, cleaned up, and then dismantled and packed away before they moved on.

In Tel Aviv martial law had been declared and curfew was fixed at an even earlier hour. All Tel Aviv seemed new, or in construction, and, if possible, even noisier than Jerusalem. They were held up in a mad traffic jam made up of every possible vehicle and animal. A horse was having a screaming fit. Maddy could see him rearing and hear him screaming, not neighing, screaming like a human being, and the driver of the wagon cursing out the animal and whipping him wildly. The horse had an enormous erection, inconceivably enormous, and the other inconceivable element was that this brutal driver, so cruel to animals, could only be Jewish, since he was cursing in Yiddish.

The hotel smelled of new wood and fresh paint. Maddy spent the early part of the evening in Vidhya's room, reading to him from an English-language newspaper published in Jerusalem, but he fell asleep almost immediately. When she joined the others on their terrace, they were deep in a political argument, Elsa against Jag and Mr. Singh, Ram against all of them, Rosamund and Jag listening silently, Milli asleep on a chaise. They spoke in a shorthand that baffled Maddy: the British Mandate, the Balfour Declaration, Paolo Zionism, the Stern Gang, Gandhi and nonviolence, independence and Home Rule, the Comintern and all those numbered Internationals. Ram barged in with a denunciation of reform tactics and social democracy. Mr. Singh's wrath turned his lips a purple so dark it was almost black.

"You call me a pawn in the hands of the imperialist oppressors? And what are you? Nothing but an irresponsible who would rather see the people deluged in disaster, see India lying helpless and bloodied."

"And now?" Ram said. "And now? You like our present situation better?"

Bobo emerged on his adjoining terrace to hush them.

"You're disturbing the entire hotel with your pointless, ridiculous politics," he said coldly. "You're disturbing Lady Pansy."

In the silence that followed, a sound of shots fired was all the more startling. Then, the military rattle of hooves on pavement. But it was a riderless, unarmed horse that appeared on the quiet street of their hotel, running downhill at a gallop. Like a displaced element in a dream, its pale mane and tail floating on the soft night air, the animal thudded below the balcony on which they stood and disappeared around the curve of the city street, fully illuminated, in its last magical instant, by the dim street light just mounted by the new electrification project, financed by American money.

It got away, was Maddy's first exultant thought.

265

She had brought into one image the horse on the boulevard with its enormous erection and human screaming and the maddened driver beating it senseless, and the wild, beautiful creature that had just passed by. But then as in a dream, the riderless horse was herself and its thudding hooves the thunder of her own heart and it was she who was running, running away, running free.

In an oversized atlas in her daddy's study in the house in Iowa City, there had been a map that so distorted the shape of the world Maddy could not then imagine any civilization, however exotic, inhabiting those flattened, elongated, cross-hatched spaces — the ends of the earth, strung out to the right of the two-page spread. The United States, almost off the map at the left, was a mere flying rag of white tatters rimmed with salmon pink, but she knew the real thing, knew the United States to be solid ground, flat and habitable. Now, moving steadily eastward toward a dot on the map that marked the Society encampment on the shore of an unimaginable sea, intersected by fixed lines of latitude and longitude and the imaginary lines of the equator and the Tropic of Cancer, the unimaginable daily became mundane. The ship plowed ahead, the exotic names of the curved, lined, and pastel-colored spaces — the Arabian Sea, the Indian Ocean — flattened out into manageable sea below and sky above, and, finally, into earth, the Society's sacred earth of India, on which she placed her foot as if it were any old earth, God's earth under God's equal light.

Perhaps she had lived here in an earlier incarnation. Visually, it was so right, colors just what one would have chosen to make the scene a scene, and the faces were family faces: Grandma's beaked nose, witty eyes, and faintly dissatisfied mouth reincarnated on dozens of elderly women, and dark-skinned, serious, big-eyed children like her baby cousins, everywhere marred by filth and swarming flies and the disfigurement of a blinded pale blue eye. In this India, where she had expected an increase in wisdom and spirituality to wrap her in the tranquility of the East, she was instead back in the street life she had lived on the Bronx stoop, here monstrously exaggerated, but the same noise, energy, anxiety, hope, and hopelessness, the same rich gossip and the same dalliance, the self-satisfied incompetence, the wild impatience and despair.

If she was at home in the street life, she was lost again in the grand places of New Delhi and Agra. These she connected to England — even the Taj Mahal seemed English, since the English made so much of it — and she was discovering that England was the factor she was hoping to lose in India. The pull she felt in this strange country was a tug toward home and her origins, and it called for putting aside the splendid — and the quarrelsome. Ignorance was the key, willful ignorance. She didn't want to learn any of the dozens of Indian languages or to try to fathom the labyrinthine politics and sticky ties that roped together the English and the Indians in their never-ending affair.

She had expected Vidhya to bloom in his home country, expanding into a more expressive self, more Indian, as had happened with Ram and Jag and Mr. Singh, instantly darker skinned, showing more body through looser clothing and softer faces under a sheen of sweat and radiant smiles. Vidhya had tightened. Distaste, impatience, and, yes, revulsion ruled his responses. Did he hate India, then?

Perhaps he only hated traveling, being on tour.

They traveled on splendid trains in a luxury that could and often did turn instantly into disaster, through mechanical failure or social disruption, or a herd of cows on the train tracks, not to be disturbed at any cost. They had crossed inward from one coast and were now bound outward to another coast. She had seen so much of this overwhelming land that she believed she had seen it all, until Vidhya informed her that they were covering only a portion, the British portion, immense enough.

The country was a work of art, of theater. It was no

longer a wonder to her that Vidhya always put on a good show. He had only to turn his head to the landscape, in the markets, on the streets, to fix on a stock of enchantments usable as drama, poetic gesture, myth, spirituality. In the cities they descended upon as a party, he dazzled his listeners at elegantly small, correct gatherings. Almost none in his audience were Indians.

"Gurus are a dime a dozen in India," Victoria had said to her in Spain. "Why should Indians gather to listen to Vidhya?"

One city would be too hot, the next too cold. The air steamed and stank or was so fresh and rare it hurt the lungs. Yes, there were people living on the streets and dying, beggars everywhere, train stations an ordeal of noise, smell, crowds, endless waiting. The most surface observation of the push and pull to survive among these multitudes was exhausting. And exhilarating.

But soon she was ready to call it quits. She wanted to stop being a tourist. If she could have chosen, she would have holed up alone with Vidhya to live a commonplace existence in a noisy city neighborhood or isolated in the countryside, anywhere, where they could learn to forget the English and live for each other. Stop the striving after martyrdom and sainthood, or whatever it was Vidhya was reaching for. Seeing Vidhya here with her own eyes, she thought she recognized the harm done him by these English. He had been plucked from his natural ground, tended into an exotic growth. She would help him replant himself where he belonged. They would live out their plain lives in India, she and Vidhya, as a man and a woman, simply, anonymously. Such a life surely held the highest good.

She was so carried away by this concept that she spoke out.

"But what shall I become here, Maddy? What are you talking of?"

Her plan had startled him.

"You could be a teacher. They must need a lot of teachers here. My father was a teacher."

"Do you know what teachers, Indian teachers, earn? We would not have enough money to buy rice. You are having some kind of dream, a nightmare. In a few days, you would come to hating it and hating me with all your heart."

"I have an annuity. And you," she said, "you would be rich here, you have a lifetime annuity."

"But if I tear myself apart from them, from the Society? How are you thinking? What would I do without them?"

He was whispering, though they were alone in his compartment having tea. The very comfortable train sped along the tracks with a minimum of jogging and lurching. They were crossing a trestle above a wide, placid river. Downstream, a group of women in the meltingly soft colors of their saris and head scarves stood in the shallow water below, beating dirt out of garments. Naked men waited in groups on the golden, muddy ground for their clean clothing, their skin lit up and burnished by the late-afternoon sun. She held the scene in view for a few minutes until the train moved on. Why couldn't they live that life?

"What harm can they do to you?" Maddy said. *Or to me?* she did not say aloud.

"They could humiliate me. They might make me a laughingstock," he said. "Don't you see that I am no longer a nobody? I am no longer a dirty, ignorant village boy. You wish me to become a village boy again?"

"No, of course not."

"Are you trying to destroy me, too?" Vidhya said.

"I want you to be happy," Maddy said. "I can't bear to see you so unhappy." And added, "How can you say 'destroy' to me?"

"Please, pour me more tea, and let us stop this foolish talk."

She placed his refilled cup before him.

269

"What do you want for yourself?" she said. "Really, what do you really want, not what they've dreamed up for you, but —"

He interrupted, frantically whispering.

"You know perfectly well what I want. I want you to believe in me. That is what I *really* want, as you put it, that is what I *really* want, and you know it, but that is the last thing —"

"And if I believed in you, and nobody else did, if only I believed in you, would that . . . ?"

Vidhya said, "You know perfectly what I am saying but you pretend to misunderstand. You prefer to mock me."

"I love you, Vidhya. How can you say such bad things of me, 'destroy,' 'mock.' I want you to be happy. It's you who's miserable. It's you who clearly wants to escape this fate they've dreamed up for you."

"Happy. Happy," he said. "Women always talk of such things, of happiness, as if it is our highest task in life to be happy. It is not. Our task is not to be happy but to be useful, to be good. Only fools and adolescent girls talk endlessly of happiness."

"I want to help you, I want to help. If I'm of no help to you then I have no business here, I'm just a silly tourist, a lost person like Milli, hanging around," she said.

"I think I shall never learn to understand you girls, never, you baffle me," he said.

He was angry with her; that was why he had used the phrase *you girls*. She hated that. She was Maddy, not part of an anonymous coalition of *you girls*.

He began again. "I am doing something very difficult. I am studying how to live up to my fate, I am studying how to do my fate justice, to be worthy of the fate that I have been called to, not dreamed up by others, as you put it. If you can help me — if you would only help me with that."

"Tell me how," she said.

She slipped her hand in his. He lifted it in both his

hands, caressing and kissing her palm. She kissed his bent head. His silky hair had a faint spicy smell. When he looked up at her, his strange light eyes were filled with tears.

"We shall begin our real work, Maddy, darling, when we reach the encampment, then our true work shall begin."

They arrive late at night. Vidhya is sick, silent, and running a high temperature. An infection? Or his mysterious spiritual ailment returned?

She wakes to the routine of the house in Hampstead, but in a setting so different it is another experience. The usual breakfast, under the familiar rule of silence, but on a terrace open to the perfumed air, trilling with birdsong and the soft clash of hanging chimes. An intense, languorous heat. The effect of a village square with the buildings grouped about a central courtyard of trees, gardens, terraces, alive with movement, color, motion, like a stage, a theater of life, of dance and song. At the same time everything is simple, unadorned, natural. She is enchanted.

Vidhya's room is in the most elaborate central bungalow. Maddy is situated at the other end of the compound, in the young people's house. She has been demoted? She is told by Lady Pansy that she is free to acquaint herself with the encampment for the next few days while Vidhya recuperates. Bobo has gone into a private retreat in the main bungalow. The others have all been here before; they scatter to their favorite spots, their favorite activities.

Maddy wanders about through the gardens surrounding the low buildings, and then along an avenue of palms to an astounding beach that extends endlessly in both directions. She has permission to swim whenever she likes; it is a substitute for daily walks. To swim in these tepid, silky, colored waters is as good as making love. To lie on this fine white sand and think of nothing is better than meditating. She spends hours here, her head resting on her arms, tuned to the music of the sea, one hand sifting between her fingers the magical sand that strains and flushes away all fleshly tensions.

Because of her special editorial work with Vidhya, she is excused from household tasks and from learning to operate the primitive spinning wheels. Transcribing Vidhya's speeches comes to a stop when he is suffering one of his fits. Her work becomes the easing of his pain, trances, weakness, and despair. Then suddenly he is well again in a burst of unbounded energy. He calls for a gathering of the entire compound and, sitting cross-legged under the banyan tree, discourses speculatively in a manner different from his usual talks, and each new talk different from the ones before, as if he is trying on varieties of approaches. She takes down his words in shorthand, but often by the time it is returned, he has again retreated into illness.

From time to time, he seems entirely cured. He joins them at meals, at games of croquet on the lawn in the late afternoon, or statues on the terrace, or blindman's buff around the banyan tree in the evenings before dark.

When he is well, he is ingenious in finding spots for lovemaking: a cavelike retreat on the beach, sheltered by a dune, a cool, dark, secret place; a field above the compound, resting between kitchen crops allowed to go over to wildflowers and sweet grasses.

There is his room during the day, but that's chancy. Rosamund or Lady Pansy might come poking in, checking on Vidhya's state. And with their bedrooms so far apart, he never signals Maddy to come to him at night.

The cave and the field are magical places. They mingle sand, sea, sun, lovemaking, flowers and grasses, the golden light of India, herself and Vidhya in a mix of drunken bliss.

Out of nowhere, then, Vidhya leads her to the banyan tree one evening and in a ranting discourse argues that he cannot reach the spiritual being he must become while mired in carnal passion. He swears himself and Maddy to a vow of continence. She is bewildered and as hurt as if he had rejected an advance, but she swears.

Around her, the swarmings of the pilgrims, the comings and goings, the passing events coming to a boil and simmering down, the politics and gossip of Society life, ceased to occupy her as they had in Hampstead. The ranks of the Society thinned and swelled. The entire German section of the Society withdrew, under the pressure of its own national problems, or so Ram speculated. Lord Harkness arrived, swept up his daughters, gazed at his wife with reproach dripping from his eyes, did not speak to Maddy at all, and left within a few days, Milli and Daph clinging to his sides, each under a huge, protecting arm.

Bobo took off too, turning his back on the problem of Vidhya by leaving for Australia, the United States, and Canada. Word came back months later that California had proved so wonderful he was still there. *It is indeed the promised land, just as the Elders said in their messages,* he wrote, and added the postscript, *How goes it with Vidhya and with his mysterious spiritual manifestations?*

And Ram was gone, following a series of fierce political arguments with Jag on nonviolence and Gandhi, on the failure of Soviet communism, the cause of the worldwide depression, the nature of imperialism and colonialism and the immediate withdrawal of the British from India. Jag was opposed. They argued Home Rule, pro and con, night after night. Ram called Jag's position *deranged Eastern Marxism, infantile leftist idiocy.*

"You think that the worse matters get, the better for the revolution, but what you forget in your calculations is human misery. Let the British go at once, while there is still some order in the country."

Lady Pansy would not allow either young man to be alone with Vidhya, and they themselves shunned the messages Vidhya delivered under the banyan tree.

"They are letting him waste away in body and mind," Ram said to Maddy. "I cannot watch this senseless suicide taking place."

Was he accusing *her*?

One morning he was off to join Gandhi, or the Congress party, leaving behind a letter denouncing the hypocrisies of the Society and churning up once again all the old charges against Bobo. Lady Pansy sent the memo to Bobo, and that was the end of it, so far as Maddy heard.

Not that she was listening in the old intent fashion. For her the Society had spiraled down to a pinpoint that contained her whole world — Vidhya. She was tied to Vidhya. They were joined. Even their metabolism matched. She grew thin along with him, dark skinned, silent, and remote. There were no proper mirrors at the compound except for a small, blotched glass hung too high in the hallway of the young people's bungalow. It returned her a dark image of a thin, morbid stranger. Perhaps she was merely dirtier. She bathed in the sea every day, and washed her hair in rainwater once a week. Under the banyan tree she labored at cleansing the impurities of her consciousness, but instead of her brain emptying itself in meditation, it filled with buzzing fancies.

The huge old tree frightened her. It grew downward, sending forth a massive tangle of branches to root in the earth, a tree of darkness and writhing power, especially at its immense trunk, where Vidhya sat every evening now in silent meditation.

With her own eyes, she saw Vidhya rise through that tree one night. He floated upward through the mist to a topmost branch, where others found him in the morning, sitting cross-legged on an upper limb, bathed in sunlight, and found Maddy on the ground, her face turned to the magic light filtering downward from Vidhya's dominating presence.

She lived with the notion that she might be going mad.

It was the hours under the banyan tree that made her crazy, the long hours of sitting, watching, waiting, listening for Vidhya's messages from the Elders to come through. She grew stiff and cold, her brain, her teeth, her tongue and eyes penetrated by mist. She saw visions. Vidhya ascending to the top of the tree. The Elders materialized, a group of menacing, shadowy wraiths. Bobo appeared in a robe and funny hat. At the worst moments, Grandma came to comfort and warm her. Grandma was a good vision, the only one.

It was under the banyan tree that Vidhya led her to regularly renew their vows of abstinence. It was to the wide field of grasses and wildflowers that Vidhya led her to break the vow one brilliantly clear morning. With an urgency more like rage than love, he entered her for the first time, but pulled out before he came and burst into tears when he did. She comforted him, lying under his weight on the sweet-smelling rough ground, noting a cloud move lazily across the sky, God's sky, under which, at the moment, she felt herself and, yes, Vidhya too, singularly abandoned.

It was back to the banyan tree that night for penance and blame.

Vidhya extolled chastity, celibacy, the benign influence of sexual abstinence on the spirit, lamenting the body's inevitable fall into sin and the existence of those dark forces which tempted lapses from the higher states of being.

He sat cross-legged, facing the trunk, in his filmy white garments, confiding in the hanging branches reaching downward to root. Twenty young petitioners, mostly females, were gathered at the outward reaches of the great tree, listening less to Vidhya's actual words than to tones, as if he were a singer. They were an Australian group, on a short pilgrimage, under the supervision of the Voynows.

"Women have great power to do good in the world," Vidhya said, "greater than men, but misdirected and abused, women exert great power to harm. Passion is violence, passion misdirected becomes a weapon of abuse against the highest aspirations of man."

She felt each word was a knife flung directly at her.

"We must subdue the violence within ourselves first and then think how to help others subdue what is violent within them . . ."

275

She looked around self-consciously, but nobody was looking at her. It was that morning that the great thing had happened between them for the first time. The real thing. And now Vidhya repenting, wiping it all out. She fixed her eyes on the bare ground, starved of sun by the huge, shadowing tree, and with the tip of her finger scratched letters in the dry, black earth. LOVE, she wrote, and then rubbed out the word with the palm of her hand, before anybody noticed.

She wrote LOVE in the sand at the beach, too, where it instantly faded, crumbling and erasing itself in the sugary substance. Alone, settled close to the water's edge on a sunbleached madras cloth smelling of sea air and soap, she was bothered by a sense of being observed and kept herself covered with the loose garment worn over her bathing suit, usually discarded. Face down, head turned to the sea, one hand stretched beyond the reaches of the spread, sifting the sand, she fell asleep. She woke groggy with sun. There was some hubbub farther up the beach.

In the distance, on the deserted shore, two men struggled, shouting in a dialect she couldn't understand, interspersed with English curses and un-English wails and shrieks. They were moving in her direction. She snatched up the cloth and ran toward the cave at the upper point of the beach to hide, but swerved before she reached it. She had seen the barest flash of white and dark skin, but she knew that Rosamund and Vidhya were in the cave. The cave of their lovemaking, her cave and Vidhya's.

Of course Vidhya and Rosamund Keats were lovers. And Vidhya and Lady Pansy Harkness. And Vidhya and Bobo. And Vidhya and Maddy Brewster. And Vidhya and God knows who else.

She took it all in at one gulp, swallowing it whole, with difficulty, like a lump of ice. And indeed she was very cold, a reaction to the extreme heat and of having fallen asleep under the burning sun. Her horror was genuine, inspired by the abysmal embarrassment of her position, and of theirs,

276

Vidhya's and Rosamund's, of the immense gap opened up between what was professed and what actually was. She was terrified of coming face to face with them, and between her fear of that possibility and her fear of the scene taking place now directly before her, she crouched in the tall grasses of the dune, shuddering.

A stocky British soldier in khaki uniform was gripping an Indian with one closed fist and hitting him about the head with the other. The Indian was naked except for the strips of torn and bloody loincloth dangling from his crotch. The soldier wore heavy boots and kicked the Indian in the backside, in the groin really, as they moved forward. The Indian squirmed and slid from the soldier's grasp as much as he could manage under the rigid hold of the fist. The Indian was taller, broader, stronger looking than the British soldier, except that his back was curved like a beaten dog's and he yelped and screamed like a dog. At each kick of the boot, bright blood seeped into the mess of rags at the Indian's crotch.

The soldier cursed in a mixture of dialect and English, the same curses, over and over.

"Damned bloody bugger. Filth. Damned filthy bugger. Bloody bugger."

The fine white sand spurted up from the foot movements of their violent dance. Their struggle carried them into the soft, shallow waves and the water splashed and played with them, as in a child's game of running to and from the waves. Squirming, squealing, kicking, the two stick figures, indiscriminately silhouetted black against the gleaming sea, might have seemed comic, except for the bright red blood seeping into the Indian's loincloth.

Later she told about the scene she had witnessed, pretending to address Mr. Singh and the Voynows, but it was to Vidhya she was speaking. They were on the verandah of the main bungalow, resting between games of statues. It was Vidhya who responded first.

"But Maddy, you were not a witness to what the fellow

might have done. He might be a hardened criminal. How do you know?"

"Arrest him. Try him in a court of law. Don't beat him to death on a deserted beach," she said.

"Oh, come now, Maddy. Beat him to death! The soldier was tapping him with his boot. No more than a tapping."

"You saw them, then," Maddy said.

He continued as if he hadn't heard.

"You have no facts, no details. How do you judge without facts or details?"

"I saw with my own eyes," she said. "The violence. How can you look away from that? You, of all people. And take sides against your own kind?"

Mr. Singh said, "Perhaps you misunderstood a disciplinary act between an officer and his servant. Servants here can be very irritating when they are insubordinate."

"You compare me with that, that, that . . ." Vidhya stammered.

"You saw him, then?" Maddy repeated. "You saw the Indian on the beach."

"These are very subtle matters," Mr. Voynow said. "We Westerners shouldn't —"

"I am too tired to go on with our game," Vidhya said. He walked away rapidly.

Rosamund sought her out, next morning, after breakfast. Maddy was sitting on the verandah of the young people's bungalow, going over some notes she had transcribed.

"I want to explain about yesterday at the beach," Rosamund said.

"No, no," Maddy said.

She would have run away if she had had any warning. She wanted no part of a false drama between herself and Rosamund.

"There's nothing between *us*," Maddy said, "nothing to explain."

"I just want to explain to you that —"

"You can't. It can't be explained. There's nothing plain about it. It's hopelessly mixed up. Please, let's not talk about it."

The sound of her own voice rising out of control was unpleasant.

"I'm not the least bit in love with Vidhya in the ordinary sense of *love*," Rosamund said. "I want you to understand that."

"I don't want to hear this," Maddy said.

"In the way that *you* are," Rosamund said. "I have none of that sort of feeling. Mine is a different sort of love entirely."

How wonderfully calm and cool Rosamund appeared to be. She was wearing a simple blue dress and had bound up her hair in a white kerchief. Her skin shone as pure as her convictions and her eyes held Maddy's in a sane and steady gaze. It was Maddy who must look the mad fanatic.

"Please," Maddy said. "I really don't want to hear this."

She covered her ears with the palms of her hands. The touch of her own hair sticky with sweat was as revolting as an unwanted contact with a stranger.

"It's all a part of the work I have been selected — I have been honored —" Rosamund said.

"I'm hot," Maddy said. "I'm too hot."

". . . My duty to the Elders and their commands, to the Society and its precepts, to carry on in the light of these great spirits . . ."

"I don't see any point to this conversation," Maddy said.

"I come with a message of love," Rosamund said. "Spiritual love."

Quiescence offered itself as the quickest way out. Maddy sat still and listened. The slow-moving life of the compound around her made for a bearable distraction. A scene of arrested time, as on a stage, a play set and costumed in the filmy whites and brilliantly soft colors of the saris, with just the right spottings of red in the turbans and head wrappings, the elegance of gold trim, or a vivid embroidery on a menial's clothing, looms and frames scattered about, symbols of the simple life, the blue smoke of the cooking fires, dark-skinned gardeners tending the flowers and among these, the Westerners, self-conscious actors trying too hard to blend: Mr. Voynow emerging on his verandah to breathe deeply and move his arms in a mysterious incantation of his own; at the far end, under the banyan tree, Miranda, a large, red-faced Canadian woman with grizzled hair in a mannish cut, looking incongruous in a sari, composing herself before a loom into a pious vision of industry and peace.

She was part of this tableau, *of* it as much as any of them — Rosamund and Mr. Voynow and the Canadian woman — part of the play and the play-acting, part of the true effort and part of the posturing.

She shivered, in spite of the heat, or because of it, and forced her attention back to Rosamund's long introduction. To what? What was this scene a prelude to? What did Rosamund really want? A truce, a working arrangement, to fit them all nicely into Vidhya's complex pattern of desire and spiritual ambition. Fine, fine. Anything to stop Rosamund talking. Agreed, agreed. She had been ground down to a fine dust of agreement. But no more talk.

Reporters swarm on their arrival in New York. Newspaper readers need a lift. Life is dreary in the fall of 1931; all the news is bad. A skinny, black Indian Messiah and his fervent followers are excellent candidates for amusing copy. Dozens of reporters have gathered on the deck of the *Île de France* while it is still in the harbor. It had been determined earlier that Lady Florence and Mr. Voynow would act as press representatives, but reporters howl for Vidhya and he is called forth.

Vidhya wears a white flannel suit, Panama hat, white silk shirt, white Liberty tie, and matching handkerchief in his breast pocket. He has been advised not to speak. He smiles and raises his hands in blessing, affecting a saintly expression, which in the news photos makes him look sickly and sullen.

There are also cameras present, the real thing, movie cameras for Pathé News. They take film of Vidhya, and of Lady Florence. These two are the stars, particularly Lady Florence, the former Fabian, Suffragist, Socialist, and advocate of free love, the former companion of George Bernard Shaw and Gordon Craig, the present friend of Mahatma Gandhi, an advocate of Indian Home Rule and the sponsor of Vidhya as the coming Messiah.

When the cameras have finished with Lady Florence and Vidhya, they turn to Lady Pansy in her white sari, Mrs. Voynow in an English tailored summer suit, and to Maddy leaning against the railing, flanked by Mr. Singh and Jag. Both men are in Indian dress, Mr. Singh's outfit topped by an elaborately pleated turban and Jag's by a neat triangular cap. Maddy is dressed in an ensemble she bought in Paris during the return journey, a white crepe dress covered by a flower-print coat. For some reason the coat is called a *redingote*, and coupled with the word *ensemble* these terms make her feel fashionably attired. She is unaccustomed to high heels and leans against the ship's rail, where she is less likely to totter.

She is not the gloriously pretty girl who left four years ago. Too thin and drawn, for one thing, and the smiling serenity and bursting good health are no longer evident. Even the exuberant hair is subdued. But she's striking enough to draw the cameras. They stay on her and a woman reporter comes around asking questions. It had been agreed that Maddy would remain in the background. If questioned she was to respond that she was an American returning to her homeland after an extended stay at various Society encampments. She thinks she manages very nicely with the woman reporter, certainly as well as Lady Pansy and Mr. Voynow do in their rambling discourses.

In the evening papers, nobody comes out well. The photographs are particularly hideous, everybody out of focus and dark skinned and the Indians blacker than black. In the Hearst paper a caption under a photograph of Vidhya asks: SAVIOR OF THE WORLD OR SKINNY KID? Under a photograph of Maddy, Jag, and Mr. Singh: AMERICAN HEIRESS WITH INDIAN BODYGUARD, and the written account hints of white-slave traffic.

Other text devotes itself to Vidhya's clothes, the cut of his hair, "parted in the middle and slicked back Valentino fashion," and carries detailed descriptions of his silk suspenders and monogrammed silk socks, etc., etc., etc. Maddy's clothes also come in for minute descriptive attention, though the term *redingote* is utilized by only one newspaper. Vidhya is called "the alleged, self-appointed Messiah of the world," and he is characterized as "foppish, sullen, sickly, retarded looking, and effeminate." Maddy is "an heiress," "the mystery girl behind the scenes," "the handmaiden of the alleged coming Messiah," and is variously described as striking, plain, angular, aesthetic, pretty, sensual, and nondescript.

The more sedate morning papers, the *Times, Herald, Tribune,* and *World,* carry no photographs. In print the Society is derided as "a cult awaiting the end of the world" led by "fanatical believers in the Second Coming"; and all the old charges against Bobo and Vidhya are rehashed: ". . . rumors of perverted practices, sexual orgies, and immoral influence on the young."

Reporters camp out before the building in which their party is housed, a handsome, large apartment on Fifth Avenue, overlooking the park. A retired surgeon and his wife, Dr. and Mrs. Janssen, are their hosts, not themselves members or even followers of the Society, but good friends of the

Voynows. They clearly regret their present offer of hospitality. They hadn't bargained for notoriety and scandal.

In this spacious apartment, Maddy had been assigned her own room, a study with a sofa-bed, a desk, a leather chair, and its own white tiled bathroom. Formerly used as a consulting space, the quarters retained a tense remembrance of anxious waiting periods and tragic confrontations, an overbearing sense of oncoming death, if not her own, then another's. Not even the view of the park eased the feel of that room. She fled it.

Leaving the building meant wading through the reporters at the door. *Plain* and *angular* had bothered her. She fussed with her dress and her hair and tried to move gracefully. Both words meant *awkward* to her, meant Milli. Had she grown into Milli merely by proximity?

The reporters hounded her with questions she smilingly refused to answer. It was Vidhya they wanted anyway, and they never pursued her beyond the corner.

She was free then.

She had not expected to be enchanted with her own country, her own city, beginning with the sight of the celebrated New York City skyline from the ship's deck and the sound of New York City speech. She had not expected to respond with this gush of relief. She was home. Home. She walked all over Manhattan, drinking in the city, its surprising corners, sudden astonishing buildings, little bits of park. The elevated trains were glorious. A bird's-eye view. And more. The intimate glimpse. The immediate touch of another's life. A child standing at the window, looking directly into Maddy's face. She made a promise to the child. *I know you. I know your life. I have come home to you.*

The period of time spent away, the variety of places she had visited and lived in, had been a preparation, an intense schooling in coming to rest in her own true spot, a corner of this startlingly original city. She was determined to stay, somehow, anyhow. She would manage it, convince Vidhya.

There had been a message that Victoria and her troupe were performing at a theater on Fourteenth Street, but she put off going the first day. The first day was for the celebration of coming home, for roaming, for filling her pores with this city where she had been born, and torn from, without her consent.

Among the men crowding the entrance when she came back that evening, there was a face she knew. The American with the rectangular-shaped smile and the deep dimple in his chin.

"Welcome home," he said. "I'm Dwight Phillips. Remember, in Spain?"

"Of course," she said. "Are you a reporter?"

Others were crowding them, listening to the exchange.

"No," he said, "but they wouldn't let me in anyway. Take me into the lobby with you, so we can say a quiet hello."

"Swear you're not a reporter?"

"Cross my heart and hope to die," he said.

"What are you?" she said.

"I'm a full-time paid Party organizer," he said. "At the moment undercover, organizing the unemployed. Unemployed Councils — that's my Mass Org. And I teach a class at the Workers' School."

They had entered the marble lobby and were seated on a dusty, shabby couch in a hidden corner. She didn't know the Workers' School or what a full-time paid Party organizer was, or what Unemployed Councils were, either, or what Mass Org. meant. She knew it was pleasant to be with him, chatting, sunning under his smile and his admiring blue eyes. He scribbled an address and a telephone number.

"I knock around in a broken-down flivver. We could go for a spin anytime you say. Go out to Sheepshead Bay or City Island and eat some seafood," he said.

"I'm a vegetarian," Maddy said.

"Do you still believe in fairies?" he said.

"If you're going to make fun of me," she said. "How did you know where I was?"

"Are you kidding?" he said. "You're plastered all over the papers. 'Mystery girl.' 'Heiress.' 'Handmaiden of the coming Messiah.' That stuff. It was easy to get the address. Anyway, I know one of the guys covering the story, he's a pal."

"Please don't talk to him," she said. "Don't tell him anything about me."

"If it were up to me," Dwight Phillips said, "I'd have you out of this whole mess before you got into it. I'm not talking to anybody but you. May I call you?"

She shook her head. She would call him, she promised.

There was a message from Victoria, too, and from Elena Dasinov, to come to the theater on Fourteenth Street. She went the following day, after a long sightseeing trip on the Ninth Avenue el and a short one on the Third Avenue. She was afraid to enter the theater. All the doors were shut, and though the street was lively, it was also dirty and seedy, with a tone she was suspicious of but couldn't translate into terms of familiarity.

She walked up and down for a bit, looking into the shop windows, getting used to the people again, her people, Bronx-stoop sort of people. She mounted a few steps into a park and listened to a public speaker addressing a crowd that melted and reformed as he harangued them. She couldn't follow his talk but his tone made her brave. When she returned to the theater, she had determined not to hesitate but to barge in.

Temporarily blinded by the change from sunlight to blackness, she halted. The door screeched. A wraith ran up the aisle, calling *Maddy! Maddy!* Elena, in still another incarnation: masses of curly hair; long, flowing skirt; rows and rows of beads; a leather jacket. It was cool in the dark theater. The lights had come up onstage and she saw Elena in the moment before she became engulfed by hair, smell, beads, slightly sweaty flesh, sharp, intrusive bones, and the fishy smell of leather jacket. It was so good to be hugged, to be touched, she almost cried. Nobody had touched her in months.

And behind Elena, Victoria waiting with open arms for Maddy to come running: Victoria — tall, erect, queenly, more queenly than ever.

She sat next to Elena in the almost empty theater when the rehearsal resumed. An all-women dance, Victoria at the center of the advancing, turning columns, a slow, stately, courtly movement, plain, spare, American Quaker, Amish. Simple full-skirted costumes with a winglike yoke. Democratic nuns professing their pioneer faith. It was a dress rehearsal. They were opening the following night.

Then a cup of tea at a miserable dive on University Avenue, Elena overflowing with old feeling, as if they had never been apart, Victoria her commanding, separate, passionate self, taking control of Maddy with spare warnings and advice. Maddy must leave the Society at once. She was nineteen. Time to go. Time to protect herself from the kind of stories the papers were having such fun with. There was an apartment on Tenth Street between Fifth and Sixth (one of the dancers was marrying) and a job as Victoria's assistant. Ten dollars a week.

"You can be out of their clutches tomorrow," Victoria said.

Elena was Victoria's stage manager, but Victoria would release her for a couple of hours. Elena walked Maddy to the wide, tree-lined street where the brownstone stood behind an iron grille. The hallway was dingy, peeling, a little scary. One flight up, very dark (not in the morning), a large single room, a real fireplace and two big windows, an alcove large enough for a bed and dresser, a sink, gas stove, and electric refrigerator shoved against one wall behind closet doors, a cubicle of a bathroom, but complete.

She could take a day to decide.

The possibility of living alone in this setting enchanted her — and terrified her.

She was tired when she returned to the Fifth Avenue apartment. Her Parisian shoes had blistered her feet, and the dirt and heat and the terrible excitement of being with Victoria and Elena had given her a headache. She wanted a cool drink, a bath, a rest, and time to think, but she was immediately hauled into the immense living room before a tribunal of Vidhya, Lady Florence, Jag, Mr. Singh, Lady Pansy, and the Voynows. It was a shabby room, beautifully so, the upholstery on the many cushioned pieces fading along with the Persian rugs, the walls yellowing away from white, the gauzy curtains at the window gray with city soot. A cooling wind blew in from the park across the street.

A strategy session, she had surmised. Not at all. A Criticism/Self-criticism event, with herself at the center. What had she done? She looked to Vidhya for a hint. His eyes were cast down and his face blank.

But first, a long digression as to the propriety of the participation of their hosts in the session. Mrs. Janssen, as spokesman for herself and her husband, expressed their "keen interest in this most original technique about which they had heard so much," and pledged that both she and Dr. Janssen would be absolutely discreet about what occurred during this "unique self-learning experience."

Vidhya was opposed to the Janssens' presence. Lady Florence was in favor. The Voynows agreed with Lady Florence. Lady Pansy had no opinion. Jag and Mr. Singh thought it impolite to shut out their hosts. Maddy wasn't asked to comment.

Dr. and Mrs. Janssen remained, seated on a love seat placed to the side of the room, spectators at a performance.

The crux of the matter? Maddy was shown the headlines: "MESSIAH" SECRETLY ENGAGED TO AMERICAN HEIRESS; WEDDING BELLS FOR "MESSIAH" AND TEENAGER; MYSTERY GIRL AND "MESSIAH" TO BECOME MR. AND MRS.

And under a picture of Maddy and Vidhya artfully spliced together from two separate shots, MR. AND MRS. MESSIAH?

"What is this?" Maddy said. "Where did this come from?"

"My girl, you were seen talking to them," Lady Florence said. "Walking down the street, talking to them."

"I said nothing to them," Maddy said. "I never said a word to them."

"And your manner of dress, my dear. We asked you not to be conspicuous. Those high-heeled shoes," Lady Pansy said.

The offending spike-heeled shoes pinched her feet, and the blisters they had caused were tormenting her at that very moment. But she loved the shoes. They were an elegant shade of deep green with an elegantly thin T-strap, and they had come from an elegant shop on the Place Vendôme.

"My shoes have nothing to do with this," she shouted.

Vidhya lifted his head from its drooping position but did not look at her directly, fixing his gaze somewhere above her face, in her hair.

"Maddy," he said. "I have told them there is some misunderstanding. Just explain that these reports are nothing but lies, total lies."

"I never spoke to the press," she said.

"The entire story. Secret engagements, that nonsense. Tell them, just as I did, that it is a monstrous lie."

"Monstrous?" Maddy said.

"I will not be made a laughingstock. Me! Me! They are turning *me* into a laughingstock. The *New York Times* has called twice. Twice. They have insinuated I am covering something, not telling the whole truth. They want to speak to you, to the 'mystery girl,' as they call you. You must deny it, you must."

"Did you imagine I might confirm it?" Maddy said.

"How do I know what you have said to them? Who told them this monstrous story?" Vidhya said.

Lady Pansy reached out a hand and placed it on Vidhya's shoulder.

"Vidhya," she said. "Do not let this silly incident destroy your inner peace. You must not allow unworthy matters to gain an ascendancy over your —"

"Oh, for Christ's sake," Maddy yelled. "For Christ's sake, what are we talking about, why are we paying any attention to these ridiculous reports? And why am I being punished? I have nothing to do with it, with any of it. I wash my hands of it. What is it you want me to deny? I'll deny it gladly, anything, anything you say. You want me to deny that Vidhya loves me? Good, I deny it. And that I love him? I deny it. Everything, everything, totally denied. Tell them I said love doesn't exist. Now, have I satisfied you?"

"Maddy," Vidhya said, "why are you distorting the entire sense of these proceedings? And of our love, the love of colleagues and companions on the Path to the Good? What has such love to do with silly talk of secret engagements? What has our important work to do with cruel gossip in the tabloids?"

"I don't know," Maddy said, "if you don't."

She was exhausted and wanted only to get away from them.

"I'm very tired," she said. "Perhaps we can continue this some other time. I had nothing to do with it, whatever it is, I spoke to no reporters."

She had remembered in the middle of her speech that she had told Victoria in Spain. Would Victoria talk to reporters? *Had* Victoria talked to reporters?

Nobody attempted to keep her from leaving the room. From the hallway she heard Mr. Voynow explaining to Dr. and Mrs. Janssen that this session had been atypical, on a lower level than their usual Criticism/Self-criticism meetings. At the end of the hall, Mr. Singh intercepted her. He had come round the other way.

"We must talk together, Maddy," he whispered.

"I'm tired," she said.

"No," he said, "we must. You must come with me. We have only twenty minutes before dinner. This is a terrible misunderstanding. Vidhya wants to explain to you what has happened."

She was too exhausted to resist him. He led her to a library behind the living room. They could faintly hear voices through the wall. The pain of her shoes pinching was unbearable and she bent down to work them off her blistered feet. Vidhya came into the room, closing the door behind him, whispering as he approached.

"Have you told her?"

Mr. Singh shook his head.

She stood holding her French high-heeled, green leather, T-strap, not very utilitarian shoes in one hand.

"Maddy, you must understand. I must do this in this manner. In a few weeks" — his whisper fell so low she had difficulty hearing him at all — "I am renouncing all the non-sense. The Messiah nonsense, all of that part. Jag and Mr. Singh and I have worked it out. But there must be no stigma attached. You understand? We must clear up the gossip about secret engagements before I make my announcement. That is why I spoke to them as I did. Now all you must do is confirm my story."

"What story?"

"Maddy, you must understand that the important thing is that I not be discredited. Otherwise we are all ruined. You see that, don't you? If I am made a laughingstock, then I am ruined. My whole life and future — it can be ruined. And what of the people who believe in me? I have an obligation to those good people, my followers, do I not? To present myself to the world in the proper light."

"What did you say to the reporters, Vidhya? *Tell* me."

"I thought that you had given them a lot of false information. How do I know even now that you did not? Only your denial will convince me, your public denial."

"What did you say to them?"

"It will all appear in tomorrow's newspapers."

"What? What exactly will appear in tomorrow's newspapers?"

"And perhaps nothing will appear. Perhaps they will decide that this story is not interesting after all, not interesting enough to waste newspaper space on such foolish stories . . ."

He paused and began again. She knew he was distraught because of the whites showing under the irises of his eyes.

"The important thing is your denial of all that foolish engagement talk, Maddy. That is what is important."

"If you don't tell me what you told the reporters, I will absolutely refuse to talk to them. That's it," Maddy said, "my final word on the subject."

"I told them that you were one of many young girls attached to the Society," he said. "I told them we were bringing you back to the United States because it is your home. I told them that you were, unfortunately, a habitual liar, though one who meant no harm by it, a romantic girl who made up fanciful stories, whose head was easily turned, a girl who made up fantasies, love fantasies —"

He broke off. They stared into each other's face.

Mr. Singh interceded. "Come, finish up. Finish up. We have only fifteen minutes now."

"Why are you looking at me with big, blaming eyes?" Vidhya said to Maddy. "I was protecting myself and you, too, yes, can't you see that I protect you with this story? Because we want you to stay with us. We have planned everything very well, the finances, everything."

"Now we are properly discussing," Mr. Singh said. "Now we are reaching the important matters . . ."

"I promise you, Maddy, you will always be part of us, part of the New Vidhya Foundation. Let Bobo keep his Universal Society of Brotherhood. Once I have disassociated myself from this Messiah nonsense, we launch with absolute dignity the New Vidhya Foundation, and those who believe in the true precepts of harmony and brotherhood —"

"Hurry, hurry," Mr. Singh said.

"I don't know what you're talking about," Maddy said.

"We must be careful," Vidhya said, whispering frantically. "Lady Pansy we need not worry about. We have her support. And Rosamund's support. Perhaps Rosamund will also influence Lady Florence, though so far we do not trust Lady Florence enough to tell her anything. She is too thick with Bobo, and Bobo — no, Bobo is intractable, we cannot manage him, he wants always to lead. Bobo mustn't know until all our plans are safely accomplished. We must proceed step by step with caution. First we must retreat with dignity, turning aside from talk of Messiahs and Levels of Perfection, talk of Masters and Elders, all that nonsense, then I shall begin to speak to my followers truly and simply of individual spiritual growth . . ."

"Hurry, hurry," Mr. Singh said.

"Then everybody knew of these plans? Everybody but me?" Maddy said.

The two men hoarsely whispered "No, no" simultaneously.

"Nobody knows," Mr. Singh said. "Circumspection was essential, essential."

"Hardly anybody knows," Vidhya said. "Maddy, why are you being obtuse?"

"Until the design is complete, nobody but us must get wind of our plans. Only those who are with us know. You, now we have told you. Perhaps we will tell Mrs. Dasinov when we reach the West Coast. Her support would be invaluable," Mr. Singh said.

Her money would be invaluable, Maddy did not say.

"How long has this been going on — your plans? Why did you come here pretending seriously that you were called to be a Messiah and all along —"

Vidhya whispered his scream.

"You see us as conspirators, plotters, evil beings. We are good, *good*. It is the good of all we're concerned with, not only my followers, believe me, it is the good of the world, and your good, Maddy, your good."

"Why did you lie about me?"

"I did not lie. An exaggeration. A slight exaggeration. You *are* a romantic girl, you know you are. If I had said something else ... Just think what you said to them, just think, Maddy."

"I told them nothing," Maddy said. "I didn't speak to any reporters, except on the boat, and that was nothing about engagements. But suppose I had, suppose I had told the reporters, 'Yes, Vidhya and I are secretly engaged'?"

"You're lying," Vidhya whispered in a screeching panic. "Stop this stupid lying. She's lying, she's lying."

He was pleading with Mr. Singh to believe him.

"We have no more time," Mr. Singh said. "It is time to act like grown-ups."

"I'll be leaving," she said, "as soon as I'm packed."

She turned to Mr. Singh.

"We'll need to arrange about my finances."

He was so taken aback by her grown-up manner that he half bowed.

"At your convenience, Maddy," he said. "But it will take a day or so. Your finances may be a little complicated. Bobo has control of the money your father —"

"I've already spoken to a lawyer," she said, improvising. If she was going to be tagged a liar, she'd earn the name.

"Maddy, you should not rush into precipitous action. We have no problems between us. These are public matters we are discussing, not our personal concerns. They are not our true problems," Vidhya whispered. "How can you even think of leaving us, leaving me?"

"If you try to hold me," Maddy said, "there are lots of things to tell, lots of things I could tell about."

She was instantly ashamed of herself for having said that, and ashamed of Vidhya for pleading with her.

"Maddy, please remember our love, remember what we meant to each other."

What an unreal and ridiculous scene. Shoes in hand, in the library of a retired rich doctor's Fifth Avenue apartment, whispering and plotting with two men who were lying to her about everything, because, she realized at that moment, they were afraid of her, afraid that she would tell what she knew, ruin their business, their business of salvation.

She said, "I'm not talking to any reporters, Vidhya. I haven't talked to them and I'm not going to. Ever."

She meant her words as reassurance. The men heard a threat, which she read in their alarmed exchanged glances.

"I expect my annuity to come to me intact, except for what I've drawn from it, and I know that's very little," she added. "And then I'll be off as soon as everything's settled."

"Maddy," Vidhya said — and for a moment she was moved by what seemed to be true concern — "what will you do? Without us? Without our work and our cause? Without me? There will be no reason to live."

"We'll see," she said.

She knew she would cry once out of Vidhya's sight. The losses were too great. Everything was going at once as if the floor of the world had caved in.

"We'll see," she said again, and left the room.

16

T HE thing I loved about the first moon flight," Maddy
said, "was seeing the world on television."
Nobody answered her. They were dozing on
either side, Victoria slumped against the window of the plane,
Dwight folded over his seat belt, looking a million years
old, looking as if he would never wake again.

The descent into La Guardia had been announced.
There was still nothing out there but solid fog. Then the
plane broke through to a clear sight of upper Manhattan, the
Hudson River and the Harlem snaking along on either side.
They were coming in from the north, not over the water
from the east. Her first view of New York City from the
air had been from an old propeller plane that shuddered
and danced with every maneuver, the city below a grid of
colored illumination shimmering under a light rain. She
couldn't remember when. Nineteen forties, early fifties?
Those old clattering planes, swooping and banking into a
landing with style, made you feel you were really *flying*. In a
smooth jumbo jet you might as well be on a bus or train; you
felt nothing, until it blew up and you were dead, in one
stroke, under the anesthesia of the PA system.

Consider the well-known phenomenon of one's life passing before one's eyes in the moment before death. Would it work in her case? Quite a bit to cover. Not only the life, the life in the Society, her life with Dwight. Try flashing her friendship with Victoria in a split second! The geography alone in the life story of Maddy Brewster Phillips, formerly Bessie Bernstein, would take a feature-length film to flash by, counting the places all over the world that they'd traveled to for Dwight's lectures.

Forget geography. Now one saw the real world, a tangible spinning globe, seen whole in its blue-and-white enameled perfection. A perfect orb. *The earth is round! It's really round.* A jeweled ball. Rilke's sweet apple earth. All of a piece. No tearing it apart anymore. Save it all or lose it all. See it flash by our eyes, the whole world, everybody's life, in the last seconds before . . .

"Yes, yes," Dwight said, awake and disoriented. "The moon, yes, all that space exploration nonsense, I agree. And the terrible waste, the shuttle, the waste of human life, the money."

He took a deep breath and a new tack.

"The search for intelligent life in the universe is a very serious undertaking, however they may ridicule the endeavor and obscure the issue. We have never been properly informed on the subject of UFOs," he said. "They have been feeding us disinformation steadily . . ."

Victoria had also awakened.

"Ah, yes," she said. "*They, they,* the all-powerful *they* and *them.*"

The plane had landed and was taxiing to a stop. Two teenage girls stood in the aisle, talking in a storm of gestures, hair, drooping garments, nomadic piles of soft baggage slung on their bodies.

"So he goes, 'What? What?' and I go, 'You know what, you know what,' and he goes, 'What? What am I supposed to know?' like I'm demented and then I get really mad and I go,

'Yeah, well you know, you know,' and he doesn't even let me finish, he starts fishing in a drawer and he takes out a roach . . .''

Dwight said, "*Now* what are we waiting for? I spend all my time waiting, wasting my old age. What the dickens are we waiting for now?"

"I'm going home to soak in a cool bath," Victoria said. "Then I'm flopping out in front of the TV to watch that ridiculous soap that's nothing but clothes."

"Are you leaving the demonstration?" Maddy said.

"It left me," Victoria said. "I can't go on chasing it. I'm tired."

"It's my opinion," Dwight said, "that there will be nothing to connect with in New York but confusion. This wasn't properly planned, this demonstration. Too many young people barging in without proper preparation. It's probably fizzled out already."

Victoria stretched and yawned.

"Oh my *God*, oh my *God*," a voice screeched.

It was the other teenager in the aisle, the silent, listening one. She was alternately flinging out her arms in the direction of Victoria and clutching her own head.

"I can't believe it. I can't believe it. It's Victoria Younger. It really is Victoria Younger. Wait. Wait."

She rummaged through her collection of stuffed receptacles and came up with a battered notebook.

"Oh God, Miss Younger, if you would sign here in my diary, I'll fill in the rest later, I would be the happiest . . . To get your autograph, Miss Younger, I can't even begin . . . Oh my God, I can't believe it, I'm such an admirer, you're a role model for my mother, she's not going to believe this, I swear she'll say I forged your name, oh God, nobody is going to believe this, we all thought you were dead, especially after that PBS film, that was brilliant . . . "

"Young lady," Victoria said, returning the signed notebook, "you're giving me a headache."

Jeff Bernstein was waiting for them with a red VW bus. Traffic on the expressway was heavy but moving steadily.

"They've rounded up so many people, they're shoving them into sports arenas and school playgrounds. There's been nothing like this on the streets since the seventies, since May Day. We're putting all we got into this. It's wonderful that blacks and Hispanics showed, it's great, but we can't let them take the brunt. We have to publicize what's going on — to the hilt."

"Certainly not," Dwight said.

"What?" Jeff said. "Why not?"

"They must not take the brunt," Dwight said. "Certainly not."

Maddy said, "I think Dwight needs to rest now. We're not needed anymore, are we?"

"We hoped you'd appear at the UN, as we originally planned, all of you or the two of you or one of you. Whatever. Whatever we can get."

He turned around and grinned at them.

"These VW buses make me sick to my stomach," Victoria said. "You should face front when you drive."

He paid no attention to that.

"The resolution still hasn't come to a vote, and we're holding back on troops, unless of course we're lying, they're lying, the administration I mean, keeping the action secret, like in Grenada."

"*We, they.*" Victoria sighed. "Ah me. I must go home," she said. "I give up."

They left Victoria at her East Side apartment house, then drove to a hotel on Forty-second Street.

"Glitzy," Jeff said.

They were moving slowly across a huge lobby, half carrying Dwight between them.

"If I go to the UN, I'll need someone to stay with him here," Maddy said.

"No problem," Jeff said. "I'll get on the phone. No problem."

Within the enclosed vault of the hotel atrium there are stores, restaurants, trees, plants, banks of telephones, banks of elevators, banks of flowers, banks of money, models walking about displaying costumes, people sitting on deep couches, riding up and down escalators, telephoning in ranks, sitting at tables eating, writing, reviewing sales material, drinking, dealing in business and sex, signing contracts and breaking vows, wandering, promenading, boulevarding, window-shopping, wasting time, enjoying themselves. An instrumental group on an island of greenery makes music, and people sit at little tables drinking and listening.

She looks up to see if it is this hotel that runs a train directly into the lobby; she remembers a clean, noiseless vehicle on tracks that deposited guests at a terminal high above the floor of the lobby. In Montreal, perhaps. Or Disney World. The soaring balconies display splendid shops, restaurants, bars, trees, plants, flowers, waterfalls. Lights dazzle and blind.

"New York looks quite undisturbed," she said.

"Business as usual," Dwight said, and brought on a coughing fit.

Jeff handed her a heavy key hanging from an oversized wooden slab, along with a hotel passport, a sheaf of invitations, and free-drink vouchers. She laughed and unlocked the door.

Beyond the foyer, the room opens into an amazing L-shaped immensity. Big, big, big. The bed is also outsize, as are the sealed and draped windows and the TV, the couch, the dresser, the telephones, the red numbers on the digital clock, the dressing room and bath.

"Who booked us in here?"

"The owner's a friend," Jeff said. "And it's close to the UN."

"Intolerable," Dwight said, and collapsed on the bed with a long expiration of breath.

299

Call me, was the last thing Victoria had said, as she left the VW bus. *So I'll know how to reach you.*

An answering machine responded. Where was Victoria? Soaking in a cool bath?

She was hungry. With some difficulty, she convinced a reluctant and suspicious room service clerk to send up fresh fruit, rice, cooked stringbeans and carrots, yogurt, fresh orange juice. She woke Dwight, propping him up against the extravagantly huge pillows. They ate watching the national news coverage of the demonstrations and arrests: a fleeting glimpse of the march in East Hartford, then a shot of blue-helmeted police moving in on a group of mostly blacks and Hispanics on the West Coast.

"Not since the late sixties and early seventies . . ." An anchorman talking, then a rerun of Dwight at the press conference that morning, cut to Maddy in the back of the truck the day before. ". . . a throwback to an earlier generation, though this contingent of distinguished former left-wing leaders of that generation is no longer a part of the demonstration . . ."

"It's not news," Dwight said, "it's mystification. They word it as if we've withdrawn from the action."

But the news had already left them behind and moved on to shots of department store bombings in Paris, indictments of top officials in the Housing Administration, a flareup in the Persian Gulf, death by overdose of a film actor they didn't know. The latest hijacking turned out a fizzle: a hungry passenger cutting baloney and cheese with a sharp knife; a worried steward and an over-careful pilot.

Victoria called, excited, reinvigorated. A friend in the State Department had been in touch.

"Bunny says the action is having an impact. He thinks the administration will pull back. There are demonstrations all across Central America and in Argentina and Ecuador. There's a rumor that the generals are about to step down."

"You see," Dwight said. "You see." He had broken out

in white blotches of excited triumph. "Saved from a truly awful blunder. We were backing the wrong people, backing the cutthroats, the murderers and criminals. We have spared many innocent lives from imprisonment and torture."

Saved all kinds of lives, even those committed up to their guilty necks. Saved a threatened corner of the world, not one of the great corners, hardly worth saving at all, according to those who weighed and judged these matters, one of the odd corners she had never seen with her own eyes.

International crises were more harrowing when the terrain and the people were familiar. What a way to think! The hidden advantages of travel. See the world, learn to love it, the better to suffer when it is wronged. The Spanish Civil War had been unbearable. The bombardment of England. And the partition of India. The Bay of Pigs and the Cuban Missile Crisis. She had met a mayor of a small Cuban city who had been educated in the United States and loved the writings of Salinger, met him when he was attempting to teach himself how to govern a tiny corner of a new world in a new way and probably failing; there was the sunken valley of Vinales, with its strange outcroppings of giant earthworks under the vault of the sky, or the foolish, lovable children's park outside Havana, with its fairy tale castle; there was the Cuban poet with green eyes, living in middle-class comfort in a house in Miramar, scrounging for shoes for his wife and grown kids, screwing all the young American women tourists who arrived at his door gaga with revolutionary nonsense. She had gone through those few terrorized days visualizing particular people and places in instant ruins. KABOOM. Over and done with. The idealism, the faith, the stupidities, hypocrisies, and hopes, wiped out equally.

Did it mean anything — her whole long, agitating life? First in the Society, then with Dwight, when their activity was all political in the early years, and during the later years of the long retreat to the good life, the natural life? She had struggled to protect life in its spiritual, societal, and natural spheres. Had she accomplished anything? Could she clearly point to a single triumph, even a single solid advance? Had her efforts made the world one whit better? What a load of dedicated busyness. What good were they doing right now with this current demonstration?

Blow up the hotel. That would do something. Shake things up. Make a splash.

She could never become one, but she understood terrorists. Because life and property were sacred to her? Well, they were, they were sacred. Somebody's home, somebody's faith, somebody's memories, resided in a hunk of land or structure. She couldn't stand it that anarchists had burned churches in Spain, though she was capable of hauling down Franco's Valley of the Fallen Monument, stone by stone, with her own hands.

A memory came unbidden, a demonstration more than forty years earlier. Late thirties or early 1940s. Before the Second World War. Its purpose to protest U.S. business as usual with Nazi Germany. A demonstration to impede the sailing of a great German luxury liner. Was it the *Bremen*?

There were no bystanders. The docks were deserted except for hundreds — thousands, maybe — of demonstrators and cops. Was it dawn or dusk? Midnight, she seemed to remember. Sailing time. Pitch blackness surrounded them; the ship had been darkened, its great hulk loomed above.

She and Dwight were part of a group of eight comrades who were to chain themselves to the rail of the ship and to the dock and make it impossible for the ship to move off. She recalled the event much like one of her recurrent nightmares. Fear dominated. Irrational, rational fear. She knew by then what the Nazis were doing to Jews. They would know instantly that she was a Jew. She would be caught and spirited away on the *Bremen* to imprisonment and death. The blackness added to the nightmare quality of the immense, impossible effort to climb the side of the ship, as did the faintly rotten smell of the water, rusted metal, sodden wood, of comradely struggling bodies, pushing, pulling, in a silence of grunts and hard breathing, her heart skittering in her chest, then the sound of the chains clanking, the shocking discomfort of her position, the chains tightened and locked and with it her fear, the paralyzing fear of never again escaping a chained fate, and then, the exhilaration of having done it — it was done — they had done it!

She remembered a long, silent wait and the return of uncontrollable fear. They would never be discovered. The great ship would take off and tear their bodies apart. Then, at a given signal, they shouted out a slogan she had long since forgotten. Lights, shouting, commotion, pain, Nazi sailors in Nazi sailor uniforms, young men as frightened as she, running about screaming warnings. What were they afraid of? Defenseless bodies, chained to the ship's railing.

New York City cops arrested them, and Communist party lawyers had them loose on bail in a couple of hours. Her memory didn't bring up anything else.

Dwight had fallen asleep again. And when Susan called Maddy was also asleep, in an armchair, fully dressed. Susan reminded Maddy that she was Susan of "Susan and Jeff, remember, yesterday, and today in Boston?" Yes, the pretty girl who had helped with the press conference, waiting with them through the long morning, asking questions, adoring and ignorant. Jeff had asked Susan to call because he was tied up, arranging another press conference, to take place in an hour. Maddy and Vidhya were to be there. He hoped to get others. The committee had decided to call off further actions, but the press had fallen in love with the contingent of the old. The press couldn't get enough of them, and another show on the late-night news might be useful.

"Where?" Maddy said. "Where is it to be held?"

"Right there. At your hotel. Vidhya is registered also, so we're sure of you two."

"Here?" Maddy said. "He's here?"

"Yes," Susan said. "Would you like his room number?"

She half expected Mr. Singh or Jag to pick up the phone in Vidhya's suite. That was ridiculous, naturally. Even Jag would have been ninety, and Mr. Singh . . . A woman with an English accent answered.

"The Master does not grant any interviews in the United States," she said. "I'm sure you understand."

Maddy said, "I'm an old friend. We'll be appearing at the same press conference."

"There appears to be some misunderstanding," the woman on the phone said. "We will not be attending the press conference. The Master does not attend press conferences in the United States."

"I'm an old, old friend," Maddy said. "Would you be good enough to give my old friend Vidhya the message that Maddy, Maddy Brewster, is here in the same hotel and would like very much to say hello? No interviews. No press conference. Just me and him. Maddy and Vidhya. I'd like to see him. And I'm sure he'd like to see me."

She hadn't known it when she started this telephone call, but she was desperate to see Vidhya once more.

"May I have your room number?" the woman said. "And the spelling of your name and your nationality?" And then, "May I ask when was the last time you saw the Master?"

Maddy considered for a moment. "I guess it was September or October of nineteen thirty-one," she said.

"Just a moment," the woman said, and left the phone. When she returned, her voice was clipped and distant and on a set spiel. "As you may know and as has been reported many times, Master does not recall any of his life before the date of November nineteen thirty-one, when he repudiated the role of Savior of the world, claimed for him by the leadership of the Universal Society of Brotherhood —"

"I don't care about any of that," Maddy said. "We were very close. I just want to say hello. Tell him Maddy Brewster is on the phone and wants to say hello. Did you tell him that? Just ask him, ask him to get on the phone for a minute. Tell him I want to have tea with him, for old times' sake."

"It is quite impossible, madam," she said. "Master is very weak because of his hunger strike, and he does not see anybody who claims an acquaintance with him that goes back to those days."

" 'Claims an acquaintance'! Listen, put Vidhya on the phone. We're too old for these silly games. Tell him it's Maddy. It's Maddy, and I must see him. My name is Phillips now. I've lived a whole life apart from him. I don't want anything from him. But it's unnatural — it's vile to deny what was. Come on, who is he kidding? He knows who I am."

Dwight was sitting up, listening to her. The agitation in her voice had probably awakened him.

She wondered at her intensity herself. What did she want? She didn't care about urging Vidhya to attend the press conference. Events were moving ahead of any influence she and Vidhya and Dwight might exert. This need was personal. She craved something for herself, damn it, some satisfaction she had never reached with Vidhya that she would wrench from this moment.

"He's turning everything we were into garbage with that line of his," she heard herself say.

The woman said, "Will you hold please?" and disappeared for a long bit.

"Madam, Master recalls nothing of those days and of those times. He asks me to send you greetings of peace, and his regrets," she said when she returned.

"Stop calling him by that ridiculous title," Maddy said. "And tell him he can palm those lies off on his public but that he's talking to Maddy now, who knew him when —"

But the woman had rung off.

305

"Do you believe this?" Maddy said. "Victoria would never let him get away with this."

"What do you hope for?" Dwight said.

"I don't know," Maddy said. "A rounding off. Something. He was my whole life, once. Doesn't that mean anything? Even if nothing else does?" And, after a moment, "It's ridiculous. We're old, two old people. Death is right ahead of us, a step away. If we don't accept reality now, then when? What is he afraid of now?"

"He was negotiating the rest of his life," Dwight said. "He had to do what he did then. And now he must believe whatever he invented was real."

"You're not excusing him?" Maddy said.

"I? I don't even know the man. But I'll tell you one thing," Dwight said, putting his head down on the pillow, "that man's no gentleman."

"Gentleman! Who cares about that?" Maddy said. "It's love and faith and truth that matter. The good guys and the bad guys. That's what matters. I don't care what anybody says. That's what matters."

"Yes," Dwight said. "That's exactly what I meant."

ABOUT THE AUTHOR

Helen Yglesias's first novel, *How She Died,* won a Hougton Mifflin Literary Fellowship in 1972. She has written two others, *Family Feeling* and *Sweetsir,* and a nonfiction work, *Starting.* Her stories, articles, and reviews have appeared in *The New Yorker, Harper's, The Nation,* and the *New York Times,* among other publications. She has taught creative writing, lectured, and read widely at a number of universities, including Columbia University and the universities of Iowa, Massachusetts, and Maine, among others. Helen Yglesias is a member of the well-known family of writers that includes her daughter Tamar Cole, her sons Rafael Yglesias and Lewis Cole, and her husband, José Yglesias. She and her husband spend part of each year in Maine and in Manhattan.